ROMILLY C
BENEATH THE VISITING MOON

ROMILLY CAVAN, the pen name of Isabel Wilson, was born on 13 July, 1914. She was the daughter of writer Desemea Wilson, who wrote under the name Diana Patrick.

She met her husband, journalist and author Eric Hiscock in 1934, at the launch of her debut novel, *Heron*, when she was only 21. Romilly went on to write six novels in all. The last, *Beneath the Visiting Moon*, was an *Evening Standard* book of the month in 1940, the same year she married Eric.

During World War Two, and on the encouragement of Noël Coward, she turned to the theatre. She eventually wrote twelve produced plays, including the Coward-titled *I'll See You Again*.

Romilly Cavan died of cancer on 5 August, 1975.

NOVELS BY ROMILLY CAVAN

Heron (aka *The Daughters of Richard Heron*) (1934)

To-morrow is Also a Day (1935)

The Splendour Falls (1936)

Characters in Order of Appearance (1938)

Mary Cloud (1939)

Beneath the Visiting Moon (1940)

ROMILLY CAVAN

BENEATH THE VISITING MOON

With an introduction by
Charlotte Moore

DEAN STREET PRESS

A Furrowed Middlebrow Book
FM34

Published by Dean Street Press 2019

Copyright © 1940 Romilly Cavan

Introduction © 2019 Charlotte Moore

All Rights Reserved

Published by licence, issued under the UK Orphan Works
Licensing Scheme.

First published in 1940 by William Heinemann

Cover by DSP

ISBN 978 1 913054 25 0

www.deanstreetpress.co.uk

To

MARION SPRING

young boys and girls
Are level now with men: the odds is gone,
And there is nothing left remarkable
Beneath the visiting moon.

Antony and Cleopatra

INTRODUCTION

"After this summer, the world may end" he said.

THE SPEAKER is Bracken, ageless, all-purpose family friend of the Fontaynes. It's the summer of 1939. The Fontaynes are a "linked family" whose aristocratic connections make up, socially at least, for their lack of cash. Their ancestral home, also called Fontayne, is on the market, though nobody really expects to find a buyer for a place so large, decrepit and outmoded. Meanwhile, international disaster is brewing. Breakfast on the sunlit terrace is disturbed by the daily newspaper hanging over the morning "like a guillotine ready to cut it to shreds", but the Fontaynes drift along in a "dream-like atmosphere of unaccomplished things".

The central character is seventeen-year-old Sarah, a restless beauty longing for change. Her twin brother Christopher wants to fly aeroplanes; to the older generation, shaped by the Great War, young men like Christopher seem in "good shape for slaughter", but he's too young to sense the doom. Shy fifteen-year-old Philly, in perpetual retreat from her over-exotic full Christian name Philadelphia, keeps hens, loves her cat Ernest, the villagers' babies and reading comics, and harbours socialist opinions, but will do anything to help Sarah fulfil her romantic ambitions. Little Tom, the eccentric nine-year-old with a quaint turn of phrase, slips by ungoverned and virtually uneducated, bewitching everyone with his dark eyes and blond fringe. Elisabeth, their unworldly mother, can hardly focus on anything beyond gardening and flower-arranging. For her, "yesterday's dismays were screened now by the lilies in white bud below the terrace." Elisabeth is a widow. Fontayne was once an intellectual Mount Olympus, but when her gifted husband Marcus died, its glory days died too.

An English family house, a rural community, a shifting class system, all poised on the brink of war- these rich ingredients have been well used by novelists. One thinks of the solid pleasures of, for instance, Elizabeth Jane Howard's Cazalet Chronicles. What's striking about *Beneath The Visiting Moon* is that it was written in 1940, as events unfolded. Romilly Cavan, writing in her London flat that would be bombed twice, must have believed, like Bracken, that the world might very well end.

Romilly Cavan was born Isabelle Wilson in July 1914, on the very eve of the First World War. Her mother, Desemea Wilson, produced thirty gorgeously-jacketed romantic novels under the pseudonym Diana Patrick, and when Isabelle began to write she also adopted a pseudonym, "Cavan", perhaps in homage to her Irish heritage. Her first novel, *Heron*, was published when she was only twenty-one. At the launch party she met the literary journalist Eric Hiscock, pronounced Hiscoe. They married six years later, by which time she had written five more novels, of which *Beneath The Visiting Moon*, *Evening Standard* Book of the Month, would be the last. Eric Hiscock claimed that the wartime paper shortage was the reason Romilly gave up novels for plays. Encouraged by Noël Coward, she wrote twelve.

She is a shadowy figure. An early dust-jacket photograph shows thin, fine-boned intensity. Eric described her as "dark Irish, very secretive"; she wouldn't let him read anything she'd written until it was finished. She aimed high, and was jealously competitive with other female authors. She couldn't stand to have Edna O'Brien mentioned, said Eric, wouldn't allow her books over the threshold – but after Romilly's death (from cancer, aged 61) he opened a cupboard and found O'Brien's complete works concealed within. Perfectionism, as much as the paper shortage, may have prematurely ended her novel-writing career.

This is a great pity, because *Beneath The Visiting Moon* is glorious. Though Cavan kept the details of her life private, her tastes – one might say, her loves – blaze from its pages. Weather, colour, scents, food, clothes, cats, gardens, houses, the sea . . . all are described in exact, fulfilling detail; "It was the full peacock hour of mid afternoon"; "this side of the posturing yews, tall shaggy hollyhocks made a bright little wilderness, with shadows lying in long lines like palings overthrown"; "all the débris and fluff of August going through a squalid phase"; "Ernest [the cat] buttoned up his eyes for slumber". She has an acute eye for social detail. Village life on a warm day has "a friendly laziness of football, speech, laughter", but she also notes "a width of class-dividing road". One knows just what she means by "the sherry pause". When the Fontayne girls learn that the Christian name of their old, revered, aristocratic neighbour is Bunty, they are as shocked as if they had seen her in the bath. She skewers characters with her verbal precision. Sarah is in love with handsome Sir Giles, a politician always flitting off to try to put the world to rights. Can this suave individual really be right for her?, we wonder. "Sir Giles stood dark against a background of sunlight, like an advertisement of the Riviera" tells us that no, he can't.

"Living at Fontayne is so soft. You sink into it, as if it's a sort of warm mist", complains Sarah. Comic characters arrive to break into the softness. Lupin the pretentious artist ("'He says I'm golden', Philly said humbly"), Harbrittle, whose novels sag "like a Dachshund, in the middle", Lady Pansy, an ageing beauty of spider-like selfishness, feckless Mrs Rudge who cheerfully blows the money her infant triplets win in a beauty competition, the plump prodigy Bronwen who publishes her memoirs at the age of thirteen and finds herself yoked to the Fontayne girls in ill-assorted step-sisterhood; these and many more leap off the page. But the comedy is tinged with something darker. What are the choices available to girls like Sarah and Philly? Sarah strikes out independently and finds herself a menial job, but is sacked after a few weeks; Philly falls back on reading fairy stories to the village children. Marriage, then? "You're either shrivelled and quite sweet and harmless or else tight and wound up, if you don't get married", declares Sarah. Sweet, vague Elisabeth has a second go at marital happiness with Bronwen's mild musical father, who bears "just a hinted resemblance to that so reasonable and kind Metro-Goldwyn-Major lion"; this union allows the Fontayne ménage to muddle on for a little longer, but the blended family in the oversized house feels like "tiny dwarf groups going their own ways, never warmly mingling". "I'd rather have fried bread" declares little Tom at the sumptuous wedding breakfast, summing up the "rising tide of filial resentment" afflicting them all. Cavan refuses to stitch happy endings together, and never lets us forget that "a gas mask won't save Ernest or any of us".

Beneath the Visiting Moon's surface sparkle illuminates sombre depths. Lonely, unfulfilled adults, traumatised children, and, most convincingly of all, girls on the exhausting treadmill of adolescence are created by Romilly Cavan with something of Dodie Smith's lightness of touch, something of Virginia Woolf's sense of human tragedy. The combination leaves us sharing Elisabeth's feeling that "all, (with the exception of the world) was well with the world". Cavan's achievement is the very essence of bittersweet.

Charlotte Moore

CHAPTER ONE

THE CHILDREN hung perilously over the beautiful curving staircase.

"The front door has opened and shut—"

"I can't see—"

"I didn't see. What was he like?"

"Rabbity but determined. Would never offer a sum worth having."

"Why did Cruddles let him in, then?"

"You know what Cruddles is. Ever hopeful. Anyway, I don't think Cruddles is such a good judge of character as we are."

They continued to hang limply, although the cause for their curiosity had vanished into the flower room which led off the hall. Nobody at Fontayne could have explained why the flower room, at once so dank and so frivolous, was used for the interviewing of prospective buyers of the place.

"I hope we didn't leave those decayed daffodils around," Sarah said. "It might prejudice him."

"If he isn't going to buy, that won't matter," Philly pointed out.

"But he might think we were a dirty horrid family," Sarah said sadly. Her own untidiness chastened her spirit sometimes, and for brief periods she longed to be able to describe herself as "fastidious."

Tom gave a rich chuckle deep in his throat. It was a mature lubricated sound, wonderfully unsuited to a nine-year-old boy. The two girls laughed sympathetically. Christopher sighed faintly.

"It's awful that we should *want* to sell Fontayne," Christopher said.

"We can't go all over that again," Sarah frowned at him. "Sentimentality is supposed to be a vice, anyway."

"I'm not sentimental," Christopher said hotly.

"Don't let's quarrel," Philly said equably. "Christopher will soon be going back to school."

All four were silent for a few moments. Sarah, who, as the eldest, had the vantage leaning space, stared down on the remote plateau of the hall floor, spacious and full of a dark gloomy light even on this morning of busy spring sunlight. April will go and Christopher will go and summer will come and nothing will happen. . . . She felt a not unpleasant lassitude of melancholy creeping over her.

"A lot of money must be going out on Christopher's education," she said dreamily. "If we don't sell soon, he won't be able to go to Oxford."

"I don't want to go to Oxford," Christopher said amiably, almost placidly.

Often that near-placidity, which he shared with Philly, exasperated Sarah to the depths of her being. They were together in it, apart from her, strong in their twinship, formidably united.

"It's no use staying here," Sarah said restlessly. "I said I'd go shopping. I'll go down and see what we want."

Their sudden downward impetus held an unconsidered rhythm. Down, down, the dark light of the hall seeming to rise up to meet them. The domestic warmth of the upper floors gave way to the chill ceremony of the ground floor. In spiral flight they came, like a single body, a mindless force.

"I'll go and get the list from Mrs. Bale," Sarah said breathlessly, as she regained her own identity at the foot of the stairs.

The kitchens were unimaginably bleak. Mrs. Bale considered herself a martyr for putting up with them. Nobody minded pandering a little to her martyrdom, if it would prevent her leaving. Even Philly, who was essentially honest, fell into automatic cunning commiseration when she was with the cook. The rest of the indoor staff consisted of Cruddles and a succession of very young housemaids, one at a time, and for not very long at a time. This was one of the frequent occasions when there was no housemaid. Mrs. Bale was "managing," with the help of Sarah and Philly. Mrs. Moody, who came in twice a week to do odd jobs and sewing, scarcely counted. Neither, of course, did the old governess Miss Janies.

"Are we having anyone for the Week End?" Mrs. Bale asked accusingly.

"*Are* we?" Sarah stared. "Oh dear, it is possible, isn't it?"

"Quite," Mrs. Bale agreed grimly.

"In that case we'll have to augment the shopping list," Sarah went on grandly.

"I don't expect it would be anyone but Bracken," Philly said, sitting on one of the cosier, less dwarfing of the kitchen window sills. "Tildy is out there looking sinister, Mrs. Bale. Did you leave any safes or anything open?"

"I did not."

"Because she's licking her whiskers and rolling her eyes," Philly went on imperturbably.

"Be quiet, Philly. I believe Mother *did* say Bracken was coming for Easter. It's an excuse to have some nice meals . . ." Meeting Mrs.

Bale's eye, Sarah's words faltered: "I don't mean any blame to you for our meals being dreary. You-do-what-you-can-in-impossible-circumstances." The last was a gabbled formula, in deference to Mrs. Bale's martyrdom. It was used with as little regard for sincerity, and with as facile a tongue-wagging, as some formal mouthing of grace before meals. "Leave it to me, Mrs. Bale," she continued zestfully. "I'll get something interesting. Are you coming, Philly?"

Mrs. Bale eyed the two girls inimically. They were a nice pair, she thought; meaning that they weren't. Always thinking of themselves and their stomachs, and that Sarah had begun wearing a lot of powder on her face. They loitered, their expressions relaxed dreamily, in what Mrs. Bale called their idiotic moods.

"You'd better be getting along," she said stonily.

They smiled at her politely, irritatingly, from the midst of their idiotic dreams.

"I don't think she's ever been married, although she calls herself 'Mrs.'" Sarah said, as they went along a damp tunnel of a passage toward the hall.

"Do you think it can *show*," Philly asked, her heart sinking.

"Of course it does. You're either shrivelled and quite sweet and harmless or else tight and wound up, if you don't get married."

"Oh. . . ." Philly was not yet quite sixteen, but she knew she would never get married. She was terrified of all men except a few quite old ones and one or two who didn't seem particularly like men. "Well, don't let's talk about it," she sighed.

Sarah had already forgotten what they had been talking about. She was filled with a nervous energy of mingled desires and fears. The Easter weekend, imaginatively embellished, loomed dazzlingly. She knew how it would really be: a cold-mutton atmosphere which Bracken, as a too old friend of the family, would scarcely bother to dish up into something more exciting. Nevertheless, her heart and mind continued to rebel against that dull inevitability. Her thoughts contrived a shopping list to provide a brilliant social Week End with everything it could need.

They were walking down the weedy driveway. Green budding trees shot up to the pale blue sky. Philly's long black stockings stalked like solid shadows in the path of the sun.

"I wish you wouldn't wear those stockings to go into the village," Sarah said, her entrancing thoughts diverted. "You look like a schoolgirl."

"I ought to be a schoolgirl," Philly said equably.

"It isn't fair to me," Sarah said sternly. "Everyone classes us together; and what do you think I can make of my life if I'm classed as a schoolgirl? And don't ask me"—she paused to stamp her foot—"what I *am* making of it, because I know the answer is nothing at all." She glared angrily at her younger sister's offending stockings.

Philly would not have dreamed of asking Sarah such a leading and impertinent question. She squeezed Sarah's thin little hand with her own broader stronger one.

"I'd go back and change now," she whispered, "but my only decent pale ones are full of holes."

"What? Oh, stockings . . ." Sarah laughed, the tension gone. "You've broken all the bones in my hand."

They walked on, unperturbed by this catastrophe.

"Sometimes I wake up in the night and think it can't be true," Sarah said conversationally, after a short silence.

"What can't?"

"That I'm seventeen. I mean, it is utterly grown-up, whatever way you look at it. But nobody treats me with respect. Look at Mrs. Bale just now! Look at Cruddles, Mother, everyone! I might as well be Tom—"

"You're awfully pretty," Philly ventured.

"Pretty! I'm either beautiful or nothing at all."

"Beautiful—" Philly added hastily.

"Oh, Philly, you are sweet. How about some salmon? Oh and we must have melon. We could have ice cream with it. I think I've got the trick of how to make it, if Bale doesn't interfere. I can't think *how* we got that refrigerator—"

"Could you get some stockings for Easter? If Bracken's coming. I ought to have some for the evening, I suppose, even if I go without any during the day."

"Yes, Mother said to get you some next time we were shopping," Sarah said, quite graciously. "She meant about three pairs, I expect, so don't you think it would be a good idea if we just got you one very cheap pair and then bought some gingham with the rest of the money we would have spent? We must try that new pattern that Mrs. Moody gave us."

"I think it would be a lovely idea," Philly said.

"Then if the dresses turn out seemly we could wear them for church on Easter Sunday."

"I don't suppose they'd be quite seemly enough for that," Philly said, speaking from a wisdom of experience.

"Well, you needn't begin being horrid and dampening before we've even cut them out." Sarah glared.

They were out of the drive now, beyond the imposing and far too promising gates, and on to the road that led down to the village. It was a small town, really, but so small that the word "village" seemed a much more friendly way of describing it. It was further described, by the local guide book, as being full of quaint charm. This was true, but most of the more intellectual of the inhabitants chose to make fun of such epithets. When the wind was in the right quarter, other more rustic inhabitants had often told the children, you could smell the sea, which was a good ten miles away. But through the years the young Fontaynes had sniffed in vain, the scent of sea eluding them. "I'm afraid we haven't very discerning noses," Sarah had come to excusing herself and her brothers and sister.

The place often had a satisfactory depthless look, with light and shadow lying in neat lozenges of effectively thought-out patterns. Times when windowboxes, slung casually from the second-story windows of houses that were shops on their ground floors and residences above, were not the mere artistic whims of nature-loving dwellers, but the very expression of a street made from a child's single-minded design and carried out with the expert aid of scissors and paint-box and glue. Walking, you felt the steep pull of exacting two-dimensional demands. You were flat with the road and the buildings, at one with a paper-flat aspect of life, as if you were no more than sketched in lightly, as brief human interest, on the final architectural design. This point of view, the girls had found, left you with a most pleasing sense of release from the ordinary irksome pressure of daily life.

"Talking of ice creams," Philly said with precision, "do you think we could have one before we do the shopping?" Sarah, in another phase of the dream of a glamorous weekend, didn't answer. They were approaching the feudal rounded rose-coloured walls that enclosed the home of their old friend Mrs. Oxford.

"We'll call on the way back, if we have time," Sarah said socially, nodding at the wall.

"I wonder if she has any of those beautiful biscuits still."

"*Don't* keep thinking of your stomach, Philly. And *don't* call biscuits 'beautiful.'" It made Philly's former admission of her own beauty seem rather pointless.

The main street of the little town was the only shopping street. Beyond the haberdashery it tailed off into the common and then to open country. There was no wavering suburban line of "outskirts" to the town. One moment you were in it, the next it was gone; a clean break. On either side of the shopping street, there branched quiet dull little residential roads of varying degrees of respectability. The two girls had at least one special friend in most of these byways. Mrs. Moody, who had her particular connection with Fontayne twice a week, lived in the crude pink cottage with the solitary and funereal cypress tree stuck bang in line with her front door. And there was Mrs. Rudge, who had, on rare and desperate occasions, obliged with some scrubbing. Mrs. Rudge was a cheerful slatternly woman whose scrubbing had been scamped, to say the least; but all the children had a special warmth of feeling for her and her incredibly beautiful offspring. Even Bracken had admired them when they were pointed out to him. And Mrs. Oxford herself had been heard to say that "they looked like a trio of cherubs in improbable association with their separate niches on Mrs. Rudge's deplorable yard wall."

Shopping was a great success this morning. Still dazzled by her inward picture of the brilliant Week End, Sarah gave her orders with such an air of clear authority that even the shopkeepers, who knew all about the Fontayne finances, were impressed. The ices were left to the last, so that one could relax in a cool teeth-on-edge dream with the knowledge that all one's duties were done.

"I wish we lived in a large town where you could get music with your ices," Philly said, scooping the liquid yellow last drops of her threepenny vanilla from its plate.

On their way home, carrying some of the purchases most dear to their hearts, they met Bracken himself walking toward them.

"Have you come *already*?" Sarah cried out to him. "It isn't Easter yet."

"It is Good Friday tomorrow," he cried back.

"Even so—" The two words expressed reproof only thinly veiled.

He was near enough to them now to see Sarah's frown and Philly's dawning smile. How grown up they looked! How shall I talk to them? he thought quickly, coldly. Sarah's silky dark hair appeared to his simple eyes to have a new sophistication. Her small-boned patrician slenderness seemed to conserve a new kind of vitality, more conscious, more arrogant, than before. His eyes were grateful for Philly's still reasonably child-like appearance, but on the other hand she was growing so tall. Already her light brown head topped her sister's dark one. She was slender too, but not with that extreme tense fineness of form which

individualized Sarah. Really individualized, Bracken thought, eyeing
Sarah. Spun glass . . . , he added silently, deliberately exaggerating.
Both the girls wore thick old skirts and sweaters, not highly suited to
the warm spring morning.

"What have you been doing?" he asked.

"Buying champagne and gingham and things."

"Champagne!"

"Well, Bob Norbett, who works at the wine merchant's is quite a
friend of ours," Sarah said.

"Quite a friend indeed if you feel obliged to buy his champagne."

"Only one bottle. We really went in for some mineral water for
mother."

"And for whom is the champagne?"

"For you, we thought," Sarah said disarmingly.

She accepted Bracken, loving him as almost a part of the family.
He was not the sort of man she would have expected to be a great
friend of her father; but he had been. He was small, with blue eyes,
a bald spot, and a tranquil spirit; he was also American and, Sarah
supposed, about fifty.

"Mother is selling the house again this morning," Philly said.
Bracken was one of the few men with whom she was at ease.

"Any hopes?"

"Oh, no," Sarah said lightly.

"You'll be horrified when it does get sold."

"Our lives *hinge* on selling Fontayne," she retorted reprovingly.

There was silence for a while. The white road threw up little
powdery clouds that suggested, oddly, a greater heat than the April
day gave. The country seemed sheathed by some idyllic patina; nothing could possibly be wrong with the world, it improbably proclaimed.
The girls were in accord with the landscape, Bracken felt. It was
extraordinary how their general ignorance could suggest single-mind-
edness. . . . He laughed aloud.

Their eyes questioned him.

"I was thinking of you with far more respect than you deserve," he
said.

"Did you come out to meet us or haven't you arrived properly yet?"
Philly asked.

"I haven't arrived properly. I left my suitcase at the station, 'to come
up later,' whatever that means."

"It means what it always has meant—Proctor's cart," Sarah said. "Then why were you coming in the wrong direction?"

"Because I looked back and saw you and turned to meet you."

"Then you'll be tired," she said kindly. "We'll stop at Mrs. Oxford's and rest for a few minutes."

Mrs. Oxford was a very rich old lady. She had heavy aristocratic eyelids and a quantity of huge diamond rings which she wore all at once and always, in a way that might have been vulgar ostentation in most people, but was not so in her, even though her fingernails were frequently slightly dirty. She was in fact highly conventional and circumspect. Each morning on awakening—even before her tea—she read a chapter of her Bible. It put her in excellent benevolent countenance for the day, the more so for the special emphasis in her mind on its being *her* Bible. She had one orphan grand-daughter, Emily, who lived with her and whom she bullied for the child's own good. Her greater indulgence was allowed to the Fontayne children, to whom, in former days, she had occasionally been known to extend the privilege of stroking her in the little soft plushy hollow under her chin.

Emily was playing docilely by herself in the garden as they went in at the gateway in the rose-coloured wall. They asked if her grandmother were in, and were shyly told yes, she was trying on some new hair. It was no secret that Mrs. Oxford experimented with wigs, and nobody would have dreamed of laughing at her because everyone knew she *had* some hair of her own; neither had anyone ever questioned this thin line of reasoning which separated what was legitimately humorous from what was not.

Yes, it would be quite all right for them to go in, Emily assured; Grandmother would be pleased. She said this faintly wistfully, knowing what favourites the Fontaynes were. *Their* father had merely died, whereas her own had left her mother, which seemed to make an enormous difference in Grandmother's estimation. Nothing that Emily ever did or ever would do could be quite right, because her father had left her mother.

Mrs. Oxford watched Emily almost morbidly for signs of the inferiority of her dead mother. That Emily's mother had been her own daughter was a constant source of shame to the old lady. Although the women of her family had never been conspicuously beautiful, they prided themselves on their decorous powers of magnetism. The fact of Emily's mother so far forgetting herself as not only to lose the regard of her husband but to allow herself to become so distasteful to him that he could no longer bear the sight of her, was so humiliating that Mrs. Oxford dwelt upon it only in the strictest Bible-preserved privacy of her bedroom. But Emily, like the poor, was always with her, a humbling admission of the failures to which her sex could sink.

Emily herself was an extremely nice little girl, only too anxious to please in all ways. But her very anxiety told against her, because it suggested she might be going to follow in her mother's lamentable steps. She was already a very tidy little thing, which was all the more reason for her grandmother to view her with consternation as a born good housekeeper and trusting believer in the notion that man's deepest respect and love was invariably for a nice capable homemaker. And nothing, in Mrs. Oxford's estimation, could be farther from the truth than that.

Emily, without resentment against fate, led the lucky Fontaynes toward the house. Her knobbly little knees showed beneath her short frock. Her small face, serious between her dark plaits of hair, had an elusive loveliness, but she was quite unaware of this. She was nine years old, and extremely thin.

"Why don't you come and see Tom if you feel lonely during the holidays?" Sarah suggested kindly.

Mrs. Oxford appeared almost as soon as they were into one of the dark heavily-furnished rooms that was typical of all in her house. She kissed the two girls and held out a diamond-flashing hand to Bracken.

"But how dear of you all to call!"

Sarah loved the immediate atmosphere the old lady created, as of some imminent vast reception wherein there could be no one who was not witty, handsome, and compelling.

"We're on our way back from shopping and Bracken has come for Easter," Philly said.

"The town is not at all what it was. Far too much give and take. Far too much voluntary discarding of privileges. Mr. Bracken, you will take a glass of sherry? And the biscuits—go and fetch the biscuits, Emily."

The girls were glad their old friend had interrupted herself in her favourite theme of the disintegration of one class of society into another. They were guiltily sure that she would see it as a betrayal of her class if she knew they had bought champagne for the reason that Bob Norbett was such a good friend of theirs.

"The town seems quite full," Sarah said, making conversation, and accepting a biscuit from the box Emily proffered.

"Too full, perhaps," Mrs. Oxford took her up. "I hear that some people have temporarily taken that ugly place Copley's Green, and they are looking for a more attractive place around here in which to settle down. Though from what one hears they are not the settling down kind."

"Who are they?" Sarah asked.

"I forget the name, but I hear they are dreadful musical artistic people out of a book."

"Not *really* out of a book?" Philly stared at her, startled, for some reason thinking of the fairy tales Bracken had written for them when they were young.

"I can guess the type," Mrs. Oxford said distantly, ignoring Philly. "Colourful and erratic and improbable."

Like the Sangers, Sarah thought hopefully; but no, Mrs. Oxford had most likely got it all wrong.

"Not the sort of people one would want to know, my dears. Another glass of sherry, Mr. Bracken?"

"No, thank you," Bracken said, enjoying himself.

"But would you want to know us if you didn't know us?" Sarah inquired, with a certain pointedness.

"Your father fought for England, dear, and then helped to rule her," Mrs. Oxford reminded her, as if to say, "What more could you want?"

"But he practically died of debts, it seems."

"England should have seen to it that so devoted a son was not worried by tiresome details," Mrs. Oxford said magnificently.

"But you couldn't really expect England to bother with us."

"No. Think of poor Emma," Bracken said.

Emily looked up from her biscuit, wondered if they were talking of her, decided they weren't, and went on crunching unobtrusively.

Sarah rather liked being classed with poor Emma. It made her feel romantic. But, then, Emma had got fat and seen Naples and died, or something. It was nicer to be alive and slim, even if you weren't a hero's mistress.

"Apart from these people at Copley's Green, I hear Mr. Harbrittle has a distinguished friend staying with him," Mrs. Oxford said, in her social-register voice. "But of course he always has *someone* at the holidays. At Christmas it was that Indian prince, you know."

"For someone who writes such blood-thick earthy novels, Mr. Harbrittle does seem to like illustrious people," Sarah said. "I'm afraid we'll have to go now, in case Mrs. Bale needs any last-minute help with lunch."

"Poor children," Mrs. Oxford said compassionately, quite shattered to think of her young friends in contact with the Fontayne kitchens, which she was personally convinced contained cockroaches.

Mrs. Fontayne and the boys were already in the dining room when the others reached home. She greeted Bracken without attempt at ceremony, and smiled at him sweetly and vaguely.

Elisabeth Fontayne was beautiful and romantic and good. Knowing that she had no brains she was amazed that her children should be even as clever as they were. For she had never, in her heart of hearts, been able to believe that her husband had any brains, either. After all, a clever man should have left one with enough to live on. (Not that she ever blamed him for not doing so.) She did what was possible with the meagre income that had been rescued from the midst of his debts. But the proper upkeep of Fontayne was not one of the possibilities. She kept accounts and reminders of her various commitments but, as nothing by any chance ever balanced, it was little more than a nice gesture, like going to church on Sunday morning. Fontayne had a great number of rooms, including a ballroom seventy feet long and suitably wide. It would have been enough to take the heart out of a much stronger character than Mrs. Fontayne.

"We're sorry we're late. Mrs. Oxford kept us," Sarah said breathlessly. "Did Mrs. Bale manage?"

"I suppose so, darling. Bracken, will you sit at the end? Make Ernest get off your chair."

Philly rescued her cat and sat down with it on her knee under the table. Bracken took his seat meekly in a residue of cat's hairs.

"Grapefruit!" Christopher said, in a tone of simple and general congratulation.

"Mrs. Moody is coming this afternoon," Tom said, with a brooding contentment.

"Good!" Sarah exclaimed with more brisk pleasure. "She's really coming to make some curtains, but she can give us a few more hints about that pattern, Philly."

"Mrs. Moody seems extremely popular," Bracken said.

"She taught us all we know about dressmaking," Sarah said with quiet dignity.

Thereafter the conversation was restricted. The children were abstracted to all except the meal, which was not bad for once. The four had a peculiar resemblance to each other when they fell into this dream state which separated them from all else except one another.

Tom was in some ways the best dreamer of the lot. His colouring—fair hair and very dark eyes with astonishing dark eyelashes—helped to create a dramatic effect. Philly and Christopher, with mere grey eyes, were not so fortunate in their fairness.

The best silver forks and spoons—Sarah gazed at them with almost tender pride. It was a pity Cruddles would never let them be used except when there were visitors. And, for once, the sort of tablecloth that could be described as snowy damask. How lovely life could be, in spite of people saying it was nothing but a nightmare nowadays. . . .

"Mother, Bracken hasn't got anything to drink," she said, her bliss interrupted.

"Oh, dear! What a pity we had to let the cellar go. And they were such horrid men who came to buy it. They *criticized* it. After Marcus had put it down with such loving care, too—or whatever it is one does to cellars."

"But Bracken wants a drink *now*, Mother," Christopher urged. He sometimes suffered agonies of humiliation because the Fontayne hospitality was not what it should be.

"I really prefer water at lunchtime," Bracken quietly insisted.

"Perhaps he hasn't got over Prohibition," Sarah said.

Tom's mature mellow chuckle rolled through the room. "I hate old water, that I do," he stated simply. "But I hate old lemonade even more."

Silence came in again with the pudding.

"Do you think Cruddles would make us some coffee?" Sarah said, when the final regretful scraping of plates came. "If so, I shall have a cigarette," she announced as a matter of general interest.

"I'll go and ask him," Tom said, sliding from his chair. "You could have it on the terrace with talk."

"Tom is the only one with a sense of organization in the family," Mrs. Fontayne said.

"Philly and I can cut out our dresses on the terrace; and you can read aloud some of your tales to us if you like, Bracken," Sarah said graciously.

Years ago, when Tom was a baby and even Sarah was very young, Bracken had written some astonishing fairy tales specially for them. Of such a blending of the exquisitely macabre and the fantastically humorous had they been that the children had always looked upon them as a very part of their lives. They had never allowed their mother's unthinkable suggestion that the stories ought to be published so that other children might have the pleasure of them.

* * * * *

When the coffee was finished and the gingham cutting out was in full swing, Philly, after profound meditation, said: "Those people-out-of-a-book may be artistic, but they must be rich too, if they've taken Copley's Green. Why shouldn't they buy Fontayne?"

Sarah, brandishing the scissors perilously over Philly's serene fair head, eyed her younger sister admiringly.

"What a marvellous idea, Philly! I suppose you didn't sell to that man this morning, Mother?"

"No, darling, I'm afraid not. He didn't seem to think the kitchens would be convenient."

"And I expect he smelt mice and dead daffodils and the gas escaping in Bracken's bedroom. But I don't suppose artistic people would mind about little things like that."

"Did you say gas?" Bracken asked, in the voice of one who merely wanted to know.

"Oh, it's all right," Sarah reassured him. "It's not *half* enough to kill anyone. I think we ought to call on Copley's Green, Mother, and be awfully social and blameless, and then gradually and subtly *inveigle* them over here and push the place down their throats, as you might say."

"It doesn't sound very nice," Mrs. Fontayne demurred. "You can't be nice and business-like at the same time. Can you, Bracken?"

"I suppose not," he said, only half listening. His contentment was clear and sharp-etched, which was rather reprehensible, he thought, for there was little that was admirably decisive in a weekend with the Fontaynes.

"The thing is to find out all about them." Sarah slashed viciously through the gingham. "Mrs. Moody will know. I'll go and see if she has arrived. She will know all about Mr. Harbrittle's visitor, too."

"It's Sir Giles Merrick, the diplomat or something," Philly said, not looking up from matching notches in the material.

"What do you mean? How can you know?" Sarah shot out a thin hand and clutched her sister's knee urgently. "How do you get to know things?"

"I just listen," Philly said placidly. "I heard Cruddles talking to Mrs. Bale. Cruddles said he shouldn't wonder if he'd come to think over a major Cabinet move, in peace and quiet-like."

"Whom are you talking about?" Sarah sat on her haunches and rocked her knees: she was frantic with impatience. "Cruddles or Sir Giles Merrick? Besides, he isn't in anybody's Cabinet, is he?"

"I don't know. I was just telling you what Cruddles said." She went on with her work, taking up great swooping stitches with tacking thread now.

"I must go and find out—"

Sarah swept herself to her feet. Sir Giles Merrick was always having his pictures in the paper. He was poised, utterly adult, and—her mind paused in its flight for a suitable word—and, surely, a little decadent.

It seemed as if the terrace settled down with relief to its peace again when Sarah was gone. Down below, away from the house, the clipped yews had sprouted a little from their proper symmetry, so that the dodos (or whatever the fantastic bird-growths were) seemed tipped with feathery green haloes through which the sun came shimmeringly.

Sarah has become a beautiful young lady, Bracken thought, as he closed his eyes and gave himself up to the increased peace; but she does not yet act too much like a young lady.

Mrs. Moody was in the sewing room when Sarah got there.

"Hello, duck," she said casually, absent-mindedly, her thoughts on curtains.

"I have a lot to ask you, Mrs. Moody."

"If you're using that pattern, be sure you don't get it too tight under the arms—"

Mrs. Moody was short, thick-set, and middle-aged and had a perceptible, not to say pronounced, moustache. On the face of her, it would have been difficult to know why the children were so devoted to her. Perhaps of all of them Tom was the most alive to her excellence. Tom, when he came out of his dreams, was given to inventing spectacular useless things and doing secret unfathomable sums. There was a special affinity between him and Mrs. Moody, so that all his inscrutable works went much better when she was near. Crouched beneath the sewing table, while she whirred along seams, her hand turning the sewing-machine handle at enormous speed, all sorts of ideas came to him and were the finer for Mrs. Moody's presence.

"I want to know all about the people at Copley's Green and Mr. Harbrittle's guest," Sarah demanded. She stood in the doorway, framed in the heavy greenish light of the narrow second-floor passage, which led also to the schoolroom and the nurseries.

"Well, their name is Jones, dear, and they're clever." Mrs. Moody grappled with a pin which she seemed to have, as she had most people's affairs, at the tip of her tongue.

"Jones!" Sarah wilted slightly.

"As for Sir Giles Merrick, my cousin who sometimes works for Mr. Harbrittle, says the house has been fair turned upside down for him. Talk about the Indian prince, he wasn't in it, except for that special food he ate. But there's Mr. Harbrittle picking out special books for this Sir Giles's bedside. Crisis books and that."

"That must be very bad for him. I'd give him a nice light novel to go to sleep with. But these Joneses—have they any money?"

"They do say they have."

"Then they can't be musicians."

"I've heard they are. They are a widower and a son and daughter. I'll have to go and measure these curtains. Going to be a nice hot Easter, it looks like."

"Spring weather can be too nice," Sarah said soberly. "It makes you . . . I don't know . . . want all sorts of things to happen."

"Yes dear, I know what you mean. I used to feel the same, I think. Love and that."

"I didn't say that," Sarah said haughtily.

"That's what it boils down to, dear. And if you want to boil it down still more, it's *sex*, that's what it is."

For a moment Sarah almost hated Mrs. Moody, sitting there in her smug certainty of life's consequences. Horrid thing, with her gas-fire-mottled legs and the petticoat frill that always showed. Hated her, creaking with knowledge, her solid corseted frame so sure of itself, swaying in boned stiffness, complacent in ugliness.

"Whatever happened I could never wear corsets," Sarah said passionately.

"Doesn't look as if you'll ever need to, duck," Mrs. Moody said calmly, glancing at the girl's taut body. "I must go and do my bit of measuring now."

Good Friday was the smell of hot-cross-buns and the aura of an almost pious tranquillity over the gardens and the contrast of the girls still busy with their sewing. Tom had an enormous chocolate Easter egg. The others said he was broody over it; he fondled it, but wouldn't dream of eating it.

Bracken looked out of his bedroom window, early, and saw Philly on the terrace, stockingless, stroking her cat. Ernest was a large and lustrous tabby, a normal cat in all ways—Philly had said—except that he didn't like cats. Philly pandered to him with a fierce maternal affection, in contrast with her usual cool sweet-tempered manner. Greyish cloud broke for a moment and a gleam of sunlight fell on the girl's golden-brown arms and legs and her pale brown severely brushed-back hair. It wouldn't surprise me if one day she turned out wholly and unintentionally beautiful, Bracken thought. . . .

They drowsed the day away. Christopher brought out to the terrace one of the little books his father had written (the slimmest he could find), but he couldn't read it. Politics didn't seem to be up his street, as Mrs. Moody had correctly suggested only the other day.

Sarah wondered about the champagne. Good Friday definitely wasn't the day for it. Then it ought to be opened tomorrow, because neither did Easter Sunday seem suitable. Nothing was happening, after all. It was just any old Week End, with Bracken's white eyelids closed against the sun, his being remote in incredible polar regions of cold thought. It was dispiriting and unnerving. What was the use of having made a special chocolate mousse for everyone's pleasure when Bracken probably had his mind pitched to the miserable history of man throughout the ages?

Saturday was altogether a more invigorating day, although it began in much the same way, except that the hot-cross buns were done with and Tom's smooth egg now had a blurred and dissipated appearance.

Mrs. Fontayne awakened with a certain distaste for the day. During Good Friday, she had resolutely, even reverently, put the thought of bills out of her mind; but now the memory came back with redoubled energy. And Mrs. Oxford was coming to lunch with Emily. And the girls had made her promise to call at Copley's Green this afternoon. And when she got downstairs there would be the morning papers as large as life but surely more terrible than life could be. Those morning papers uncovering the wounds of the world; she could not be sure that even breakfast on the terrace in the now brilliant Easter sunlight could put the seemly bandages in place again. . . . If only Marcus had lived, she thought helplessly. Her mind never went so far as to specify how Marcus's frantic urgent ideas (so like Sarah's) could have solved the frantic urgent problems of the world; but nevertheless that "If only . . ." helped her.

And when she came downstairs she found that after all everything was surprisingly gay. But so gay! The children teased the hours, stretching them, dismissing them. Misery was all beneath, decently hidden. In any case, Mrs. Oxford's presence at lunch would be a talisman against all but the most seemly phases of living.

Sarah had decided that they should not confide to Mrs. Oxford their plan to call on Copley's Green.

Philly agreed without argument. She was more concerned about her new pair of stockings, already in holes; but the weather was too exquisitely warm to worry much about anything. Often, she drifted into this sense of irresponsibility, although she did not approve of it in herself. When she got into this mood, she always tried to get out of it by fixing her mind on her gas mask; but even this didn't invariably work.

Mrs. Oxford's Daimler rolled up the drive punctually at one. Emily sat on the edge of the seat, leaning forward, her hands clasped.

Christopher was there, opening the door and helping the old lady out, before the chauffeur could get to her. He was a lovely boy, Mrs. Oxford thought, with a voluptuous sort of sentiment. The presence of young men warmed her heart with an innocent fire; and Christopher, though scarcely sixteen, she saw as a young man. With his fair-brown skin and his free young limbs he made her think of the Bible, though she could not have said why.

Tom came running up, pulling at his socks, so that there seemed something hiccupping, drunken, in his progress.

"We have been cleaning up," he said cheerfully. "Cruddles said we'd have a spick-and-span Easter or die in the attempt. I dusted and Sarah broomed."

Mrs. Oxford winced. These poor children in their menial roles— And here came Sarah, with a smut on her cheek. Marcus Fontayne's daughter, who should be having a season in London, befitting her position. Oh dear, oh dear. . . .

"Tom, take Emily and show her your inventions or something," Sarah said in her grown-up voice.

Mortification was too deep in Tom to be shown by any visible signs. He did not bat an eyelid. But he felt his teeth freeze with distaste both for his sister and the little girl with the plaits.

"Come with me," he said with a terrible politeness, and Emily, abandoning herself to the ultimate of despair, went with him.

Cruddles always dressed perfectly to receive Mrs. Oxford.

He was at the door now, exuding his matured, even welcome, the chill just sufficiently taken off it, like good claret: a calculated personal temperature which he reserved only for those for whom he held a deep respect.

The perfect butler—Sarah wanted to giggle. Mrs. Oxford would be horrified if she knew what a malignant nature Cruddles could have in private.

Mrs. Oxford waited expectantly after Mrs. Fontayne had greeted her and before luncheon began. Of course!—the sherry pause. And they had forgotten to get any. The dry sherry pause passed over as if it didn't exist—how awful! Poor Mrs. Oxford.

"Will you have champagne with lunch?" Sarah burst out, with a frantic desire to put things right.

"My dear child, no!" Momentarily off guard, the old lady's tone gave the impression that champagne was still a Gaiety chorus girl's drink, and nothing else, to her.

Bracken came in and somehow, miraculously, managed to fill up that all too dry sherry pause. He was actually bothering to be social. How sweet he was!

"—dining there tonight," Mrs. Oxford was saying. "Mr. Harbrittle has a small house-party."

"To meet Sir Giles Merrick . . ." Sarah said dreamily. "What will you wear, Mrs. Oxford?"

For some reason they all laughed, though Sarah didn't know why. But Mrs. Oxford said quite kindly:

"Can it matter, dear? An old woman such as I. Sir Giles, I am sure, likes beautiful young women."

The sudden appearance of Philly interrupted this intriguing theme.

"Could we please eat at once?" she said anxiously. "Mrs. Bale has made a fish soufflé and it may sag or something if we don't get to it quickly."

"Do you mind?" Mrs. Fontayne turned to her guest, her large grey eyes full of an undirected compassion.

"Who else besides you is going to dinner at Mr. Harbrittle's?" Sarah asked wistfully, halfway through the meal.

"Mr. Lupin, I believe," Mrs. Oxford said. "Emily, keep your shoulders up."

Emily shot bolt upright and knocked over her glass of water. Fire and water drenched her, her face bathed in a scarlet blush and her lap in well-iced moisture.

"I'll mop you—never fear," Tom said, chivalry uppermost, his hate for her gone.

Mrs. Oxford, after one pained glance at her granddaughter, went smoothly on about Mr. Lupin.

"You know him, don't you, my dears?" she addressed the girls.

"He comes down to his cottage most Week Ends. We sometimes meet him in the village," Sarah said, without enthusiasm.

"He's always making fun of people who hike or are literary or social or who dress for dinner and things like that," Philly said comprehensively.

"I believe he's literary himself," Sarah accused. "And I know he hikes. But he makes a big point of calling it *walking*."

"Yes, he tramps through vineyards," said Philly, who often knew the oddest things about people. "I suppose that *would* make you feel superior."

"There aren't any vineyards here," Sarah added, "so he just fishes and vents himself on people who aren't simple. He ought to like us, because we're simple, but somehow it doesn't follow."

"He hates modern girls and people who don't eat and drink gar-gar-gantuanly," Philly continued from her secret fund of knowledge.

"Then he *ought* to like us," Christopher insisted. "We aren't literary and we do eat a lot when we get the chance, and I shouldn't think we're modern." He took a gulp of water. "He sounds pretty bogus, anyway," he pronounced with finality.

Mrs. Oxford was privately disconcerted by this summary of Mr. Lupin. Never mind the rest, but—not dress for dinner when invited to meet Sir Giles Merrick? *That* was unthinkable. . . .

"Do you mind if we rush on with our sewing while you drink coffee?" Sarah asked the old lady, after lunch. "We rather want to wear these dresses this afternoon." It seemed deceitful not to tell her where they were going, but she would probably find out soon enough.

Mrs. Oxford sat at the drawing-room window—the sun outdoors was too strong for her—and watched the two girls putting the last-minute touches to their gingham, as they sat outside on the terrace. The shoulder-length dark curling hair of the elder, and the shorter satin-straight light hair of the younger, took her eye. Charming, charming. . . .

"The age of innocence," she murmured aloud, benevolently.

How can she? Sarah slashed savagely at a dart on the shoulder. She spoils it all. How can I think of being glamorous if she says things like that?

"The most precious of all gifts—youth," Mrs. Oxford went on, unable to leave well alone.

Philly, her mind hovering on the horrors of growing up and having to talk to young men, glanced up in amazement at such a dictum.

"Oh, but I'd like to be old!" she cried. "I can't imagine anything nicer."

Mrs. Oxford, who had forgotten (but did not know that she had) what it was like to be young, was shocked.

Bracken sat a little apart, on the terrace but removed from the family grouping inside and outside the house. The heat was that of midsummer. He sat in a bright red deckchair, his eyes enjoying the pretty scene. Yet, without knowing why, he had a surface sense of doom upon it all. Only surface, because the doom, whatever way you looked at it, would be as ephemeral as was the scene itself. Fontayne, decayed by the times, had scarcely even a minor significance. He stretched his arms. How shocked poor Elisabeth would be if she knew he were thinking like this; she would see it as a disloyalty to her dead husband.

The children patterned the early afternoon with their stillness and energy. Tom was still, rapt, standing in the drawing room at the window, his feathery-fair head against his mother's arm, his dark eyes blank-sweet. Christopher lounged alone, outside, and Bracken felt a current of something dimly but deliberately forlorn passing from him to the open window.

"What was the name of that noted young débutante of a few years ago, Sarah dear?" Mrs. Oxford said, leaning forward at the window.

"How should I know?" Sarah retorted shortly.

"Virginia Welwyn, that was it," the old lady went on imperturbably. "She married, but the husband died. Her photograph was everywhere for a time. But these beauties don't seem to last as they did in my day." She concluded casually: "Mr. Harbrittle said she would be there tonight."

"I've seen a picture of her," Christopher said unexpectedly. He remembered it; pearls at the throat and awful long dark painted fingernails. He turned his mind away, disconcerted that he should have remembered this at all.

He shuffled his shoes among the bruised little flowers that grew between the flagstones on the terrace. He felt a faint aloof jealousy of Tom snuggled so unself-consciously against his mother. The sight of her serene hand stroking Tom's hair up from his bony forehead disturbed him. He could not remember how he himself had felt when he was only nine.

Emily sat in the shadow of her plaits and watched Ernest watching birds. She was at peace. Nobody was talking to her, and her grandmother's eye wasn't on her. She retreated to her own country, within her mind. The Queen was riding in the Palace grounds. She was dressed in a purple habit and her hair was purple like a grape—

"Would you like one of these sweets?" Christopher asked rather gruffly.

"Thank you." Emily smiled shyly down at the box he offered. (Thank you, said the Queen, accepting a sweetmeat from a courtier. . . .)

Mrs. Oxford said it was time they went. Sarah sewed the last stitch and thought how well the day was working out. A clock struck three. Cruddles was collecting coffee cups. She glanced through the drawing-room window and raised her eyebrows at him, hoping he would interpret this correctly as a request to him to put up the ironing board for her in the so-called butler's pantry, as she had already warned him it would be needed. Mrs. Oxford rose and adjusted the diamonds on her gnarled fingers. Ernest lolloped in unconvincing pursuit of a bird. The terrace bloomed with a burst of chatter, farewells, and the sun spread like a tropic glaze on the green leaf and unopened buds of the magnolia sprawling up the house. It was the full peacock hour of mid-afternoon. The actively leisured passage of these minutes was a peacock's tail-spread mincing progress across the day. In electric blue and green and ardent splashes of orange, time was traced in a flare of colours that seemed to hold the absolute of light. The day might have been born to this peak, without beginning and with no threat of any end.

CHAPTER TWO

COPLEY'S GREEN was a large prosperous-looking house, solid and unimaginative. It stood in a symmetrically bedded garden that exuded a dazzling efficiency.

"Think of anyone artistic living there," Sarah said wonderingly. "Do we look awfully hot and dusty? You look beautiful, Mother. Anyone would think you had just stepped from your Rolls."

"If you had let me tell Mrs. Oxford where we were going, she would have dropped us here in her car," Mrs. Fontayne said, but without complaint.

"She's such a gossip, darling. Philly, *must* you keep hitching your arms about? The sleeves can't be so tight as all that."

"I think they got put in back to front. They seem to be sort of hunched in to the back of my neck." She took this predicament placidly. "Perhaps it will pass off."

"How can a solid thing like gingham 'pass off'?" Sarah demanded, annoyed.

"Couldn't you remake the sleeves?" Mrs. Fontayne asked. "We can't do it now. And it's now we want to make a good impression."

"But why should we bother whether we make a good impression?" Mrs. Fontayne said, suddenly fired with a lovely arrogant disdain, as she remembered she was Marcus Fontayne's widow.

"Because, if they seem rich, we are going to sell Fontayne to them, darling," Sarah explained again, patiently. "Have you got your cards? They're sure to be in on such an inopportune day for callers."

As they walked through the garden and drew near the house, they saw a man standing by one of the major and most bracing flower beds, staring at it rather ruefully.

"Good afternoon," he said gently, undemandingly.

"Good afternoon," Mrs. Fontayne returned waveringly.

"Are you Mr. Jones?" Sarah plunged for his not being the gardener, judging that his butcher-blue shirt and corduroy trousers, though suspicious, might just as well be artistic as horticultural.

"Yes," he said, bowing his tall thin body slightly.

"Oh, well, we've come to call. This is my mother, Mrs. Fontayne, and I'm Sarah and this is Philly."

They did not make use of the cards, after all.

"That's very nice of you," Mr. Jones said. "Will you—won't you have a drink or something?"

This was so unexpected that they all laughed; including, after a moment, Mr. Jones himself. He waved a thin hand and said he supposed he wasn't very good at callers, but wouldn't they at least come in?

They went into the turkey-red and chocolate-brown house, furnished by the former owner, now dead. Mr. Jones had longish greyish-red hair and velvet-dark eyes, and was nice-looking except for his old-world droopy-silky moustache. Or does it *make* him? Sarah considered this, eyeing him. He caught her eye and smiled so gently that she felt vaguely ashamed.

"Perhaps you'd like to meet my children?" he suggested diffidently.

"But of course," Sarah said in her Mrs. Oxford voice.

"I wonder if they can be found. We go our own ways, you see—" He smiled apologetically. "Peter is just eighteen, Bronwen thirteen."

Bronwen. . . . Sarah and Philly eyed each other.

"I'll just go and see—" Mr. Jones made a dive for the door and escaped.

"Is he very shy?" Mrs. Fontayne wondered, in a whisper.

"Just erratic, I expect," Sarah said. "Look at his trousers!"

In imagination, they looked at them.

"Bronwen—" Philly began.

"Yes, I'm afraid they're a bit Welsh or something," Sarah said, slightly distressed. "They'll probably slip through our fingers by being mystic. We won't know where we are with them."

"If you two young people would like to pop into the next room, you'll find my boy and girl," said Mr. Jones, entering the room as precipitously as he had fled it.

He looked so pleased with this suggestion that Sarah wondered if he could have evil designs on her mother, and whether it were safe to leave them alone together.

"They seem rather busy, but I daresay they'll be pleased to see you."

This decided Sarah. Busy indeed!

"Come along, Philly," she said curtly.

They pushed open the door of the next room. Sunlight danced over green plush curtains, a very upright piano, and a typewriter. The atmosphere seemed full of sprightly endeavour, so that for a moment Sarah felt: Here's an answer to all our endless drifting in and out of days. . . . But the feeling passed and was succeeded by something more wary. The young man (he was really more than a boy) stepped forward; and his eyes (Sarah stared in his face) were both fiery and absent-minded, which was not only disconcerting but exasperating.

"Good afternoon," Sarah began, with dead formality, "your father said—"

"Yes, I know." He smiled sombrely. "Do sit down if you can find a spot." The place was picturesquely littered with books and sheets of music and gramophone records. "This is Bronwen."

As he spoke, his sister was very slowly laying down a pen and casting a last loving glance at a writing pad on the table by the typewriter. There was a massive deliberation about her, a portentous solidity of movement. She had a broad rather flat face, a sallow complexion, long colourless fair hair, thick wrists on which barbaric bracelets jangled, and fat hands that wove the air like little plump doves in constant flight. For so plain a child she was filled with an awesome self-possession.

"You are the Fontaynes," she said.

"You are the Joneses," Sarah said, not to be put at any disadvantage.

"I have read things about your home—"

"Good," Sarah said, remembering the purpose of this mission. "It's a nice old place," she added, putting into her voice the sort of casual tender note she felt would appeal to people who had no ancestral home.

"In your father's day it was sometimes nicknamed Mount Olympus," Bronwen stated. "Sandleton mentions it in his autobiography, doesn't he?"

"I don't know," Sarah said shortly.

"We don't care for biographies," Philly put in hurriedly.

"It's an autobiography," Bronwen said, in a tone as flat as her face.

It was an unpropitious beginning. Sarah's gracious Mrs. Oxford manner froze within her.

"This is a terrible house," Bronwen went on easily, "and yet in a way it *has* something. You know how some Victorian houses are?—so gorgeously typical that they can give you quite a thrill? There's the most delicious stuffed pike in a glass case in the hall. Peter and I simply *fell* on it, didn't we, Peter?"

What was this? Falling on delicious stuffed pike with a thrill—Philly hitched at her self-willed sleeves and gazed respectfully at the stuffy riotous carpet.

"Your name is Peter Jones!" Sarah cried out, with inspired pointedness. "But it can't be! Peter Jones is a shop. We have bought lampshades and things there." *I can easily hold my own with them. . . .* She gazed triumphantly into the youth's dark melancholy eyes.

"It does sound rather silly, put that way," he admitted. "What are your names?"

"Mine is Sarah, I'm afraid," Sarah admitted, disliking him somewhat less. "Of course it's a horrible name, but I don't really hate it."

Why must we dwell *on names? . . .* Philly kept her eyes on the carpet; but it was no use. Sarah was telling them—

"And what is Philly short for?" Bronwen asked.

"Philadelphia!" Philly burst out, loud in self-persecution.

There was a pause and then Bronwen said:

"But I think that is rather delicious."

Was she a stuffed pike? If she said nothing, perhaps it would pass off. No, Sarah was explaining—

"You see our late father was in America when she was born. He rushed back from Washington and—"

"Why wasn't she called Washington?" Bronwen pinned her down.

"I don't know," Sarah said brightly. "Philly sounds better than Washy, anyway."

Oh, how could he, how could he? Philly rocked her silent grief to her heart. Such a lovely bold dashing man, as she vaguely remembered, but capable of such things. . . .

"But America is attractive," Bronwen said, as if this were compensation. "I suppose you know it?"

"No."

"Father was doing some conducting there," Peter said quickly, thinking the visitors would become utterly implacable if Bronwen went on being so devastating. "So we had a chance to see many of the big cities."

Philly was incurably sensitive on the subject of America. Even Bracken, by coming from there, could be a thorn in the flesh. Joneses' Conducted Tours of the States . . . She tried out the words in her mind, wonderingly. But they were musical Joneses. That was the clew.

"A musical conductor," she said, surprised to hear her own voice. "Like Stokowski." She had read something in the paper about him, lately.

"Not necessarily like Stokowski," Peter said.

"I think America really gave me a lot of ideas for my book," Bronwen said meditatively, her bracelets clanking.

There was another silence. Then Philly (Sarah could have strangled her for falling into such a trap) asked politely:

"What is your book?"

"It's more or less a scrapbook of my life," Bronwen said, a conscious, modest smile flickering over her wide lips.

"Your life? I thought you were thirteen," Sarah said.

"She is. But most people seem to think that makes the book all the more interesting," Peter said, not exactly with pride but certainly not with the sense of shame one would have expected a brother to express.

"Do you mean you have *shown* the book to anyone?"

"But of course. It is shortly being published." The bracelets seemed to take up her casual words on a brilliant counter-theme of metallic jazz.

There was nothing to say. There was nothing on earth to say to this.

"Are you going to the dance in the Hall on Easter Monday?" Sarah changed the subject vigorously, but she felt the spirit had gone out of her.

"Should one? But how delicious," Bronwen said. "I simply love this place!"

"Father wouldn't let you go out at night," Peter said.

"I thought an authoress would be quite . . . emancipated," Sarah said venomously.

"You see, I'm not very strong," Bronwen excused this conventionality. "I often get feverish when I write poetry."

"Are *you* going to the dance?" Peter asked.

Sarah said that it depended on her friends, which seemed a good enough answer.

"I think your home must be extremely interesting," Bronwen said, with a sallow smile.

"You must come and see it," Sarah got back on the right tack. "I shall arrange a little party." She felt herself to be spectacularly, her father's daughter. On this fillip, she rose to go. "We must go back to Mother, Philly."

The Jones brother and sister followed them into the next room. Mr. Jones sat at a perfectly decorous distance from Mrs. Fontayne. They were talking about gardening; and through the opened windows came suitably the warm drowsy scents of flowers whose sharp spring ecstasy seemed already to have given place to a relaxed full summer contentment. Over all, the rich Victorian smell of wallflowers was dominantly mellow.

Bronwen and Peter were introduced to Mrs. Fontayne in the midst of amiable suggestions for the exchanging of cuttings and bulbs and roots. It was all, in fact, charmingly rustic and simple, literature and music gone by the board. For the rest of the visit it was all this figurative good clean earth beneath the nails and country breezes through the hair. And nobody mentioned Bronwen's forthcoming book.

Bracken saw them coming up the hill and went to meet them. The afternoon was full and rounded like a ripened golden peach. The air around Fontayne seemed smug with unruffled beliefs and comforting certainties. How simple and easy was the emphasis here on the trivial intricacies of personality! Even the trees of Fontayne and near about seemed to possess this pat acceptance of their inevitability here; founded in ground rich with feudal privileges, however hopelessly useless the privileges themselves might have become. . . .

"How did you get on?" He captured the delicate essence of their petty-urgent little pilgrimage.

"The little girl has written a book, and they have a delicious stuffed pike in the hall," Philly said, exactly.

"As for Fontayne," Sarah said, "I don't know. They have sinister likings for the ugliest things."

"The man will like the gardens. I think he may have a green hand," Mrs. Fontayne said.

"Then they are coming to see you?" Bracken asked.

"Oh, yes. Next week, I thought," Sarah suggested. "Could you stay on, Bracken, to entertain them?"

"I'm afraid I'd be more a handicap than an asset."

Fontayne seemed very still and spacious after the heavy fulsomeness of Copley's Green. Christopher and Tom were unimpressed by the Jones family.

"I won't play with the little girl," Tom said moodily.

"Play with her! She wouldn't dream of playing with you," Sarah cried. "She is a . . . cosmopolitan."

Tom's rich incredible laugh flowed out, steeped in unfathomable ironies. They sat on the terrace, all of them, and watched the green spring twilight settling in the trees. And this will go on and on, Sarah thought, and will never change. (But she no longer quite believed it.) A moth settled on Philly's stiff cotton skirt, its wings folded in a grey prayer. A deliciously stuffed pike, Philly repeated over and over— silently, dubiously.

Sarah's voice broke the calm of the deepening evening.

"Will you take me to the dance on Monday night, Bracken? It is quite respectable, truly. Anyway, you'd make it so."

"I should hope so." She sat at his feet on the terrace, her outline seeming restively taut even in this wavering light. "Does one dress?"

"What do you mean?" she asked anxiously. "We wear what we like, of course."

"What are you going to wear? Something you ran up, I suppose? I'll come if Philly will come."

"Oh, no!" cried Philly.

"Don't be silly. I'll go if you will," Christopher said. "We could go, I suppose, Mother?"

Very slowly and gently Mrs. Fontayne roused herself from a melancholy imaginary scrutiny of the household bills. Her guileless "calling frock" was woven into the increasing intricacies of the green lace evening.

"But of course you can do as you please, darlings," she said, in an echo of all Marcus's passionate pleas for freedom in living.

"Anything in reason," Tom said, plucking a phrase from memory with a nice discrimination.

*　　*　　*　　*　　*

They hired a car to drive them to the Hall on Monday night.

"If a thing's worth doing, it is worth doing well," Mrs. Moody said, in approval of this measure.

"It's better than tramping through the elements in galoshes," Sarah agreed in a muffled tone, as she dived into the crinoline "foundation" of her dance frock. "You don't think we tried to be too ambitious, do you?" The plural was not so much the one of Royalty as of conspiracy: she had made the frock, but Mrs. Moody had tendered some advice.

"Well, your father was an ambitious man," the seamstress said with brisk irrelevance. "I'd say it was a good fault."

The spring evening flowed sweetly in at the bedroom window. It was like getting ready for a *real* party. What jewels will you wear, Madam? . . . If the Joneses did turn up, one would be casually friendly, but reserved.

"Don't lose your heart," Mrs. Moody said, as they put the finishing touches.

"I would if I possibly could," Sarah said coldly, "but it isn't likely, at the Hall."

Bracken, Philly, and Christopher were waiting for her when she came downstairs.

"You can't wear that," Christopher said quickly. "You look like Cinderella going to the ball."

"I think she looks lovely," said Philly, who was wearing something short, white, straight and severe, and looking, Bracken thought, somehow like a choir boy.

"We won't quarrel about it," Bracken said impartially. "I am pinning my faith to Sarah's assurance that one can wear what one likes."

But how cold he is! As the front door opened and they stepped first into the ripe cool of the evening and thence into the near-luxury of the hired limousine, Sarah's mind exclaimed against Bracken. In spite of being so kind as to take us to the dance, how cold he really is to us. . . .

The Hall was wooden and unprepossessing. It was set in the middle of the little town, ready to embrace all causes, from rowdy football dances to pleasant Sunday afternoons for mothers and babies.

Light clouds swam on a light sky as Bracken and his charges got out of the hired car. It was the familiar moment of anticipation: the band crashing out beyond the portals, the murmur of voices, the cars, motor-cycles and pedal-cycles crowding the gravel space surrounding the Hall. Sarah shivered in her meagre wrap and hoped her lipstick looked all right.

Bracken bought tickets from a sulky young man who seemed to resent the fate that had cooped him up in a sort of cage at the doorway.

"It's the *good* band," Sarah whispered, as they went in.

"Good," Bracken echoed inadequately, his words drowned by a deafening excellence of jazz. "Where should we sit?"

"Oh, anywhere—I'm just looking round." Sarah looked round.

"Any of your special friends here?"

"I'm just looking. Only Bob Norbett. He dances quite well. Smile at Bob, Philly."

Philly smiled shyly. The last time they had seen Bob was when he sold them the champagne. What would she do if he asked her to dance?

They sat down at one of the little tables that edged the hard uninviting-looking dance floor. A dance had just ended. A group of young men stood around the door in an animated fringe. The sexes were inclined to fall into a voluntary segregation between dances. The air was arid with chalk dust and the innocuous smell of the soft drinks bar.

"It doesn't seem to have quite warmed up, does it?" Christopher said, wondering why he had allowed himself to come.

He would dance with Philly, if she liked, but not with Sarah in that bloated skirt.

"There's Mr. Lupin, coming out of the proper bar," Philly said, referring, though one might not have guessed it, to the one that sold beers and spirits. "He has a lovely purple shirt."

"Awful," Christopher said, wincing ostentatiously. "I think he must be awfully bogus."

"Do we smile at him, Sarah?" Philly begged unhappily. "We don't *exactly* know him."

"How extremely intricate are these social distinctions in the country," Bracken said. "Would any of you like any refreshments?"

"Oh, not *yet*," Sarah frowned.

The band struck up, on two taps of the drummer's stick. "You had better dance with me first, Bracken," Sarah said, kind again. "If you can dance, that is."

It was scarcely what she called dancing, but she bore with him. He was too small and he held her at a distance and he was inclined to guide her against the current of the other dancers. They paused near the door to clap for the encore, and saw a stirring of new arrivals.

"Who is it now?" Bracken asked, breathing rather hard.

"I don't know." She shook her head. "We often get strangers here."

There was a man in the foreground of the group and, though the dancing had begun again, she did not move or take her eyes off him. He was tall and slim, with black hair cut rather long, high cheekbones, and what could only be called a distinguished mouth. There was a lightness in his eyes that made him seem more alive than most people. Without the faintest ado—with scarcely even a quickening of breath and heart-beat—Sarah fell in love with him.

"I think it's Sir Giles Merrick. Yes, I think it must be. He's some-thing in politics, you know." She waited for Bracken's interested comment, but he made none.

"Yes, there's Mr. Harbrittle, and two women. They must have made up a party for the dance," Sarah went on gravely. "I *told* you it would be a good dance."

Bracken felt rather overwhelmed. Sarah's mind no longer seemed to be on her dance with him, so he led her back to their table. Philly and Christopher were still prancing adolescently, enjoying themselves for these moments that were free of ordinary partner etiquette.

Bob Norbett bowed by the table.

"How about a dance, Miss Sarah?"

"Oh, I don't know—Oh, yes, of course—" She was torn between the fear of disappointing Bob and the fear of losing sight of Sir Giles.

She rose and abandoned herself to Bob's elegant handling of a waltz.

"Quite a do," he remarked pleasantly. "It does make for drawing the community together, a do like this. A hall like this seems to be a symbol for good, if you know what I mean."

Sarah nodded. Bob was rather an earnest young man, really, but a perfect dancer. He belonged to all sorts of organizations in the town; he was treasurer of things, and secretary of things and captain of things. It was amazing how he found time for it all, with his work at the wine merchant's, too.

Bob held her firmly but with chivalry. Never would he overstep the bridge that he himself had fixed between himself and his friends the Fontayne young ladies. Bob was inclined to be a communist in theory, but scarcely so in practice.

"Do you know that's Sir Giles Merrick over there?"

"Is it, in fact?" Bob allowed himself. "I heard he was staying here over the holiday, but I never thought—You know him, of course, your father being such a big shot in politics—I mean—" Bob hummed the dance tune, not quite sure of his ground.

"Father has been dead almost ten years," Sarah said forlornly. "Besides, I believe Sir Giles is a 'diplomat.' I think there is some subtle difference." She didn't exactly say she *didn't* know Sir Giles. . . . "Of course I know Mr. Harbrittle," she added, recalling the various occasions on which the old novelist had given Philly and herself a passing remote attention.

"The old fellow looks a bit out of place in this meal-yer, doesn't he? Can't say I've ever read any of his books."

Mr. Harbrittle sat with his friends at a more or less secluded table, and looked distinctly put out. Whoever it was had had the whim to attend the dance it was not he. It was not his idea of a becoming gesture. Mr. Harbrittle lived on devious, yet innocent, poses. His old yellow-white moustache drooped with a *fin-de-siècle* sort of elegance over withered lips. His high-pointed collar rose up in a rigid challenge to his parchment face. His mottled eyelids gave him an air as of some peculiarly worldly bird. Philly was terrified of him.

Now the ladies of the party were in the light and in Sarah's line of vision. The younger one wore a very simple, very severe black frock, and she was (there was, unfortunately, no getting away from it) extremely good-looking. The older one (Sarah recognized her) was that Lady Pansy Bysshe who had herself, so legend and Mrs. Oxford had it, been a famous beauty in her youth.

"I'm going up to talk to Mr. Harbrittle," she whispered dreamily to Bob. If it kills me . . . she added silently.

"Shan't I escort you back to your friend?" Bob asked doubtfully, liking everything to be in order.

"No. I'll just sort of sidle round the room back to him and pause at the Harbrittle table on the way. Bracken's busy buying Philly an ice just now."

She made her way around the edge of the people still dancing and stopped dead with her wafting skirt against Sir Giles's chair.

"Hello. You remember me, Mr. Harbrittle," she said, as much like Mrs. Oxford as possible.

His eyelids flickered alarmingly as he focused his gaze. Sir Giles rose; and there was a moment of nerve-racking still life, with Lady Pansy's eyes fixed immobile within mascara, and the young woman's cigarette poised in mid-air, and Sir Giles like some very graceful leaning tower of Pisa above one.

"Dear me," Mr. Harbrittle said somewhat querulously. "The years seem to have made you grown up, young lady."

"Well, of course," Sarah said, tart with nervousness. "What do you expect?"

"My dear Lady Pansy, this is one of Marcus Fontayne's young daughters. Merrick, you know all about Fontayne—"

"Are you here *alone*?" Lady Pansy asked, raising the remains of her eyebrows.

"Oh, no, in a party," Sarah said icily.

"Sit down," the young woman said, with an alarmingly dazzling smile. "I met a friend of yours at dinner the other night—Mrs. Oxford."

"Oh, did she talk about us?" Sarah said gratefully. This then, must be Virginia Welwyn, who had been a "noted débutante," but who was now merely a young widow.

"Your father was a handsome man," Lady Pansy said with authority.

"An able man," Sir Giles said, speaking for the first time. "I would have given a lot to meet him. I never did."

Sarah's being was suffused with warmth for all of them, even Mr. Harbrittle. How beautiful life was, she thought again, as she had thought the other day at lunch.

"Do you live here all the time?" Virginia Welwyn asked, her voice slightly husky and melancholy.

"Yes, all the time. But soon we may sell Fontayne and go away."

"Dear me." Mr. Harbrittle's conscience smote him—no, not exactly *smote*, but at least placed some vague and ghostly finger on him—that he had never bothered with Fontayne's widow. One had heard they were a linked family, which seemed just as well, as they had been left no money; and one left it at that. After all, the give and take of hospitality was a very serious thing; you could not meddle with unalterable laws. Any form of charity in one's own class was an extremely dangerous and subversive thing. He wished, quite without malice, that the young woman would take herself and what he described to himself as her unhinged gown away from his table.

"You must have a drink," Merrick was saying.

"No, I think I must go now," Sarah dared to look at him.

"What finally happened to those memoirs your father wrote?" Mr. Harbrittle asked, suddenly remembering he had one possible common theme of conversation with the girl.

"I don't know," she said cautiously. Memoirs! Pictures opened like interminable fans in her mind, full of wonderful possibilities.

"They never *were* published—You know, it was I who advised him against it at the time."

"This is extremely interesting. I never heard of them," Sir Giles said.

"Few people did, I believe." Mr. Harbrittle began to enjoy himself.

"But how astonishing to *write* memoirs and then not publish them," Lady Pansy said simply. For years she had striven to write her own, but the golden period of her youth seemed never to be conjured to life by words of hers.

"Brilliant as they were, they had a certain satirical scandalous turn to them which made me feel—which made me advise him—that it might prove detrimental to his career should he publish them. He was rising, of course, but not sufficiently risen to risk anything. One was not, naturally, to know then—"

"That he would die," Sarah said, high and clear.

"Exactly." His eyelids acknowledged her. He had forgotten it was Marcus Fontayne's daughter to whom he spoke. "I admired him for taking my advice, for in some ways it must have been a temptation not to do so, if only for the fact that America would have paid immensely for them."

"'If only!'" Sarah echoed.

"I think it is thrilling," Virginia Welwyn said quietly. "What became of them?"

"I could not say," Mr. Harbrittle said reservedly. "They doubtless have their private place in the Fontayne papers."

But it is like a plot. . . . Dazedly, Sarah eyed in turn each person at the table. It is like a plot, with the "Fontayne papers," the measured words among people of importance, and things out of the past suddenly catching up with you.

The waltz chorus was repeated for the final time; and was emphasized by soft-coloured lights playing across the hall. Now Lady Pansy was a witch swathed in green scarves, with a green-powdered face and shocking green eyelids. Even Virginia Welwyn's looks suffered. As for Mr. Harbrittle, he was a phosphorescent saffron corpse painted with a dreadful levity. Only Sir Giles triumphed, shadowed and hollowed like an amiable devil, but still perfectly master of himself.

"I must go." Sarah heard her voice crack a little. I shall grow old and ugly like Lady Pansy, with fat green arms and two green double chins. And then I shall die.

She came up blankly against that fate as she rose composedly to her feet.

"Perhaps you could spare me a dance a little later," Sir Giles smiled.

"That would be nice," she said sedately, her thought of death scattered into a million frolic-winged pieces. Oh joy, oh joy!

She reached the others as the plain glare of yellow light returned.

"We saw you," Christopher said. "What were you up to?"

She didn't answer. She said to Bracken:

"Did you know father wrote some memoirs?"

"He once told me he was writing them, but I never heard of the end of them."

"But how could you never mention them? How could you come to Fontayne now and again through the years and never mention them?"

"I'm afraid I never thought of them," he confessed.

It was no use—it was simply no use—being angry with Bracken. You had to take him or leave him.

"Mrs. Rudge is serving the ices," Philly pointed out as a matter of general interest. "She says she likes some odd canteen work now and again. She calls it canteen work—I've persuaded her to enter Jimmie and Johnnie and Georgie for a children's beauty competition."

"I don't see how they can help but win," Sarah said, her mind not on Mrs. Rudge's cherubs but upon the older, subtler beauty of Sir Giles.

"It's funny how Mr. and Mrs. Rudge go in for having such beautiful children when they are so plain themselves."

"Oh, Philly, be quiet! Do we have to talk about the Rudges when we come to a dance?"

"Have an ice," Christopher said tactfully.

"I don't want one."

Another dance had begun. Covertly she watched the Harbrittle table to see what Sir Giles was doing. He rose with Virginia Welwyn. Sarah turned her eyes away.

"There are the Joneses!" Philly exclaimed.

"Where?" She couldn't be bothered. She would find her father's hidden memoirs and make America pay immensely for them, and then the Jones finance wouldn't be needed. But money was sordid, anyway.

"Not Bronwen, only Peter and Mr. Jones," Philly added. She looked up, feeling an impending doom upon her. Bob Norbett was smiling at her.

"Come along now, Miss Philly. Mustn't sit out, you know."

"No," she said humbly; rising humbly. She cast one despairing glance at Bracken, but he failed her with a little smile of encouragement.

The Jones father and son came across the room. Sarah made listless introductions between them and Bracken and Christopher. Christopher wondered if they were a bit bogus, but couldn't make up his mind.

"And where is your mother?" Mr. Jones asked.

"Oh, she never comes to these affairs," Sarah said sweepingly, her eyes morbidly picking out one couple among the dancers. "She wouldn't dream of it."

"She isn't very strong," Bracken said, putting things right.

"Isn't she now?" Mr. Jones looked rather too genuinely sorry.

"Will you dance?" Peter asked Sarah.

"If you don't mind, no. Not just now."

Bob bunched Philly's dress up with his supporting hand. The dress was the wrong length, anyway, but he made it worse.

"Just take it easily," he said kindly. "You're doing fine."

She wanted to sink through the floor. Why couldn't she dance? She could walk and swim and play tennis—She trod on Bob's toe.

"Oh, do you mind if we sit down?" she entreated. "I'm so hot."

He paused instantly at an empty table, and insinuated her into a chair. This wasn't what she had meant—away from the others. Now she would have to think of things to say.

"Let me get you a lemonade," Bob said gallantly.

"Oh, no—please! No thank you." (Oh, to be at home with Ernest, and reading *The Gem* or *The Magnet*. Oh, for Tom Merry and Arthur Augustus D'Arcy. . . .)

"Mrs. Rudge is serving the ices," she offered miserably, after an interval, as Bob's gifts for small talk seemed to have deserted him.

"Oh, yes. She works for you, doesn't she?"

"Sometimes, when we're in a hole. She has triplets, you know."

"M'm. You take an interest in the good of our little community, don't you, Miss Philly?"

"Well, I—" She swallowed. "I just know people, you see."

Neither did Bracken make much of an effort at small talk with Mr. Jones. It must be all those icy wastes and things he's used to, Sarah thought resentfully. Perhaps blubber and ice picks and things make you so you can't bother to *try* to be attractive.

"Mr. Bracken sometimes explores," she said coldly.

"Only sometimes," Bracken agreed mildly.

"Really?" Mr. Jones's dark eyes showed faint astonishment. "Will you have a drink?"

Bracken had a drink. He had no objection to the Joneses. When, after a few minutes, the father and son departed from the table, he said: "I expected something more extreme."

"You haven't seen Bronwen," Sarah retorted.

The dance was over and Bob, like an anxious hen, deposited Philly with her native brood.

"Oh, thank you," she said, in a reaction of heartfelt relief. "Thank you very much for the dance."

"You shouldn't overdo the gratitude," Sarah rebuked, when Bob was gone.

"But I *am* grateful," Philly said, a slow smile dawning on her wide beautiful mouth.

"Well, don't argue," Sarah retorted, her eyes on Sir Giles, who was walking across the floor to the opening notes of a foxtrot. He is practically bound to stop here . . . .

"Oh, Bracken, this is Sir Giles Merrick. Perhaps you haven't met." Her voice ran too high and she was tragically conscious of near-idiocy in herself.

Her heart warmed to Bracken for his nice handling of the next few moments. He chose to be that rare being, his "man-of-the-world" self. And Sir Giles, of course, for his part, behaved perfectly. He even had a light and charming word for Philly and Christopher. Sarah felt a reticent gratitude to her late father, too. Ghostly speaking, he put everything on a proper basis of mutual respect. And when she finally glided into the dance with Sir Giles, it was as if they moved not only exquisitely in step but were also exquisitely hand in glove with each other's worlds.

"How long are you staying with Mr. Harbrittle?"

He swung her lightly around and took five paces before he said casually: "Until tomorrow morning."

"He entertains a lot." One must pretend even to oneself that one had not heard his soul-destroying words. "Mrs. Oxford says she's surprised he hasn't got a knighthood." (Sir Giles was a baronet, of course.)

"Really?" Sir Giles just, only just, smiled.

Now I've said something crude. Why can't I be well bred? "I mean, he's gone on writing such long thorough books for such a long time." (How marvellous Sir Giles smelt!) "At least I suppose they're thorough," she added dreamily, spoiling things again.

"He's what they call a regional novelist," Sir Giles said cautiously.

"Is he? I thought that was something to do with the radio."

Sir Giles looked at her as if he suddenly saw her for the first time. "How very charming it is to find that one's early heroes have left an unexpected record of themselves." He smiled; wholly smiled.

"What do you mean?"

"Marcus Fontayne was quite a hero of my youth. I always thought of him as having such—such *width* and liberality. I remember taking it as almost a personal tragedy when he died so young."

"Oh, he wasn't young. He was about forty-five. He would be quite old if he were alive now."

"Comparatively young, I meant," Sir Giles corrected himself, a shade stiffly.

"Oh yes, of course." How old was Sir Giles himself? One had not considered it until now. One had even seen him referred to as an "infant prodigy," which was in a high degree ridiculous, because now that one *did* consider it, there was nothing horribly young about him. "Do you mean the memoirs are the . . . unexpected record?" she concluded, wanting to get things straight.

"I meant you," he said with a shining pat simplicity, for which his eloquent voice seemed especially suited.

Her breath caught in her throat and she choked a little against his lapel. "Oh, must you go tomorrow?" Her thoughts broke into words. "I mean, it would have been nice if you could have come to Fontayne. I could have shown you things of my father's, and we could have searched for the missing memoirs."

"How exciting it all sounds," he said charmingly. "But sometimes I have to work, you know."

"Yes, of course." Never mind; there is this at least. And I'll go on afterwards as if nothing has happened; but nothing will ever be the same again. . . .

"Sarah's got off," Christopher remarked casually, but with an underlying relief. Her dress couldn't be as ghastly as he imagined.

"Are you ready to go?" Bracken asked.

"I like it all right so long as I can avoid anyone's eye," Philly said.

Her doom was sealed as she spoke. Mr. Lupin's rolling chubby gait brought him to rest at their table. "Good evening," he said in an ample voice.

"Good evening," Bracken said politely.

"It's the first time I've seen a Fontayne contingent here. How remarkably social our village life is becoming."

Philly resented that "our village." He was only a weekend visitor, even if he did dote on the simple life. He had sat down at the table, uninvited, and Bracken was perforce asking him to have a drink. She and Christopher looked at each other. It was a bit thick. Mr. Lupin said he would have an honest pint; which surprised Philly, who could not help but associate him with the vineyards through which he was said to walk.

"You're still at school?" he asked Christopher, coming up to breathe after an immense gulp of beer. "Well, don't let them turn you out too much in the fatal public-school pattern. God, was there ever such a country! If it isn't the hypocrisy of the great middle and upper class it is the dismal factions of those who laboriously copy the ideologies of other nations. There is no room left for a dwindling minority of free men."

Christopher, not sure whether he was still addressed, said nothing.

"You still find freedom in a few unexploited bars of country pubs, but even then you are likely to find they become desecrated by disgusting young women playing darts. And freedom, thank God, is still to be found in parts of the French wine country. I know a little place near . . ."

Now he is all right, Philly thought. She felt quite kindly toward him so long as she didn't have to speak to him.

". . . I can see it now, that solitary-placed inn, with Papa Bo-Bo— we call him Papa Bo-Bo, the good Lord knows why—standing bowing in his doorway; and God help me if he doesn't fill that doorway side to side but for the merest crack of light around his splendid swelling form. There's a man for you, who eats and drinks as if he meant it. He knows the meaning of life, does Papa Bo-Bo. You can open wide your thirsty throat and give yourself into his care when you cross the great threshold of his hospitality."

"Tramping through vineyards," Philly murmured, feeling the grapes squashing under her bare feet. But perhaps that was going a bit far even for Mr. Lupin. Besides he must have fat little feet that were probably much happier wearing shoes than not wearing them. . . .

His voice, addressing her direct, dreadfully aroused her from her comfortable dream.

"I'm damned if I'll dance with these females spoiling in their paint and powder. Come, golden child of the morning!"

"I c-can't dance." Her voice shook with terror.

"Nonsense!" With a huge gesture he swept her to her feet, but looked slightly disconcerted when he found she was taller than he.

Nevertheless he made onslaught with her against the beat of the orchestra; and, because they were at least in harmony with each other in that neither had any sense of rhythm, they did not do too badly. Away they bounded over the floor in a galloping satyr-nymph progress.

Sarah saw and giggled inwardly. Poor Philly!—but it *was* funny.

"I know your friend Bracken's face," Sir Giles said.

"He sometimes explores, but not very publicly," Sarah explained, half apologetically. "He's an American really. He went with somebody's expedition to the North Pole or somewhere, about three years ago." It set her teeth on edge merely to think of Bracken hacking his way through frozen wastes. "But he wasn't the leader, so no one has ever heard of him."

"Oh, but that expedition you speak of was most enthralling," Sir Giles said, with as much animation as if he had shared the experience. "One of the party wrote an almost epic book on it."

"Not Bracken. Writing some fairy tales for us is as far as he has got."

"Do you think our two tables might join forces?" Sir Giles asked, looking down at her with that pensive nerve-teasing little smile.

"You mean all sit together?" Her eyes were serious. "Oh, could we?" She sighed, thinking of half-grown Christopher, anxious Philly, and untalkative Bracken. "I'd love it, if we aren't too anti-social."

He laughed: flatteringly, as if she had said something witty. "Well, I expect you draw the line at anarchy," he said carelessly, yet almost tenderly.

"I meant Bracken, really. My brother and sister are hardly more than children, of course." Her head cushioned on his arm, she talked up to his clear-cut chin; and satisfactorily dissociated herself from adolescence. "Oh, but Bracken is remote. Oh, but he lives in polar regions! He—he *unbends* for us, but he is still a Thinker." She sensed Sir Giles's approval of thinkers; and knew he did not understand. "Oh, not sensible thinking about how to improve people's lots," she went on, "but thinking for the *sake* of thinking. And seeming so normal with it, as if his mind's on his food or something of the sort. It is terribly tricky. For instance, I don't suppose he thinks my personal life is any more important than a—than an ant's, for instance."

Sir Giles looked quite incensed at this.

"That may be an exaggeration, but I don't think it is," she said.

Lightly, he walked her to the Harbrittle table just before the dance ended; and lightly made his suggestion that the two little groups should join. One could just as easily imagine him patching the quarrels or bridging the indifferences of nations. How important was Sir Giles? One couldn't be sure merely by the number of times one saw his picture in the papers, for naturally it must be more of a pleasure to print his picture than that of the usual shapeless politician, but it was to be hoped that the government realized what a valuable treasure they had in his mere presence.

"By all means," Mr. Harbrittle was saying with studied courtesy, as he made way for Sarah on the chair next to him.

In a moment Sir Giles returned with Bracken and Christopher in tow. Philly eyed the procedure frantically from the arms of Mr. Lupin, who was doggedly mopping up the last bars of the foxtrot.

"We managed that very well." He breathed hard. "Very refreshing. Don't become a nauseous nicotined blood-nailed modern girl, child."

"No," Philly said docilely.

He took her to the others, then, bowed rather ironically at the Harbrittle table and retired without another word.

"That seems to me a peculiar and rude person," Lady Pansy said distantly. "Sit here, my dear. You look hot."

"I am," Philly said miserably. What an evening it had turned out, full of scarcely known people and terrible currents of conversation. But how happy Sarah looked. One must bear with it.

Sarah *was* happy. She heard her own voice flowing evenly, and did not care what it said, for everything now fell magically into place and nothing could go wrong. Mrs. Welwyn was sweet and kind, in spite of being so arrogantly fashionable, and even Lady Pansy, one now perceived, had a magnificence of beauty past and gone, yet still present in the aura of its tradition. . . . Self-possessed, Sarah engaged Mr. Harbrittle on no less a subject than Literature.

Christopher, too, was talking, and, of all people, to Virginia Welwyn. Of course he disapproved of nearly everything about her, from her long nails to her dark red lipstick, but the fact remained that she was talking to him about aeroplanes and seemed to know something about them. And she did not seem to have perceived him as a young boy, but simply as another human being. It was amazing.

"I used to fly myself," she said in her soft melancholy voice, "but I wasn't very good." It didn't seem to matter either way, her tone said, as nothing really seemed to matter either way; the weight of her natural sophistication reducing everything to a limpid sort of simplicity.

"I've never flown," he said.

"Oh, well, if you'd like to do so—have lessons, I mean—I expect I could arrange it with my old instructor . . ." She left it like that, vague, appropriately up in the air.

"Who is the man? Why did you have him to dinner?" Lady Pansy was still harping on Mr. Lupin.

"Quite an able fellow in his way," Mr. Harbrittle said tolerantly. "Quite a harmonious humourist and a bit of a painter too."

Lady Pansy gave a sniff that was so like one of Mrs. Moody's dress-making sniffs that Philly sat amazed.

"I don't like him," Lady Pansy said flatly. She had known Mr. Harbrittle since she was beautiful and he was struggling, so she could say anything she chose to him. "Perhaps it is time we went. Let us take these young people and give them hot drinks at your house." She herself always had a hot drink at this hour.

"That would be lovely," Sarah said gracefully, "but may we stay for one more dance?" Sir Giles would no doubt dance with Mrs. Welwyn, but it was worth risking. "It is going to be a waltz," she added reverently, as the lights dimmed. She felt the very soles of her feet tingle with an anguished fear of frustration. Oh, not to have to sit it out, she prayed. Let even Bob ask me for it, if Sir Giles is too much to ask. . . .

Virginia Welwyn turned her slow devastating smile on Christopher and said: "Would it be a good idea to try it, do you think?" as if there were nothing in the least extraordinary about the suggestion.

"I'll try, if you like," Christopher agreed, not over-graciously.

Oh, sweet young woman, kind brother—Sarah eyed them benevolently as they rose. Now the way is clear, unless he could possibly think he ought to ask Philly—

She glared impressively at Philly, who could not imagine what she had done.

Christopher held Virginia with a clumsy gingerliness, but he guided her with a wary concentration and there were no disasters. His fair head topped her dark bronze one. She kept up her running vague little remarks, and still, miraculously, continued to treat him as a human being.

Sir Giles was unconcernedly talking to Bracken.

"The dance is getting on," Sarah said desperately.

"Shall we catch the rest of it, then, before it vanishes?" He glanced up, his brilliant eyes on hers.

"Oh, yes. . . ."

From his arms she saw young Peter Jones revolving with a village maiden. She saw Bob twirling incomparably with the adenoidy girl from the haberdashery. She saw Mr. Lupin wiping his red glistening brow. She saw Mrs. Rudge amid ice cream and Lady Pansy amid the enigmatic pattern of her draperies. She saw her brother Christopher dancing with a modern beauty.

"I never liked a night so much," she said.

"I too find it enchanting," Sir Giles said gravely.

"And it is ending, and—" She paused.

"We must see that it happens all over again." She was as light as a feather, a quite unlooked-for nymph. And that she should be Marcus Fontayne's daughter made it all the more pleasing. "You must let me know when there is such a dance again, and we must see what we all can do."

It meant nothing, the merest pleasantry, she told herself; but she hugged the words to her heart as if she would hold them there for ever. And their magic enshrouded the rest of the lovely night.

They all left the Hall together and stood shivering enjoyably in the clear April air. The heady spring darkness of the night was sweet with an affectation of mystery. Coming out from a garish interior the contrast of tender gloom lay like a caress upon the eyelids. One lowered them in instinctive almost reverential response. And, at the same time, sympathetically dilated one's nostrils in quest of the pinched delicacy of outdoor perfumes after the too-decisive smells within the Hall. In a few moments the darkness was recast in a lesser starlit dusk. All that sweep of heaven, marked out, filled in . . . it was incredible, thought Sarah with an exalted humility, as if the whole scheme had been laid out for her especial benefit. Usually, starlight made her feel morose and insignificant. Tonight, still vaguely conscious of insignificance, she did not mind; for the wonder and glory and *point* of it was that Sir Giles was in exactly the same boat of heavenly negligibility. She laughed aloud; and for a moment or two felt herself actually his equal, a dot to his mere dot in the universe. . . . If only one were capable of retaining this vast and proper sense of proportion in all circumstances; but, alas, one was not.

Mr. Harbrittle had sent for his car and chauffeur. Sir Giles had room in his own dashing car for four people. Sarah hovered at his elbow.

"Mind those bicycles." She felt his hard slim hand on her arm, guiding her. He opened the door of his car and ushered her in beside him. Just as if it were all a matter of course. "Get in at the back," he said to Philly and Christopher.

The journey, which Sarah could have wished to last the whole night, was over in a few moments. Starlight faintly illumined the sweet old-maidish-scented flowers of Mr. Harbrittle's garden. Sarah and Sir Giles were the last of the party to walk up to the house.

"I *am* so happy," she said, sighing.

"I forget how long it is since I could say that with such conviction," he said, luxuriating in the bitter-sweet vanity of regret.

"Will you ever come again?"

"Of course. Don't you remember you are to tell me when there is another dance?"

"Oh, you were joking—"

"No, indeed." She would probably break in pieces and vanish if she were hurt. He thought that he would hate to hurt her.

"If you *do* come again, will you come to see us? Fontayne, I mean. Mother is very nice, if a bit vague. But if you come, don't be too long. It's a bit urgent, you see, because we may be leaving Fontayne."

"I'd love to come. I'll write to you."

He saw her tender rapt profile and wondered what she was thinking; wondered if she had inherited anything of Marcus Fontayne's queer, even burlesque, spark of genius. Her dark flower-like head swayed and her white frock swayed out from her form, the silk-like paper in the faint illumination from the doorway of the house.

They entered Mr. Harbrittle's respect-provoking dry-dust house, where heaven knew how those books of blood and soil got written. Books lapped over the walls of the hall, giving the effect of having overflowed there in an unquenchable rivulet of learning.

"Is Lady Pansy staying here?" Sarah whispered.

"Yes, this is our little house-party, the little Easter gathering," Sir Giles smiled.

"And Mrs. Welwyn too?" Virginia was still wearing her fur cape and was looking more glamorous than ever, standing by the fireplace, her shoulders hunched, her long hands clasped as if in some meditative prayer.

"Yes. She is Lady Pansy's niece."

"Oh, I see. Beauty runs in the family," Sarah said flatly.

"How cold this house is!" cried Lady Pansy, who stood on no one's ceremony. She swept forward into the light—the cold uncompromising light of her host's hall—which revealed the varying ginger tones of colouring that seem to be the native hues of all beauties from past eras.

"The house faces north," Mr. Harbrittle said. "Himself," he might have added, from inclination and habit also faced north.

The hot drinks came and all stood dutifully sipping under Lady Pansy's eye. Sarah never knew what she drank. It was nectar warmed at the hearth of gods. It was one's second baptism, marking the final escape from childhood.

"AH the old tradition is gone," Mr. Harbrittle said to nobody in particular. "No villagers left to dance to the scraping fiddles of happy amateurs. The old country life is gone."

"I expect people do what they want," Virginia said indifferently. "I don't suppose jigs on the green would be many people's cup of tea." She yawned delicately. One felt she could, merely by being so casual, get away with any sort of murder in her so lightly-expressed opinions.

"It is a debatable point whether people nowadays have the least idea what they want," Mr. Harbrittle said crisply. He knew what they ought to want: all the old simplicities of folklore and blood lusts and feudal superstitions, as one could show them the way oneself in one's own uniform edition. But they would take no notice, so what was the use? He took a somewhat peevish sip at his cooling drink.

Sarah turned to the bookcase with a worldly-wise eye.

"What sort of things do you read?" Sir Giles asked, rather foolishly.

"Anything that comes into the house. But nothing much does come in, so I have to read old stuff. Sometimes I buy a magazine, of course. . . ." When I have sixpence or a shilling; but there's no need to go into sordid details.

"I see." He nodded politely, discounting the wistfulness at the mention of magazines. He had an unaccountable wish that he might have danced with her again.

Virginia's yawn had spread. Christopher didn't repress his. Philly was half asleep by the fire.

"I like descriptions," Sarah said dreamily.

"What?" Sir Giles's attention had wandered.

"I say I like descriptive books."

"Oh." He smiled a little and stepped to the hall window and pulled back the curtain. "There's a slight description of starlight here . . ."

She sat on the window seat beside him and stared out on the garden; and listened to the others talking.

Lady Pansy was telling the unalert Philly and Christopher of some fantastic moonlight paper chase in the spring of her life. She gave the impression of expurgating it a little for the benefit of their young ears. Virginia talked to Bracken, as simply and coolly as she had done to Christopher.

The prolonged hour of festivity was at last disintegrating. Where could one ever find it again, sophistication and scholarship and beauty thus mingled, the stuff of adult life at one's fingertips . . . ? Sarah sighed.

"If I could have known the evening would end like this—" She stared at the fine feather-stitching of dark hairs on the backs of Sir Giles's hands.

"Yes?" he said, prompting.

"I don't know—Well, I would have looked forward to it more suitably."

He laughed; impulsively laid a hand on one of hers and gave it a light squeeze.

"I should think you are destined to know many more exciting evenings than this," he said.

Those words stayed thrillingly with her all the time they were being driven home in Mr. Harbrittle's car and after they had entered the cold silence of Fontayne. From force of habit, following an evening outing, they congregated in Cruddles's little pantry, where he had left milk in a pan on the gas ring. But only Christopher had the indecency to accept this nourishment after the Harbrittle nectar.

"I like hot milk," he said unanswerably.

Sarah snorted; and wordlessly took her way up to bed. On the landing she danced a few steps. Yet it was not so much in frivolity that she did so as in a grave sense of dedication to Sir Giles, as if her dance steps with him had been part of the ritual of a new religion. As indeed they were.

CHAPTER THREE

BRACKEN WAS LEAVING soon after breakfast. He hardly expected to see any of the children down in time to say good-by to him, after the exhausting excitement of the dance. He got up early and saw the fluid pallor of the morn become gradually shaped into another blue-and-gold day. The garden displayed itself with unexpected assurance, not one young green shoot out of place, the leaves laid out with dew-soaked light and shadow, as if brushed there in orderly paint. The serene season and hour well became the place, which could with such unhappy ease look desolate.

He walked on the terrace, his small figure as neat and alert as the day. Today, even the ancient monk-ghost-ridden central part of the house would have no part of desolation. In the old priory foundation the emanation of round smug placid monks must persist. There were no tales of moaning unquiet spirits either there or in the chapel ruins within the Cedar Ring in the lower garden. Perhaps the later, more worldly sections of the house, despite dilapidation, held the balance of mood. The dirty white and gold of the neglected salon-ballroom would be a snag to any pure-minded medieval spectre. That great unwieldy room had an unmistakably ostentatious-decadent Georgian worldliness.

He went down from the terrace across a long leisurely slope of grass, then paused, turning his eyes back to the house.

The sun came now in lithe morning leaps across the lawn, cut off abruptly by clear dark shadow at the terrace edge. The abominable yews were let into the new decisive day like some sprightly jigsaw that missed indecency, it seemed, by the merest accident of final assembly. From here, the house spread curtsying skirts in pale unhurried sweeps. Decorum and grandeur were graciously at one, cast imperturbably on a bland background. Coming up once more towards it, however—seeing it slowly emerge in line on line of detail—that distant glamour vanished, its place taken by a pathetic and quite misleading aspect of refinement. Now, it seemed thinned, diluted, bloodlessly aristocratic, set in a middle distance of polite threadbare dismay. It was a shell, with no more than a robust core of tradition, its present empty, its hope of future gone. Rising yet again on the sloping ground, one came to a last stance before it and found still another persuasion of view: the poignancy abruptly cut off and ridiculed by the near-focus return scrutiny from numerous gleaming close-set windows, rich and crystal in the sun. Decayed, yes, Fontayne might be, but still with a disconcerting eye to zest. Defeated, letting the grass grow under its feet, lazy to death, but not yet dead; old and materially quelled by the invasion of corruption, it was so gently purposeless that its spirit emerged in a final feckless innocence. There was something lively within the very impression of its hopeless invitation to death. It threatened to rise up again and again from the pall of last ignominy, to refuse again and again its own pose of listless age lying down meekly under circumstance.

Returned to the terrace, Bracken stood, unnumbered windows winking at him, lidded here and there by curtains still drawn against the day. Fontayne yawned and reluctantly awakened to another morning.

There was no sign of breakfast on the terrace, this morning, so he went indoors and found all the family already at table in the dining room.

"Bracken, dear," Mrs. Fontayne smiled compassionately. "Did they wear you out last night?"

"No. But I thought the dissipations would keep them all in bed this morning."

"What dissipations?" Tom asked, stirring his tea frenziedly.

Nobody answered. Philly and Christopher were quarrelling happily over the morning paper and Sarah was dreaming over a plate of corn flakes.

"Yes, how was the dance?" Mrs. Fontayne poured tea for Bracken and dropped three lumps of sugar into the cup. He did not take sugar.

"Yes, how was the dance? Have you nothing to tell us?" Tom demanded severely.

"It was all right," Christopher said. "Not bad."

Philly shuddered and pressed Ernest tight down on her knee under the table. Morning was here and the horror was over. Without being too deceitful, one could even join brightly in the chatter.

"Mrs. Rudge was there doing the ices," she said.

"Did you all dance?" her mother asked.

"Oh, yes." Sarah roused herself from rapt oblivious contemplation of corn flakes. "Philly was quite the belle of the ball, with loads of partners!" She smiled slyly but kindly.

"I danced with Bob Norbett and then with Mr. Lupin," Philly mumbled, her face half hidden by a pale brown wing of hair.

"Not to mention me," Christopher added.

"And as for Christopher, he danced with the most glamorous creature any of us has ever seen." Sarah felt she could afford to be generous.

"Well, her face looked awful really, of course," Christopher said judicially, "with all that paint and what not, but she isn't bad."

"I don't call that paint. It was simply a perfect make-up. I only wish I knew how to do it so well," Sarah said. "You ought to be flattered to death at having a dance with someone who was a famous débutante."

"Well, I *said* she wasn't bad." He could not admit the humility of gratitude he felt to her for having treated him as a human being. "She didn't seem too bogus."

Why can't they say what *I* did? I lead them on and flatter them, but they leave me to blow my own trumpet. Even Bracken says nothing. It isn't fair—

"I danced with Sir Giles Merrick," Sarah said, with indifference.

"Was he nice, darling?"

"I think he was, Mother, but that really isn't the point." What is the point . . . ? "I mean, he is so many other things."

"Even so, it remains important to be nice," Mrs. Fontayne said serenely.

"He's very handsome in an old sort of way," Philly offered helpfully.

"Handsome is as handsome does," Tom remarked, clashing two spoons together deftly.

"He's very handsome in *any* sort of way," Sarah said icily.

She was all ice and fire, dismaying the temperate morning. Her dark hair hung in silky uncombed loops against her shoulders; she wore a cotton kimono that was at once forlorn and dashing. Bracken felt an odd compassion for her, but faintly resented it, for one should not pity the young and lovely and the self-important.

"I rang up to order the . . . conveyance," he said to his hostess. "Was that all right?"

"Oh, are you really leaving us? Must you go?"

"When will you come again?" Sarah asked, one eye on Cruddles, who had brought the letters in. It wasn't humanly possible that he could have written to her yet, but her heart beat wildly for a moment of unreasonable anticipation.

"Bills . . ." Mrs. Fontayne sighed.

"We must have the Joneses here." Sarah roused herself. "If we have them before the weather changes they will see how beautiful Fontayne can be, and they may want it. Couldn't you stay on to tide us over their visit, Bracken? You were awfully good with Mrs. Oxford."

"That must have been purely an accident. But I am sure you will manage the Joneses perfectly." He evaded Sarah's compelling eye.

"I know what it is. When you think of us, you say to yourself, Enough is as good as a feast," she said resentfully. "You don't care that we shall have nobody to talk to Mr. Jones."

"Don't worry Bracken, Sarah. *I* shall talk to Mr. Jones," Mrs. Fontayne said with surprising briskness.

"Is there any more jam?" Tom muttered to himself. "Is there any more jam for my little bit of butter and my little bit of bread?"

"Oh, I wash my hands of trying to sell Fontayne," Sarah said grandly. She had suddenly recollected the memoirs again. "Where are Father's Papers?"

"Papers, darling? What papers?"

"Everyone of any importance leaves Papers behind when they die."

"But, darling, your father has been dead for nine years. However, you had better ask Cruddles—" This was how Mrs. Fontayne usually shelved puzzling questions.

"Come again soon, won't you, Bracken?" Philly said, feeling that if the parting guest were not exactly being speeded neither was he very pressingly being detained, unless it were to suit Sarah's purpose.

"I will," he said, smiling at her.

"It may be our last summer at Fontayne." Ernest wriggled upright on her knee and viewed the table disdainfully. Not a kipper carcass in sight.

"And I'll be back at school for most of the summer," Christopher said glumly. "Leave the jam alone, Tom."

"I was only scraping the scrape," Tom said moderately.

"If we sell," Sarah dreamed, "perhaps we could give a house party before we leave." The derelict ballroom coming to life and no expense spared and Sir Giles in tails and a dark red carnation . . . the Fontaynes going out in glory, come what might. . . .

They rose and drifted out on to the terrace, Sarah still in her kimono, Philly in her obdurate gingham. The conveyance would soon be here. Bracken strolled, with a girl on either side of him.

"It turned out a good Easter," Sarah said reflectively, "although we never drank the champagne."

"And we never read any of the fairy stories this time," Philly said.

"Perhaps you have outgrown them."

"We could never do that," they said decidedly.

"Yet everything changes," Sarah added. "After this summer—"

"After this summer, the world may end," he said.

Their shadows stalked the morning boldly. His words settled quite tidily into the scene. Mrs. Bale's kitchen cat endeavoured to fraternize in a classless amiability with Ernest, but was not successful. Somewhere to the side of the house Tom could be heard talking pleadingly to his donkey and Christopher's fluting brooding whistle spread sweetly on the air.

When Bracken was gone there was a sense of blankness which Sarah, at least, had not expected to feel. It was as if, in going, he left a veil of lassitude upon the place. He did not say much, but there seemed a silence and a somnolence when he was gone.

She roused herself and went in search of Cruddles.

"Did you ever hear there were any of my father's private papers left unsorted here at Fontayne?" she demanded.

"There's a lot of old rubbish in the south attic," Cruddles said grandly, "but you'll only go mucking yourself up with cobwebs."

He had a sour face, she thought. Tom was right when he called it (out of the blue, one day) a Dundreary face, although Cruddles was passionately clean-shaven.

"Will you come and help me look?"

"I've no time for wild-goose chases."

"Cruddles!"

"Yes, Miss Sarah?" he said suavely, switching his tone without the flicker of an eyelid.

"Can't you even try to be helpful ever?" She did not wait for an answer, but flung herself off alone to the attics.

She found a great many unexpected things during her morning of exploration, but not the memoirs. The attics were knee-deep in incredible forgotten things. The air was thick with the silted dust of years. She sat on the floor and looked around it all. All these pasts laid out in trivial little bits and pieces . . . even mine. I have my own dismal corpses here among the rest. That toy grocery store I used to play with: the ladles, and the bins marked "Sugar" and "Tea" . . .

She rocked herself on her haunches, meditating.

They would leave it all here behind them if ever they left Fontayne. It would crumble to dust, all this, when other people were beneath the roof. The years would go over it all. On and on, rising, falling. On and on until the grocery store was quite crumbled away. But why stop at that? On and on, until Fontayne itself wavered and weeds choked the garden and the creepers grew into the house and a fungoid growth spread over the floors.

"What are you doing?" Cruddles asked with asperity.

"Oh . . ." She rose slowly. "I can't find anything. It's too late for you to come and help me. I was just going down."

"There's a big smut on your nose."

"There's a cobweb on your hairs." To refer to his hair in the plural emphasized its scantiness.

"Well, run along down now," he said, rather at a loss. "I'm sure I don't know what you're up to."

"Cruddles!" Mechanically, she glared.

"Yes, Miss Sarah?" he said mechanically.

They went down weary flights of stairs together.

The house seemed at sixes and sevens. Even such formality as Bracken had given it was gone. Meals would begin to be utterly haphazard again. Miss James, the old governess, who did her best to bring order into the life here, was still away on her Easter holiday. She still taught Tom, and Philly was supposed to do a few lady-like lessons with her, but she had long outgrown her, and it was only a question of time. Like everything else, Sarah thought restively.

The midday post came, but there were only circulars.

Tom elected to have lunch with Mrs. Moody on a tray in the schoolroom, where she was doing some sewing. Sarah went in there for a moment, before going to have her own lunch. The seamstress and the little boy were sitting in silence, but in obvious contentment. The tray was already there, shoved down on the work table amid reels of silk and pins and scissors and a tape measure.

"Hello, duck. Tom and me are just going to have a bite."

"Several bites," Tom said. "Hard-boiled eggs and pineapple chunks. I'm going to eat mine both together. There's a wooden thimble floating in the pineapple juice, did you know, Mrs. Moody?"

"Well, who'd have believed it?" she said, as if it were indeed incredible.

"Don't eat any pins," Sarah said, rather nervously.

"How did it look, last night?" With professional interest, Mrs. Moody referred to Sarah's frock.

"All right." She was cautious. If she mentioned Sir Giles, Mrs. Moody would probably be horrid and talk about sex.

"Oh, it's a nice little hard-boiled egg," Tom crooned lovingly.

"You didn't lose your heart, then, love?"

I knew it, I knew it! "Of course not," she said shortly. I simply daren't risk telling her, with the dirty mind she's got. . . .

The sun poured into the room, full on Tom's light feathery hair and the yolk of a bitten egg. For no reason at all Sarah suddenly felt mad with gladness. She laughed aloud. The sun shone and anything might happen. It was a lovely life.

"Now we can settle down," Tom said thankfully, when his sister was gone.

Having the Joneses to lunch was considerably more than the mere statement of the fact. There was Mrs. Bale to be propitiated, there was Cruddles to be cajoled into assuming the role he properly reserved only for Mrs. Oxford, and above all there was the tidying-up of what seemed like yawning acres of untidiness.

"They may want to see all over it, so we daren't neglect it," Sarah said. "Christopher and Tom must help, too."

"What's happened to Polly? Has she gone?" Christopher asked protestingly.

"No, but it doesn't look as if she's going to *last*, so we have to treat her delicately."

"Is she going to die?" Tom asked, with interest.

"No; leave," Sarah returned curtly. "Come on, now. I'll begin on our bathroom and you do the schoolroom, Philly. And dust the bookcase. Horrible Bronwen is sure to go snooping around to see what our literary taste is."

Tom tore the carpet sweeper up and down the sewing room in a passionate massacre of pins and bits of thread. How pleased Mrs. Moody would be! Ernest gathered his tail unto him in the nick of time and fled before the onslaught. Tom glanced round to find out if Philly had seen, and then permitted himself a brief private smile.

Philly did her dusting and then went to see how Sarah was getting on.

"You've only half-cleaned the bath," she pointed out.

"I've done the higher tide mark, which is mine. I've left the lower one, which is yours, for you to do," Sarah explained unemotionally.

The Joneses arrived in a haphazard sort of sports car, driven by the father. Bronwen, wearing a peculiar velvet frock that practically matched her long lank straw-coloured hair, was the first into the house.

"I'm getting the *feel* of the place," she greeted Mrs. Fontayne. "It really is most lovely."

"These are my two boys." Mrs. Fontayne passed obliviously over her rhapsodies.

They were all warily polite. Mr. Jones, smiling mournfully, charmingly, beneath his old-world moustache, said it was very kind, very kind . . . his words, hanging in mid-air, hinged to nothing. The sherry pause was dryly, adequately, filled by an Amontillado that Bob had specially recommended. Mr. Jones drank with a boyish zest and Peter gravely sipped. Sarah had a half glass to keep them company and to allow Bronwen to make no mistake that at least one Fontayne was quite grown up.

Lunch went well. Bronwen, it seemed, enjoyed her food and talked very little while she was eating. The Jones father and son conversed blamelessly.

"I should like to have a permanent home in this part of the world," Mr. Jones said.

Sarah kicked Philly under the table. Tom gave a deep pre-meditated chuckle.

"Copley's Green begins to pall," Bronwen said, her remark coinciding with the end of a course.

"It's pretty dull around these parts, really," Christopher, who would have no part of the odious commercial enterprise of this lunch, said flatly.

"It is nothing of the kind," Sarah said sweepingly. "It is a richly diverse community." Bob Norbett had earnestly said something of the sort.

"Oh, it's a beautiful little place to live," Tom said, still chuckling.

"If you are interested in old houses, perhaps you would care to look round," Sarah said, as soon as lunch was over.

Mrs. Fontayne took charge of Mr. Jones to look first at the garden. The rest of them trooped upstairs for the first round of inspection. Bronwen seemed disposed to loiter in the schoolroom quarters. While her brother politely tried to discover Christopher's interests, she made play with her bracelets and broke into reminiscence for the benefit of the girls. Her pallid muddy skin took on a faint flush of animation.

"I can't imagine how anyone can *not* have an urge to be creative here. The only time I ever had such a sense of harmony was when we stayed in the old south, at a place in Virginia."

"Would you like to live in such a house?" Sarah asked pointedly, passing over the old south.

"Here? But of course." The bracelets were expressive.

"There's supposed to be some sort of ghost that snoops about the old Keep ruins." She piled it on rather.

"It's perfect. . . . I wish I'd known this place before I'd finished my book. But it's too late to add anything. I shall be getting proofs soon."

"Are you writing another?" Sarah asked with generous, if not exactly disinterested, interest.

"Well, of course I'm always *writing*." She produced, with a conjurer's dexterity, a large flat notebook from somewhere about her person, and fluttered the leaves before the girls' horrified eyes. "I'm jotting all the time, you see." Without altering her voice at all, she added:

> *"Sometimes, looming on a curve in a cloud,*
> *I've seen the moon of her splendour sloughed.*
> *Thin craven moon, measuring my disillusion*
> *And mirroring only my emptiness."*

"The last bit doesn't rhyme," Sarah pointed out. One had to say something.

Tom, who had been listening in brooding silence, suddenly gave a laugh of shocking timeliness.

Bronwen eyed him with pale displeasure. "It isn't meant to. That's how we write poems nowadays."

"Then the first bit shouldn't sort of rhyme."

"Why not?" Bronwen was sullen. "To be really free, you've got to be able to rhyme or not, just as you feel inclined." She went on somewhat hurriedly: "Of course I really prefer prose. I have a 'Hollywood Interlude' here. I describe how Daddy conducted a symphony in the Bowl."

With great self-restraint the girls did not inquire what on earth "the Bowl" was; but Philly asked:

"Did you meet Shirley Temple?"

"No," Bronwen said curtly.

Peter had sat down at the old schoolroom piano and was strumming lightly as he chatted to Christopher, who looked uncomfortable.

"I have written of some of my very early memories in my book," Bronwen said. "We were in Paris then. I think you may find that part interesting."

Does she expect us to *read* her book . . . ? Sarah and Philly caught each other's eye in a wary horror.

"I have a fortunately long memory," Bronwen said complacently.

"I remember being born," Tom said impassively.

"Of course you don't. No one remembers that."

"I do. I got born in the middle of a storm. There was thunder and lightning."

"It's true he was," Sarah said. "He has heard people mention it."

"I remember," Tom said inscrutably. "Oh, it was very dark. And the thunder came boom-boom-boom and I think I was frightened. Oh, it's awful getting born when you remember it."

"You tell the most appalling lies," Bronwen said cuttingly, yet hatefully feeling she had not truly managed to have the last word.

Christopher, fearing that Peter might become more involved in his strumming, tactfully but resolutely made an opportunity to switch on the radio. The room became flooded with the full tide of a cinema organ recital.

"God!" said Peter, simply.

"What's wrong?" Christopher increased the volume.

But Sarah guessed. "We *like* organ music," she said coldly.

Peter smiled almost apologetically, his long thin hands drooping between his knees.

"Doesn't your mother care for music either?" Bronwen inquired.

Christopher was too innocent to notice that sly "either," but he knew that he thought Bronwen was the most utterly bogus being he had ever met.

"She's not high-brow, anyway," he defended hotly. "I think it would be horrid to have a clever mother."

"Our mother was a genius," Bronwen said. "She had a salon."

"What's that?"

"It's where you receive people and talk."

"People talk everywhere."

"It is special talk in a salon."

"Talk can't be *special*. It's just how it happens to come."

"That's what you think," Bronwen closed the topic pertly.

"Shall we go and look at the ballroom?" Sarah suggested. This wasn't selling the house.

They descended one flight of stairs to the first floor. Bronwen forgot all else in seeing the sad splendour of the ballroom.

"It's so *tarnished*," she said gloatingly.

"It could be done up," Sarah countered hopefully.

"Oh, but it has such glamour like this! This green shadowy light, everything dimmed down. . . . It's such a thrilling not-quite-tawdry decay."

She spoke, Philly thought, in exactly the same tone as she had used for the delicious stuffed pike.

"There's a smell of mould," Christopher said bluntly. "I expect all this gilt and plaster stuff will break up if someone doesn't get at it soon."

"But how can you bear to let it go to rack and ruin?" Bronwen accused them all.

"Because we are extremely poor," Sarah said precisely.

Bronwen did not blush, but it seemed as if her pale eyes became suffused with a noticeable darkness of confusion.

In a moment or two they continued their descent to the ground floor. It had begun to rain a little and Mr. Jones and Elisabeth Fontayne came in breathlessly from the garden. (Surely Mother couldn't have been *running* with Mr. Jones?) Her fair hair was ruffled; she peered short-sightedly, absently. She was wearing a white angora wool sweater, very fluffy and delicate, which would have made her look like an alluring rabbit if that had not been a too contradictory description.

"It is enchanting," she said seriously, wiping moisture of rain from her face. She spoke with simple sincerity, not remembering the "sales talk" Sarah had urged on her.

"Indeed it is," Mr. Jones agreed, as seriously.

Bronwen was less insupportable when grown-ups were present. She found an old music box on a side table in the drawing room, and for a few minutes became like a real little girl as she played with it. Mr. Jones confided that he had had some sort of nervous breakdown and had to rest for some time.

"It must seem very dull to you here after your engagements all over the world," Elisabeth said simply. She was thinking of Marcus, who had loved Fontayne, but who had so hated ever to be still.

"No, I like it more than I can tell." His moustache lifted almost sprightlily above a deprecating smile. "In the most unlikely places I have felt the urge for gardening."

"You must ask me for anything you like that you have seen in the garden," Elisabeth said, her heart going out to him.

"At the moment I have no place to plant—"

"Then you won't stay at Copley's Green?" Sarah rushed in.

"That arrangement is purely temporary," he said gently.

She eyed him calculatingly. I could suggest something purely permanent if I were sure the moment were ripe. . . .

"We must really be going now," he said, as she was hesitating.

There was a general casualness of farewell that made it seem inevitable it would be quite soon when they met again. The rain had stopped and the sweetness of spring was redoubled for having known it. The Fontaynes stood at the door to watch their guests depart. Mr. Jones turned the car inexpertly, and lost and found his engine. His sombre sensitive face was all wrong above the steering wheel. They careered off down the weed-studded drive, a cloud of exhaust smoke obscuring their passing.

"It went off fairly well. The thin end of the wedge, anyway," Sarah said. "Did he try to talk of music to you, Mother?"

"No, darling. We talked of flowers. And even vegetables."

"You never talk to me." Tom pressed close to her angora softness and then sprang away, clawing at his face. "I'm furred up! I'm all furred up! Go away!"

He ran away into the garden as if possessed. The others still stood, loitering. The day seemed to have come to an end in its middle; as so many days at Fontayne disconcertingly did. There would be more little showers and in between the sun would shine. And more fruit blossom would bud and fall and more daffodils would come out and live and die, and Mrs. Bale's venom would increase more and more against the kitchens, and the gardens would show more and more their green neglect as the prolific season deepened.

Sarah sighed, and began to think about the afternoon post.

The last ripple of Easter was gone, leaving a dead calm. Sarah had had two letters since then: one from Bracken and one from a girl she vaguely knew in London, but she had not heard from Sir Giles. Her moods alternated between elation and despair, but now despair was beginning to get the upper hand. She loved the pale cool mornings when she awakened to breath-catching anticipation; and hated them when the zero hour of post time came; and only began to warm toward the day again when the moment of the next post loomed.

Then, too, she despised herself for having broken down and confided in Mrs. Moody. What miserable lack of self-restraint. Now she was tortured by the intolerable conspiracy of tongue-clicking sympathy with which the seamstress all too appropriately hemmed her in.

Mrs. Moody blossomed on the confidence. She would whirl up to Fontayne on her bicycle (Tom still believed that that was why her visits were called "bi-weekly") for a positive orgy of sewing and mending, and full of the most outrageous suggestions.

"What I would do is make yourself a set of really nice undies," she would say.

"Why?"

"Well, it would keep you calm. Nothing like a good job of whipping lace on to undies for keeping your mind tranquil."

"I don't wear things with lace on them."

"You would, when you saw how dainty they were. Or," she added lamentably, "you could save them for your bottom drawer."

"Oh, do shut up, Mrs. Moody," Sarah said wearily.

"Well, it's best to be prepared. You're the kind to get married young."

"Oh, do you think so?" she relented slightly.

"M'm, it stands out a mile."

"Why do you say that?" In spite of herself she was intrigued.

"Well, I've noticed how you lap up any little thing you read about love," Mrs. Moody said, hardly tactfully.

"I do not!"

"It's only natural. But I'd like to see you married young to some nice man. Better," she added obscurely, "than running around."

"I think you're horrible," Sarah said, but too depressed to put much feeling in her tone.

"And, then, you being so innocent—"

"I am not," she interrupted coldly. "I know all about everything."

"No doubt," Mrs. Moody said enigmatically, biting off a thread.

What had Mr. Moody been like? One never heard of him. And had Mrs. Moody had such a moustache and such mottled legs when first she met him? One felt that he must have been put aside long ago, like the laced boots and the pleated petticoat Mrs. Moody used to wear.

"Then there is the Jones family," Sarah said, getting on to less agonizing ground. "I somehow feel things aren't going quite the way I meant them to." Mrs. Moody of course knew all about the Jones plot too. "Perhaps I ought to start an advertising campaign for Fontayne. I think I can do the estate agent's language. We won't call it a bijou gem this time, because no one seems to think the kitchens in the least bijou."

"Well, it might do you all good to get away from here, and then again it might not."

"And I've searched and searched, but I can't find any trace of those memoirs."

"If you'd start making those undies you'd be surprised how it would take your mind off your troubles," Mrs. Moody said.

The girls accompanied Christopher when he called to say good-by to Mrs. Oxford before he returned to school at the end of the Easter holidays. Sarah was glad to go. Mrs. Oxford knew Mr. Harbrittle, who knew Sir Giles. It was a far-fetched crumb of comfort, but it was something.

Their mother had said at first that she would come with them, and then had most peculiarly excused herself on the grounds that she had promised to go and look at the Bayswood Nurseries (whatever they were) with Mr. Jones. Even for the sake of trying to sell Fontayne, Sarah felt this was carrying courtesy rather far.

"It's funny how you wouldn't dream of calling on anyone but Mrs. Oxford," Philly said to her brother, as the three of them trudged down the road toward the town.

"Oh, she's a decent old girl. I don't mind her."

Sarah kept her head low against a bluff wind. One could almost smell the sea in it today. There hadn't been a single letter to the house either in the morning or at noon; and she was in a mood to find poignancy in all things. Even her brother, tall and fair and stepping out sturdily, seemed to her pathetic. Even her sister, chatting cheerfully about the possibility of a gas mask for Ernest, was sad to look upon.

"A gas mask won't save Ernest or any of us," Sarah said, with a morbidity so dark that it was nearly pleasurable.

"Everyone can't be killed off," Christopher objected.

"That isn't the point. Don't be so callous."

"Well, but—" It was no use. He couldn't argue; and was in any case ashamed of his own feelings. It wasn't as if he wanted bombs to fall on blameless people like Mrs. Oxford and Emily, for instance. It was just—well, it was simply that all the things they said about war couldn't really touch him. He wanted to fly. And he thought that he would like to fly in a war. Oh, yes, it was awful to kill people, but they were pretty *dull*, most of them. He didn't really like people much. Few people made him happy. . . . Not that he could talk to the girls about any of this, of course.

"You know nothing about world problems," Sarah said crushingly, thinking of Sir Giles. She had been thinking of him, too, when she ploughed into an old copy of *War and Peace*, this morning.

"What do you bet that Mrs. Oxford gives us some of that brandy-snap stuff for tea, Philly?" he asked, leaving Sarah alone.

"I don't know. I mean, I bet she does."

After the shaggy-bearded look of the Fontayne gardens, Mrs. Oxford's place was quite a dazzle to the eyes in its neatness and symmetry.

"But this is delightful to have my young friends around me," she greeted them, instantly drawing them into the social-matriarchal atmosphere which surrounded her. "How you grow, dear boy."

"Mother had to go out with Mr. Jones," Philly said.

"So she let me know." The old lady's eyebrows gave a preparatory twitch but did not quite rise. "I hear you have made friends with the musical folk."

"It isn't exactly friendship," Sarah said delicately.

"You, no doubt"—she turned to Christopher again—"find the boy a congenial companion." She seemed to be doing her best to explain away the Joneses for them.

"He's older than I am. He's eighteen, and awfully old for it." He added without censure: "He doesn't seem to have been to school."

"So one would gather," Mrs. Oxford said smoothly, taking it all in. "Still, I suppose it is nice for you to find young companions."

"We don't want them," Sarah burst out. "We don't get on with them."

"Indeed? I believe I said in the first place that I did not think you would." She dismissed the Joneses. "I have tea laid in the dining room where there is plenty of space."

There was plenty of food too. I wish she would leave off treating us as gluttonous infants, Sarah thought sadly.

Emily sidled in shyly and said how-do-you-do. She was intensely, secretly, relieved that Tom had not come. She had just spent a happy but exhausting hour riding side-saddle on her bedhead, with her courtiers pounding along behind her.

"You are eating nothing, dear," Mrs. Oxford reminded Sarah.

"I'm not hungry, thank you."

"She's feeling Russian," Christopher said.

"Dear me!" The old lady looked genuinely distressed.

"Not communistic," he added hurriedly. "Old Russian. Tolstoy."

"In that case she might like to take her tea with lemon," Mrs. Oxford said with a clear intention of humour.

"Have you seen Mr. Harbrittle lately?" Sarah changed the tiresome subject.

"I hear he is much involved in his middle chapters," the hostess said, somehow making it sound more anatomical than literary. "I think you were the last to see him, at the—er—dance." She had not yet quite got over the fact of his presence there.

"Oh, yes, the dance . . ." Sarah said wistfully. Much good it does me to get back to that. . . . "Lady Pansy Bysshe and her niece were still staying with Mr. Harbrittle then." Her mouth was too dry with undesired madeira cake to speak Sir Giles's name.

"Yes. Pansy I have known off and on since youth, of course."

Sarah gave a melancholy nod. One saw the on-off movement of their acquaintance over the hurdles of the endless years since they were young. Over the first hurdle of their first season they went: up and over and down. Over a neck-and-neck hurdle of engagement, marriage, then back to ground and settling down. Lady Pansy had been the beauty, but Mrs. Oxford had made the better marriage. (One had heard somewhere that Lady Pansy was poor.) Over hurdles of births and deaths and age, to finish up with diamonds and green eyelids and gingerish hair and experimental wigs and beautiful nieces and brandy-snap for tea. . . .

"Pansy always was difficult. Emily, sit up." She noticed now, as she had noticed previously, that her granddaughter invariably and incomprehensively blushed at the mention of Lady Pansy's name.

Emily sat up, the blush deepening. How tell anyone of the sense of shame brought by that name? How tell anyone that for years you had mistaken a picture of Lady Pansy, in the awesome fashions of her youth, for an authentic portrait of God, and had said your prayers to it accordingly, night after unnumbered night? That great plumed hat and shawl-like robing, and the prominence that Grandmother had given the picture: was it really any wonder that you had gone on praying to Lady Pansy for so long? But now—when the truth had at last come out—it was not only that Lady Pansy no longer seemed to have any real identity. Neither, alas, had God.

Emily's head drooped between her plaits which were tied at the end by one grey ribbon and one tartan one.

"If you can't sit up, Emily, you will have to leave the table. Well, Pansy has gone back to her poky little flat in London now. She still tries to be in the swim of things, I believe. One would think she was too old to bother. It is different for the niece, of course, who has a position of Beauty to maintain—"

"She flies," Christopher said, drinking his fourth cup of tea. "She told me so."

"Yes, they do everything nowadays," Mrs. Oxford said, not altogether with approval.

"All *I* do is ride a bicycle," he said. They all laughed, but he didn't think it funny. "I think we'll have to go now, Mrs. Oxford," he said politely but firmly. "I have to get my things ready for school." He knew Sarah was frowning at him, but he wouldn't meet her eye.

Mrs. Oxford, the perfect hostess, made little murmurs that might have been of disappointment or commiseration. Jet and diamonds caught the light as she rose from the table.

"Mrs. Rudge's triplets have gone in for a beauty competition," Philly slipped into an awkward pause as they all left the table.

"Indeed? I should consider that rather a presumption." But on the part of whom the old lady did not say.

Emily, standing on one leg like a petrified dark stork, shook hands with each Fontayne. Mrs. Oxford kissed them on the brow, including Christopher.

"Well, that's what I call a disastrous call," Sarah said, as soon as the front door shut on them. "You simply *can't* stuff yourself full and then just get up and leave."

"I'm not full," Christopher objected.

"I can never face her again. I don't suppose she'll ever invite us again. I'm utterly mortified."

"I wouldn't be."

"It's all very well for you, if you've no finer feelings."

"No, but really I wouldn't be. I mean, she can't feel so bogus toward us or she wouldn't have slipped me two as I came away."

"Two pounds!" the girls said together.

"She knows my birthday comes in term time. Very decent of her."

"*Our* birthday," Philly corrected, a trifle wistfully.

"But it makes your behaviour worse than ever."

"Don't you see she wouldn't have given it to me if she didn't still like me?" he explained patiently.

That was just it; everyone *did* like Christopher. Here I wear myself to the bone to get a little affection, Sarah thought; here I would go through fire and water for just the tiniest letter, and Christopher gets two pounds for being rude. . . . She still felt extremely Russian.

They left the walled garden and came into the full slapping tide of the wind, and met a soft grey hat whirling in their path.

"Got it!" Christopher caught it on his toe-cap.

"Quick—it's Mr. Harbrittle," Sarah whispered.

"I've caught your hat, sir," Christopher said, wiping it tenderly on his cuff.

"Thank you." The incident had not ruffled Mr. Harbrittle. He took the hat and adjusted it on his head as if at some invisible mirror, his knees bent a little, his yellow-white moustache lifting in the wind. He said carefully: "Ah, the young Fontaynes."

"We've been calling on Mrs. Oxford," Sarah said.

"And I have walked to Hogshott Farm. Every afternoon at this time I walk there from my house and back again."

"Do you?" they said.

The topic seemed incapable of yielding more. I must do something, say something. . . . Sarah stared desperately around.

"How are your middle chapters?" she asked loudly, over the wind. She could sense there would be no response to this, so she rushed on: "I can't find a trace of my father's memoirs."

"He probably destroyed them," the novelist said, without emotion.

Sarah hid her bubbling rage. "It was terribly nice seeing you at the dance and meeting Sir Giles and everyone." I've said it—I've said his name, after all these years—

"Ah, yes. I've just been writing to Merrick." It was a topic that held his interest. Quite benevolently, he waved an envelope at them and said emphatically: "In these difficult times I shall be very surprised if Merrick does not make a considerable place for himself, to the benefit of us all."

This was dazzling; but not so dazzling that one could not keep oneself down to earth enough to take a lightning glance at the address on the envelope. Once seen never forgotten. You will find it written on my heart—

Mr. Harbrittle naturally approved of people who had a considerable place in things. He himself had one in literature. Even so, and even though Sir Giles was his friend, he needn't be so uppish about it.

"If my father had lived he would probably have had a very considerable place too," Sarah said gravely. For surely the Fontayne home had not been nicknamed Mount Olympus for nothing.

Mr. Harbrittle stared at the girl, so slight that the wind, not content with flinging her hair into dark spirals, seemed to go right through her, too. Charming fellow Fontayne had been. Unstable and charming. The girl was probably growing up to be unstable and charming too. Pity these young people seemed to show no sign of culture, let alone brains. Still, she would most likely marry well, her pretty face her fortune.

"No doubt he would," he said courteously.

The rest of the day, already built up in their minds to some pattern of their several pursuits, had no such neatly destined conclusion. Hurrying up the drive, Christopher was already harping on the crucial problems of what he would take back to school, Philly was thinking she must feed her hens, and backward and forward in Sarah's mind Sir Giles's address was running like a poem, with *War and Peace* sinking into obscurity and taking the last tinge of her Russian melancholy with it.

Tom, meeting them on the terrace, gave the first hint that normality had been disturbed.

"Mother wants to see you all as soon as you get back," he announced.

"We have got back, stupid."

"Well, she's in the flower room and she wants to see you."

"In the flower room?"

They were disturbed. What was it about the flower room that made it not only the place where all prospective buyers of the house were interviewed, but also the haven of unlooked-for confidences? It aroused a willy-nilly sense of guilt. But surely none of us has done anything beyond the bounds of decency lately, Sarah thought perplexedly.

"Come clean, Tom—what is it?" Christopher demanded.

Tom looked inscrutable, but he knew no more than they.

Elisabeth Fontayne was "doing" the big hall vases. Her white hands went fluttering among cool green leaves. She herself, in her pale green linen dress, looked as cool as a cucumber. But a cucumber with something on its mind, Sarah decided with dismay.

"The laburnum will drop," she said regretfully, "but I could not resist it." Pale gold fountains showered over her gentle cunning fingers. All the children sat watching her as if she were a conjurer casting yellow spring spells. The little room was as oddly dank and lively as ever, full of elusive magic.

"Well, what is it, Mother?" Christopher prompted.

"Darlings"—she placed a frond deftly, gold curved within a bower of green—"I have something to tell you."

"Oh, it is a long time coming, so it should be good," Tom said.

"Shut up, Tom." The elder boy began to feel upset. He couldn't stand the flower room.

"Darlings, I'm going to marry Julian."

"Who?" Four voices pounced in unison.

"Mr. Jones," she added, in anti-climax.

Still her hands wove golden spells, and still she gazed short-sightedly at her handiwork. It was too much. It was monstrous. And there seemed nothing on earth to say. The silence might have gone on for ever if Tom had not laughed.

"But why? How could he make you?" Christopher then burst out.

"Oh, you needn't, darling," Sarah said. "Fontayne doesn't matter all that much."

"But I *want* to marry Julian," Elisabeth said, with an extraordinary dignity.

"But, Mother, you can't," Philly spoke for the first time. "What about Bronwen and the delicious stuffed pike?"

"Yes, what about Bronwen?" they all said.

"I'm not marrying Bronwen," she retorted, still with that amazing firmness and dignity. "In any case, she is undoubtedly a very clever little girl, whatever you may say about her."

"Oh, Mother, don't say you are going to be a beautiful understanding stepmother to her," Sarah beseeched. "I can't bear it."

"I think you are extremely unkind," Elisabeth rebuked, with a gentle sort of severity.

"What beats me is how people can marry people they don't know," Christopher said dully.

"Yes, you've only met three times," Sarah added.

"Four," Elisabeth corrected.

"Then there must have been one secret meeting," Philly said sadly.

"Yes, I went out for a drive with Julian one afternoon when you were all out."

They gazed at each other in despair. It had got as far as that—There was no hope left. It had got to stolen meetings, romantic rendezvous. Sarah made a last effort:

"Darling, are you quite sure you aren't sacrificing yourself for the sake of Fontayne, so that we don't have to sell?"

"Sacrificing myself! Where do you pick up such expressions, Sarah? Will you all kindly leave me to make my own decisions and try to be a little less vulgar?"

"Oh, Mother!" They gazed at her more in sorrow than in anger.

"I think you should at least try to understand my new happiness," she relented a little.

"But what will Mrs. Oxford say, for instance?" Sarah said.

"And what"—Philly thought of something even more disastrously to the point—"oh what on earth will Cruddles say?"

CHAPTER FOUR

SARAH HAD one comfort in the midst of calamity: the London address of Sir Giles. She did nothing with this until Christopher had returned to school and she and Philly had settled down to a monotonous despair at the situation. When she did at last write to him it took her two days and two nearly sleepless nights to compose the letter. First, there was the attitude to be decided on: resentful, humble, amusing, or one of quiet dignity? She spoilt a dozen or more sheets of notepaper.

Dear Sir Giles,
I know you are very busy, but—

Dear Sir Giles,

When we met at the dance here, you told me to let you know when there was another one, but I don't suppose you meant it—

Dear Sir Giles,

I haven't discovered my father's Memoirs yet, but there are several clues I am following up—

Dear Sir Giles,

You promised to write to me, but I expect you have been too busy helping to get us over the Crisis—

Dear Sir Giles,

My mother is going to marry Julian Jones, the conductor—

No, "the conductor" certainly wouldn't do. If Mr. Jones couldn't stand on his own two musical feet, he would have to remain anonymous, professionally speaking. If Sir Giles did not know who Julian Jones was, she was not going into details.

Finally she wrote out a fair copy of her least depressing draft:

Dear Sir Giles,

I was talking to Mr. Harbrittle the other day and he said it seemed quite a while since we had the pleasure of seeing you here (God forgive me for such a lie . . .) *and I wondered if you would have any free time in the near future, because Fontayne is looking very nice just now with all the rhododendrons* [she had looked it up in the dictionary] *and things coming out, so if you had a free Week End we would all like so much to show you the various things of my father's that I feel sure would interest you* (I wish it didn't sound so like the "bijou gem" advertising angle . . .), *and I have several clues to the whereabouts of the missing Memoirs. My mother is going to marry Julian Jones shortly, so we shall probably be having quite a lot of week-end parties* (I think that's what Bracken calls a *non sequitur*, but it can't be helped), *so it would be so nice if you could join us for one of them. In fact, we shall probably give a dance at Fontayne to celebrate the engagement, so if you could come*

*down for that I should be very pleased because I did enjoy our
dances together.*

Yours sincerely,
Sarah Fontayne.

Tense and frowning, she read it through. There seemed an appallingly frequent use of "and" and "so," but it would have to do. And the idea of the dance was certainly the one bright spot in the disgusting engagement. Mother would hardly like to refuse the suggestion, having done her best to ruin their lives.

Sarah sighed as she licked the envelope flap and affixed a rather tattered-looking stamp. What would one do for money when Mr. Jones was the head of the household? Naturally one would rather die than butt in on dear Bronwen's inheritance. Presumably Mother could still keep them going on the remains of the Fontayne money, while she herself would be entitled to spend the Jones wealth.

Philly stuck her golden-brown head in at the doorway. "Are you coming down to the town? I'm going to take Mrs. Rudge some eggs my hens have laid."

"How busy they are," Sarah said sarcastically. "I simply loathe your hens to the depths of my soul."

"Never mind, darling." Philly thought the condemnation a trifle strong, but she made allowances for Sarah's depressed state. "Don't bother to come."

"Yes, I will. I have a letter to post." Languidly, she rose from the table and languidly powdered her nose at a mirror on the schoolroom wall. "We must go the long way, to avoid Copley's Green. I don't feel quite up to seeing Bronwen today."

"Perhaps it won't be so bad," Philly ventured. "Mr. Jones really is very sweet to us all."

"They have to be, at first," Sarah said wearily, as if she had made a lifelong study of the habits of prospective stepfathers. "After all, Mother, even in the midst of this unsuitable passion she has formed, would hardly let him ill-treat us."

"Oh, Sarah, you can tell he would never hurt a fly!"

"If he hadn't minded hurting a few flies perhaps Bronwen would have been less ghastly," Sarah said perversely. "Anyway, don't let's talk about it. Let's go and perform your good work. You will become full of smug good works if you aren't careful, Philly."

Philly flushed with dismay. Of course she didn't think she was doing a good work by taking eggs to Mrs. Rudge and she knew Mrs. Rudge would never think such a horrid thing, either. But nevertheless it made her take up her little basket with a forlorn self-consciousness. She felt like a mixture of Red-Riding-Hood and the vicar's wife.

"I hate that basket—come along," Sarah said irritably. "I want to catch the post."

The May afternoon was soft and drowsy. Houses in the little town were washed over by a sort of pinkish glow that made everything seem a little larger and kinder than life. Distances were deceptive, bathed in this rosy suffusion, so that the whole long street seemed more intricately related in its parts than usual, in a serene democracy of light. There was a friendly laziness of football, speech, laughter. Awnings over shops were like tolerantly dropped eyelids over slumbrous eyes.

The two girls turned off to the side road where Mrs. Rudge lived. Noise was sharper, clearer, here. Children screamed and laughed and cracked tops smartly with flying whips. The yard outside Mrs. Rudge's cottage looked more hopeless than ever. But there was nothing hopeless about Mrs. Rudge herself. She greeted them with an enthusiastic, if somewhat tooth-lacking, grin. She was as thin as a rail and her hair was as straight as a poker and about as stylish as a teapot.

"Here's a few eggs from my hens," Philly greeted her, trying to dissociate herself from the gift, after Sarah's discouraging suggestion.

"There now—how kind!" Mrs. Rudge exclaimed, with appreciation for the hens' forethought. "Come in, do. I haven't quite got through with my tidying up, but you'll excuse that."

She never has, and we always have to. . . . Sarah gazed round the chaotic Rudge living room with disapproval all the stronger because she was untidy herself.

"I've got a present for you, too, Miss Philly," Mrs. Rudge said, her mind far above any ignoble suspicion that Good Works were being practiced on her. "My Georgie has knitted you a tea-cosy."

"How terribly nice of him." Philly's eyes sparkled with pleasure.

"Jimmie and Johnnie were each knitting you one, too, but they haven't finished yet."

Philly looked overwhelmed by the magnificently wholesale proportion of these gifts. Sarah, in spite of herself, felt rather out of things. A diversion was caused by the appearance of the brilliant triplets themselves, playing with an old clockwork train of Tom's. Their red-gold curls made aureoles of radiance over their identical soiled petal faces. Six violet eyes gazed placidly.

"Thank you very much for the tea-cosy, Georgie," Philly said, looking at all of them, because she couldn't tell one from another.

An appreciative general squeak was the only response. They were not quite five, and not yet at school.

"Didn't they win anything in that competition?"

Philly was amazing, Sarah reflected. She could still take interest in other people's affairs, in spite of their own lives having been nipped so tragically in the bud.

"Doesn't seem like it," Mrs. Rudge said without rancour. "You know what these competitions are. I keep telling my husband not to put all his heart into his football pools. Doesn't pay, does it, Miss Sarah?"

"I suppose not," Sarah said.

"What I say is, there's enough trouble in life without setting your heart on things as never comes to be. You'd think my husband was wrestling with demons or the like when he gets down to his coupons every week in the season. Can't make up his mind, you know. I tell him, Put anything, it's all the same in the long run, but he thinks that is"— she paused for a word—"well, mutiny, or something."

"I expect it keeps him happy," Philly said wisely.

"I daresay. How's that new Jane of yours doing, Miss Philly?" Mrs. Rudge kept in constant touch with the domestic arrangements of Fontayne.

"Well, I'm afraid she's practically on the brink of leaving. She doesn't exactly get on with Mrs. Bale."

Jimmie (or Georgie or Johnnie) hit Georgie (or Jimmie or Johnnie) over the head with the caboose and a minor case of pandemonium ensued for a few minutes. Sarah made it the excuse for leave-taking.

"Thank you for the eggs, Miss Philly!" Mrs. Rudge called after them, as she chastised the triplets impartially.

"She doesn't deserve such beautiful children," Sarah said severely, as they walked away. "Did you notice how dirty their faces were?"

"Yes, I know, but they seem perfectly happy. Do you know, Sarah, I think she's going to have another one. Didn't she seem to you to stick out a bit more than usual?"

"I'm sure I never noticed," Sarah said loftily.

Everything was wrong today. There was something *extra* on Sarah's mind, as well as the Joneses, Philly decided. She knew Sarah was weary of the Rudges, but nervousness made her harp on the subject:

"I wish Mrs. Rudge wouldn't call us 'Miss Philly' and 'Miss Sarah.'"

"Why not?"

"I—I don't know. I just don't like it."

"Perhaps you'd like her to call you 'Comrade Philly,'" Sarah suggested, with heavy sarcasm, "and then perhaps you could convert her to communism. Here's some hens my eggs have laid, Comrade Minny Rudge."

"No, but"—Philly passed over this display of humour—"I just don't like being called Miss Philly by anyone. Not even by Bob, though it is only being sort of gallant with him."

"How subtle of you to note the difference—"

"Oh, Sarah, darling, do be nice."

Sarah's heart, against her much-confounded will, misgave her. There was something about that little pleading husky note in Philly's voice—

"I'm sorry. I have a lot on my mind." Oh, why did I post the letter? Now it is gone and I am shamed for ever. It is prisoned in that monstrous pillar box and I must die of shame.

"There *is* Bob," Philly remarked, as they re-entered the main street.

"Good afternoon." He fell into step beside them. "How have you been keeping since the dance?"

"A lot of things have been happening," Philly said, not going into details.

"A lot of things have been happening everywhere." Bob looked portentous. "Outlook doesn't look too good. I don't know, I'm shu-er. I give up." He abandoned the world to its fate.

"That's what I keep saying," Sarah said distantly, fatalistically. "We shall all be blown up soon, so what does anything matter?"

"Oh, now, you mustn't say things like that, Miss Sarah. It doesn't do, you know. That was a nice little dance we had on Easter Monday. I hope we'll see you at the Hockey Dance. I'm the treasurer, you know."

Philly shivered, feeling as if she were squeezed between the two dances, in memory and anticipation. What were bombs compared with that?

"I'm afraid our future movements are rather uncertain," Sarah said obscurely.

Bob was far too polite to press the point.

"I see Sir Giles Merrick has gone in for some new secretaryship post," he said, with a sympathetic fellow-feeling of responsibility because of his own new task as the hockey club treasurer.

"Oh has he?"

They had reached the wine store and Bob paused for a final word, but Sarah hurried Philly off with only the briefest farewell. Feeling the brusqueness demanded some explanation she said curtly to her sister as they walked away:

"I felt rather sick."

Sarah sat with her eyes fixed resentfully on Mrs. Moody, who was darning a pair of Tom's socks. How incredible it was that not only had one broken down and confessed one's love, but had also admitted posting that letter. What was it about Mrs. Moody that extracted these wholly unwilling confidences?

"Don't fidget, duck. Let's have a look at your hand."

"Why?"

"Let's see it." She seized Sarah's thin beautiful hand. "M'm, you've got all kinds of nice things coming to you. Surprises and things. I wouldn't be surprised"—she peered so closely at the young lines of the hand that her moustache brushed over the palm—"no, I wouldn't be surprised at all if you had an answer to that letter right away."

"What letter?" Sarah asked haughtily, her heart nevertheless quickening its beat.

"Yes, it's there. Oh, and I see you wearing fine new clothes, and—"

"You're making it up." She snatched away her hand, depression settling on her again.

She left the sewing room and went forlornly downstairs to examine the noon post. It was a doleful sort of game to get there before Cruddles and discover the delivery unflawed by prying eyes. Bills, of course, as ever. A letter from Tom's godmother; one knew the old spidery writing. And . . . *Miss Sarah Fontayne*: very neat but masculine. It cannot be. I shall go mad. The hall smells of somebody's polishing wax. I feel sick and if the postmark is London I shall almost certainly go mad. It is.

"What are you doing?" asked Tom's voice, near.

"Go away," she said fiercely. "Get out of my sight."

"I want to see the letters."

"Here—take them." She flung the bills and circulars in a scattering around him.

"Oh, for shame," he said sedately.

She opened the massive front door and flung herself away into the garden. Family persecution seemed still to trail her like some persistent ghost. Through the kitchen garden to the little orchard. The green little orchard, poised still within blossom. Peace, here, beneath a pear tree, the long grass wafting over feet and legs as one sat down.

The thick paper crackled in sunlight. She shaded her eyes with a trembling hand, and read:

Dear Sarah,

How very nice of you to write to me. At the moment I am abnormally busy, but there is nothing l should like better than to come and see Fontayne. Perhaps I could run down one afternoon before so long and call on you all.

I, too, enjoyed our dances immensely.

Yours sincerely,
Giles Merrick.

She laid the letter in her lap, then seized it and read it again. "Dear Sarah," he said; was that good or bad? Good, because it meant he felt he knew her well. Bad, because it might mean he thought of her as almost a child. He enjoyed our dances, though. And there's nothing he would like better than to come and see Fontayne.

She lay back in the long grass, staring up through a pattern of pear-tree branches clad in frills of pink-tipped blossom, to the bland milky sky. Dear God, how kind of You to make him reply. . . . The grass had a dry sweet smell, nostril-tickling. The world was full of peace and the amiable twittering of birds. I shall not rest on my laurels; I shall follow up my advantage. And now I shall be nice to everyone. I shall even be kind to Mother about getting married.

"What's the matter, Sarah? Don't you feel well?"

"Oh, Philly, darling!" She sat up slowly, dazed. "It's so lovely, just lying here quietly."

Philly was amazed by the return of temperate sweetness to her elder sister's manner, but she naturally knew better than to comment on it.

"I've just been along to feed my hens. It's about lunchtime, you know."

"Is it?" Of course I couldn't eat a thing. "By the way, I had a letter from Sir Giles Merrick. He says he enjoyed our dances immensely. Wasn't it nice of him to go on thinking of me?"

"Yes," Philly said. She felt anxious and puzzled. There was something unnatural in Sarah's high clear tone.

They walked slowly from the cramped little orchard, across unmown lawn and up terraces toward the house. Sarah set her gaze in a consciously aloof valuation of the house. It was really far from imposing, viewed thus, with the huddled ancient centre bit squashed between the more spacious Georgian wings. Long ago, she remembered Bracken calling it a fine example of the higgledy-piggledy, and her small child self had seized on the word as an enchanting tribute. Our house is a fine example of the higgledy-piggledy period . . . had she truly and in all seriousness said that to somebody, as a family legend had it . . . ? But the point, the crucial point, was how would Sir Giles view it? How could one persuade him into seeing faded dilapidated Fontayne in the enthralling light that Bronwen (give her her due) saw it? Even the roof didn't match. From the lower garden it presented a patched, darned appearance, and the colour had run, blotty pink into red, with yellow undertones. Nothing was sharp and decided about Fontayne. Everything seemed faintly blurred and furred at the edges, except the kitchens, which were simply stark. And not only the dimensions, but even the atmosphere seemed perpetually at sixes and sevens. Nobody ever quite caught up with things, whether with dusting, bill paying, or simply living. Sarah's own bedroom was an example of the dying still hanging on; never a clean sweep. Dying faded roses on the wallpaper, now so pale a pink that one felt exhausted even to look at them. More roses woven into the carpet, long obscured by the treading feet of years, yet still visible as ghosts of their former selves when the sun plundered rudely across the room. In all the rooms it was like that. The past was allowed to accumulate for ever and there was no question of ever trying to catch up with the present.

"Mrs. Moody is really very clever," Sarah said, as they entered the hall, "She has an occult touch. She should have been a fortune teller."

Elisabeth sat at the drawing-room window in the twilight, her thoughts pattering out like little moths into the approaching night. How *dear* Julian was . . . she had never known anything about music, but it was surprising how little it seemed to matter . . . and the children would get used to things . . . and . . . yes, even if one had to hear about music some time, it was wonderfully out of the world, not in the least like politics, which was a relief, as the daily papers were full of worse and worse things . . . and the household bills . . . but lately one had been able to put it all out of mind and concentrate on the evolving pageant of summer. . . .

Working in the garden in these leisured lengthening days was an everlasting delight; and showing Julian what she had done. The children never noticed. Because the garden, as a whole, had an inevitable shabbiness, they could not pick out the created gems of preciously rescued corners here and there. However, she thought, gratefully, the children had been nicer to her in the past few days. Sarah had been gentle and charming, retreating within some dream of her own. Philly, of course, had a naturally lovely nature. It was all so restful and almost spellbound, that she hesitated to break the calm. And yet it seemed wisest to have the marriage as soon as possible.

The larches were perfect from this distance. She seriously believed that the trees of Fontayne would have been quite sufficient as a common interest between herself and Julian, even if there had been no other. Surely to any people with a sense of proper proportion (not the sort of people one read about in the papers, of course) trees could be a topic of endless delight. The light on them now was cold and green and brought to the final pitch of purity before the dusk would invade and dilute it.

She heard the voices of the children, unseen on the terrace, quite close to the open window.

"It's all very well for you," Sarah said. "At nine, you can get used to anything. You'll be calling him Daddy before we know where we are."

"I shall not," Tom said, with dignity. "I shall call him Mr. Jones, as I always do."

"You don't call him anything," Sarah said scornfully. "You just look at him sweetly from under your lashes, making the poor man think you're a nice little boy."

"I *am* a nice little boy, and," he added serenely, "Mr. Jones is prob'ly a nice little man."

Sarah snorted. Sometimes, of late, the heretical thought had come into her mind that the Fontayne family was scarcely less dreadful than the Jones family.

Indoors, Elisabeth Fontayne gently sighed.

Gradually, in those few weeks of spring and summer advancing and retreating as if in some uncertain figure dance, the Joneses had ceased to be ordinary visitors to Fontayne, and, while not exactly presuming to be a part of the family, had gained an all too positive familiarity with the place. The truth of it was that scarcely one secret dreaming place remained intact in all Fontayne. Even the most unassuming hidey-holes in the kitchen garden were ruined by Mr. Jones's conscientious, almost morbid, interest in vegetables. As for the house, Bronwen had trailed her personality over it to such an extent that nearly every spot seemed smeared by her gloating rapture. The pianos—the old grand in the drawing room and the rickety upright in the schoolroom—were continually wakened from their seemly silence to protesting life by Peter's fleet fingers. One day he had even gone so far as to suggest to Sarah that a piano-tuner would not come amiss. Naturally, this idea had come to nothing. . . . The attics still brooded undiscovered, but it was impossible to know how long such a state could last.

It was definitely decided that Mr. Jones and Bronwen and Peter should come to live at Fontayne after the marriage. For the present . . . The future was mercifully vague. Anything might happen when Julian Jones had finished with his rest cure and got back into the swing, or whatever it was called, of conducting.

The girls wrote each week to Christopher, reporting on the general progress of the Jones suit. He wrote back (irritatingly) after a while to say none of it seemed so important now he was back at school; which in turn inspired him with the brilliant notion that, if they could smuggle their mother out of the sight of Mr. Jones for a while the whole affair would probably fizzle out ignominiously. Against this, he added the gloomy warning: "But I suppose distance does lend a sort of bogus enchantment to some people. . . ."

Elisabeth went on several occasions to London for the day with Julian Jones. She always grumbled faintly at leaving all the peace-drenched custom of her home, as if to miss the ripening scent and colour even for a day took something precious from her heart. But "there were things to see to, arrangements to be made." Even the simplest weddings seemed pretty chaotic, Sarah decided gloomily, when one got down to it.

There was that particular occasion when gall ran bitterest to the soul; the day when Bronwen went to visit her publisher. ("Her" publisher—as if the poor man, whoever he might be, existed only for the purpose of bringing forth her mouldy Scrapbook of Life!) It was bad enough to be associated with this even through a "step" relationship, but that one's own mother should be numbered in the despicable excursion was the last straw embedded in the gall.

It made no difference that Elisabeth said she would not actually accompany Bronwen and her father to the publisher's office. Peter, who was staying at home, was to spend the day at Fontayne with the two girls and Tom. Sarah maneuvered to have a sewing day with Mrs. Moody on this date.

"But we ought to be decent to Peter if he's a guest," Philly said, troubled.

"Very well, *you* can look after him and talk to him," Sarah retorted.

"Oh, no! Oh, Sarah, promise you won't leave me alone to think of things to say to him!"

"Well, don't be difficult, then. Peter is quite capable of looking after himself. You know how he goes on at the piano."

Mr. Jones and Bronwen arrived in the erratic car early in the young May morning to call for Elisabeth. Bronwen seemed rapt within a beatific coma of self-esteem and had little to say, beyond mentioning that she was "going to have a friendly little chat with her publisher." It was no part of her intention to appear sophisticated. Her drab-fair hair fell in lank chunks over her shoulders and her short stocky frame was clad in a plain white frock. She had even discarded the bracelets. Her shoes were patent leather, heel-less, strapped childishly round her ankles.

"Peter is walking up a little later to have lunch with you," Mr. Jones said to Sarah. "Send him off if you get bored with him."

He took the wind out of your sails. . . . Sarah stood near the house and watched her mother, unfamiliarly smart in black, get into the car and sit between Bronwen and the driver. One felt wretchedly out of it, being left behind. Tom ran forward to kiss his mother good-by again, leaning firmly on Bronwen's hair as he did so.

The girls were left with the familiar empty feeling as of life cut off short in the middle of a sentence. Do the flowers in the drawing room, Mother had said, almost her final words; but she would be sure to criticize the effect gently, when she returned. Down below the terraces, there was a hedge of pale new blossomed lilac, and laburnum drooped and wept its golden crocodile tears everywhere.

"Flowers or some more sewing?" Philly asked, with a show of briskness.

"I feel too squalid for flowers," Sarah said, "and perhaps for sewing too." She flopped onto a seat on the terrace and closed her eyes against the sun. "This gingham has never quite got over being scratchy, in spite of being washed. I suppose you can't expect much for sixpence a yard."

"My sleeves still hitch up my shoulders. I think if we aren't going to sew I'll go and look if there are any more eggs."

"All right. You're getting very morbid about those hens." Ernest flicked across the lawn after Philly, his belly almost brushing the ground in an affected prey-stalking progress. Sarah closed her eyes again. She opened them to see Peter walking gracefully, silently toward her.

"Hello," she said unenthusiastically.

"You look very comfortable and lazy." He sat down in a deck chair and, with his olive skin and dark hair against a red cushion, looked quite decorative.

She did not answer. After a few minutes he gave an obviously pre-meditated sigh.

"Doesn't the—the narrowness of life here sometimes oppress you?"

No words could more aptly have coincided with her feelings, but all the same she was incensed by them.

"I love Fontayne," she said forbiddingly.

"But of course." He gave his exasperating little Gallic shrug. "Yet, even so, to be young in a highly circumspect village is inclined to be an irksome thing."

"I suppose you are yearning for your cosmopolitan freedom?" She ground down a weed in a crack of paving with her shoe heel. "It's a town, not a village."

"There is a happy mean between the cosmopolitan and the bucolic." He feared she was somewhat prejudiced against his family's kind of freedom of capital cities. "The thing that one does not particularly want is to be treated as a child, a schoolboy. At eighteen!"

"Boys are always younger than girls," she said more comfortably.

"Not I." Again he sighed; and stretched his long thin body in the sun. "Your mother is charming, lovely, but I wish she hadn't begun to try to find me suitable boy companions. I don't care for boys—"

"It's like Philly's Ernest not caring for cats." She smiled. "What do you like?"

"I like women," he said sombrely.

"Aren't you rather young for that sort of thing?" she said as starchily as Mrs. Oxford might have said it.

"I feel I can talk openly to you," he said disarmingly.

"Yes, I do agree eighteen is a terribly misunderstood age," she admitted.

"I've lost all inspiration since we've been here and I've met no new people. I don't even practice, let alone attempt to compose. The incessantly monastic atmosphere is getting me down."

"I expect we could find you someone to talk to, if we look around." She was beginning faintly to enjoy his confidences.

"Dear Sarah, I don't think you quite understand. I want neither your village maidens nor the young ladies at tennis parties."

"Then what do you want?"

"I want," he sighed, "a woman like Claudine."

"Who's she?"

"Claudine was tender and warm and civilized, and she was my mistress."

Sarah opened her eyes extremely wide, with some idea that this would prevent the threatened mounting blush.

"That seems rather unnecessary," she said coldly.

"There, you see, dear Sarah, you won't try to understand. But I was in calf love—twice—at fifteen; at sixteen I was conducting a pathetically abortive little intrigue with a mannequin; and then, at seventeen, I had Claudine for three perfect months in New York."

"Did your father know?"

"Apparently not, or he could scarcely have been so cruel as to drag me off to Hollywood at a moment's notice. But I could not discuss it with him, which may seem strange to you; but he is a peculiarly reserved shy man in some ways."

It did not seem in the least strange to Sarah; any more than it would have seemed strange that she couldn't discuss her lover with her mother—supposing she had a lover.

"So what is one to do?"

She gazed with disapproval at his lazy sun-tanned form. "I think you need some work to take your mind off yourself," she said tartly.

Philly and Ernest were coming back across the lawn below.

"On no account say these things in front of Philly," Sarah said.

"I shouldn't dream of it," Peter agreed, so promptly that Sarah felt more adult and apart from her sister and brothers than ever before.

Lunch was a dreary meal. Old Miss James, the governess, was there, "to put spokes in us," as Tom muttered darkly. He had wanted to eat with Mrs. Moody, but Miss James wouldn't let him. Oh, it was a hard life.

"Oh it is a hard life," he said aloud. "Give me the salt, Miss James."

"'Please,' Tom."

"'Please, Tom,'" he said.

"I don't think little boys should take salt, in any case."

"Being a little boy has got nothing to do with liking salt," he said patiently. "In *any* case."

Miss James always looked cold, however warm the day. She seemed slung into her clothes, as if she were wearing a hammock. She had an ancient but somehow shockingly still pretty face, pink and white beneath a coronet of white hair; like a shrivelled Dresden china shepherdess who had lost her way in time.

"Mrs. Bale takes revenge on us when Mother is away," Sarah said, grimacing at her plate.

"This afternoon, Philly, dear, I think we might run through those essays again," Miss James said, not too hopefully.

"Oh, please not today. I'm doing needlework with Mrs. Moody." Said like that it sounded almost like lessons.

Not even a clean tablecloth. . . . Sarah cast an eye over the ill-appointed table. How sordid life was. And just look at the sweet slimy custard with tinned tough apricots. One even felt sorry for Peter, who was far too good-mannered to appear even to notice the monstrous nursery fare.

Cruddles came in and Sarah made a valiant effort to rescue some remnant of normally civilized living.

"I think we'll have coffee on the terrace, Cruddles."

"Oh, do you want coffee?" he said.

She could have cried.

Erotic bursts of music came from the drawing room. Peter was working off the effect of lunch by plunging the house into a bath of sensuous sound. It was his unaggrieved revenge against the day for being so dull. Sarah crossed the hall on the way to going upstairs to the sewing room. The day was a failure, draped in a depressing pall; better to accept it so.

The sudden urgent note of the telephone bell made her jump. Cruddles would take *years* to rise out of his afternoon pantry sloth, straighten his back, and plod along the passage. She picked up the receiver.

"Yes, it is Fontayne. No, it's Sarah Fontayne. I *can't* hear what you say." Her irritation with the day came to a bubbling head.

"It is Sarah I *want* to speak to," the voice said very softly but amiably. "Giles Merrick here. I have been lunching here and wondered if I could call for a few minutes?"

"Oh, yes!" she cried, to deafen her drumming heart. "Oh, yes, do come. Are you with Mr. Harbrittle? Bring him, too, of course." Tom ate the last of the cake, and I don't suppose we have any China tea. Or would a diplomat drink whisky and soda . . . ? "How soon will you get here?"

"Almost at once. No, he begs to be excused." It must have been Mr. Harbrittle's own phrase that he used.

"I see. Well, then, I—Well, we'll expect you—" How did one end? "Quite soon, then—" Mercifully, Sir Giles said a clipped good-by.

She was left in the mid-air of a dream. She stood still in the hall, the cunning notes played by Peter lapping around her. What a moment it was! Flowers and music and love. Mother had done the hall flowers this very morning, before she left for London. I should have told him she was away—An eloquence of pink and gold spoke through the perpetual dull greenish light of the great arching hall, like a limpid voice echoing and re-echoing on a silence that yet persisted. It was not (she decided in one lucid critical moment) so much the world well *lost* for love as utterly transformed by it. . . .

She tore upstairs to find Philly.

"You won't leave me alone with him?" was all Philly said.

"As if I would," Sarah said from her heart. She was tearing around her bedroom, changing frock, shoes, and stockings all at once. "I've come to the end of my face powder!" she said frantically.

"You don't need any," Philly said soothingly.

"How *can* you be so silly! I'll have to borrow some of Mother's."

"She hates having her things messed up, you know."

"She said I could always go into her room if it were a genuine emergency."

Philly wondered rather sadly what the world and Sarah were coming to, that face powder was now an emergency.

"And this horrible dress!" Sarah gazed despairingly in the mirror. "I don't know that it isn't worse than the gingham." It was dark pink linen, made by Mrs. Moody. "It looks like a Sunday-school treat."

"He's here." Philly peered from the window. "In the dashing car. He's getting out. He's wearing a grey-striped suit and a white silk shirt and brown suede shoes. Fancy daring to have lunch with Mr. Harbrittle in suede shoes!"

"Oh, be quiet, Philly! You'll send me cuckoo. Where's the nail buffer? I wish Mother liked nail polish. I'll have to go down—Oh, no one has told Peter—he's still playing."

She floated downstairs on the wings of a waltz, flow odd of Peter to play anything so nice. A "Blue Danube" sort of waltz, swelling and sinking in great flamboyant waves. Oh, lovely . . . pink and gold like the flowers wreathing and curtsying in the huge hall vases. Cruddles was opening the front door as she reached the foot of the stairs. Sir Giles stood dark against a background of sunlight, like an advertisement of the Riviera. It was almost more than one could bear.

Bless darling Cruddles for assuming the rich bouquet of his Mrs. Oxford manner. He put her in countenance, making even her frock

achieve dignity. She advanced on the mermaid-mannequin equilib-
rium that blended swimming with trundling.

"How delightful of you to call," she said, her voice going satisfactorily, amply, through the arched and scalloped distances of the hall.

"Why, Sarah," he greeted her so lightly that she blushed for her
appalling hostess tone.

He was not, of course, in the least as she had remembered him.
Memory had been placed so slyly upon memory that the natural living
semblance of Sir Giles had become quite obscured. By infinitesimal
degrees he had become saturated with the personalities and appear-
ances of Lord Byron, Gary Cooper, Anthony Eden, and characters in
old-world Michael Arlen novels. To rediscover Sir Giles in the flesh,
the suede, and the white silk of reality was, Sarah thought, the most
unnerving experience of her life.

"I'm awfully sorry, my mother is away for the day," she gabbled.
"There are only Philly and Tom and me; oh, and Peter." The waltz
chords came fulsomely still.

This did not seem to worry him. In fact, the dominant thing about
him—if this could be—was his exquisite casualness. She was lost in
his reality, beyond the necessity of making conversation. The eyes of
the actual Sir Giles were greenish; that had been black for her through
all these yearning weeks. He had a little scratch on his chin, which
reminded one that he, like lesser men, must also shave. Imagination
had played her false all round; it had never taken her beyond the first
moment of getting him to Fontayne. But what now? To the luminous
aspect of the hall, bathed in its eternal twilight, she silently beseeched:
What now, what now . . . ?

"It is a remarkably fine staircase," he said easily.

"I'm glad you like it," she said gratefully. "Would you—I wonder if
you'd care to look at the good bits of the house?" Oh, shades of the bijou
gem, the unique property, the opportunity of an historic dwelling not
to be missed.

"I'd love to see *all* the bits," he said with smiling lazy generosity.

"No, you wouldn't," she contradicted sadly. "There are acres of
bleak monotony."

She was humiliatingly glad of the approach of Philly. One clutched
at the mere fact of Philly, still in her unadorned gingham, as at a raft in
a raging sea. "You know my younger sister?" she said formally.

"Yes." The two shook hands. "Your brother plays very well."

"That's not Christopher," Philly said. "He's at school. That is Peter."

"A friend," Sarah added. How gay and informal it *ought* to have been. A friend strumming idly at the piano, like a young man in a Noel Coward play. Witty conversation bandied about over tea in delicate china, the young man still playing brilliant snatches sandwiched between each *bon mot*. . . . Oh, dear, why could such things never be?

The music stopped and Peter stood at the drawing-room door. He had not heard a whisper of the visitor. He neither knew nor cared who the stranger was; but Sarah, he noted with approval, was looking perfectly lovely, which was a triumph in that rural strawberry frock.

"Peter Jones—Sir Giles Merrick," Sarah said. If it went on like this, Mrs. Moody would be coming down and getting introduced, too. . . . But Peter was already leading the way back to the drawing room.

It was a bad second impression of Fontayne, this room, with its fitful faded colouring, its fussy blurred outlines. A room more resigned than positively vanquished; not a cushion that was not deflated, frayed, and deprived of all ambition. Not the hundredth part of an inch of pile on the worn patterned carpet. Nothing that was not poised by the merest hairbreadth this side of absolute defeat. Occasional tables ran riot down its long narrow length. The easy chairs were woefully uneasy to the behind. And altogether the room was pitched on a minor key, notwithstanding Peter's playing and the spring bursts of flowers.

"We may as well have tea," Sarah said, defeated. She rang the bell, hoping that Cruddles might supply some missing quality in the afternoon.

In the moment her back was turned, Peter had begun to talk to Sir Giles. When she stepped back to them the air was already trickily heavy with art. Sir Giles wandered vaguely around the room as he talked, his words broken up, semi-detached, still held by an expanding thread to the subject Peter had introduced. He picked up a photograph of Sarah. "That is delightful," he said, putting it down again and passing on. (But the words would surely stay when all the other words of the day were dead for her.) "Ah, your nice friend the explorer." He paused at a picture of Bracken. How funny! Philly thought. It made you see somebody with a beard, saying, Dr. Livingstone, I presume. . . .

Cruddles's conduct was unblemished, and of his own accord he brought out the best china and the silver; the bread-and-butter was a fine art, and now if the tea were China all was incredibly in order. But now Sir Giles was standing still, by the window, glancing down to the terrace, and the subject of modern art seemed hatefully fixed and permanent. One was lost, utterly lost, cast up on a desert island of ignorance. How well the party now was going and how humiliating it was that one had no part in this—

"Do you take sugar?" Sarah intruded sadly upon layers of thick invisible paint that seemed to clog the very air she breathed. Paint laid on with a trowel . . . as Mrs. Oxford said of women who used too much make-up.

"Two lumps." He smiled at her through a knowledgeable sentence Peter was speaking.

There were no modern paintings at Fontayne, only scraped-thin water colours, vaporous seascapes, and misty sketches of heather. A wonderful pictorial effect of numerous busy maiden aunts, someone had once said. . . .

Ernest came in at the window and was even more affected than usual, ogling the cake and purring with his throat in guttural low gear. But it seemed that Sir Giles liked cats, which enormously disposed Philly in his favour.

"If you would *like* to glance at the garden—" Sarah began, when the last fluid ounce had been got out of the teapot and the subject of art. Even Peter, smoking a Turkish cigarette, had dried up.

Sir Giles responded with an encouraging air of alacrity. They stepped straight out on to the terrace into a fount of warm air. How does Mother show people round the garden and make it seem like an enthralling adventure? Never mind; gardens at least are Nature, which is a thousand times better than art. . . . Peter had been left behind; Philly tagged on for a while, but her presence wasn't irksome.

"I don't quite gather who the boy is," Sir Giles said confidentially, playing into her hands.

"He's Julian Jones's son—"

"Mother's going to marry him," Philly said.

Sir Giles did just lift his eyebrows, but only, as it were, in passing.

"Going to marry Peter's father, she means," Sarah said.

They all laughed, ice cosily broken, the family tribulations coming to light.

"You see, it really is all rather ghastly," Sarah said, hurrying down the terrace, entirely forgetting to point out special flowers and vistas. "Peter is not too bad, in some ways, but Bronwen—"

"She has written a book," Philly said.

"And we shall have to live with that for the rest of our lives."

Sir Giles had begun to enjoy himself. It was delightful; the forlorn aspect of Fontayne, as if one viewed it through an impersonal myopic eye, all the fire of Marcus Fontayne diluted, dissipated, on intricately antagonistic domestic scenes. And lovely Sarah, with all her father's fervour and energy misdirected at a score of different humorous tangents. His own life, he was fond of saying, was Organized up to the hilt, and his personality was trained to exact and never overlapping compartments, but he could thoroughly appreciate this dream-like atmosphere of unaccomplished things.

Philly, warmed by the guest's uncondescending response to Ernest, seemed surprisingly at ease. She nodded approvingly when Sarah said:

"She has no regard for the seriousness of the times, for one thing," still harping on Bronwen. "If she must write poetry, don't you think she ought to bring in something about the Crisis and the Coming War?" She appealed to his professional awareness for political events.

"Oh, I don't know," Sir Giles said, smiling. "Lots of true artists don't go in for that sort of thing, you know. Look at Jane Austen."

"Why look at her?" Philly asked, wanting to know.

Sir Giles frowned. He disliked all explanations as being necessarily clumsy things.

"Down there is the Cedar Ring." Sarah waved an arm. "The monk's ghost usually walks there, they say, but lately it seems to have taken to haunting the sewing room, which is utterly unsuitable."

"No, I think it's mice," Philly disagreed. "Tom and Mrs. Moody have such a passion for snacks of cheese."

They had reached the orchard. Sarah had felt sentimental for this spot ever since she had read Sir Giles's letter there. Trees were shaking the last of the blossom in a pink-veined ripe confetti to the ground. The scent was so sweet that it filled the nostrils and left one almost gasping. It was the setting of a film Sarah had recently seen, with hero and heroine outlined on a close-up of blossom.

"I'll just run down and look at my hens as I'm near."

Sarah felt she had never loved either Philly or her monstrous hens so much. Alone with Sir Giles, her spirit felt wonderfully calm. Never mind about conversation. Silence was now as pure and tender as the fruit blossom. Tranquillity stretched in an endless avenue, away down the rhododendron-hedged paths to eternity.

"It is beautiful, peaceful," he said, aware of her mood. "I don't like having to leave it."

"Oh, you aren't going yet! I have shown you nothing of the house. I have shown you nothing of my father's, yet. He used to sit here in the little orchard." She added wistfully: "Perhaps he composed speeches or something here."

"I'm afraid I shall have to go soon."

"Do you have to go back to Mr. Harbrittle's?"

"No; but I have an appointment in town."

Of course: inevitably. Appointments following thick and fast on one another, the little engagement at Fontayne fitted in neatly as in a jigsaw puzzle. . . . She sighed.

"Perhaps you don't want to wait for any more?"

"My dear girl, yes."

Her heart rebounded in joy. His dear girl. . . . Going back across the lawn his hand swung very close to hers.

"My brother Christopher tells me you are a Boxing Blue," she said out of her bounteous joy.

"*Was*, long ago," he corrected with light ruefulness. "It's a sport for the rudest of rude youths."

"But you still look very strong."

He might have winced at "still," but did not. He was full of well-being and never for a single wistful moment regretted his vanished teens and twenties.

"My brother boxes at school. But he likes aeroplanes best. Mrs. Welwyn"—she hesitated—"said she might be able to help him get some flying." Not for Christopher that one introduced the tantalizing enigma of Virginia Welwyn. "I—I suppose you see her in London a lot?"

He seemed amused. "London is rather large. I scarcely know Virginia Welwyn."

The tour of house inspection ended in the attics. How this could have happened was impossible to trace except by mere physical means. Mentally, emotionally, the progress was immeasurable from the stilted scene in the drawing room to this fluent communion of mind and spirit. He sat on an old travelling trunk, while she knelt on the dusty floor and sorted yellowing curling-leaved papers as if they were priceless documents.

"If only I were clever I would like to write a book about my father. He was a brilliant man, wasn't he?"

"Undoubtedly," Sir Giles said.

"Or if only I could *quite* find the memoirs, I might . . . edit them." She did not know what this meant. "They are terribly elusive, but I'm sure they are here somewhere." She could tell him practically anything now. The unsunned attic gave the strangest air of intimacy. She gazed at him sitting there on the trunk in his beautiful suit.

"You know, I *did* enjoy that dance," she said meditatively.

"So did I." He watched, fascinated, her tender white hands hovering over the somehow pathetic little piles of papers. So cool and slim and ineffectual . . . he felt his heart lift on a spasm of undeniable sympathy. He knew and sometimes deplored the generous streak of sentimentality that ran through him. Her irresponsibly thoughtful little face between its frames of dark hair . . . suppose she had more in her of Marcus Fontayne than met the eye? Harbrittle insisted that all the family was appallingly uncultured and brainless, but—In any case, it was an attractive subject for speculation.

"Isn't Fontayne a mess?" She took her eyes off him at last and stared away to dim cobweb-looped far caverns of attic. "Not only up here, but all over. Sometimes I feel that *we* personally are what is meant by the 'twilight of civilization.'"

"You really mustn't say such things," he said, slightly ashamed for her.

"But we go drifting on, and now we aren't even going to sell Fontayne, and when the war comes—"

"You must not say *when*, as if it is a foregone conclusion." His habitual smoothness came within an ace of breaking into irritation.

"Well, then, the revolution," she amended. "A friend of mine, Bob Norbett, says that it well may come to pass." (Here her mind went off at one of its fascinating shocking tangents, he noted.) "We shan't be able to keep Cruddles as a slave any longer after the revolution."

"'A slave'?" Sir Giles repeated, shocked to the depths of his liberal conservative soul.

"Yes. I don't think we've paid him any wages for years," she said simply. "Of course, as a twilight I quite see we deserve to die out."

"My dear, I'm afraid it's time for me to go. We'll have to postpone the search for the memoirs." He held out a strong fine hand to draw her to her feet. He continued to hold her thin fingers long after (as Mrs. Oxford would have said) there was any excuse for it. "Your hand is cold," he said.

"So is yours."

That moment was the apex of felicity. It was a perfection so delicately poised that the faintest extra touch, by word or gesture, might have ruined it. The chill stuffy attic was the shrine of this accomplishment; to remain here now would be folly. She was so painfully sensitive to his own feelings now that she could believe the thoughts of her mind were mingled mysteriously with his. Any more of the attic and he would lose his feeling of whimsical incongruity and realize that he was getting cold and stiff and that he needed good company again and a drink. So sensitive was she, now, that illusions fell away and she knew that he was thus wonderfully amiable mainly because life had always fitted him so amiably; and—even—so handsome mainly because life had always treated him handsomely. This consciousness, far from arousing condemnation in her (as it might have done in Philly), merely filled her with a passionate hope that his fortune would never deviate an inch from this admirable norm.

"Now we shall go down for a drink before you go," she said, a crisp hostess again.

How right she had been in sensing that such a peak could not be regained.

Downstairs, she discovered that her mother had returned. Bronwen was in full possession of the drawing room. Not even the tinkle of glasses and the display of cocktails in a genuine cocktail shaker could take the iron from this discovery. The Joneses monopolized the scene, but Mother held her own, Sarah felt with a glow of family pride. Mother in her London black, not forceful of course, but somehow illumined, impinging faintly even upon Sir Giles's world in an unexpectedly gratifying manner. Mother, without even the aura of her individual gardening gloves with their awful worn leather fingers in perpetual dowdy curves; but wearing, for once, high heels and sheer stockings and a tracing of lipstick; and, as if these adjustments did indeed (as promised in the Beauty Column of Sarah's favourite magazine) give that essential poise for the older woman, accepting Sir Giles as if he were all in the day's march, dropping in for a casual friendly cocktail. Mr. Jones had at least introduced the idea of cocktails to Fontayne, though this was the first time they had put in an actual appearance.

Yet Bronwen managed to spoil even this fool-proof worldly pause, and to reduce it to a milk-and-biscuits personal childish success. She was a little girl, weary but ecstatic beneath a future stepmother's generous praise, ankle straps drooping, genius forgotten. She curled up on the couch by the big fireplace in which a leisured evening log fire had been lighted.

"Mr. Tulsey said she had a big future—" Elisabeth herself wielded the shaker with a desperate sort of aplomb, while her fiancé handled the filled glasses.

"Who is Mr. Tulsey?" Sarah and Philly asked.

"Tulsey and Flewkes," Bronwen said, catching a skin of hot milk skilfully with her fat tongue. "My publishers."

"I know Tulsey," Sir Giles said.

Why must he say it?—playing up to the milk and biscuits and the tedious bedtime hour? Naturally Bronwen responded to the encouragement. She turned to him and said: "He *has* a sympathetic personality," as if she were agreeing with something Sir Giles had said.

From publishing the talk turned to writing and then to Mr. Harbrittle.

"Isn't he rather hidebound?" Mr. Jones said, with his nice air of diffidence which so well became the silky modest downward curve of his moustache.

"He's calf-bound," Bronwen said sleepily. "I've seen his uniform edition."

The older ones laughed, though Sarah was not at all sure Bronwen had meant to be funny.

"Surely it's terribly dated stuff," Peter said. "Conventional movements and repetitions and repercussions."

"He has a great following even in the most out-of-the-way places, I believe," Elisabeth said kindly. "And he has had the same secretary for years."

There seemed little to add to such a recommendation, so they left Mr. Harbrittle at that.

Sir Giles had finished one cocktail and refused a second. His neglected appointment loomed with ghostly reproach. Sarah's thoughts floated in the strength of half a cocktail: "up to the trimming on the glass, darling," as her mother had unnecessarily pointed out. Sir Giles would get outside the door, and he might never return, but she was doing nothing about it. . . . He was saying good-by and already retreating into the aura of some brilliant beyond.

"It was so nice of you to come," Elisabeth said, going vague again, her own personal aura of gardening gloves slipping back into place. "I'm so sorry there was nothing to show you, but you probably liked to see Marcus's home, as you knew him."

He did not tell her that he had *not* known Marcus. He murmured compassionately, as if he imagined Elisabeth were still emotionally entangled with her widow's weeds as well as her horticultural ones. He was the perfect guest, as he would doubtless have been, in given circumstances, the perfect host.

"Good-by." Bronwen lifted a tired podgy paw and smiled up at him from amid cushions. She had even left a wistful fringe of shortbread crumbs about her lips to give greater realism to her role of poignant little prodigy.

"I hope the book will be a great success," he smiled.

"Mr. Tulsey is such a lovely publisher and they are going to have such lovely drawings that I think it may be," she said modestly.

"I hope we'll see you again when things are more settled," Elisabeth said.

"For that I'm afraid we shall have to wait a long time," Sir Giles said, fashionably in line with pessimism.

"She meant, when we are married," Mr. Jones explained in his wouldn't-hurt-a-fly tone.

"For *that* I hope we shall not have to wait a long time," Sir Giles amended, smiling again.

"No, it is all fixed," Elisabeth said gaily, like a girl. "We have been arranging for it today."

Ah, treachery. . . . Sarah's glance, cocktail-venomed, sped to Philly's; but she, fresh from her unfruitful hens and an intimation from Mrs. Bale that, without eggs, there was little hope of an evening meal, did not meet the challenge.

"Then perhaps he'll be able to come to the dance you said you'd have here after you are married." Sarah seized a cigarette and flung the words in a desperate fresh challenge at her mother, leaving Sir Giles in a third-person isolation.

Elisabeth had not gone beyond saying they might possibly have a little party, but this was too much even for the aplomb of a cocktail drinker and lipstick wearer. Her beautiful face flushed to the tender peak of her soft fair hair, and she was hopelessly outmanoeuvered.

"There is nothing would please me better," she said with such promptitude that Sarah's heart went out to her and left a chill void of self-reproach for the trick she had played.

"That will be delightful," Sir Giles said in farewell.

The dance began to bud for Sarah from that instant and to promise ambitious fabulous fruit. It was a forming tree ready to put out many branches that would stretch out over and almost obliterate an intervening prospect of the lamentable wedding.

"Would you like to come out this way by the terrace?" she asked Sir Giles, the triumphant moment blended in a mystical communion with the attic moments.

Without ceremony she drew him out to the cooling evening air, his farewells cut off in their prime, his departure without benefit of Cruddles.

The terrace described the hour lovingly. Young green sprang in tender shoots from the grooves between stones as warmly uncoloured as the sundown sky. The moment was scraped clean of hue, the evening folds of twilight not yet gathered. A scene so balanced and unemotional that even Sarah's emotions were whittled of their agony and exultation. Plane on plane of green blocked in the pattern of the day, shaped it in uttermost serenity. In the receding of afternoon and the holding off of night, passion lay down and died.

And in the rhythmic fronds of lilac, flowering currant, and wistaria, it was not so much the being of deepened spring that was trapped there as it was the essence of the hour straining colour from all things, reducing and diluting, until the purest quiescence of pallor was achieved. It had damped down the flame of the tulips to so guarded a fire that they seemed no more than a temperance reflection seen in cool shallows of water. All over the garden there was this lucid unlustred calm.

"Good-by, Sarah." He stood beside his car.

"You'll come again?" But her voice was robbed, exhausted.

"I'd love to."

"Next time I'll show you the Cedar Ring where the ghost walks."

"It sounds thrilling."

"It isn't really." Exhausted, quenched, there was nothing else to say.

. . .

CHAPTER FIVE

AFTER THE VISIT of Sir Giles (or A.S.G. as Christopher, with mingled respect and flippancy, referred by letter to the occasion) events moved on a rising tide of filial resentment toward the crescendo of the wedding.

Mrs. Fontayne went forward with her plans on a note of persistent humble gaiety. The children, never having known such stubbornness in her, were gradually forced to the conclusion that she must in fact love Mr. Jones.

"It's as if he is a Golden Fleece or something," Sarah said bitterly, "and her mind is ever fixed on the goal of getting him."

The wedding was fixed for Whitsuntide, when Christopher would have a holiday. It would take place in London, to avoid fuss, Mother said (did not this prove she was in some way ashamed of her conduct?), and they would spend a short honeymoon abroad.

Peter and Bronwen were so often at Fontayne nowadays that it was difficult to conduct family discussions in privacy. Once in a while it was impossible to exclude them.

"Of course your father is a very nice man," Sarah said with admirable fairness, one afternoon when they were not to be dislodged from the house all afternoon, "but what can he be thinking of, to want to get married at his age?"

"What most people think about when they want to get married, I suppose," Peter said, with a faint disarming smile. "It's the same for your mother, anyway."

"No. No, not exactly," she differentiated delicately; "Mother is only a little over forty. Your father is at least fifty, for some reason or other."

To this, even Peter could find no worthy answer.

Now, the fatal day loomed ominously. "We are getting warmer and warmer," Tom said cheerfully, as if it were a game of hide-and-seek. He at least had relinquished all rancour against his mother. The first traitor in the camp. . . . New London-bought frocks for Sarah and Philly had arrived, but they were no consolation; indeed, they both missed the familiar touches and flourishes of Mrs. Moody, and—not content with her twice-weekly visits—they sent her a stream of telegrams describing their dissatisfaction with what they called their loathsome trousseaux. The telegrams themselves were no novelty. Whenever there was a crisis at Fontayne it was the custom to telephone a telegram to Mrs. Moody, though it very often happened she was herself again with them in the flesh before the post office had got around to delivering the message to her end of the little town.

Bronwen had decided to wear white, the bride being in black, as she pointed out. White, with subtle hints of Chinese green here and there. It was, she said, an ensemble. She also said she had not much time for clothes, now that her book was so nearly forthcoming. Her complacency was now and again broken by nervous crises. This particular afternoon, inclined to be thundery, had brought her to the edge of one of these. She sat with her elaborate notebooks spread around her, waiting sullenly to be delivered of some presaging literary theme. Philly hemmed listlessly at dreary table napkins while Sarah twiddled her thumbs. Peter's hands flickered periodically over the piano. They sat in the drawing room with windows wide to a stifled terrace. Elisabeth and Mr. Jones were off on some youth-inspired jaunt of their own.

Cruddles came in with ostentatious silence to ask where they would like to have tea. His voice suddenly coming from nowhere caused Bronwen to start clean out of her muse.

"The devil damn thee black, thou cream-fac'd loon!" she said conversationally. "Where gott'st thou that goose look?"

Sarah and Philly were horrified and incensed. After all, Cruddles belonged to *them*. It was humiliating. Not to think of what it must be for Cruddles. They dared not look at him.

"*Macbeth* . . ." Peter murmured somewhat shamefacedly.

"That is scarcely the point," Sarah said, her voice as frigid as Cruddles's rapidly retreating face.

"It should be a wedding of young people," Elisabeth said, when she looked on her garden and saw the mid-May flowering. "Spring will still be here at Whitsun, if we aren't careful." The season would dog her steps romantically and deprive her of her sensible autumnal blossoming. Whitsuntide itself conspired to fall this side of the end of May, as if with impish malice aforethought.

"I hope spring *will* still be here," Mr. Jones said stoutly.

Then the heat of summer fell on house, garden, and town for the last flurried days before they all departed for London. A new moon hung in the glassy-still nights. The flowering currants rioted all along the edge of the higher lawn, and rhododendrons (attaining their full and vaunted glory without Sir Giles to approve) defined the driveway with their assured definite pink. The magnolia opened voluptuously on the face of the house and basked, inlaid in the sun.

Sarah waited with a scrupulous patience to hear from Sir Giles again.

All the town knew of the coming wedding. To the girls' too sensitive feelings it seemed as if the place could never cease to buzz with gossip of the subject. Surely it must run like wildfire through cottage, villa, shop, and slacken its pace only a little at the decorous portals of such homes as Mrs. Oxford's and Mr. Harbrittle's. Mrs. Moody (infallible oracle) had it that the old novelist had given an exclusive little dinner party at which literature and art and politics had been a poor second fiddle to Mrs. Fontayne's second marriage. In the Week End before the wedding, when Mr. Lupin was in residence at his cottage, he met the girls in the town and the wearisome topic was once more renewed. Philly, remembering the dance, was glad that he should talk of anything rather than call her a child of the morning again; but Sarah was deep-pressed in melancholy.

"So you are placed in romantic limelight at the moment?" he began.

"It isn't our limelight," Sarah said.

"Even a proxy limelight is something," he suggested.

They were hurrying to the haberdashery when he (all too suitably) buttonholed them. A vast surge of impatience drove Sarah on past his figure planted tubbily in her path. Let Philly wrestle alone with him as she had at the dance—He was always mopping his rubicund brow and he always conscientiously smelt of good honest tavern drink.

She was consulting earnestly with the shop owner, Mrs. Pratt (whose moods ranged with the temperament of a *prima donna* from excessive amiability to excessive dourness), when Philly followed her into the shop. Mrs. Pratt, exuding terrifying charm, would have turned every knick-knack in the place upside down today, should Miss Fontayne have expressed a whim for it.

"Well, you escaped?" Sarah interrupted herself in her finical order.

"Yes." Philly shivered, her grey eyes wide. "He says he would like to paint me."

"—Or we have an even *tinier* size," Mrs. Pratt said vivaciously.

"I'd rather die . . ." Philly muttered hopelessly.

"Don't be silly," Sarah said crossly. She was hurt that Philly was the chosen one. Not that she wanted to be painted by Mr. Lupin, but nobody had ever suggested that Philly was a quarter so pretty as herself. "Though I can't imagine why he wants to paint you."

"He says I'm golden," Philly said humbly.

Sarah snorted into the safety pins.

Cruddles, naturally, had pointedly avoided Bronwen since her lamentable Shakespearean lapse. He had been reserved about the prospect of the wedding from the beginning, but now he was positively inimical toward it.

"It isn't as if," he said, in a confiding moment to Sarah over silver-polishing in his pantry, "they are old friends of the family, like. Why, we hardly know them. It is not what you could call an acquaint-anceship ripened with the years. It's *raw*, that's what it is."

"I know. But it's too late now. We have got to marry them."

"It's certainly a mill to have round our pond."

"Yes." The meaning was clear, but hadn't he got it a bit wrong? "It seems all wrong you can't divorce relations. I can't see why anyone wants to get rid of a husband or wife—because it must be so easy to settle down to being a nice wife or husband—but *relations* are utterly different."

Cruddles cordially agreed.

Mrs. Moody, coming in to make herself a cup of tea, was surprised by his unbending manner. "Quite showing himself with his back hair down and his stays loosened, so to speak, wasn't he?" she said with blis-tering inaccuracy to Sarah, later.

Bob Norbett, on the other hand, respectfully thought the marriage a good idea.

"People need a bit of company for the evening of their days, Miss Sarah. Think how lonely your mother would be if she was all alone when you all left the nest."

"Her days don't seem to have very long evenings yet. And I don't see how, by any stretch of imagination, you could call Fontayne a *nest*," she retorted.

"No, but you know what I mean," he said.

The Fontayne wedding caused Mrs. Oxford to brood over marriage in general and Emily's mother's failure in particular. It brought it all back . . . the funereal return, to the maternal roof, of poor Caro-line, husband-bereft, tagged by Emily in a mask of orphan gloom. How distasteful it had been in a well-ordered household such as Mrs. Oxford's own! How disagreeable it had been to see Caroline at every turn, with her moist little handkerchief and her mock-widow mourn-ing! Naturally one had felt to the full a mother's grief when she died, but Emily was at least once removed from the relationship of the broken marriage, though a yet painful reminder of it. On the whole it was easier to cope with the errant-fathered Emily alone.

Talking over the Fontayne-Jones wedding details with her young friends, she was inclined to give Emily a little extra bullying. Really, the child was most odd. One would expect a properly frivolous feminine little girl to take interest in the sketches of Sarah's and Philly's frocks, if not in the subject of marriage itself. But no, she merely sat smiling politely and obviously between her dark pigtails when she wasn't riding the end of her bed and talking to herself.

Sometimes Mrs. Oxford went even beyond the conviction that Emily would marry a man who would inevitably leave her; beyond that to a further dread that Emily would never marry at all, but would become a . . . a Lesbos or whatever it was those queer people nowadays called themselves. . . .

"Well, dears," she said, offering Sarah a glass of her sherry for the first time and handing her biscuits to Philly again and again, "in many ways it is not what in *my* day would have been called a marriage made in heaven, but one must not feel too strongly that as a simply temporal arrangement it may not work out fairly well."

Temporary . . . ? wondered Philly, mis-hearing the word. Is Mother, then, to remake her marriage with Father (who named me Philadelphia) when she gets to heaven? And Mr. Jones, perhaps, with that intellectual lady with the salon? It was an intricate matter. On the whole, since they had got so far, it would seem best for Mother now to stick to Mr. Jones through thick and thin of eternity.

But this, Philly decided, was not an opinion that she would convey to Sarah.

It was only two days off. Christopher was home for the brief respite of Whitsuntide and tomorrow they were all going to London. Christopher was taller, browner, fairer, and more silent. He was very polite to Mr. Jones and simply ignored Bronwen and Peter. Sarah could arouse him to no demonstrations of any kind.

"You're crammed to the brim with stodgy school," she accused.

"No: I *ought* to be cramming, but I'm *not*," he said equably.

"Life here," she said, "is nothing but school ties, hens, and trousseaux." And love . . . she might have added. She was shaken by the aspect of love upon Fontayne. As if her own secret letterless love for Sir Giles were not enough without Mother and Mr. Jones!

This very morning it was brought home to her again.

Elisabeth sat on the sun-glittering terrace and drank mid-morning coffee with her fiancé. She sat full in the sun that never tanned her fair white skin, and her words rippled out so smoothly, so unimportantly, that they made no greater stir than the fallen petal of magnolia that lay beside her chair. Occasionally she took a few stitches in the embroidery on her lap. When she did so, she placed a mild-looking pair of glasses on the innocent tip of her youthful little nose and placidly peered over the top of them. The garden was alive with limpid birdsong that seemed to enclose the two in an elusive privacy. Mr. Jones glanced at one of his high-brow artistic weekly papers, but passed no comment on its contents. Once or twice Elisabeth drew his attention to her embroidery and explained the name of a certain stitch. This information he received with an air of gentle but profound interest.

Can this be love. . . ? Unknown to them, Sarah sat near, closely observing. Didn't the magazines always say that people must have interests in common if they were to be happy? Yet when did Mr. Jones ever fly into authentic paroxysms of music enthusiasm, demanding Mother to share his exultation or depart from his sight for ever? When he played the piano, he did it so reservedly that nobody would have thought of remarking on it. If this were love indeed, then Sarah felt she had wasted her time by conscientiously reading the newspaper leaders every day since she last saw Sir Giles.

"I think it would be a good idea to have some more aromatic plants near the terrace," Elisabeth said serenely, pressing a pungent leaf of lemon verbena between her fingers.

Can this (Sarah hurled herself indoors in a tempest of impatience) indeed be love . . . ?

On their rare visits to London the Fontaynes stayed always at the same hotel in Curzon Street, a place with a pleasing old-fashioned air. It would never have occurred to Mrs. Fontayne to go elsewhere. Only Philly was faintly uneasy in the place. Its name reminded her of her father's long-ago visit to the United States' capital, and the peculiarly disastrous humour in him that had led him (by further devious geographical routes) to arrive eventually at *Philadelphia* as a name for her. It seemed to her an extra, spun-out cruelty that he had not even been content to leave it at Washington. . . .

Still, Philly liked London in some ways. She liked going out after breakfast and meeting "Lord Curzon," the black-and-white lady cat of the Curzon Cinema. On a previous visit she had ventured to ask a commissionaire what happened to "Lord Curzon's" last season's kittens (but mentioned no names, of course, as the man probably thought the cat was called "Tibbies") and had been charmed to hear that one of them had gone to live at the Empire Cinema. A dynasty of cinema cats seemed to her to be an entirely satisfactory thing.

The morning of the wedding was peerless, shimmering gold. Sarah got out of bed early and saw Curzon Street brushed with that particular feathery blue light which she had noticed before seemed peculiar to it. Roofs were mysterious in it, their irregular pattern branching off into an oddly near sense of the infinite. It was strange how an effect of *blue* light could be so clear and radiant. The prospect and perspective filled her with yearnings and fabulous ambitions; but all cast within the spell of dreams untouched by a shadow of reality. But, surely, how *alive* one would be, living here all the time. It is time I did something, high time I found a job and worked for my living; but my sort of job would hardly keep me in Curzon Street. . . . Milk in neat arrays of bottles still stood on doorsteps, giving a homely touch. An arch that led into Shepherd Market was boarded to its right with bills full of the morning's usual awful news. Traffic moved sparsely. Away up the street a flower-stall glowed.

She drew her head into the room again and saw Philly in the far-side bed, rubbing sleep from her eyes.

"I dreamed that Bracken turned into a lobster."

"I thought you would," Sarah said, unsurprised.

Bracken had taken them all out last night, including Tom, while Mother and Mr. Jones had an evening on their own. Bracken had been sweet, but the outing had been a strain, with Bronwen at her most adult and braceleted. Unfortunately she had taken an unexpectedly discerning liking to Bracken and had even received Philly's mention of his fairy stories with a tolerant kindly interest. . . . Bracken, as Bronwen had pointed out, was to be the only outsider at the wedding. Sarah had said that she preferred to call him the only *un-family* person to be present.

"Oh, Sarah, it's a lovely day!" Philly got out of bed.

"Yes . . ." Her pristine enthusiasm for it was already dying down. To what point was it such, after all? She herself had dreamed she was marrying Sir Giles: but dreams were not things to be carelessly bandied about in public, at her age.

"Didn't Peter look funny in evening dress?"

"Did he?"

"Your dress looked nice, Sarah."

"Better than our bought ones for today."

"I think they'll look all right now Mrs. Moody has touched them up."

Sarah's silence was not so much for doubt of Mrs. Moody as indifference to the whole affair.

"Do we get properly dressed now, or wait until after breakfast?"

"I should think this is the kind of place where they *expect* you to be properly dressed," Sarah said.

"No—you know what I mean. Wedding clothes or old ones?"

"I don't see any point in toiling into squalid garments to eat breakfast and then taking them off and toiling into our wretched trousseaux," Sarah said wearily.

"Mother's having a tray in her room."

"I wish we were. But you and Tom would insist on the bacon-and-eggy dining room and full publicity."

"I'm sorry," Philly said meekly.

They bathed and dressed themselves in full finery; and Sarah spent so long with her face cream, powder, and meagre sixpenny lipstick that Christopher came and banged impatiently on the door before she had finished experimenting.

"Hurry up. I'm starving." He came in. "Sarah, you aren't going down with your mouth got up like that."

She ignored his remark; which was the more insulting for being a statement rather than a question.

Christopher sighed. Sarah got up like that was the last straw. "I can't see why Mother couldn't be satisfied with one husband," he glowered, re-knotting his tie. "Father seemed all right, as far as I remember. Why couldn't she be satisfied with his memory? Oh, blast this tie! It's your fault this ever happened anyway, Sarah. What with you trying to sell Fontayne, the whole thing was most bogus and unethical from the beginning."

"Oh, come down to breakfast," Sarah said.

Elisabeth called them into her room when the dignified lift brought them up again. Sarah had only toyed abstractedly with a cup of coffee and smoked a cigarette, but the others had eaten heartily.

"Oh, you look pretty good," Tom said, making a rush at his mother.

"Mind, darling. Even now, I don't think my hair is too steady." It never was. She had never had it bobbed, and it was so fine and soft that it would take to no style decisively.

"Yes, you look very nice," Sarah said soberly, with dignity. "You ought to wear black more often."

"Somehow, it doesn't seem to suit Fontayne." She closed her eyes a moment. Would the white rose by the sundial be out by this morning?

It would probably have lived and died before she saw it. What a pity honeymoons were considered the thing—

"I have the stomache," Tom announced economically.

"Oh, Tom!" Elisabeth's eyes were moist with compassion and reproach.

"It's no use saying, 'Oh, Tom—' If you've got the stomache, you have *got* it," he said decidedly.

"Don't be silly, Tom," Christopher said sternly. "Buck up and forget it. It's nearly time for us to go."

Tom gave a hollow groan.

"Yes, darling, do try to forget about it."

"Yes, Tom, do," they all said.

"It's all very well for all you. You haven't got it." He backed away from them, eyeing them darkly. "It's me that's got to be the . . . Stoik."

"*Sto-ic* . . ." Elisabeth murmured absently.

"Stoik," he repeated firmly.

"Oh, my hair isn't going to stay—I told that hair dresser yesterday that it never would." Elisabeth moved to her bedroom, holding two fingers tenderly to her coiffure. She had both sitting room and bedroom for this pre-nuptial occasion. A whole suite; very grand. "Sarah, ring the bell and see if they can get anything for Tom . . ."

"Has it gone?" Sarah asked resignedly, when Elisabeth had disappeared.

"Has what gone?" Tom looked indignant. "My stomache hasn't gone. I wish Mrs. Moody was here."

"Well, she isn't." Sarah's eye fell on a little flask of brandy. Mr. Jones must have left it for Mother in case she had any proper fainty-wedding feelings; but of course she hadn't. "Here, have a sip of this."

Tom obediently opened his mouth and threw back his head.

"Only a sip," Sarah warned.

Tom took a gulp and recoiled with a spluttering yell.

"You've killed him," Christopher said cheerfully.

"I'm sorry, Tom; but I told you only a sip."

"It was all right," Tom said, weeping tears of shock from his dark eyes, and mopping brandy from his fair feathery hair. "Very nice," he added.

"Has it *cured* you?" Philly gazed at him with morbid interest.

"Give it time," he said importantly.

They stood watching Tom in silence, giving it time.

"What a terrible smell!" Elisabeth came back, wearing her unexpectedly cute little bridal hat. "Do you feel better, darling?"

"I've been cured," Tom said grandly. He gave a laugh that was more exquisitely rich and mellow than any he had ever achieved before.

Elisabeth was still sniffing the air, her head poised like a wary bird's, but before she could make further inquiries the door opened and Bronwen came in. No ankle straps today. She wore her expensive outfit with an air; only the falling greenish-drab blond strands of her hair cast her as a little girl. She went straight to Elisabeth and kissed her prettily and pressed a flat box into her hands.

"Peter and I came here, so that we could all go together." Palely, she looked the Fontaynes over.

"For me?" Touched, Elisabeth opened the box and found a waxen writhing spray of orchids that seemed to eye her with an inimical speckled stare. Quite unreasonably they reminded her of Cruddles.

"Terribly hackneyed, I know," Bronwen apologized, "but what else is there?"

Privately, Elisabeth thought there was every flower in her own sweet garden, for preference, but she would not for the world have said this to Bronwen. Meekly she stood while Bronwen expertly pinned the spray on her, while the others gazed in implacable silence. Only Sarah appreciated orchids. They reminded *her*, elusively, of Sir Giles.

"Peter is waiting downstairs. Are we all ready?" Bronwen took charge.

"Those aren't flowers!" Tom laughed abandonedly.

"Indeed they are," Elisabeth said severely. "You must not be a rude little boy." In her anxiety to be fair to Bronwen, she forgot that he was still entitled to an aftermath of sympathy because of his recent pain.

"I never saw such flowers," Tom said. "Never in all my born days," he clinched the matter, staring balefully at the spray.

"You had better all go downstairs, now. Bracken will be here for me in a few minutes."

"Bracken gets all the odd jobs in our family," Christopher said, as they went out. "Even giving Mother away, if you can call it that, at her age."

"Poor Bracken. He's neither fish, fowl, nor good red herring. He must be glad when he has time off in America," Philly sympathized.

Tom laughed immoderately. Bronwen stared at him; eloquently said nothing.

Peter, in the hotel lounge, rose to greet them. He wore a dashing well-cut suit and a dark red carnation in his buttonhole. He sought the time, expensively emblazoned on his wrist.

"What an array of beauty," he smiled. "How is the bride?"

"Mother is the same as usual," Christopher said.

"What a relief the show isn't being pitched in a church," Peter said, persistently amiable and casual.

Sarah didn't particularly care for churches, but she resented this remark. "Your father said churches stifled him," she accused. "Personally, I think he should have told Mother at the beginning that he is an atheist."

"Not being able to breathe in churches does not necessarily make one an atheist," Peter pointed out, civilly. "The actual phrase might suggest asthmatic rather than atheistic tendencies."

Bracken came in. Bronwen ran up to him, hung on his arm. He smiled at her as nicely as he does at us, Sarah thought, surprised she could feel jealousy over Bracken. . . . He looked the same as ever, small, wiry, brown, encased within that secret orderliness of being that no mere wedding would change. Or no mere exploring, either, Sarah decided.

"Mother's waiting for you. We are just going."

"Need I come?" Tom subsided on a chair. "I do feel tired—that I do."

"Oh, *don't* keep on being so silly!" Sarah vented some unfathomably-sourced woe upon him. "Let's go and get it done with." I shall never marry. I can feel it in my bones. My life is pointless. . . . I know that I shall never hear of him again. And even Bracken goes over to the enemy. . . .

She led the way from the restrained light of the lounge to the radiant outdoor dazzle. The six of them piled into one taxi. Peter seemed amazingly undisturbed by the awful school-treat sort of feeling over everything. Tom had regained his hilarity. "This isn't London," he pronounced. "It wasn't like this last night. We never passed *that*."

"Shut up," Christopher said, his tie still irking his neck.

The registrar's office was bleak, forbidding. Sarah, her heart in an empty, coffee-tinged pit of her stomach, wished she had eaten some breakfast. How terrible life was . . . you were born, you got married, you died; and what was it all about, except a lot of meals and getting up and going to bed, and only a grudged letter or two to vary the monotony . . . ? She fostered her Slav mood, dissociating herself from the occasion for festivity.

"What do we do now?" Christopher asked. "If we go in now, we shall have to explain who we are and who's getting married and other bogus things like that."

They were saved from further discussion by the arrival of the bridegroom himself. Tom began to laugh, but a glance from Sarah quelled him. His hair still smelt most embarrassingly of brandy.

"Good morning," Philly smiled shyly. She felt weakly sorry for Mr. Jones, looking thin and delicate in the full sunshine, confronted by so much youth. Nobody ever seemed to bother much that he wasn't strong and was supposed to be having a rest cure.

"Good morning. Are we"—his dark glance winged fleetly over them all—"waiting for anything?"

"Only Mother," Tom said, beginning to laugh again in spite of Sarah's eye.

They trooped into the building after Mr. Jones. Out of the sun again, Sarah's Slav mood grew by melancholy leaps and bounds. How cold and grey, how bleak and unsympathetic the eye of the registrar, how thickly folded in gloom the little room in which they sat! And her new shoes looked faintly common, after all, with those loopy little bows on them. There was an unearthly silence. Even Tom—She glanced sideways. He seemed, incredibly, to be fast asleep in his chair.

Elisabeth and Bracken arrived, bringing with them a breath of the now almost-forgotten brisk outdoor world. The orchids swept forward, awakening the registrar to the fact that this was in fact a wedding and not a young people's outing. He shook himself out of a coma and, with relief, treated Elisabeth as a queen. As if nothing would have been too much trouble, in her service, even to the producing of a different bridegroom at a moment's notice. He was with her in the spirit, his nostrils twitching with the tensity of his spiritual sympathy. Nobody would have been really surprised if he had clasped her to his bosom. Don't be nervous to say if you would like it all stopped even now. . . . He fingered his books of office, loitering deliberately. You have only to say the word. We all make mistakes sometimes. No?—well, then, there's nothing left but to get on with the job. . . . Light trickled, mote-dotted, through a high window on to the orchids; on to the little veiled hat. Happy the bride the sun shines on. Might as well get on with the job.

Tom slept, his lips just parted, the sun on his fair brandy-stiff forelock.

"The ring?" the registrar inquired reluctantly.

Bracken produced it. Mr. Jones seemed vaguely surprised. Elisabeth was extraordinarily self-possessed. Christopher scraped his chair and Peter kept on glancing at his watch. Sarah looked at the bows on her shoes and Philly looked anxiously at Tom. The wedding was well into its stride. The registrar, personal regret nobly put on one side, was working up to the finale. Under cover of his vivacity, Philly nudged Sarah and nodded at sleeping Tom.

"I think perhaps he is a tiny bit drunk," Sarah whispered primly, praying the Joneses had noticed nothing wrong.

Sunlight again. . . . The day was nothing but a prolonged hide-and-seek with sun and shade. Nothing was any different. Life would never be the same again. . . . Kissing Mother and shaking hands with Mr. Jones was a ghastly ordeal. Tom was unobtrusively awakened in time for the departure to the wedding breakfast.

"I don't see why they call it a wedding breakfast at lunchtime," Christopher said. "I'm not eating eggs and bacon again for anyone."

"Of course you won't have to," Philly said wisely. "We are going to drink champagne."

"All of us?"

"I expect so."

"I'm not," Tom said, with all the fervour of a reformed drunkard. "I'll have a little hard-boiled egg with plenty of salt, and then I'll have a nice little sardine."

"You had better try *hors-d'oeuvres*," Bronwen said condescendingly, "as your tastes seem to run in that direction."

The four younger ones shared a car this time. The bride and bridegroom drove alone, and Sarah and Peter went with Bracken. Sarah hovered on the edge of a dream. They would go into the fashionable Mayfair hotel for the lunch and find Sir Giles there, lunching in lonely ceremony. Won't you join us? Mr. Jones said. I do feel honoured to be invited into the midst of such an intimate family gathering, Sir Giles said. He was terribly witty and amusing, making the party go. We can't let such a good thing come to an end, he said, when they rose from the wedding breakfast. Mother and Mr. Jones went off alone, and Bracken said he had arranged to take the others to the Zoo or somewhere. And what about you? Sir Giles said to herself. While she hesitated, he added, I ought to go to the House of Commons or something, this afternoon, but shall we try a matinée instead? What have you seen—?

The car stopped and she got slowly out ahead of Bracken and Peter, her dream falling to pieces. Even the authentic glamour of the hotel, with great tubs of flowers at its portals, could arouse her to no fresh enthusiasm. Only an impersonal gladness remained with her that they were to eat in the public restaurant, not in a cramping private room.

They were received with gratifying attention by a horde of suave waiters. There was perhaps something to be said for the Joneses being cosmopolitan. Mr. Jones wore the same gently absent air in this glittering worldly restaurant of white and crystal as he had had in the red plush interior of Copley's Green.

"Daddy, there's Jacques again," Bronwen breathed ecstatically. "Isn't he *marvellous*."

Sarah's eye, following Bronwen's, saw the very suavest and darkest and most ceremonious of all the waiters. She tried not to feel impressed at Bronwen's being on terms of such equality with him.

The meal was beautiful, there was no getting away from it. Philly's and Christopher's meeting eyes congratulated each other on it.

"A little champagne for everyone, I think," Mr. Jones said, when it arrived, magnificently clanking in icy depths of bucket.

"Oh, not for Tom!" Elisabeth said, awakening from a pink soft dream of renewed married life.

"Oh, not for Tom . . ." Tom said bleakly.

"Why don't you ever come to Fontayne?" Sarah sighed to Bracken. "You're going back to America soon, and we'll hardly have seen you."

"Not until the fall," he said. "Of course I'll come."

"Come during the honeymoon," she pleaded. He would smooth some of the first awful prickles of living with Bronwen and Peter.

"How long does that last?"

"Only about a fortnight, I think, but it is going to seem much longer."

"I'll see what I can do," he promised. The champagne had fired her, tautened her. Her eyes moved restively, over table, people, room. If she would learn the advantages of stillness, he thought, she would find a very useful weapon. Even her dreams moved at a terrific rate through space. Her hair, beneath her slight and, to him, shapely hat, was nearly blue in its curves against her neck; and her eyelids, when her eyes were contemplatively lowered to her dancing golden drink, were faintly, fragilely, blue-white, delicately weary and glazed with lost illusion. She was as inspired with tragi-comedy as ever.

Peter was scarcely less than valiant. He might have studied a special course on behaviour at wedding breakfasts. His ready words fell on all sides, yet contrived also to reserve some of themselves individually for his new stepmother on his one hand and Philly on his other. For Elisabeth he had a smiling gallantry, a chivalry touched by teasing; and for Philly an elder-brotherly protectiveness with which she had not the least idea how to cope.

"You'll have to try skiing," he said decidedly.

"Yes," she agreed.

"It's *the* biggest thrill."

"It must be."

"Of course there's the most *terrific* sense of a sort of exalted *purity* of snobbery about real experts. As if mere immensities and *heights* of snow go to the head."

"Yes, I expect so," Philly said, far out of her depths, let alone heights.

"A perfectly chosen meal, Daddy," Bronwen complimented, munching thoroughly and appreciatively.

"I'd rather have fried bread," Tom said, lowering his eyelashes; being difficult. He resented the fact that he remembered nothing of his mother's wedding. For all he knew he had missed some splendid entertainment.

"Fried bread!" Bronwen wilted so effectively that it was almost possible to see her appetite draining away from her and her gorge rising to take its place.

"It's Mrs. Moody's fault," Philly said. "She and Tom get up to such funny snacks."

It was Mrs. Moody also who had bred in Tom his topsy-turvy habits at table. Everything was held, if not upside down, at the very least in the wrong hand. Not content with being more or less reasonably left-handed, he contrived to drink from the far side of his cup or glass, as if he were entering for some tortuous handicap competition. Guests at Fontayne had been known to lose control of their own table manners through confused mirror-like contemplation of Tom's contortions.

During the ice pudding Elisabeth grew more and more *distraite*, her mind catching erratically at all the things she had forgotten to pack, all the orders she had forgotten to leave for Cruddles and Mrs. Bale. And was there a hope of their ever getting the boat train? Julian probably was used to such things, with all his travelling, but the train would scarcely wait especially for him. His grey-red shaggy head was leonine, but not too much so; there was that comforting mild surface within the bold outline; just a hinted resemblance to that so reasonable and kind Metro-Goldwyn-Mayer lion. . . .

Bracken was hurrying on the coffee. She shot him a grateful glance. "What's this?" Tom demanded haughtily. "Coffee, darling," she said patiently. She did not flatter herself that Tom's mood was caused by sorrow at losing her for a couple of weeks, but there was undoubtedly something unusual about him. "You don't want it, do you, darling?"

"Now who said so?" Tom asked, exasperated. With perilous independence, he dashed the cream jug tipsily against his cup. "I *never* don't have coffee if it's there."

"I think—" Bracken began.

"Yes—" As if she had been awaiting just such a signal, Elisabeth began to sweep together her handbag, gloves, glasses. Her lovely little nose glowed faintly pink. Powder never seems to take *root* with her, Sarah thought, impersonally irritated.

"Yes," Julian repeated.

They all began to rise.

"I haven't finished my coffee," Tom said, sitting tight, mortally offended.

In the great glass-and-flowered hotel entrance the unnerving farewells took place. "Good-by, sir," Christopher said firmly. "I hope you have a nice time." He wondered if it were the thing to have said. "Good-by, Mother," Sarah said, and whispered: "Do powder your nose." Bronwen and Peter, self-possessed, continental, kissed Elisabeth on either cheek. "Good-by, Mr. Jones," Tom said, still balefully offended. Philly gave Julian's hand a warm little squeeze, when Sarah wasn't watching.

It was all over. The car drove off into the sunlit green richness of the park, and Mother's hand vanished, and Mr. Jones's moustache, against the little rear window, blurred into the distance. . . . They were left with a great weight of silence and ice pudding upon them.

The journey home was cast in a thrall of poignancy. They stayed on with Bracken until early evening; and even then it was not the whole party that got into the train for home. At the last moment Peter, as unconcerned as you please, said: "I shall stay in town tonight with a friend. Expect me at Fontayne some time tomorrow." He took not the smallest notice of Sarah's suspicious scrutiny; still wore his bold wedding manner as surely as he wore his carnation. He got as far as the station without a word about these plans, and then casually turned aside from them all, as if it were the most usual thing in the world to stay on in London alone.

"You mean, you are leaving *me* to look after everyone?" Sarah said crossly.

He seemed amused. "I don't think you'll find Bronwen needs much looking after, for one."

"Get in," Sarah snapped to the others. How unfair that Peter (no older than herself) should possess this independence of being and purse, able to drift off unshackled to the carefree sweetness of a London summer night. . . . Bracken had gone off by then, so one could not appeal to him. Not that he would have interfered, anyway.

They settled themselves in the stuffy compartment. Bronwen fanned her face with her hand. "I'm sure Daddy intended us to travel first class."

"You can do what you please," Sarah said. "*We* can't afford it." Bronwen, sensitive to any vulgar mention of money, flushed darkly.

It was better when the train moved and a light breeze flickered. But how sad the country looked, at the end of its long afternoon, as if summer were wilted already. How sad the little merging fields and rippling hedges, the sweet-sick thirsty taste of champagne in the mouth, Fontayne waiting inevitably to draw one into its twilight. Sarah closed her eyes against it all. We could go to the pictures when we get back—no, too late, too tiring.

Philly had taken off her new shoes. "As we have the carriage to ourselves," she explained. When buying shoes, it was always taken into account that her feet were bigger than Sarah's, but seldom taken into account quite enough. "I wonder how Ernest has got on?" Nobody passed any opinion on this.

"I suppose Mrs. Moody will pack for me?" Christopher's mind hovered uneasily over school. Whitsun was too short for you to get acclimatized to holiday.

"Oh, but it'll be nice to get back to Mrs. Moody," Tom said, from his heart.

Sarah looked out of the window again. Shadows were lacing the scene. How sad, how *unearthly*, the darkening earth, the train flying on. Cruddles will have milk ready to *goad* us with. How different even milk can seem, in different settings . . . this morning in gay bottles in Curzon Street. I must search for the memoirs again. I *know* they are there somewhere. I wonder if Mr. Harbrittle could find me a job in London.

"I hope they'll be happy," Bronwen said, with an adult margin of doubt. "Of course there are differences of temperament."

"I suppose if you love people, nothing matters," Philly said diffidently.

"*Love* cannot be so simplified," Bronwen informed her. "*'There lives within the very flame of love a kind of wick or snuff that will abate it . . .'*"

Against her will, Sarah was mournfully impressed by this astonishing remark. She said: "*Macbeth*, I suppose?" with sarcastic intent, but the strange words, not to be escaped, sank into crying depths of her being, making her voice tremble mournfully.

"No, *Hamlet*," Bronwen said complacently.

CHAPTER SIX

NOT A MOMENT was wasted before the Joneses made their presence felt at Fontayne.

Sarah awakened to find Bronwen standing by her bed. She had been given the bedroom next to the schoolroom, the largest on the floor; too good for her.

"Do I have to use your bath?" she demanded, without preamble.

"What do you mean?"

"There's a *huge* crack in it."

"You'd better use the other one, then, down below, if you're so squeamish. It's for Mother and any guests, but I expect everyone would love you to have it." Sarcasm fell flat in the cold light of morning.

"Thanks, I will." Dressing-gowned and sponge-bagged, Bronwen hurried off, her sallow face still creased with sleep.

"What cheek," Christopher said, when he heard. "It's only a crack, not a definite split."

During breakfast, which Philly and Sarah had laid on a table on the terrace, Peter rang up from London. Sarah answered.

"Don't expect me till fairly late," he said. "How is everything?"

"All right. How is London?"

"Quite attractive." There was almost a Bronwen-like complacence in his voice. What had he been up to . . . ? "You'll have to try and curb your sister in some ways," she slipped in. "My dear, we aren't a family to interfere with each other," he protested.

She went back to continue her breakfast. Ernest was sitting on the table, but perhaps this was permissible as it was an outdoor meal; it seemed to make some subtle difference. Bronwen was absorbedly reading a scrap of paper. "Look! They've sent me a cutting about my book. It's under the heading, 'To be published shortly.' It says it's the unconventional account of the adventures of a girl of twelve, written in her own words. . . . I don't like 'adventures' or 'written in her own words.' I wonder who writes up these things? Would you care to see it?" Graciously, she passed the cutting to Sarah.

"Very interesting." Sarah laid it down. "Philly, do you *mind* asking Ernest to take his feet off the bread?"

"Of course I'm really thirteen," Bronwen remarked.

"I'm really nine," Tom said. He had recovered his normal well-being, his dark eyes serene, unclouded. His fair hair was still wet with the washing Sarah had rather secretively given it as soon as he was up. He missed the nice smell it had had when he first awakened.

"Things seem very dull," Christopher grumbled. "I must do *something* before I go back to school."

"We'll have to go and tell Mrs. Oxford about the wedding," Philly said. "Do you think we could go to the pictures tonight, Sarah?"

"I expect so," Sarah said listlessly.

"What is the film?" Bronwen asked Philly.

"I don't know."

Pale eyebrows shot high. "You go to the movies without knowing what's *on*? How extraordinary."

"Don't you like the pictures?"

"I sometimes like the continental films," Bronwen admitted. "Peter and I used to go in London and"—she sighed—"Paris, of course."

"Don't you like Donald Duck?"

Bronwen sipped her tea meditatively. "I wonder if it could be arranged for me to have coffee for breakfast in future?"

"I suppose you had it in Paris?" Sarah suggested wearily.

"But of course." Bracelets flashed.

"Don't you like Donald Duck?" Philly repeated patiently.

"Oh, Disney was all right until he began pandering to too-popular taste."

"But surely you liked *Snow White*?"

"No, I didn't. Those awful ubiquitous dwarfs!"

Philly sat in silent horror at such sacrilege, but Sarah spoke up bravely, icily: "It happens that we *particularly* like the dwarfs."

There seemed something forlorn, dead-endish, about them all when Peter got to Fontayne that evening. He felt an impulsive pang of pity for them all. "Couldn't we all do something absurd and amusing tomorrow?" he suggested.

"My last day. Yes, let's," Christopher said promptly.

"The car's here. I expect you all hate motoring as much as I do," (What could Sarah do but nod?) "but it's bearable if one has an object. What about this ostentatious seaside neighbour of your modest village?"

"Oh, *yes!*" Bronwen cried. "Isn't there a lovely vulgar pier with entrancing old-fashioned peep shows?"

How surprising that Bronwen, of all people, should appreciate the pier, too . . . Sarah and Philly both thought. It must be in the same sort of way as she liked the delicious stuffed pike . . . Philly additionally and discerningly thought.

It rained a little in the morning, but they decided not to abandon their outing. The fine rain slanted over Fontayne, turning everything to grey-silver, sombrely radiant.

"Well, I don't call it much of a day for a trip," Mrs. Moody, alighting from her bicycle, greeted them as they stood at the door, ready to go.

"I think I'll stay with you," Tom said.

"No, duckie, you go and have a look at the sea. You can see me any time." She looked at Sarah. "That collar has come up nice, dear. I like you in that blouse. See anyone you knew in London?"

"We don't know anyone."

"Thought perhaps *he* might have taken you out." Her bright brown gaze practically nudged Sarah in the ribs.

"I don't know what you mean."

"Well, he seemed pretty keen, coming all this way to see you," Mrs. Moody persisted, unabashed. "Write to him again, I would, and see if he wouldn't come down while we're all on our own."

It was an idea, Sarah admitted to herself; but not a very nice one. A bit . . . clandestine. No, she couldn't. She'd rather die than force herself on his notice again.

"I think perhaps it is going to clear up," she gave Mrs. Moody the hint to shut up.

"Oh, I daresay you'll manage to enjoy yourselves. What is it, duck?" She turned to Tom, who had sidled up to her again.

"I think I *will* stay with you and do a bit of inventing while you are mending."

"You're coming with us," Sarah said ruthlessly. "Come along. The others are ready."

She was uncertain of Peter's driving; and also of whether he even had a driving licence. His airy remark that he had driven in Paris and New York did not reassure her, for wasn't it *correct* to drive on the wrong side of the road in those cities? The rain sped in a fine persistent veil over the windshield. Peter drove debonairly, one hand on the wheel, the other gesturing with a cigarette and making ostentatious road signals. Sarah sat in front with him and Bronwen. The other three were crowded on the cramped back seat. Nobody talked and Christopher whistled, sweetly, mournfully.

The damp sea air came up to meet them as they reached the wet coast road. The green sodden country fell away from the vaporous seascape.

And then, as they parked the car near the beach, the sun came waterily out to meet them. It flung rays over the grey sea, picking out pools of radiance.

"Shall we go and have some ice cream and see what happens?" Philly said, for once taking the initiative.

"A good idea," Peter agreed, determined to carry out his treat to the end.

"I haven't any money," Tom said forlornly.

"I'll look after that," Peter smiled. He exuded a spirit of tolerant generosity.

They found a glass-façaded café, filled to the brim with strenuous selections of swing music. How lovely and gay it was, but the Joneses would be sure to wince at it and say it was an unholy din. The place was full of a wet rubbery sea-weedy smell that intoxicated the nostril as the music did the ears. And the ices had cool green layers within their pink.

"This is jolly nice," Christopher said, expressing for the other Fontaynes a reserved appreciation of Peter's decency.

"It will clear up," Peter said, successfully stage-managing even the weather. Sunlight trickled tentatively amid the blue smoke-laden air. It was too early in the season for the place to be full of people, but those who were there had a superb holiday zest. The bucket-and-spade, canvas-shoed, swim-suited, sand-in-the-hair tradition was worthily, if sparsely, upheld.

"That's an attractive number," Bronwen said, humming lightly.

"You don't *like* this music?" Philly asked, amazed.

"The band is rather bouncing and crude, but I simply *adore* Cole Porter."

You never knew where you were with them . . . they didn't like cinema organs, but approved this which was no less nice and understandable. . . .

The increasing light was like a golden liquid filling the expanded goblet of the morning. Presently, it splashed over the rim and the sun dripped down the café walls and lay in pools on the floor, a squandered yellow flood. Not only the sun, but the quality of the very sea, invaded the place; exhilarating, mysterious. A sea as aloof and clear as if it washed a desert island instead of so populated a shore. Aloofly, tenderly, it betrayed every object, person, to its cool luminous eye.

"Oh, but it's a nice little ice," Tom said.

Sarah laughed. Her own swift gaiety of spirit amazed her. She could have coped with any situation, any problem, at this moment. She was awake, alive, thirsting for event. The moving pattern of sea light over people filled her with ardent sympathy. People so *full* of themselves, so strong, so sure in enjoyment. Perhaps I could begin again, forget the past. . . . She threw off her light summer coat, the even heat of the room enclosing her.

"And now what?" Peter asked.

"Oh, the pier," Bronwen said. "The loud dank lovely disgusting pier. . . ."

The outdoor air met them with a soft courtesy. "We went in at one end of the day and came out at the other," Tom said. The rain was miraculously dried from the ground already. Along the front the brazen little bungalows gleamed shining red and white; and behind, across a width of class-dividing road, the tall hotels put their noses high in the clean bright air. A man was selling coloured toy balloons that struggled from long strings in his hand and threw their weightless willful energy up in vivid globes. Down below, on the sands, donkeys dragged their patient muffled tread and children screamed and shuffled on their backs. A few bright-haired young ladies strolled self-consciously on the promenade, wearing flimsy beach pyjamas and floppy downcast hats. ("So obliviously hideous," Peter said with catty glee. "Why is it always the ones with *colossal* behinds who dress like that?" Sarah smiled, agree-

ing, feeling pleasantly superior in her unbulged pencil-straight black
skirt. . . .) The sharp clarity of the atmosphere contrasted oddly with
the paper-strewn, orange-peel-desecrated way to the pier. The waves
slurred lazily in, trimming the sand with lengthening widening scrolls
of froth.

"We haven't been here for *years*," Tom exaggerated.

When they did come, it was treated as a town for special shopping,
not as an authentic seaside resort. It did not occur to their mother that
they could love it for itself alone, apart from the things it sold. It was
ages since they had been able to find any excuse for going on the pier.

Now here it was, unchanged, eternal. Here the clanking turnstile,
the suddenly deepened sea smell, the salt raw upon the lips, the eyes
smarting with the essence of brilliance here distilled, the ears alert for
the pseudo-military band. The weighing machines, sheathed in the
isolation of their rust, had long retired from active life, but the children had always paused, whenever they had the chance, to calculate
morbidly what their correct weights should have been. There were so
many things to be taken into account, age, height, and so on, that the
answers were trickily arrived at. Once, Sarah, with astonished delight,
had announced that she ought to weigh eleven stone. It had stayed in
the memory . . . a beautiful burlesque moment: a memory of skipping
joyfully on damp pier boards, conscious of the spare freedom of clear-
cut unhampered grace, imagining phantom flesh bulked full upon one.
. . . But today she suggested no pause here. Bronwen was short and
thick, and might not appreciate the old family joke; and even Bronw-
en's feelings were not to be dismissed without charity on so fair a day
as this.

"We *must* see the shocking peep shows." Bronwen laughed.

"They're on the other side," Christopher said knowledgeably. "I
wish we could fish."

"You can fish for presents on that stall," Tom said, with polite disin-
terest.

"Here you are." Sarah hurriedly gave him a few coppers, embarrassed by Peter's continuous generosity. "Don't go out of sight."

The peep shows stood neglected, hungry for pennies. Not until
August would they really come into their own again. They stood with
their backs to the sea, the spirit of holiday not on them, drably clothed,
without illusion. The winds of winter might still have been upon them,
so indifferent seemed their stance. Everyone stood back while Bronwen

inserted the first coin, as if there were some ritual about it. There was a pause and then she spun around, rocking on her heels with mirth.

"A *gorgeous* ninetyish lady in—I *think*—her knickers; or should one say *drawers*? Oh, quite perfectly archaic!" She wiped from her eyes tears of amusement and sea breeze. But her interest soon palled. She wandered off alone, hugging (as it were) all the garish *typicalness* of the pier to her bosom.

Seagulls screamed overhead. On the sands parties were opening lunch packets. Philly, ashamed, began to feel hungry again, in spite of the ice. She moved up to Bronwen on the parapet at the far end of the pier.

"Only a few threadbare boisterous pierrots are needed to complete the scene . . ." Bronwen murmured, gloatingly.

"Yes, I like pierrots," Philly sincerely agreed.

The afternoon was somnolent, heat-stored. They lay on the sand, replete. Peter had come up to scratch with amazing proficiency. Lunch in assured elegant surroundings, with lobster mayonnaise. It was spiritual as well as physical expansion. Sarah saw two young men watching their table with interest. Are we being too noisy? No, they're looking at *me*. They like the look of me. . . . She rose with this certainty upon her, so elated that she could have flirted even with Peter without any undue effort.

The hot sands closed softly round their languid bodies. They lay remote in their own concerns. Christopher, far from the thought of school tomorrow, dwelt in a singular lassitude of joy. The sky was blank, cloudless, to his upward-squinting glance. The heavens unused, so much clear blue going to waste, not a 'plane in sight. Would Virginia Welwyn have done any flying, all these fine days? Nothing had come of her plan to get in touch with her flying instructor. It hadn't been anything as definite as a plan—nothing half so definite. How funny she'd been, so un-bogus, so ordinary, as if she really *were* that. Quite un-bogus except for making up her face like that. Why had she to? Not because she was old, surely. He didn't know how old she was, but she was young. Twenty-five . . . twenty-eight . . . perhaps . . . he couldn't say. You couldn't tell. It was a pity about her lips and nails, because she had been nice. Quite decent, really.

His limbs sank into the sand. Now the memory of school came back, threatening, half-sweet, half-irksome. Now the sun burned his closed eyelids. Somewhere at the heart of his quiescence was a queer desire to get up and run and jump and vent his nearly-sleeping energy upon the passive day. Yet he didn't really want to move. He wanted . . . he wasn't sure . . . perhaps not to be himself for a little while, to stand aside, to be released. If I could fly. . . . It was that, of course, but something else as well as that? He couldn't think, couldn't be sure. Something teased and twisted at the back of his mind; found no response from his contented stomach, no yawning void to provide an answer. Lunch had been jolly good and sustaining. No, it wasn't food, this quick-dead feeling, at once livening, stifling.

He sat up and scanned the pale horizon and then began to skim pebbles at the retreating waves. Presently Philly sat up too and joined the pastime, quickening it to competition. Hit that mound of sand; three goes at it. They hit, missed, laughed. He glanced swiftly into his heart and found to his relief that the stirred urgent feelings were gone. He pounded the target with overwhelming energy. He was well away with it, beating Philly all ends up. The day was strictly in line again.

Sarah was left alone, the others walking away, treading among the groups of people still idle on the shore. Still sitting, she stretched herself, sand dancing off her black skirt. The afternoon was ridged with heat. On the pier a band played, poignant, tinny, the tune dogged by a limping echo. Its bright melancholy satisfied her. Bronwen's stocky figure had separated from the others and was plodding off with an ostentatious appearance of desire for privacy. To commune with her soul or to be sick? She had gloated over her lobster with a concentration that did not deceive by being so seemingly discriminating. Sarah yawned. The skin on her cheeks and eyelids felt as if it were contracting, tingled by sun. She peered into the little mirror in her handbag and thought she saw a freckle forming in solitary state on her nose. Her eyes, she noticed without special interest, were as blue as the sea and the sky were now blue.

A nice-looking young man in a highly-striped blazer sat carefully down on the sand at a respectably measured distance from her. He rustled a paper, but did not seem able to keep his mind on reading. He gave a little cough and rubbed sand through his fingers.

"Too hot to read," he said discreetly to the air.

Sarah was mildly surprised by this eccentricity. He looked so pinky-brown and normal.

"Not that the news is anything to write home about, these days," he said.

She felt she ought to say something, to make it look as if there were nothing queer about him, poor young man. Then it dawned on her. He is actually trying to pick me up! She had no idea what to do about it; and yet her heart was gentle and full of charity. I must have sex appeal, after all. . . .

He floundered on, his confidence dying: "If there *is* going to be a war, I'd rather we got on with it."

She wondered briefly how Sir Giles would view that remark. "Oh, would you?" she said, as if it were the most natural thing in the world to reply; "I'd rather put it off to the last possible instant."

His object attained, he no longer cared in the least when, if, or how, the war began. But he pursued the profitable theme. "You get tired of it in the papers all the time, anyway, as if it's actually happening."

"Yes, the leaders are mostly depressing," Sarah said grandly.

"Yes, it doesn't make very pleasant reading." The topic was beginning to fail.

Whom was he like? Bob Norbett, a bit, but with a snubber nose, and not so earnest.

"One thing, you can always turn to the amusement page," he struggled on. It was the local paper that he had. "I see they have a good picture on at the Globe." He paused.

"Have they?" Far off she could spy the others returning.

"Yes, it's on at four. I suppose you don't happen to have the time on you?"

"What time it is, do you mean? No, I don't know."

"Must be nearly four, I should think."

"I should think so," she said.

"I suppose"—his eyes sought the ultimate ribbon of horizon —"you haven't time to take in a movie?"

He's obsessed with *time* . . . time on me, time to take in a movie. Take in?—gobble up, digest? Oh, poor young man. . . .

"No, I haven't time," she said, snubbing him so tenderly that he would undoubtedly have come back for more if the others had not stalked close to her as she spoke. Christopher came so close that he nearly trod on her fingers lying in the sand.

"Are we ready to move off?" He frowned down at her. "Peter says we'd better be getting off."

"Yes, if you can find Bronwen." She kept her eyes on the sea, but was conscious of a striped movement to her right: the young man softly, silently, stealing away.

"You were *talking* to that chap," Christopher accused. "I saw you."

"You can't *see* people talking to people," she said coolly.

Peter laughed. His dark eyes were on her appraisingly, malice-tinged, applauding.

Bronwen sat alone on a rock, bereft. Chin on hands, she stared down on swirling interlocking pools of green within the blue. The sea always filled her with brooding; she had been steeped in brooding during all the voyage home from New York. She hated, yet was fascinated, by the sense of inferiority it forced on her. Physical inferiority, of course, never mental. Here, her stoutness became like some iron running deep to her soul, flaying her, torturing her ever-forming muse. Her fat wrists mocked at her as she held them up against her face. To the depths of her being she deplored that Sarah should possess the long pale thin hands of a Chinese princess, while her own were like pastry puffs that had disastrously risen all too well. Only her hair, falling in its straight heavy waterfall down her back, seemed to her in the least like a worthy attribute for a poet; the almost seaweed-green tint within its dull fairness pleased her. To herself she called her hair "mermaid-blond." But there was nothing else about her that was even remotely right; and the Fontaynes had shown up the lack more than ever. She envied them their height and grace; tall slim beautiful Philly and less tall but even slimmer beautiful Sarah. And they were fortunate in other ways too. In spite of being so brainless and ignorant, she knew they held some assurance of knowledge denied to her. They were grown-up and seemingly quite easy in their minds about it. They would have no dreadful recurring sense of shame and fear. They seemed already women, taking the awfulness of life without dismay. They shrank from nothing; not even from the kitchen cat having kittens. Philly had unthinkably held its paw through the last happy event. . . .

Tom appeared round a jut of the rock. "We're all going now."

She did not answer, but, after a moment or two, she rose. Plodding through the sand, her back to the sea, her feelings began to regather their pugnacious normality. Everything could be explained, really, by the Fontayne girls being so devastatingly insensitive and their having not the smallest gift of imagination. And what was mere beauty in the face of such defects . . . ?

Peter exemplarily stayed all the time at Fontayne for the rest of the honeymoon fortnight. He had spent nearly all his allowance and was irked by his empty gaping pockets. Christopher was back at school; and Peter was amazed to receive from him a brusque-embarrassed little note of thanks for the day at the sea. He was touched, and amused at himself for being touched, by it.

Postcards came from France, the last one from Paris. "We shan't stay long. Everyone says there is going to be a war—"

Sarah bent her head studiously to the newspaper leaders. How busy Sir Giles must be; naturally no time to write. Her soul was possessed within a protection of comfort and patience. It could *still* all come right in the end. . . . She had a note from Bracken to say he would come down for the Week End. Good! Time was filling up, rounding out; somewhat less awful than one had expected.

The day before Bracken came, she opened the morning paper and stared straight at a photograph of Sir Giles. Luckily this was after break-fast, or it might have been noticeable that she would not have been able to eat another mouthful, after seeing it. Herself, Philly, Bronwen, and Peter were all in the schoolroom, where Peter had just discovered the old treasured gramophone of childhood. Torturingly, he shuffled the loved ancient records with derisive fingers. Philly watched him in agonized silence.

Bronwen looked over Sarah's shoulder. "Why, it's our friend Sir Giles Merrick," she pointed out.

"I know," Sarah said. Go away. Leave me alone. Oh, take your pale horrid gaze away. . . .

"A nice man. Of course he's only *someone's* secretary, not an impor-tant *State secretary* or anything."

"I don't see any difference. He often has his picture in the papers." He smiled at her, clear-cut, black and white.

"*Yes*, in the gossip columns. Not because he's *done* anything. He is really just a gay brilliant amateur of politics."

"You know nothing whatever about it!" Sarah went white with fury.

Bronwen eyed her with dawning and enchanted fresh discovery. "Of *course* I admit he's fascinating. I'm not saying anything about *that*." She smiled gleefully, her gaze fixed firmly on Sarah's self-betraying face. "No wonder the gossip columns often report his doings. I expect *lots* of people like to look at his pictures and read what he's doing, don't you?"

"I expect so," Sarah faltered.

"Just as you were *devouring* it all just now. Does it quote a witty remark of his?" She was not surprised when Sarah did not answer. "'O *wicked wit and gifts that have the power so to seduce . . ."* she quoted appropriately, if without technical accuracy.

"I don't know what you mean," Sarah said, two flaming spots clown-marking her cheeks with the intensity of her anger.

"The Gondoliers!" Peter exclaimed, amusing himself with the dusty old gramophone discs. *"Where are the Lads of the Village Tonight?* and what's this . . . *In a Monastery Garden,* played by somebody's Mighty Wurlitzer. And *Poet and Peasant.* We must try one of these." He fitted a needle and set the old turntable in motion.

"What a *shocking* gramophone!" Bronwen said, in an almost thrilled tone, forgetting about Sir Giles.

"I like the sad cracked pre-electric-recorded note," Peter smiled. "It's exquisitely lugubrious."

How dared they . . . ? Philly wondered helplessly. Their mockery broke up the cherished monotony of a thousand memories. I shall never *really* be able to use the gramophone again, she thought sadly. They had spoilt something, ruined it irretrievably. Their superior laughter would haunt the old records, get within the very grooves.

"Here's Offenbach's *Barcarolle* with a crack in it," Peter said. "That should add to the general poignancy."

"They're absolutely prehistoric!" Bronwen seized on them rapturously, as if they were stuffed pike, no less. "And the high, breathless speed of the machine—there seems to be *no* regulator!"

"It broke a long time ago," Philly said dully.

"Don't think I *mind.* I think it's enchanting. Oh, where *are* the lads of the village tonight? I think they've run clean off the record in their abounding haste!"

"We'll try a tenor. He will turn out a falsetto by all the laws of this machine. Mind your head, Bronwen. Do you think we need another needle?"

"I *think* the scratchiness adds to the charm." She considered the point. "A scratch at the bottom of an echoing hollow—And then that exhausted gargle as the engine runs down. And the furious dentist's drill at the beginning, before the tune gets going. It's all part and parcel of a perfect *whole.*"

Philly got up quietly and left the schoolroom. Sarah followed her out.

"Oh, Sarah, couldn't you have stopped them?"

"I wouldn't interfere." She was too shaken by her own skirmish with Bronwen to bother; but this she couldn't admit to Philly.

Tom appeared in the passage.

"Will you tell Bronny to get out of my schoolroom? Miss James and I want it."

"Bronny!" the two girls echoed delightedly, something of their wrath tempered by that name.

Bracken's Week End broke up a settling glaze of animosity. He walked up the road from the town, carrying his small bag, although Sarah had said that Peter would willingly meet the train with the Jones car. Last time, he had seen the spring laid out in balanced patterns against the road. Now June, young, alert, but blurred by the branching traceries of summer, took the scene vividly, a little in advance of season, the sun having blazed in a vigilant service for days on end. Fontayne, when he came to it, seemed to sink a little in a yellow shroud of sun, a fine glittering mesh enclosing it now in one of its frequent partial deaths. The lawns were long and burned of grass, Elisabeth's green commanding hand blatantly absent. The terrace, rising frontally on his view, was fringed and starred with faint neglect upon neglect. A pair of shoes, chalked liquid white, lay drying in the sun. Ernest, emerging by the drawing-room window, jumped down on them and left his paw marks imprinted in the white. A lawn mower stood to brisk attention, but only a single green track lay smoothly bared amid the risen grass. Heat was thrown up from the baking terrace in a visible shimmering and the magnolia flowers died lingering white deaths upon the hot wall of the house. All over the garden Elisabeth's magnificent roses were opening and coming into their own.

Bracken went straight in by the long drawing-room window, without ceremony. Peter, limp on the piano stool, rose to meet him with an expression of cordiality. Fontayne was upon him, draining him, flattening him.

"Oh, it's you. How are you? How hot it is! I'll go and rake up a long cool drink."

"How is everyone?"

"Hot," Peter said laconically.

He left Bracken standing alone in the room, and went off for the drink. The room was stupefied with sun, scarred and raddled by it.

Sarah came in and flung her arms around him.

"Oh, Bracken, we've needed you!"

He could well believe it; but took no flattered credit to himself for it. Yet the life was not gone out of her, in spite of the heat and her trials. She was in one of her periodical processes of self-reorganization.

"We can't go on like this," she said briskly. "I shall go away and get a job. Have you anything in mind for me?"

"Well, not yet," he said, disconcerted.

"You don't know anyone who wants a secretary or anything?"

"I'm afraid not. You aren't," he ventured, "exactly trained for such work."

"I could learn," she said sadly. "I think I shall go and ask Mr. Harbrittle if he could find me a job."

How serious she must be, even to contemplate bearding that coldly poised gentleman within his authentic literary den.

"Do you want to take your case to your room or wash or anything, or would you come straight up to the attic?"

"I'll come to the attic if necessary," he said mildly.

"It *is*, rather. I think I've discovered a bit of Father's memoirs. I want you to come and look." Her voice, dropped low, made the suggested project an uneasy one, as if the memoirs might at any moment go off like a bomb.

"Perhaps I could drop my bag on the way up?"

"Yes, it's the usual room."

"The one into which gas leaks and seeps?"

"Yes," she said indifferently. "You won't be able to have the good bath whenever you want it, because Bronwen's always using it. She doesn't like our bath."

"Oh." He thought perhaps it was domestic rather than temperamental incompatibility that was proving the severest strain.

The attics had the evil and concentrated heat of some lesser hell. Sarah, almost knee-deep in incalculable debris, flowered in the breathless air.

"Now this is probably a bit out of the middle," she said, with strange bibliographic zeal, as she handled a curling-edged sheaf of manuscript. "It seems to be where he won some obscure election just when he got married. Not that there's a word about Mother, which seems a bit remiss." She added, with faint resentment: "I'd have liked to know what Mother was like at twenty."

"Is it only the middle part you've discovered?" Bracken asked, hoping he wouldn't expire before she was ready to let him go.

"So far; but the rest will turn up," she said confidently. "Father must have been an awfully funny man."

"He was very . . . enthusiastic. But his enthusiasm didn't always last."

"So I've gathered. Like mine," she said wisely.

"A little," he smiled. "I think perhaps he was a little late for the period that would have suited him best. He came in only at the end of the golden age of leisured fiery socialism that should have been his background. The war cut rudely into his early enthusiasm of ideals."

"But I think Mrs. Oxford approves of his memory even more for being a brave soldier than for things he did afterward," Sarah said meditatively.

"Maybe she's right. He never quite fitted in with the political patchwork that went on after the war. All his beautiful ideas for clean sweepings never had a chance. He fell between two stools of action and reaction."

"If he were so keen on clean sweepings he would probably have turned out a communist by now. *That* must be where Philly gets some of her ideas. She's all for a horrid soulless equality, you know, but luckily she hasn't the gift of talking, so she can't convert anyone."

He laughed, in spite of the lung- and throat-stifling heat. "No, his socialism was far, far too individualistic to turn into communism." By now, if he had lived, Marcus Fontayne would have missed every possible political boat, being a golden adventurer, but far above being a wary golden opportunist.

"Then I can't see there's even the excuse of heredity for Philly," Sarah said, flipping pages busily. "A lot of this part seems boring, but a few people come in at the end and it cheers up. It breaks off just where he's having a wonderful quarrel with some earl or other. It is tantalizing; I must find the rest."

Bracken furtively wiped his brow. "Couldn't we examine it downstairs?"

"I'm not taking it where Bronwen might find it. If you're bored, of course we'll go down." She eyed him coldly.

"I'm rather hot," he admitted, wiping his forehead again.

"Don't do that. You've mopped all your hair to one side and I can see a *huge* bald patch." Her tone relented. "I know some good stuff for making hair grow and it furbishes up the colour while it's at it."

"How very accommodating!"

"Yes, it is. Mrs. Moody brought it in one day. She didn't say how she came by it, but I *suspect* it came by mistake when she meant to get something for her moustache. If so, the chemist was adding insult to injury. Poor Mrs. Moody, I wonder if she minds."

Already (Bracken realized with relief), in her compassion for Mrs. Moody, she had forgotten about the superlative restorative bottle and would be unlikely to remember it again during his visit. The memoirs, too, had momentarily been edged out of prominence. She was willing to go downstairs, where Peter was presumably waiting with the long cool drink.

At lunch, Philly remarked that they had not yet been to tell Mrs. Oxford about the wedding.

"Do you think," Sarah said, inspired, "that we could invite her to dinner tonight?"

"It isn't very long notice for Mrs. Bale, Cruddles, *or* Mrs. Oxford."

"But we can tell her Bracken came down unexpectedly. She liked him very much." Sarah recollected his immediate presence at the table. "Didn't she, Bracken?"

"I have only your word for it," he said, as once before.

"Oh, but she *did*. Of course she probably didn't realize you were an American, but even so—"

The prospect of Mrs. Oxford's not unlikely eventual discovery of this fact (perhaps in the very midst of disarmed prandial cordiality) and a subsequent adjusting of subtle social and international values, was so alarming that Bracken overstepped a guest's privileges and besought his young hostess not to let things go any farther along this line of unwitting false pretences.

"Oh, that's all right," Sarah assured him graciously. "It is only out-and-out gangsters she doesn't care for."

As the afternoon advanced and cooled a little, Fontayne awakened to alert activity. Sarah and Philly had both been down to the little town to shop, Peter having kindly taken them in the car. Bracken, after an hour's respite on the terrace (Tom with Miss James and Bronwen in private pursuit of her muse), was roused by a swiftly moving spiritual and material transformation scene. Mrs. Oxford was coming; they had informally called to ask her and she had accepted. The necessary food was bought and Mrs. Bale cajoled into a promise to do her best with it.

"We've had some very good shopping," Sarah said, flopping down on the terrace for a few minutes before continuing her organization. She had ordered generously, with a decently-veiled but not wholly obscured suspicion that Mr. Jones would in future be responsible for the household bills.

Peter, ironically interested in the proceedings, followed her on to the terrace. "I've taken the rest of your astounding parcels to the kitchen."

"Oh, thank you." She was pleased with him today. "There are some more coming up later."

"Good God," Peter remarked.

"Yes. We went in to see Bob Norbett to get some sherry and he said he had a very good line of champagne, if we'd like to try a bottle. Bob said it was specially good, but we could have it very cheap because it was D.V."

"N.V., you mean," Peter said, wilting visibly. "Non-Vintage."

"Oh, yes, that was it. I *thought* D.V. seemed funny to describe champagne," Sarah said blithely.

Bracken's eye met Peter's for a moment, but the boy seemed too shaken to express any emotion whatsoever.

Mrs. Oxford's car swept up at the appointed time, to its very hour stroke. Her unstressed but formal ritual with Cruddles was exactly in time and place, too. She wore black, of course, but festively piped with violet; and about her was that faint emanation of violet scent which can be very vulgar or very seemly, according to the personality of the wearer. Her diamonds sparkled in formidable clumps, and her long black kid shoes had superior silver buckles on them. She wore a ridged front of white hair that was more than a transformation but less than a wig. She came fully prepared for the introduction to her of the younger Joneses.

Tom cheerfully agreed to have supper with Mrs. Moody, so Bronwen held undisputed sway as the youngest of the party. She wore her best midnight blue velvet dress with its long grave skirt and frolic-puffed sleeves; cunningly contrived to mingle the sophisticated with the naive.

"I haven't a long dinner dress," Philly said, dismayed, when she had seen this effort, "except that old thing like a fairy that I wore last Christmas."

"Couldn't you wear that curtain?" Sarah suggested absently, her mind on her own wardrobe.

"What curtain?" There was hope, and even trust, in her voice.

"Didn't you wear some Algerian-stripe curtain or other, in a charade, and they all said how it suited you? Yes, you did. You didn't have to say anything, of course, because you never will. You just sat still in the curtain and it looked most impressive."

"It was a long time ago." She reluctantly gave up hope. "I don't expect the curtain would fit me now. Anyway, I remember I couldn't turn round in it."

"Well, that wouldn't do with Mrs. Oxford, of course. We could ask Mrs. Moody to stick a hurried flounce on that white thing you wore at the Easter dance—"

"No, I'd better wear it as it is," Philly said, instinctively distrusting the idea of a flounce, hurried or otherwise.

"Well, at least you've got nice legs to show," Sarah comforted. "If anyone's should be hidden, it's right it should be Bronwen's; hers *are* so like table legs."

Sarah herself wore the dress she had had for the dance before the last. It was a somewhat babyish pale pink in colour, but the cut, long and strikingly slim, had turned out surprisingly well.

Mrs. Oxford had a throat-catching feeling of pleasure and regret when she saw her. *Wasting* her lovely youth, poor child, and no one, apparently, to care. If I were not too old and set, she thought, I would give her a Season myself. Pansy could do it—but then, she has no money, and would expect a suitable reward. . . . What a pity (nay, a tragedy) it was that Elisabeth Fontayne was such a singularly unworldly woman.

The evening had uncoiled and branched out leisurely from the tight heart of the day. A little breeze played loosely, slipping in at the open drawing-room window and gliding down the length of the room. Even the dining room, an oppressive place at best, had a cool luminous appearance when they went in to dinner. Revolutionarily, Cruddles had decided on lace mats instead of a tablecloth. This went with his scheme of candlelight; a consummately romantic effect in the light of day only touched, as yet, by the faintest shadows. From writhing candelabra the little crocus-like flames burned steadily, casting golden pools in the dark table and laying a frosty lustre on the cream fondants in dishes down its centre. To Sarah, it seemed an infinitely satisfying civilized scene. Even Bronwen felt that something of the proper dignity of country life was restored.

The old lady kept her distance from the artistic young people, but they were far less unconventional than she had feared. The boy, for her, had none of the Biblical good-to-look-upon quality of her favourite Christopher, and the girl was very far from beauty, but it seemed that they had moved and had their being in society not exclusively Bohemian.

"You must all be looking forward intensely to the Homecoming," she said, brooking no denial, putting the event on the level of some almost supernatural visitation.

The girls were so lost in admiration of Cruddles's magnificent behaviour that they could not concentrate on their guest while he was present; he stole even Mrs. Oxford's thunder. Neither did Bracken make such a sociable impression as had been hoped of him. Bronwen was left in command. It was not long before Mrs. Oxford knew quite a lot about her book.

"I wonder how you find time for this . . . exercise in the midst of more orthodox studies." It was a refreshingly new point.

"I have done no orthodox studies for the past months," Bronwen retorted. "Daddy thought it would be *much* better for me to do my book."

There you are, you see. . . . Sarah's glance fired Philly; that's what comes of not hurting flies. . . .

"And now that this is finished with"—Mrs. Oxford washed her diamonded hands of Bronwen's book—"he will no doubt find a suitable school for you."

"I don't think that's likely, as I have a contract for two more books. I shall probably have a French companion, at least until we travel again."

"Miss James is very good for anyone up to fifteen," Sarah said insultingly.

Mrs. Oxford took minute sips of her wine. Extraordinary, she thought, that a so reduced-in-circumstances family should so persistently try to ply one with champagne. The phenomenon was scarcely lessened by the champagne's being of such execrable quality.

"I have discovered part of the memoirs," Sarah said, sipping also, drifting into a state of careless bliss. "Do you think it would be all right for me to go and talk to Mr. Harbrittle about them?"

"I am sure he would be delighted, dear." Mrs. Oxford entered into the spirit of a new gracious little intrigue, as she could not (with the best will in the world) enter into the sparkle of the sweet champagne. "He, of course, knows all the publishers and will doubtless be able to arrange something." There was bounty in her words; it might have been that not only would she undertake the sponsoring of the posthumous Fontayne Memoirs, but that she had herself nursed Mr. Harbrittle through the first fractious teething of his career, and even that she had seen most of the publishing houses in London through a troublesome infancy to all-round satisfactory adult estate. . . .

"The best publishers of anything in the reminiscence line are certainly Tulsey and Flewkes," Bronwen said, in an admirably unbiased tone.

"Of course America is the important place." Sarah remembered Mr. Harbrittle's words.

Bracken half expected the old lady would also give the impression that she had all the American publishers in her pocket, up her sleeve, or close to her bunched yet angular bosom; but she let Sarah's words go and made no claim on them. She sat upright, without tension, her full-creased eyelids flickering; a bird of such contradictory opulent rectitude as never was on land or sea.

"I heard from Pansy Bysshe yesterday." The eyelids flickered approvingly toward Sarah. "She mentioned how *charmed* she was by you when she met you with Mr. Harbrittle."

"Me?" Sarah sat poised at the apex of her being, rapt in gratitude.

"You were a *success*," Mrs. Oxford emphasized. It was her reverent, single-minded, all-embracing word of feminine praise.

"Oh no. I didn't say anything, didn't—" But perhaps she *had*, without knowing it? "It was a lovely evening anyway," she concluded.

"And"—Mrs. Oxford piled glory upon glory—"when she happened to meet Sir Giles Merrick he remarked that the Fontayne girl was unquestionably a young beauty."

Sarah stared over the lace mats, the candelabra, and the cream fondants with dream-unfocused eyes. Why couldn't she have told me this in the first moment she came into the house? "Unquestionably!" Oh God, dear sweet God, I hope he really said "unquestionably," and that it hasn't got distorted in Lady Pansy's mind. . . .

Between the steady petal flames Bracken saw the divine unrest within her rapt stillness. Beatitude was carried in her to an edge of chaos: heaven lipped perilously by encroaching hell. She breathed in the success of the moment and held it to her; yet even now was impelled forward on further hope and triumph, whose furthermost reach was in turn already edged with expectations of despair. Slowly, her pale frail hand came out to a highly-Cruddles-polished silver dish and took a sweet; slowly (rapt within the dream that ran away with her in every gradation of bliss stretching out to the final and nearly inevitable disillusion) placed it in her mouth and let it dissolve in a moist creamy smoothness upon her tongue.

"Yes, Sarah was all prettied-up, that night," Philly said, her delight only a little less proud than Sarah's own.

"'That's an ill phrase, a vile phrase,—"beautified!" is a vile phrase . . .'" Bronwen said.

"I didn't say 'beautified,'" Philly pointed out, civilly.

Bronwen could as well have pointed out that no one ever did say the perfectly right things to be brilliantly capped by quotation; but she did not say it. Amid such Philistines, what was the use?

"Oh, it's *Macbeth*, Philly," Sarah laughed, not minding, not minding anything.

Here, too, Bronwen let the outrageous statement pass, her mind encased in layer on layer of scorn. Mrs. Oxford, with a mere negative recognition that the words were not from the Bible, was not competent to offer any correction.

Somewhere between the chicken and the coffee, Mrs. Oxford (a latter-day passive Columbus) had discovered Bracken as a part of America. She was busy, from then on, in tabulating his opinions for him. As an American, he would of course hold the view . . . as an American he would naturally believe in . . . And so on, until she had him enclosed in a tight and most disconcerting compartment, labelled "U.S.A." Her discerning eye decided at first appraisal (or at least at second or third) that he was not a gangster.

The scented English summer night and Mrs. Oxford's emphatic English tongue held Bracken captive. Even when there was a general move to the drawing room he could not evade her. Peter, boredom beginning to crack the smooth face of his amusement that had held through the fantastic dinner, slipped unobtrusively out by the glass doors onto the terrace. His Russian cigarette trailed an exotic scent over the cosy cottage smell of pinks. Bronwen sat sulkily bent over a book.

It was obvious that Mrs. Oxford thought less and less of the Joneses every moment; and all the less for their obliviousness to this disapproval. She took it out on Bracken, venting her graciousness upon him. "The trouble with Americans," she said (but scrupulously not blaming him), "is that they have no proper sense of international responsibility." She seemed to retreat behind her eyelids; as if she had made some final speech before the curtain fell. Her words were unanswerable, backed by all the weight of her knowledge of herself as one wrapped in parochial responsibility. For what, after all, was the international kind but an enlargement of the parochial . . . ?

She must go now, Sarah thought. Any more, and the evening would begin to dwindle, which would never do. "How is Emily?" she belatedly asked.

This question usually moved Mrs. Oxford to disapproval or departure. "She is not always a solace to me," the old lady said with restraint, now. "There is something about Emily that does not take kindly to kindnesses. One always does one's best, and yet there so often seems something missing. Now she says if I don't mind she would rather not eat meat. If you please! As if such fads will ever get her—" The eyelids hovered; she had been going to say "a suitable husband," but said instead ". . . anywhere."

"Bracken doesn't eat much meat," Sarah said, faintly sorry for Emily, though she wasn't sure why.

"Indeed." Up flew the eyelids, down came the bird gaze on Bracken. "I was not aware that was an American custom." Emily's elusive father, she recalled, had been at least an eighth—perhaps even a quarter—American. It was a disturbing realization. In future Emily must be made to keep in more serious contact with her roast beef than ever.

She rose to go. The summer night billowed about her through the open glass doors. The drawing room fell to pieces around her magnificent sufficiency. It was all limp cushions, faded curtains, worn carpet. She kissed Sarah and Philly, extended charity tipped with compassion in the hand she gave to Bracken. To Bronwen she only inclined her frosty front of hair; and Peter did not even return to receive any farewell from her.

Mrs. Oxford's epilogue was with Cruddles, as her prologue had been.

"What a ghastly old lady," Peter said, promptly appearing when she had gone, lighting another cigarette.

"But why do you bother with her?" Bronwen slowly raised her eyes from her book. "You can't *like* her."

"You don't understand." Sarah turned to Bracken for understanding, but for once he seemed to be going to fail her, so she switched her gaze to Philly. "She's a very old and very dear friend of ours, isn't she, Philly?"

"Yes, she is," Philly said, sincerely, from her heart.

Alone again, Bracken gone, there was a tacit agreement on retreat into strictly personal concerns. The little heat wave faded, came back, then died off into the normality of summer that neither rain nor snaps of cold could affect. It was June, assured in time, whatever the weather, with meals on the terrace the rule instead of the exception.

Bronwen pored over her notebooks, chewing over the cud of memories in search of her second book. Peter was here and there, tempestuous at the piano, drifting through the village. Philly sat beneath apple trees and stroked Ernest and ate globular boiled sweets and read *The Gem*. Sarah stitched contemptuously at the pernickety underclothes that Mrs. Moody had recommended as a solace for unrequited love. Tom rode his donkey and his bicycle and (as Mrs. Moody said) his high horse.

Gooseberries formed in pallid raw green clusters and strawberries were ripening. But the garden was a mess, as young Digby hopelessly pointed out. Without The Lady it simply didn't prosper. Nobody couldn't honestly say it was his fault . . . and besides, you hadn't a chance against it, it was that stubborn. . . . Sarah knew that the only way to treat young Digby was to goad him to the limit, but she couldn't be bothered. Only Mother knew how to put shame and pride into the youth, so that he worked like some passionate St. George upon an untidy dragon. Only Mother knew how to arouse that fine frenzy of uncalculating ambition which made him, as Bronwen had rather strikingly put it, reck not his own rede. Without Mother, Sarah retorted, he was a *broken reed*, as lost to honour as he was to labour.

Mrs. Bale produced meals which delighted Tom and Mrs. Moody by being consistently erratic snacks. Cruddles spent hours in his pantry, simply loitering. Sarah and Philly set tables and cleared away meals. After all, one couldn't blame Cruddles for being unenthusiastic since Bronwen's insult to him.

Neither Bronwen nor Peter seemed unduly dismayed by this degeneration into a state of gentle sloth; which surprised Sarah. Bronwen's kind, if formal, treatment of animals surprised her too. She had even been known to give a gingerly caress to Tom's recalcitrant donkey; and Ernest's behaviour she suffered quite without protest. She and Peter rather often discussed music and literature; but they neither played the old gramophone again nor begged any audience for Bronwen's current inspiration.

The personal selfish note—if not harmonious at least without acrimony—was maintained right on to the return to Fontayne of Mr. Jones with his bride.

The reunion was unexpected when it came: they reached home at suppertime, when, by all plans and portents, they should not have arrived until the following morning. There was no time for any of the regulation salutes to travellers: the telegram to Mrs. Moody (which she almost certainly would not receive), the hurried furbishing up of the house, the re-doing of flowers, the pulling up of a few of the more prominent weeds on the terrace. No time for any of it. They were caught unawares, Fontayne in undress. Even Bronwen had not bothered in the slightest about her appearance or the state of her surroundings all day; for that afternoon she had received six presentation copies of her book, and her eyes could hold no more than this. Peter had lately begun to compose a frilly yet subtle little prelude, and had let his hair grow long, the general disorder of the place dovetailing in a paradoxical niceness with his mood.

The impersonal separately-personal note spread over the supper table. They were eating in the scrappy little breakfast room, as it was too cold for the terrace. Bacon and eggs and sausages; with a loaf, crusty and cosy and solid, raised on its end at the edge of the table. Cruddles had kindly brought in the meal himself; and it was piping hot for once.

"It's not what you'd call etiquette to let Ernest clamber over the bread, is it?" he said; but there was no real reproof in his tone.

When Elisabeth unexpectedly came in, the scene was one of suspended yet vigorous animation. Enthralled, Bronwen turned the pages of an immaculate copy of her book and masticated sausage with solid but abstracted determination. Peter's face advanced and retreated in an olive pallor behind a mug of beer. Tom groaned pensively, placidly, swiping at his food with misdirected and eccentric implements. Philly, her back to the evening sunlight, her pale brown hair threading out to a haze of gold, was lost over the mysteries of a knitting pattern that Mrs. Moody had given her. Sarah ate in a dream, fork hovering between plate and mouth. Ernest lay stretched at his ease, nicely poised between Philly's elbow and the loaf; occasionally he lifted a moist pink nose and sniffed delicately at the flowers that overwhelmed a thin vase rocking drunkenly on its foundations.

"Darlings!" Elisabeth said, her heart not sinking, but slipping, as it were, into a minor key.

They came out of their several absorptions, then; even Ernest, so that she had not the courage to rebuke him. Time enough later, she thought weakly, to get things a little less chaotic and to get the flowers right.

"Did you have a nice time?" Tom shouted over the hubbub. "Did you have a nice time and was Mr. Jones kind to you?"

"Oh, Tom!" she said, dismayed. Peter and Bronwen waited in a polite tension, Sarah and Philly in a thrilled one. (Suppose he had turned out simply insupportable—what then?) She addressed Tom, but her voice went quietly, reproachfully, among them all: "Surely you realize he is the nicest man in the world?"

Then Julian Jones came in and the greetings began again.

CHAPTER SEVEN

"SARAH!" Philly's voice called in wild clear excitement, down from the terrace, across lawn to the orchard. "Something wonderful has happened!"

"What?" Gigantic surmise thrilled Sarah to her soul.

"Mrs. Rudge's triplets have won joint first prize in the beauty competition!"

"Oh. . . ." She sank back on her elbow beneath the pear tree.

"Aren't you *glad*?"

"Oh yes . . . but it doesn't really affect my life one way or another."

"But, Sarah," Philly pleaded, "it's about two hundred pounds, and think what they'll be able to do with that."

"They'll spend it on useless things and have nothing left to show for it in about two months' time," Sarah said with virtuous reproof.

"What would *you* do with it?"

"Spend it on useless things." She smiled up into Philly's serious face. "I wish I had won it. Then we could definitely have the dance; I'd pay for it myself, and have lots over for dresses and things for all of us."

"I expect we'll have the dance, anyway," Philly said, with dread foreboding. "But what nice things would the Rudges get if this hadn't happened?"

"They ought to save the money to educate Jimmie and Johnnie and Georgie," Sarah said perversely.

"I suppose they ought," Philly agreed. "But Mrs. Rudge likes to see something for her money."

"She won't 'oblige' us any more now—"

"Of course she will," Philly said indignantly. "You don't think she'd let this make any difference—"

"Shall we send a telegram of congratulation?" Sarah interrupted, in a mollifying tone.

"That's a nice idea, but—" Philly hesitated. "They have had one telegram already about the prize. Another one might upset Mrs. Rudge. She's a bit afraid of them."

Yawning, Sarah dropped the nice idea. In her dreams for the Fontayne dance she had seen Mrs. Rudge helping at the buffet. It showed how unstable dreams were, for—whatever Philly said—one couldn't imagine anyone with two hundred or more pounds bothering to dabble around in the cold comfort of ices belonging to someone else.

"If I had two hundred pounds I would go away to London and live there until I could find a job." She added: "Not that I'd need a job for a long time with two hundred pounds."

"I suppose even that goes, in time," Philly said, but scarcely believing it. "Do you know Bronwen is expecting to have thirty pounds of her own quite soon?"

"Why?" Sarah sat up again, shadow and sun lacing her indignant features.

"For her book when it gets published."

"Thirty pounds for Bronny's book!" Her voice trembled with scorn. She was shocked to the depths of her being. Poised ever just this side of uttermost financial chaos, it seemed to her a dreadful thing that a mere book could offer such promise of security.

"That isn't all, she says," Philly went on. "She gets something else called royalties after that."

"I don't care about that," Sarah said, dismissing the hazy Court honour that the word would seem to imply. "It's the *money* that is such a scandalous . . . profiteering."

The Fontayne dance *must* come to pass before life came to revolve completely around the publication of the nauseous book. Already she had those advance copies and was expecting one to read it. In a couple of weeks it would be all upon them. Better to combine her triumph with some triumph for Fontayne: the bitter pill crushed up in sweetness.

Sarah tackled her mother again, after lunch.

"If we have a little party—a dance—it will help to settle everything down."

"My marriage, do you mean?" Elisabeth asked.

"Well . . . yes."

"But, darling, I don't feel any need of a dance for that purpose."

"But you did half promise when"—she got it out—"Sir Giles Merrick was here. He said he would love to come. I'm sure anyone would love to come."

They were in the flower room: almost inevitably, as a discussion was on. Still, it was a good chance to catch Mother unawares, her mind nearly all reserved for roses and feathery fern.

"But Julian is supposed to rest, you know, darling. He doesn't really want any fuss and bother."

"Fontayne is still *partly* ours, though," Sarah said, with restraint. "I expect he intends to spend a lot of money on it, but even so—"

"It would be silly to spend money on it if I am going to sell it."

"Sell it?" Sarah stared. "Surely that won't happen *now*?"

"Why not? We've always been trying to sell it, off and on." Elisabeth's thoughts floated off at a tangent of white rosebuds that sprang from a bower of green.

"Yes—oh, yes, we have." Shaken, Sarah decided not to pursue this peculiar twist of conversation that might lead to any manner of unexpected revelation. "All the more reason, if there's the slightest *suspicion* we might leave, that we should give a dance to remember it by."

"It would be expensive, you know, darling."

"But surely to goodness—" But surely to goodness it was the least Mr. Jones could offer for having invaded their home and despoiled it with Bronwen's book and Peter's piano-tinkering. . . . One couldn't say it aloud, though, in the face of Mother and the clotted-cream buds of rose.

"Besides, who could be asked?"

"There are masses of people," Sarah said sternly. "Just because we have never entertained does not mean people don't exist."

"But a *dance*, darling. You have to have crowds of young men and girls strictly of suitable age. I can't imagine where hostesses find those uniform batches. Everyone we know seems to be either too old or too young."

It was a rather terrifying prospect, thought of like that. . . . "Well, then, let's have a big week-end party, with people doing just as they like, informally," Sarah amended her plan.

"But what *is* there to do?" Plenty, of course, Elisabeth thought, as she filled another vase at the little green sink, but not the sort of things guests would think proper to Week Ends.

"If we had ever had any Week Ends, we should *know*?" Sarah retorted. "In books, nobody ever seems to have any difficulty. You just get a group of people together and they talk and play games if they want to and dance and read and go on the river—"

"We haven't a river, darling—"

"No; but if one *had*—The thing is not to *arrange* anything. But you must know. Didn't you and Father have parties here when they called it Mount Olympus?"

"Well, not like that. Men used to come down sometimes, unexpectedly, and wolf sandwiches and talk through the night." Through their hats, too, she half suspected, but was too kind to encourage such a thought.

"I'm not talking of wolves," Sarah said coldly. "You'd think even Father must have known *some* civilized people. I don't think a Week End is much to ask. I'll soon be eighteen and I'll never have met anyone in my life." Wilfully self-pitying, she was astonished to find her eyes actually filling with tears. What a good actress I must be . . . or perhaps I really *am* crying. . . .

Elisabeth looked perplexed. She could not believe Sarah truly wanted her horrid week-end-out-of-a-book, but there was a possibility she did; and even that she would enjoy it if it came to pass.

"Would you like to talk to Julian about it, darling?" The great hall vases were done; this argument must end. "I expect he has plenty of friends he could invite—"

"I don't want *riots* of Jones friends. I can make a list of my own—" She caught back her words. "Still I don't mind mentioning the Week End to him," she added with discretion.

Since the return from the honeymoon, Mr. Jones had been merely accepted with civility, but without enthusiasm. There had been no attempt to 'get to know him'; but now, as Sarah informed Philly, she thought it was time they made that attempt. After all, he was a human being, she pointed out, in spite of his weak heart and the silken ledge of his moustache. Philly had never doubted this for an instant, but she did no more than make an encouraging murmur.

"He's sitting on the terrace alone now. I think we ought to go and make a bit of conversation to him," Sarah said. "There's half an hour before tea, and Bronwen and Peter are out of the way."

Julian smiled with faint surprise when the two girls sat down near him in a manner that expressed some innate formality, though the seats they took were no more than two sagging deck chairs into which one dropped straight to abrupt rock-bottom depths that affected, as Christopher had remarked, not only the bottom but the whole spinal system as well.

"How are you feeling today?" Sarah asked.

"Very well," he said, his surprise deepening.

"You find Fontayne a peaceful place in which to rest?"

"Certainly," he agreed, his kind melancholy eyes faintly restive beneath her Social Service scrutiny.

He was wearing one of his unnerving bright blue shirts, open at the neck, showing his brown throat. He looked artistic, but somehow not in the least like a conductor of colossal orchestras. Seen in evening dress, with a starched front to the world, it might have been easier to accept him, but, here, he suddenly seemed far too real and at the same time too disembodied. He was a real person, a real man, in love with one's mother. Thought of like this, his vivid shirt became the symbol of all sorts of obscure intimacies. Mother had accepted him for better or worse. He was *here*, breathing, a fly alighting on his hand, one corduroy trouser leg hitched up to his calf, his shoes ancient and earth-stained, a battered old hat pulled forward on his shaggy red grey hair, his dark eyes frowning amiably at the sun.

"Do you think your heart will quite recover if you have perfect rest here?" Sarah pressed on.

"My heart is"—he smiled from one girl to the other—"very well and happy, thank you."

His heart—the central un-physical part of it—yearning towards Mother. . . . Really, it was rather cheek, however kind one tried to be. Kissing Mother and stroking her hair—Oh, no, really it was too much! He was old, had no right to his youthful shirt and his boyish brown neck. Bracken, at least, had the decency to be getting bald at fifty. Not so Mr. Jones, his mane still sprouting luxuriantly. Virilely, Sarah thought resentfully. How awful it was. In spite of seeming so mild, he obviously ran deep . . . deep.

"You shouldn't smoke cigarettes with a weak heart," she said, her kindness disintegrating into sharpness.

"Perhaps I shouldn't," he agreed. But he was clearly going to do nothing about it.

Philly was no help at all. Ernest had come sidling sleekly up to her and she was leaning forward, delving her fingers into his thick striped fur. Mr. Jones sank deeper into his chair; sank back into the subtle persuasions of Fontayne.

"How will you occupy your time until you are well enough to conduct again?" Sarah made a final attempt. "You don't want . . . you don't want to stagnate."

"We'll call it vegetating," he corrected gently.

"Oh, but that's terrible! You don't know how it *gets* you after a while. It grows all over you and you're lost. Lost in . . . vegetation."

"Is that such a bad fate?"

It was no use. How like one's luck to get a stepfather who could not even be decently disgustingly cosmopolitan, but had to mingle vegetation with it, so that one had neither one thing nor another. . . . I always knew the Joneses were the sort to slip through your fingers.

"*I* don't want to vegetate." It's what Bracken calls my ego poking through; but I can't help it. "I want to have a weekend party."

"Well, why not?" Mr. Jones said.

"Mother makes such fusses that you wonder whether it's worth it," she said wearily. "Yet we've a lot of people we owe hospitality to, haven't we, Philly?"

"Yes," Philly said, her sigh inaudible behind the screen of Ernest's purr.

"Don't you think," Sarah said, inspired, "that it would be nice to celebrate Bronwen's book with a party, as well as your coming to live with us, and—" Well, that was enough for the moment.

"Have your party by all means, if Elisabeth agrees," he said, not committing himself on the subject of Bronwen. "Peter would be delighted, for one, I'm sure."

"That's what I mean." She smiled, transformed. "Peter, for one, *loves* to have amusing people around him." As if to seal her words, the boy himself loped in his picturesque Red Indian stride on to the terrace. "Wouldn't you like a weekend party here, Peter?"

"That depends"—he timed his words expertly to the opening and shutting of a cigarette case—"on the party."

"Oh, it will be a beautiful one!" She was impelled to her feet on an urgent belief in her words. "I think I'll go and tell Mother it is all fixed."

Philly was left on an island of despair with the silent father and son. Even Ernest went off and left her, with a faint high-pitched mew.

"What an emphatically *castrato* voice Ernest has," Peter remarked.

"I think Mrs. Bale gave him some castor oil when she was giving some to the kitchen lady cat," Philly said excusingly. "She's always doing it, out of spite. He doesn't need it."

Peter smiled. He thought there was something rather sweet about Philly, and not for the world would he now have corrected her misapprehension of his meaning.

* * * * *

First of all (before one began to make even the beginnings of plans for the Week End) there was the letter to Sir Giles. Until he answered the date must be left subject to alteration, even though one could give no reason to anyone for this. It was no use Bronwen assuming that, because her book had been artfully coupled with the party, the time should be fixed for either the Week End before or the Week End after the day of publication.

We are having a little week-end party soon. I thought I would just write and tell you this before my mother sends an invitation to you, because I thought if this date doesn't suit you we could rearrange things, as nothing is settled yet, so if you wouldn't mind letting me know fairly quickly. . . .

Something like that. It would sound a bit awkward, but there was no help for it. The Week End without Sir Giles would be—well, it *wouldn't* be, so there was no need to think what it would be.

The interim between the posting of her letter and the arrival of his answer had to be filled in somehow. Much of it was occupied by discussions with Mrs. Moody on dresses.

"Why don't you," Mrs. Moody suggested spectacularly, "get them to get you something tip-top for the dance? A model?"

"But there probably won't be a dance at all." (One had to have time to digest the notion.)

"Oh, you can always get a dance together spontaneous-like, at the last moment. Once you have the frock, the rest follows."

"Oh, I don't know. . . . I'll see." She couldn't concentrate until she had heard from him.

"Not fretting about Him, are you?"

"Him?" Sarah's tone also used a capital letter, scathingly. "You can only speak about *God* in that voice," she said distantly.

"He did say you were an unquestionable beauty," Mrs. Moody said, ignoring this gambit.

I can't have told her that—I simply *can't* have. Yet can she be occult enough to have found it out for herself? . . . "You would hardly expect him to say I was a questionable one," she said aloud.

He said he was very sorry and there was nothing he would have liked better. He said he would have rearranged his plans if he possibly could, but this visit abroad had been on the cards for some time and he hadn't a free hand in the matter. He said the whole thing was rather trying, but there it was. He said (his whimsical little smile playing almost visibly over the written words) that duty had a discourteous habit of getting in the way of pleasure. He said that he hoped they would meet again on his return some time in July. He said how sweet it was of her to have written to him specially before her mother sent an invitation. He said he would drop her a line while he was away. . . .

It was all so charming and friendly and reasonable; but it made no difference. He wasn't coming, and the Week End—the beautiful civilized June house party—was off.

"Isn't it time you sent out your invitations?" Bronwen asked, politely dissociating herself from any claims to hostess-ship.

"Oh, we aren't going to have it," Sarah said carelessly.

Elisabeth and Philly both looked across the breakfast table in astonishment. Not have it, after going on so? Philly took another piece of toast, her appetite suddenly enlarged with thankfulness.

"*Aren't* we, darling?" Elisabeth prompted.

"Oh no. It really isn't worth it. just talking and eating and drinking—and what is there at the end except good-bys and going aways and then dreary letters of thanks?"

She's feeling Russian, poor Sarah. . . . Philly's heart ached with relief and compassion. It's an ill wind, of course—But I don't want it to blow me any good if it means Sarah is sad. . . .Yet now the summer stretched on again in an endless peace. Nothing to worry about, except a necessary cautiousness of movements at Week Ends, in case Mr. Lupin might catch sight of you and remember his terrible threat of portrait painting. Beyond that, nothing but niceness, the days still lengthening and, beyond that, all July and August, nothing happening, the Joneses sinking into Fontayne life, no longer filling you with anguish for their newness and the need of things to say to them, and Christopher coming home for the holidays, and days on days of simply seeing him here, not talking to him, letting him sink in and be a part of everything again, and nothing ever changing except the weather of the days.

Philly's happiness trembled only with the misgiving that life did not give out its blessings equally: the ill-wind ever hovering, ready to turn chill on others while offering you the soft warm other side of it. If only it hadn't to be like that. If only there were some way out of it.

Marmalade rising in a sticky extravagant mound from her toast, she considered this point, but could find no answer or solution.

*   *   *   *   *

The publication date loomed, came stealthily into view. Something had to be done. There must be some accomplishment (if only of purpose, not of positive achievement) to hold up against it, to refute its threat.

Sarah went to see Mr. Harbrittle.

The morning was fluid with a mist lingering on an unconscionable time. The sun was certainly there, waiting patiently behind a pearly barrier, but unable to get through. Trees dripped autumnly; and yet the air was wholly summer air, rich and sweet and only waiting to be hot. Sarah's resolution was not to the minute, incapable of waiting. She couldn't lose the time that walking would take, couldn't wait to mend the puncture in the back tyre of her old bicycle, couldn't even wait to ask Tom's permission for her to ride his.

Trees sent drips and trickles of moisture down her neck as she hurtled down the drive, pedals whirling madly, exhaustingly, built to Tom's infantile limbs. What a machine, what a morning, what a life! Rhododendron petals lay mashed in pink pulp in the ground. Sir Giles was gone, far away into inscrutable fastnesses of "Abroad," his luggage blazoned with labels, spattered carelessly, richly, like the rhododendron petals.

Dismounting at Mr. Harbrittle's immaculate gateway, the sun at last slipped past the barrier and traced the neat grass verge outside his gate with a sudden yellow radiance. It was typical of Mr. Harbrittle to have a garden outside his garden, so that one came gradually into his domain, shedding the rude common earth in a sort of outer garden protecting the inner near-holy land. It was as if he supplied some spiritual shoe-scraper, to prepare one for the walk up his ruthlessly trim garden path to the door of his house. But Sarah, propping Tom's bicycle against the convenient raised grass verge, stepped blithely in, unaware of that invisible reminder and rebuke upon the threshold.

The elderly female servant eyed her with suspicion.

"Tell him it's Sarah Fontayne," she explained; adding enlighteningly, in case he shouldn't remember: "The older one."

"But he goes into his study at half-past ten and is never seen again till lunch," the woman said, with unintentional drama.

"Not even if the house set on fire? It's a thatched roof—it might." Not waiting for the servant's response to this interesting hypothesis, she said: "It's only twenty-five past ten, anyway."

Unluckily for Mr. Harbrittle, he also had gauged the time correctly; and now he emerged from the little sun parlour where he breakfasted and walked stiffly across the hall to his study. By half-past, calculated to a nicety, his papers would be laid out and he would be ink-deep in his theme again.

"I've come to see you for a minute," Sarah called out. "Only a minute. May I come in?"

Mr. Harbrittle felt his scalp prickle with foreboding. He detested young solitary female visitors; especially so since a buxom village wench, some years ago, had invaded his privacy and poured into his unwilling ear a shockingly intimate account of her association with some local swain and the deplorable suspected results of this liaison. What exactly, he had asked with an extraordinary forbearance, was he supposed to do about it? Well, they said ("They," he had noted with distaste), they did say he was wonderful-like in his understanding of poor folks' problems. They did say there was nothing he didn't know about hearts breaking on old farmsteads and dark blood spilling on old cold stone flags and love bruised or burning on the sweet strong earth.

It didn't bear thinking of, even now. A whole day's work ruined (for how could he regain his beautiful calm even when the young woman had been got rid of?) and the tiresome necessity of changing the colour of his heroine's hair. For the buxom young woman detestably had just that shade of morning glory red-gold tresses that was so desirable in fiction and so unsuitable in real life.

He had done his humanitarian best, of course; had sent her to his housekeeper, who, he later learned by oblique inquiry, had recommended an appropriate Home. Yet, as it turned out, he could not even have the satisfaction of being compensated for his spoiled chapter by the young female's acceptance of advice, for he had heard later (again by oblique inquiry) that she had departed not only from the little town but from all paths that could conceivably be classed as straight and narrow.

"By all means come in," he invited the Fontayne girl, as if none of this deplorable episode had re-entered his mind. The girl's hair was at least dark where his present heroine's was as yellow as . . . He eyed her sharply. There didn't *appear* to be anything radically wrong.

Sarah followed him across the hall, her heart beating fast on the memory of drinking nectar here with Sir Giles. Could it ever truly have been? . . . that enchantment which had left this thrilling painful ghost? Of all her senses it was her nose that unromantically seemed to take the lead. Crossing the hall she believed she could smell the magic elusive perfume of Sir Giles himself. Her nostrils quivered with a nervous morbid delight. Like a horse, Mr. Harbrittle thought, keeping a wary peevish eye on her. How typical of Marcus Fontayne to have beautiful offspring that quivered their noses like horses.

He sat her down in his study; because it was the hour for his study and here he must be; even if an intruder were present.

"Is there anything I can do for you, young lady?" he asked sharply, as she seemed to be ready to sink into some reprehensible stupor.

"I wondered if you could help me find a job."

"A . . . job?" Mechanically, he repeated her offensive syllable.

"You must know so many people. I wondered if you could recommend me as a secretary to one of your literary friends, or perhaps in an office, or—"

"I know nothing about offices."

"Oh, don't you? Not even the sort where they bring out magazines, where you send short stories you want to have printed—"

"I don't write short stories." He kept his tone scrupulously level.

"No, perhaps not." She gracefully went halfway to taking his word for it. "But think of all your friends, writing away all the time—Think of all the articles in papers, and the serials and stories, and then all the long books like yours—"

Like mine . . . ? He stared frostily into her large blue eyes, eloquent with mistaken zeal. "I don't quite follow where this . . . detailed enumeration is leading."

"It's leading back to me," she said, distressed. "Surely there's something I could do?"

"I fear that the published trash of current periodicals will continue to accumulate with all too facile an abundance without any assistance from you, laudable as your motive doubtless is."

From this quelling phrase she plucked impatiently at what she saw as the essential plum. "It's not laudable at all. I just want—I must have—a job."

He turned to more personal discussion. "It is unlikely you would find the working world to your taste after the ideal quality of your home life."

How does he know it's ideal? "There are difficulties," she said delicately.

Don't explain . . . he prayed. His eyes sought the clock.

It was twenty-five to eleven. "I'm afraid—" he said, his gaze returning from that white reproachful dial to her blue reproachful eyes.

"Yes, I see it's no use." His book-inlaid walls, pressing in on her, rubbing in the fact that she couldn't spell, couldn't do shorthand, could type only with one funereal finger—She rose from the chair where he had sat her down. "How is your book getting on?" she asked with sad politeness.

Mr. Harbrittle, as it happened, was not yet out of the slough of his halfway chapters. They sagged, like a Dachshund, in the middle. How could one work in peace with the macabre face of Europe peering over one's shoulder?

"It is not easy to work in peace with the macabre face of Europe peering over one's shoulder," he said dispassionately.

"No, it can't be." She nodded wisely. Covertly, her gaze searched his drooping tweed shoulder, as if she expected to see there an authentic spectre, bizarrely real as the image of Mrs. Moody's "black demon" which was known to perch at times in a fiendish tantrum on Tom's shoulder.

"Things are coming to a pretty pass, aren't they?" she said, absently, still staring at the space where Europe should have been. "I wonder what my father would have thought of it all."

Mr. Harbrittle was not disposed to enter into this remote conjecture. For the moment (bad as the situation of course was) it had not been Europe itself, but his book in relation to it that had been the point.

"It is very difficult to keep the balance," he said. "It is not that one doesn't expect to survive the cataclysm but that the interim—"

"No, I don't suppose we'd get any bombs here," Sarah interrupted, wanting to please him.

"I was not referring, one way or the other, to my personal survival," he said distantly.

"No; your books, you mean, of course," she said belatedly. "The thing is to simply keep *on*, isn't it?"

Her blithe belief that this was a simple procedure irritated him. Compared with it, even the splitting of an infinitive became almost negligible.

"That takes great strength of mind," he said.

"I'm sure you've got plenty of that." The thing was to treat him as one did Mrs. Bale, with flattery spilling recklessly over everything one said.

"I have a modicum, I believe."

He made a slight movement toward the door. It was nearly twenty to eleven, but still the girl seemed to have no conception of her enormity.

"I hear Sir Giles Merrick has gone abroad," she said, beginning to move.

"I heard of a contemplated trip."

"He has to go—not for pleasure. I expect it is . . . Europe." She glanced again for a spectral sign of it on Mr. Harbrittle's shoulder. "But he won't be away very long."

"Indeed," Mr. Harbrittle said.

"I hope I haven't been an awful bore to you."

"No, indeed," he said.

"If you do hear of a job I could do—"

"I fear there isn't the least likelihood of that."

"Well, thank you, anyway, and good-by."

"Good-by." Thankful that she did not offer to shake hands, he said: "Our friend Lady Pansy Bysshe is in this neighbourhood again, as you doubtless know."

"Is she? No, I didn't know." Vague new hopes formed in her mind. You never knew . . . she had been nice and encouraging, that night of the nectar. "She will be a happy addition to our little community won't she?" she said: a startling cordial Parthian shot in Mrs. Oxford's voice.

Philly was much too tactful to say anything else about the Week End, but she found herself watching Sarah more carefully than she had ever done before. Bronwen scarcely intruded, these last few days; her whole self was concentrated on her book now so nearly born to the world.

Sarah flung Tom's bicycle from her at the top of the drive. The sun was properly out now, and yet seemed to have half a mind to depart again. There was rain in the clouds that tipped low over the house.

"That's my bikikle," Tom said, appearing, as was his wont, from nowhere.

"I know it is."

"You've been riding it."

"I know I have." It was surprising how difficult it was to stand up to Tom's impassive scrutiny. "It's a horrible bicycle."

"It's a very nice little bikikle." His conviction was so sincere as to be infectious. "You shouldn't have taken it away without asking; I might have needed it. I did need it, because Esmé doesn't feel very well and I'm sparing her."

"It would do Esmé good not to be spared for once—spoilt beast."

"Esmé's a very nice little Esmé." To him, Esmé was merely another name for donkey. He had no part in the naming of her, for Esmé had been handed down, like cast-off clothing, from one member of the family to the next; and even, perhaps, through families before theirs. She was encrusted with tradition.

"You can have your bicycle now."

"I don't want it now. I'm having an invention."

Sarah left him standing there, small, intent, inscrutable, staring down at the fallen machine. He was rather sweet, she allowed herself to think, out of sight of him.

Philly watched her come into the schoolroom and sit down with elaborate carelessness, and elaborately yawn. "Why aren't Tom and Miss James having any lessons?" Sarah asked, through her yawn.

"Miss James doesn't feel well."

"Like Esmé. . . . Oh, Philly, I must get a job!"

The Week End was off, but now there was this; another disturbance so soon. Philly was dimly aware there might be some connection between the two.

"I must, I tell you!" Sarah insisted, as if her sister had made some demur. "I can't keep on playing second fiddle to Bronwen's book and Peter's piano."

"Peter always seems to be down in the town, lately. I wonder what he does?"

"As if I cared! Don't try to change the subject. Is that Mrs. Moody's paper?" She seized on her favourite morning picture newspaper—only seen in the house when Mrs. Moody was here—and turned to a column of miscellaneous pleas, promises, and exhortations. Her long forefinger running down the print, she read aloud:

"'Thinking of U only, but don't write.—Fe-Fi-Fo-Fum.' 'Opportunities for smart salesmen and women.' 'Same time, same place. Bring Joker. Love—Joker.' (How can he bring Joker if he *is* Joker?) 'Earn in spare time. No capital needed.' 'Ladies' superfluous hairs banished like magic. Write: Jiffy, Box 006!'" She glanced up, still holding her finger on the column. "I think I ought to tell Mrs. Moody about this. Banishes hair like magic, it says. I'll cut it out." She was glad to put off for a moment the earnest business of looking for employment.

"I expect she's tried it," Philly said disillusioningly.

"I expect she has," Sarah agreed. "You couldn't call hers a lady's face, anyway." She had turned to the Love Column. "It says if you're twenty-two it's all right for you to marry a man of thirty-five or more."

"You aren't twenty-two."

"I never mentioned me."

"No, but you were thinking of you," Philly said, suddenly miserable. "I could tell you were."

"Can't I read anything out of the paper without you putting a—a vulgar personal interpretation on it?" Sarah demanded grandly.

"Oh, Sarah, darling, *don't* be sad!"

"Sad? I'm not sad." She threw down the paper. "There's nothing here."

Mrs. Moody came in, but already both girls had forgotten the moustache cure, or even that Mrs. Moody had a moustache. She was merely a familiar presence, fully clad in reliable flesh and cosy spirit.

"So we've got your Lady Pansy here," she said chattily.

"Where?" Philly looked around.

"She's come down to open up the Continental house on the corner beyond Mrs. Oxford's. It's her niece, Mrs. Welwyn, that's taken it, but Lady Bysshe has come to get it ready."

"Lady Pansy," Sarah corrected mechanically. "The almond icing house, you mean? I didn't know it was for sale."

"It's a short let," Mrs. Moody informed. "It seems they know the old person that owns it."

"And Virginia Welwyn will come to stay, too?" Sarah asked, never doubting that the oracle would answer.

"Well, she'll slip down at the end of the Season, like. But I gather she's taken it mainly for Lady Bysshe, who she's very kind to, Lady Bysshe not being too well what you'd call provided for—"

"Lady Pansy—" Sarah said.

"Well, Lady Pansy, then," Mrs. Moody said indulgently.

"I wonder if Mother would go to call on her." Sarah had momentarily, but only partially, shelved the problem of her job. "No, I don't suppose she would. She never does." Mr. Jones had done nothing to make her less of a hermit.

"She called on the Joneses," Philly said.

"So I remember," Sarah said briefly.

"Well, we must all try to let bygones be bygones, duck," Mrs. Moody said obscurely.

They did not meet Lady Pansy again until after the publication of Bronwen's book.

Sarah awakened on the morning of that day with a sinking sensation in the stomach. It was like any other rainy summer day; yet was so different. I'm glad it's raining, anyway. If it's happy the authoress the sun shines on, perhaps she's got a disappointment coming to her. . . . Down it fell, fine and straight, dragging heaven with it. No heaven in all the sky, look where you might for a sign of it. But it was no use burrowing here beneath the eiderdown. One had to get up and face it; go down to breakfast and say, I hope your book will be a big success, Bronwen, and see her preening and taking it all in, as if it were a super sort of birthday. Yet *did* anything special happen when a book was published, except that shops began selling it if anyone would buy it?—and obviously no one in his senses would buy Bronny's book.

Sarah went downstairs. She was the last down. Rain sprayed in through the open breakfast-room window; the place smelt of roses and kippers and Tom's aggressive shoe polish.

"Good morning, everybody," Sarah said. Too high-pitched . . . oh, most unnatural! "I hope your book will be a huge success, Bronwen. I have only been waiting for it to come out before I begin to read it." (The presentation copy had been here for quite a fortnight, lying in wait, wherever one turned.)

"Thank you," Bronwen said stiffly, nervously. Extra morning papers had been ordered, but there was nothing about the book. But, then, Mr. Tulsey had said she would probably have to wait until Sunday.

So enchanted was Sarah to discover Bronwen rather less instead of more in countenance than usual that a spasm of unexpected generosity took hold of her.

"Aren't we going to have a picnic or anything, to celebrate?" (It was not, after all, *her* fault that it was raining.)

"No. Elisabeth and I are going into the town"—he meant the real town, the seaside one—"to collect the gardening things we ordered." Mr. Jones sipped at his coffee, eating nothing, and characteristically making no further explanations of what the things were, or why they had been bought.

There was one thing about Mr. Jones (perhaps one of several things, Sarah allowed), he had no awful embarrassing fatherly feelings for dear Bronwen. It might be that he considered her a genius, but, if so, he at least had the decency not to rub it in.

"I shouldn't think swallowing quarts of coffee on an empty stomach can be very good for a weak heart," Sarah said, her intention one of kindness, though her voice hit a somewhat sharp note.

"But after the first pint or quart or so, it can't be exactly on an empty stomach, can it?" he said cheerfully.

"But you never have any proper breakfast." All the Joneses shared this preposterous continental habit.

"Have the top off my little egg," Tom offered.

"Do you mind not talking about *eggs*?" Bronwen entreated.

"It's a very nice little egg," Tom said defensively.

"It may be. But I've got indigestion."

What is indigestion? Beginning her own breakfast, Sarah longed to ask. Never to have had it was perhaps to be put beyond some pale; Bronwen wore indigestion with such an air, as of some lesser martyrdom.

"Lie down on the couch, darling," Elisabeth said sympathetically. "I expect it is the excitement of your book."

She meant this kindly, so Bronwen manfully managed not to take offense; merely said patiently: "It is nothing of the kind, dear Elisabeth. All I ask is to be left in peace."

"If nobody objects, I'll take the car and—" Peter began.

"Elisabeth and I want the car," Mr. Jones said, with gentle decisiveness.

Why can't they buy another? Sarah wondered. What's one little car among Joneses? Their coming to live at Fontayne seemed to have made so little difference, financially. Even the food showed little appreciable improvement. One was not even hatefully conscious of living on charity in one's own house; because there was no change in the style of living, except for a few bottles of drink around the place, and an indefinable sense that Mother was no longer wrestling in total darkness against the bills. Naturally one was delighted to feel there was no question of robbing the musical savings, but all the same it was not exactly what one had expected.

"Well, if nobody's doing anything special, I think I shall go down and hear all about the triplets," Philly announced. "I suppose you won't come, Sarah?"

"I might."

Breakfast wavered, not rounded off by any final chair-scraping and sighs of repletion. Peter drifted off first, then Mr. Jones to the garage, then Elisabeth to put on her hat ("Powder your nose," Sarah called after her), and then Bronwen, as yellow of face as Mr. Harbrittle was (could it be a literary prerogative?) and then Tom to visit Esmé before going up to lessons; until only the sisters remained. They sat on for a minute in a luxurious dream, the house awakening to the full day all around them. Ernest, loping on to the table, seized his opportunity and an only half-denuded kipper.

"Are you coming?" Philly asked, at last.

"Yes, I'll come," Sarah said.

* * * * *

The walk in the rain down from Fontayne and through the splashed and fussily busy street to the Rudge cottage was oddly exhilarating; oddly similar to that morning of looking on to Curzon street and finding life alive as it seldom was. Added to the relief of discovering Bronwen quelled by her digestion, there was little threat left in the publication day.

Jimmie, Johnnie, and Georgie were perched on the yard wall, for all the world as if success had left them quite simple and unspoilt. They greeted Philly with an unintelligible mouthing of pleasure. "I was so glad when I heard you won the prize," she said. The triplets repeated, like some faulty echo: "You were so glad." One of them added: "Had pitcher in paper."

"I *know*," Philly said. "It was lovely."

"Lovely," they agreed, smiling cherubically, modestly.

Mrs. Rudge put her head out of a grimy window and welcomed the Fontaynes with a cracked ecstatic smile. "Come in," she said, beckoning energetically.

Sarah and Philly went in. I was quite right; the money has made no difference to the muddle, Sarah thought.

"I have all the cuttings here, Miss Philly. It comes out ever such a pretty picture except for a smudge on Georgie's nose."

"I'm not a bit surprised they won," Philly said, gazing at the angelic reproduction of the triplets' triumphant photograph. With no false sense of delicacy, she asked: "What are you going to do with the money?"

"Well, my old man wants a motorbike first thing, and then I thought I'd 'ave Jimmie learn the voyolin."

"That won't make up two hundred pounds," Sarah ventured a remark.

"No more it won't, Miss Sarah, but you know how money begins to go once you gets your hands on it?"

Sarah nodded. She did. Still, two hundred pounds—

"Why the violin and why Jimmie?" Philly asked.

"Well, have one of them learn something, I meant. It was Jimmie blew 'is whistle loudest last Christmas."

"You must have been terribly excited. What did you do when you got the telegram?"

"I got a fair turn, I can tell you. Here I was, my old man gorn to work, when in it comes at the door as ordinary as you please. I got such a turn, as I say, that I thought I'd 'ave to send for Mrs. Queevy."

Philly listened sympathetically to this dramatic account. Mrs. Queevy was the local midwife, as Philly knew; but Sarah looked so blank, so

nearly bored, that Philly wondered if she could have realized this significance. It was a good thing they hadn't decided to send the telegram of
congratulation, or *anything* might have happened to Mrs. Rudge.

"You must be very proud." Sarah did her best.

"I don't know as it's any credit to me." Mrs. Rudge fumbled at the
terrible teapot handle of hair at the back of her head. (Why on earth
not spend a bit on a permanent wave? Sarah wondered.) "It's the Lord's
doing, is what I say."

It certainly must be, Sarah silently agreed. Only a miracle of some
sort could have provided the unbeautiful Rudges with the radiant triplets.

"'Triplets Share Beauty Prize,'" Philly read the headlines aloud.
"'Money will be saved for education, says farm labourer father . . .' Did
he really say that, Mrs. Rudge?"

"They never asked, Miss Philly."

"You can't believe anything you read in papers," Sarah said without
illusion. "We ought to be going now."

"How's your mother?" Mrs. Rudge accompanied them to the yard,
half taking off her apron as a formal concession to the outdoor world.
"I'm sorry I won't be able to oblige her again for the next month or
two." It was clear that it was only the arrival of the new Rudge, not the
money, that could possibly have prevented her.

On the way home, they had to pass what they called the almond
icing, and Mrs. Moody the Congtinental, house. It would seem to have
strayed by mistake into its environment, for it bore no architectural
relationship to the Georgian-fronted street of the town, and neither
had it any place in the more emphatic residential individualities of
such homes as Mrs. Oxford's solid house, Mr. Harbrittle's ample old
high-browed thatched dwelling, nor the hideous aspect of Copley's
Green. All these houses had in common at least the appearance of
being houses. With the Congtinental almond icing it was as if one came
to a different stratum of existence, as if the place were tinged by some
fourth-dimensional persuasion. It shot up on a little hillock that should
properly have been a rock edged by the sea, so coastal was the building, so decked and painted to make a Riviera holiday. The roof was
a pale pink just against a sky that surprised it by not being a perpetual burning blue; and the walls were stucco-stiff, iced white window
ledges set into their pale yellow squares. The front door was pale green.
The garden was rocky and flowerless; small cypress trees were darkly
dotted against an outer pink wall like a stage backdrop. In spite of the
colour and the ardent invitation to light, to walk up to the house was to

feel a disconcerting blankness, as if one's foot had missed a step. For where, oh where, was the sea to whose design the place seemed surely to have been built?

The girls paused a moment at the gateway and looked in on the formal courtyard that should have lain splashed with southern sunlight, but instead lay beneath a veil of rain. The front door, however, was hospitably open and a wreath of smoke came from a chimney; and it was as if the place, long quiescent, was once more making urgent appeal to be accepted in its radiant Mediterranean right. The pink roof commanded attention, the windows were wide to some phantom sweet south wind.

"There's Lady Pansy shaking something at the door—"

"Let's wait and smile and see if she sees us," Sarah said; waiting, smiling.

"It's rude, as if we're spying—"

"But everyone looks at the almond icing when they pass. She's shaking a *duster*, Philly."

Her head bound in a purple kerchief, Lady Pansy stepped forward into the rain. She stood there, her face upturned, her breathing adjusted to fresh air, paying tribute to it. Without the girls' having realized she had seen them, she suddenly hailed them. "Are you going to, or coming from, the town?"

"We're coming from—we've just been," Sarah called back promptly.

"Oh. . . . I thought you could have reminded the dairy about my cream, if you had been going that way." She breathed regularly and deeply again. "The telephone isn't in order yet."

"We don't mind going back—"

"I shouldn't think of allowing it," Lady Pansy shouted. "Perhaps you can tell me which is the early closing day?"

"Wednesday," Philly said shyly.

"*Why* all the shops must close on the same day I can't imagine. Like a lot of sheep, isn't it?"

"Yes, it is," Sarah said. (But why should sheep be supposed to close on the same day?) "Are you sure there's nothing we can do for you?" Boldly, she stepped through into the garden.

"Don't I know you?" Lady Pansy peered at them.

It had not struck Sarah that she might not. "We're the Fontaynes. You saw us at the Easter dance."

"So I did. Charming creatures," she said impersonally. Can she mean us? Perhaps she really *did* call me unquestionably a beauty. . . . "Are you staying here long?"

"My dears, I never *plan*. It is a very inconvenient house. There does not seem to be a maids' bathroom. Or is there?"

"I don't know." It seemed reasonable to think Lady Pansy should know better than they.

"And yet there is a *back* staircase. Most confusing. I came down it this morning, by mistake, and found myself in a *totally* unfamiliar room." A purple rivulet ran from her rain-wet kerchief. "You shouldn't be standing in the rain. Come in and I'll get you a hot drink."

"Oh, thank you!" Sarah rushed Philly forward.

Within, the house seemed to shrink. The expected spacious sun-filled interior was not to be found. The sea was no longer even a persuasive phantom. Chinese curios lay a deliberate pall of antiquity on the place; there was even a faint musky smell, but this was less Oriental than mouldy. Lady Pansy wore a housecoat that caught faintly at both indoor and outdoor atmosphere: dragons sporting on a blue background less celestial than fashionable Cannes. Her eye shadow nearly matched the blue, and her lips were the lacquer-red of the dragons' small protruding tongues. She was a symphony torn between two themes.

"I don't know *what* Virginia will say when she sees how the place is furnished. You remember my niece, Virginia Welwyn?"

"Is she coming to stay?" Sarah asked.

"She will pop down for little rests. I have brought some of her things. I'm trying to unpack them." She turned with a groping gesture to a large expensive dressing case on the floor of the sitting room. "But I cannot decide which room she would like."

"Hasn't she seen the house?"

"Only from the outside. Rather a pig in a poke, isn't it?" She began to take enthralling glass bottles and filmy wisps of silk and lace from the case. "This is an emergency bag, my niece says."

What an emergency, what a blissful emergency. . . . "Can I help?" Sarah asked.

"No, child. We'll leave it all. My back is aching." She threw off the kerchief and dragged a comb through her rusty hair. "How are Joey and Bunty?"

The girls stared.

"Bunty Oxford," Lady Pansy said impatiently.

"Mrs. Oxford!" They felt as shocked as if they had unwittingly seen their old friend in her bath.

"I always called her Bunty . . ."

Sarah and Philly could not look at each other for their vicarious sense of shame. "She's quite well," Sarah said, finally.

"And Joe Harbrittle?"

"I saw him the other day. He can't get past his middle chapters with Europe looking over his shoulder."

"Nonsense!" Lady Pansy said crisply. "It isn't as if he were anything, to begin with. A clerk, or perhaps a farmer." Her tone denied him the aristocratic solace of temperament. "I must go and tell him off," she added with precise vulgarity.

After a short silence, Sarah said: "I found part of my father's memoirs."

"What?" Lady Pansy delved into her niece's case again and brought out a pair of bedroom shoes disguised with a shaggy beard of feathers. "How odd these mules smell." Her floury-white nose buried itself in them. "It's the Schiaparelli scent; they *reek* of it. What a pity. They've soaked up the whole bottle."

This tragedy effectively silenced Sarah's attempt to repeat her own remark. "If Philly and I can be any help to you, just let us know," she said, instead.

"Thank you, I will. Sweet things. If you really haven't anything to do, one of you might slip in and varnish my nails occasionally."

"Yes, with pleasure." (But what an incredible request!) "I shall be going away to a job soon, but not quite yet."

"You won't like it," Lady Pansy said flatly. "I once had a hat shop and you simply couldn't possibly imagine anything more *horrid*." Her voice rose indignantly. "All the loathsome little receipts and things people expected! And the obscene *foundations* lying in wait for you all naked in the workroom! And all the terrible trivia of velvet bows and eye-veils and quills! No—for real soul-destroying disillusion, give me a hat shop."

"I'm not going into a hat shop," Sarah said.

"I should hope not." Angrily she sniffed at the exotic mules. "Horrible little raw foundations reminding you every day how hollow life is when you get down to its bare bones."

They did not fully discuss Lady Pansy until some time later, because they ran most of the way home in the rain and had no breath for speech;

and when they reached home they found an event to take their minds abruptly off the early morning. No sooner were they in and halfway upstairs to change their wet things than they saw Cruddles going across the hall to the front door. Sarah paused, hanging over the bannister, her hair falling forward over her eyes so that she gazed through a dark mesh to those lower dimensions that always seemed luminous and mysterious seen from above.

"There's a beautiful young man crossing the hall," she whispered to Philly, with as much excitement as was proper to one with a broken heart.

"Who is he?" Philly also peered.

"As if I knew. Don't push. He's gone into the drawing room—We can't leave him stranded there, but we can't go and drip rain all over him—"

"What was he like?" Philly played for time.

"Oh, tall, with shoulders, you know."

"Has Mother come back? We must do *something*—"

Tom slowly descended the stairs and paused beside them.

"What are you looking at?"

"Go away," Sarah said mechanically.

"Don't you want to know who's come?"

"You don't know."

"I do. That I do."

"Who?"

"It's Bronny's Press," he said grandly.

"*What?*"

"They telephoned to say they were on their way and could they come. From London. Bronny said Yes. They've come about her book."

"It's 'him,' not 'they,'" Sarah quibbled for quibbling's sake. What an end to a good morning! "Is she seeing him *alone*?"

"She said she'd kill me if I came near," Tom said moderately, leaving his sisters to draw their own conclusion from this.

"But he ought to be offered sherry or something," Sarah said, in transports of anxiety. "Oh, it's terrible!"

"Mother hasn't come in yet," Tom said, beginning in a quiet way to enjoy the drama.

"She wouldn't interfere, anyway," Sarah said bitterly. "She will never be anything but a perfect stepmother. Oh, I can't bear it! I must change my shoes and then I'll go down."

"Don't you think you ought to leave her alone—?" Philly began. But Sarah had already gone off to get ready to meet the Press.

It was a tragedy that Bronwen should have been singled out for such an honour. Where on *earth* did I put my wedding shoes . . . ? It would be impossible ever to live down an honest-to-goodness London newspaper pandering to Bronwen.

Sarah did not find anything strange in the fact that the young man should have appeared so dashing and attractive. Indeed, it would have shocked her to discover that such a fascinating profession as that of "newspapermen" might be made up in any degree by the dreary, the untidy, and the unillusioned. She could not know how favoured was Fontayne in having a fashionable young columnist to wait in person upon Bronwen's muse.

Accustomed though he was to meeting what he called celebrities in the rough as well as the smooth, the young columnist was nevertheless slightly disconcerted by his assignment of the day. He had been perfectly willing to put at her ease a little girl writer awed by a sudden taste of near-fame; but he had not bargained for a Bronwen. Really, he thought, really and truly it was as if he had been put back to his greenest cub reporter days; days when he had allowed the interviewee sometimes to get the upper hand of the interview; days when his carefully prepared questions had turned sour on him. But that was years ago. Nowadays he was free of those old conventions, and millionaires and miners, priests and princes, were shaped as he chose by his agile pen.

First, he was disappointed by the girl's appearance. When he had planned his story he had hoped for one of those suitable fairy children, not above a pretty prattle in spite of precocious talent; a dancing sprite of a creature, with curls and smiles and dimples. The lugubrious reality of Bronwen, swathed in her straight seaweed hair, her pale eyes imperturbable and her thick lips set—not to mention her yellow-ochre complexion and a somehow equally yellow-ochre expression—was his idea of an implacable interviewee. He was unnerved; forced back on the old question-and-answer routine.

"Did it take you very long to write your book?"

"I don't *write* like that, from beginning to end. I can't say how long a thing *takes*. After I've experienced things they have to get shaped again in my mind before they are any use."

Chewing her cud, he thought resentfully. "Oh, yes," he said sympathetically.

"You see, my book is partly my experiences in America and Europe, and also it is the way that different places affect my imagination."

"Oh, yes," he said again. "You write poetry, too?"

"Not 'too.' I write poetry *first*.'" She felt this, today.

"Oh, yes." One simply couldn't go on like this—Why the hell couldn't she prattle prettily and let him get his page in order? How could one make one's lead paragraphs out of this turgid tripe? "What about your next book? Are you going travelling again?"

"That depends on my father," she said, suddenly a prim child; but, from the columnist's point of view, not the right sort of child.

There was a heavy silence of moments.

"Don't you," Bronwen said, her indigestion making her feel disillusioned on his behalf as well as her own, "don't you ever get tired of having to—to suckle fools and chronicle small beer?"

"Well, I—" He eyed her suspiciously. "Well, you see *my* job happens to be highly specialized journalism. I pick and choose." He implied that she ought to feel highly honoured, but he didn't suppose it would register.

There was another silence.

"This is a nice old place," he said.

"Yes. I love it, but it's not really my home, of course, I am a wanderer by nature. I'm not here for *good*. Fontayne belongs to my stepmother. My father has just married again." She had a sudden fear that the Fontaynes might somehow creep into her interview. "But that," she added impressively, "is off the record."

It is doubtful whether the young columnist would have recovered from this display of extra-worldly wariness in one so young, had not Sarah chosen that moment to enter in upon Bronny's Press.

Without seeming to notice the young man, she went straight to her stepsister. "Mrs. Moody says if you still have indigestion she has a cure."

"What is it?" Bronwen asked hopefully.

"It's something fizzy and looks like mud, but I expect it's all right." Now Sarah eyed the columnist. "One ought to try anything once, don't you think?"

"Anything and everything," he said, more cheerfully. Remembering his job, he added: "How does it feel to have a famous little sister?"

"Very nice," Sarah said demurely.

"She's not my sister," Bronwen protested. She felt like Cinderella robbed of her fairy godmother. "I'm being interviewed, Sarah. It's rather private—"

"Do you want me to go?" Sarah asked innocently.

"Don't do that," the young man said. Why the hell couldn't this one have been the girl author? But it was always the way: brains and beauty simply wouldn't fit into one skin. "Miss Jones is too shy to tell me about herself, so maybe you'd do it for her."

It would be difficult to know whether Sarah or Bronwen was the more incensed by this suggestion.

"I am not in the least shy," Bronwen said. "But I cannot talk of my work unless I feel real sympathy for it."

"How about a picture, then?" the columnist said placatingly, but not going so far as to prove sympathy with the work. "I have my photographer in my car."

His emphasis on personal property was as marked as Mrs. Oxford's on "her" Bible and "her" parish, Sarah thought. Bronwen said, with dignity, that he could have a picture if he liked.

They stepped out onto the terrace, Bronwen immediately going in again to get a copy of her book. The rain had stopped and the air seemed to have a surprised sweetness. Sarah, her face still touched by an innocent glaze of rain moisture, looked as fresh and appealing as the cleared aspect of the day. Or so the columnist thought, writing a useless paragraph on her in his mind.

"You always live here?"

"Oh, yes." She sighed; rushed on, couldn't wait: "I suppose you haven't any jobs you could give me on your newspaper?"

"Jobs?" He sounded almost as shocked as Mr. Harbrittle. "They don't just grow on trees, you know," he said, faintly offended on behalf of his profession.

"Oh, of course not," she agreed with a sort of ecstatic humility. "But you see I have pressing reasons for wanting to get away from home, and I'd take *anything*." That wasn't right, either. "I mean, I'd be an office girl if there wasn't anything else. Though as a matter of fact I think I could write answers to those people who have problems, if I tried."

"That happens to be highly specialized work," he said, a shade stiffly. (He had done it himself, for a time.) "Anyway, a newspaper office wouldn't appeal to you." He relented because she was so young and so beautiful. "Why do you want to leave home?"

"It's all very complicated. I'd rather not go into details."

He was intrigued. If only she hadn't been so obviously what he marked off as upper class he might have got a cosy little story for his column out of her sorrows. But there was nothing to get hold of, here.

Even the flowers had a remote look, and the trees were far too tall and withdrawn. He couldn't get an "angle" on Fontayne.

Bronwen came out, wearing a white bow stuck childishly on the top of her head, and carrying a copy of her book. The columnist went to fetch his photographer. This individual, in a terrifying assortment of clothing, topped by an evil greasy hat of no known classification, began to focus on Sarah as a matter of course. "Li-mo-ri," he breathed through his cigarette. "A little more to the right," the columnist translated in a disapproving cultured tone, and Bronwen obediently dropped anchor with the right side of her jaw, at the same time lifting the left corner of her lip. Sarah, fascinated by the photographer, did not move. "Li-mo-ri," he said, with a deathly patience. "I can't," Bronwen said indignantly, interpreting for herself this time. "My neck is practically broken as it is." The photographer ground his cigarette into the middle of a plant on the terrace. "Fi-tout-wi-y-sels," he said resignedly.

The columnist took command. "There is no question of anyone fighting it out for themselves," he automatically translated, though for no one's benefit. "*This* is the young lady to be photographed."

The photographer re-focused on Bronwen, without comment, but his lingering professional pride was wounded. With the other he might have got something *like* a picture, but not with this one. Furious at his error, Bronwen didn't smile at the critical moment.

Tom, daring her threat to kill him, stole out to see what was going on here. The photographer appealed to him instantly as a being on a plane of happy improbability. "Can I see?" he asked ingratiatingly.

"Go away," Bronwen said stolidly.

"Is that the Press?" He pointed to the camera. The photographer leered at him, but Tom stood his ground without a qualm.

"Will you have a glass of sherry?" Sarah asked the columnist.

"Here come Mother and Mr. Jones," Tom said. "And if there isn't Mrs. Moody just off on her bikikle. Well I never. Well, I never did."

All this coming and going, and the mature homely words of Tom, proved too much for the columnist. Not even Sarah's beauty (and he *might* have managed to make a date by a judicious appearance of interest in the matter of finding her a job; to a cad—he thought in a high-minded aside—her request would have been a heaven-sent opportunity) . . . but no, not even the girl's beauty could hold him to the place.

"I'll have to get away now." He put out a compelling hand to Bronwen. "It's awfully kind of you to have been so frank, Miss Jones." Before she could react to this he had turned to Sarah. "Thank you so much," he said simply.

Not for being frank—for what, then? Her eyes questioned him, as she smiled. For being so pretty, he let his gaze answer. Bronwen, outside this give and take of glance, was angrily silent. She had intended presenting him with a signed copy, but he really didn't deserve it. The photographer turned on a heel ground deep in one of Elisabeth's pet blooms, swept his impedimenta to his anonymous bosom, and sped off to the car, stalked by a still enchanted Tom. The young columnist, too, departed just before Elisabeth came on to the terrace to ask who had called.

"I do wish," Sarah said, "that the sherry could be left in a fairly prominent position. By the time one has asked Cruddles and he has brought it—*if* he ever does—the occasion is usually stale and pointless. You do see, don't you, Mother?"

Elisabeth, who had not gathered whence this remark led, said, Yes, she did see, and that perhaps something could be done about it.

CHAPTER EIGHT

THUNDER CRACKED over Fontayne, dividing the summer against itself. The season was old and exhausted before its time, the June not yet gone. It was old in its phase and, the storm over, would have to start all over again. We shall all have to start all over again, Sarah thought with unseasonable bleakness.

And, as it happened, she did start all over again, with Cruddles stooping for the morning letters and the thunder dying away in pettish little rumbles into the distance.

"It will clear the air," Cruddles said, straightening his back with care. "Two for you. A letter and a postcard."

"I can see that—you don't have to tell me. Give them to me."

"All in good time." He sorted the rest of the letters in fans between his fingers.

"Cruddles!"

"Yes, Miss Sarah?" Blandly, he passed her morning mail to her.

So he *had* gone abroad—Not until this very moment had she been certain. His words swam dramatically before her eyes. How emotion can affect you, she was beginning to think, with a sad pride, when she realized the writing actually was blurred; the thunder rain must have touched it before it got safely through the letter box. Behind the blur was a further blur of non-committal sentences. It was very hot, he said. He would be back in London in a week or two, he said. And that was about all. Not even his name in full; just G.M. Nothing about the international situation or what he had been doing. Yet it was something; enough to set life going again.

She turned without interest to the letter, although the receiving of any letter was an event in itself. The note, typewritten, aroused some response in her. Fancy anyone *typing* to me. . . .

A few moments later she was tearing upstairs to see if Mrs. Moody had arrived yet. It *was* one of her days, wasn't it—?

The familiar sight of the seamstress, sitting squat on her sewing-room basket chair, warmed Sarah as if she were facing a glowing fire.

"You know that job I cut out of your paper?"

"Which one?" Mrs. Moody asked. The last few days had seen what she called a holy holocaust among the adverts in her picture paper.

"The office one. The one about the junior typist. They want me to go and have an interview."

"Do you mean they've answered your letter, duck? Well, I never did!" She laughed. "You'd have to be able to type."

"I can type. Well enough, I should think. It said two pounds a week and shorthand not essential."

"I should hope not, for two pounds a week."

"But I've never had two pounds a week in my life."

"You've never had to keep yourself in your life," Mrs. Moody reminded grimly.

"But two pounds a week!" Sarah said, enchanted. "And will I be good enough to call for an interview!"

She did not talk to Elisabeth about it until a suitable opportunity occurred. The flower room, of course, stacked with the blooms of the day, gathered by Elisabeth and the boy Digby in a successful collaboration.

Elisabeth had a faint misgiving that there was something in the air as well as the insistent flower perfume. It wasn't the world news, because she hadn't looked at the papers this morning, and yesterday's horrors had been quelled by sleep. Yesterday's dismays were (as she saw it) screened now by the lilies in white bud below the terrace. Yesterday was there, mastered, behind green stems rising in long slender lines; and today was scarcely born until she put on her glasses and peered at the news. Yet, in spite of these timeless moments of bliss (selfish moments, she rebuked herself sternly), there was something in the air.

"What is it, Sarah?" She sighed faintly into the shaping pattern of colour and form beneath her hands. If only they would go to Julian, who whisked difficulties out of the way, as if he held a magician's actual wand rather than a musician's figurative baton; but no, they were stubborn, and Sarah was particularly so.

"How lovely you smell," Sarah said ingratiatingly. It was her highest compliment to anyone. Yet how useless Mother was, never having even learned to type; just dabbling away with flowers, and marrying people, and not making anything of her pretty looks.

"Philly has gone into the town. What are Bronwen and Peter doing? Is Tom with Miss James?"

"Yes, he is. I don't know what they're doing. Bronwen has been worse than ever since her book came out."

"You were very brusque and harsh about it," Elisabeth said severely.

"I wasn't brusque and harsh; and, alternatively, if I *were*, she asked for it," Sarah paraphrased the legal language of a recent enthrallingly sordid breach of promise case in Mrs. Moody's ever-to-be-depended-on picture paper.

"I do wish you would try to be nicer." The legal term, unfortunately, had no effect on Elisabeth.

"If you want me to be nice, we shouldn't all be cooped up here."

"I don't see how anyone could feel *cooped* at Fontayne," Elisabeth said gently.

"It's a spiritual cooping," Sarah retorted loftily.

"So you will be glad when we leave Fontayne?"

"But surely you'll never really leave it? Not now that you have plenty of money to go at?"

"What makes you think I have plenty of money . . . to go at?" The pause before the repetition of Sarah's words was a rebuke in itself.

"If you can't spend it, I don't know who can—"

"Whose money, Sarah?"

"Why, Mr. Jones's . . . Julian's."

"Why do you think he has a lot of money?"

"Well, he—he must have." This is awful—"It's obvious. Dashing around America and all that."

"That was his work. And he had to leave off working because he was ill. And he doesn't know yet when he will be able to work again."

"You don't mean—you can't mean—that the Joneses are living on *us*!"

"Of course I don't mean that. But I want you to put out of your mind the idea that Julian is *rich*."

"I might have known they would *riot* away their money as soon as they made it."

"That is not true. Julian has enough to live on in a way to suit himself."

"How selfish—"

"Not at all. It is my way, too. He likes Fontayne, but we both think it would be best to sell it if there comes an opportunity."

"And then I suppose you will go rioting—I mean, then you will go round the world with him?"

"We can't tell what will happen," Elisabeth said soberly, thinking of the unread morning paper.

"You won't need to take me, for one. I'm getting a job." She was no longer even apologetic; the stripping from Mr. Jones of his phantom wealth had at least done that.

"We'll have to see about that—" Elisabeth began, her admirable decisiveness weakening.

"But I've *got* it now." She produced the important typewritten note.

"Darling, you'd hate it," Elisabeth said, when she had read it. That she could not imagine anyone in his senses employing Sarah, she did not bother to add.

"I shall give it a trial," the girl said, with dignity.

"But it would mean you had to live in London and *that* would mean you had to live alone."

"I would come down sometimes at the Week End," Sarah promised kindly.

It doesn't matter because it won't happen, Elisabeth thought; but *how* can she have changed so much? I don't believe it's really Julian—nor Bronwen and Peter—but something much deeper, something . . . shattering.

"I can go for the interview, anyway, can't I?"

"I'd like to talk to Julian, darling—"

"It has nothing to do with him."

"But what use is it, darling? It's not as if you could live on the money—"

"Of course I could. Besides, I shall have to earn my living if our—our circumstances are so straitened."

Elisabeth did not even smile at this formal description; but neither did she protest any more. "If you *did* go for the interview"—"did" was so much more happily vague than "do"—"Bracken would have to meet you and go with you."

"He gets all the dirty jobs," Sarah said, but not protesting too much, having gained at least half a point.

Bronwen waited until Tom had finished his morning lessons at noon and then crept into the deserted schoolroom and pulled the old gramophone from its hiding. One of the old scratchy records grating and wheezing its way through some horrible hackneyed tune was the only thing that would fit in with her melancholy mood. Nothing had turned out as she had hoped. Her book had come out; but, so far as her present disillusion was concerned, it might as well have gone out, too. The first review, nice but all too tiny, seemed far in the background of experience now; and the lovely fillip of her name blacked vividly into the Sunday advertisement scarcely thrilled in retrospect. Fast on this pleasantness had come what should have been the ultimate triumph: a personal interview with the London Press. It was all the more tantalizing that it should have turned out, in some ways, all that she could have wished. A headline that said Child Gulliver Writes Of Her Travels. (Of course that was absurd, utterly absurd, because there had been nothing fantastic about her adventures themselves; but, still, it was a headline.) But then the awful photograph that the awful man had taken; her face burrowed in a sullen shadow of hair, her eyes and lips scowling. Worst of all, final indignity, Ernest stalking perkily across her legs, head high and preening, for all the world as if his rightful place were at her side. Indeed, the Press had taken this for granted, captioning the picture: Miss Bronwen Jones, the child author, with her favourite cat. . . .

Favourite!—as if there were other lesser Ernests waiting in a long line for her first affection! . . . Apart from this, the columnist had somehow let her down. He had two styles of writing, humorous and sincere; and, monstrously, had chosen finally to see her through a veil of humour, his complimentary phrases lined with laughter. You couldn't put your finger on it and say exactly what it was, but nevertheless there it *was*. . . .

The gramophone gave a stifled groan and the tune came to an end. Bronwen felt too dispirited to wind up the spring again.

*   *   *   *   *

"So, in any case, there would be nothing for it but to go away," Sarah explained to Philly.

Philly was silent, finding it difficult to believe in a Mr. Jones who wasn't rich. She said at last:

"I suppose it serves us right for thinking as a matter of course that we were marrying money."

"No, it's entirely his fault. He ought to have told us. Not that I care," Sarah said indifferently. "I can earn my own money."

Don't go, don't go . . . Philly's heart entreated; but she was too wise to say anything.

Naturally one had to tell Mrs. Oxford; have tea with her and put the whole reckless affair of the job on a proper basis of respectability.

"But tomorrow!" Mrs. Oxford said. "It is so sudden."

"I may not get it," Sarah said, but not believing this.

"It is all far from suitable, dear." She raised the silver teapot with a symbolic gesture. "And one cannot evade one's natural environment so easily as that."

She was all symbols. Sarah sank unprotestingly into the complicated simplicity of life as her old friend saw it. Even the heavy grey-green lustreless stockings, glancing out in brief peeps beneath the weight of skirt and underskirt, were some special symbols of caste and creed, setting her apart from lesser women.

"And then, dear, there are all the attendant snags that dog the steps of independent young women."

"I'd like to be dogged by a snag," Sarah said absurdly, feeling free and happy today, wanting to laugh.

"People—men, I might say," Mrs. Oxford pressed on bravely, "seldom take into account the delicacy of one's nurturing, however well-bred they may perceive a girl to be." Her words aroused a wistful hope in Sarah that life might turn out more exciting than she had expected.

"A pretty face—" the old lady went on.

"What is this about a pretty face?" Lady Pansy, in a short red-fox coatee (missing the shade of her hair by an inch, as it were) to guard against the sudden nip in the summer, swept unceremoniously into the room. "Yes, it *is* a pretty face." She nodded at Sarah. "What do you use, sweet girl?"

"She has too much regard for her complexion to use anything but a good soap and a little rainwater, I should hope," Mrs. Oxford answered for Sarah. "Sit down and have a cup of tea, Pansy. I regret to say that our dear Sarah is leaving us."

"Really?" Lady Pansy sought briefly for a heavenly sprouting of wings and halo, but almost immediately gave up that idea.

"For a job in London," Sarah supplied.

"Oh, the hat shop. Oh, dear, what a pity. I did warn you against it. However, I'll give you some introductions."

"*Will* you?" Oh, let them be more *concrete* than the hot drink she promised us the other morning. . . .

"You must go and see Virginia. You know where she lives?"

"No-o . . ." This wasn't very concrete.

"Oh, yes, you must. That block of flats facing the park. Windows, windows, everywhere. *Exactly* like living in a glass-house—but she doesn't seem to mind. And all mirrors inside. But that wouldn't worry you, at your age. Yes, of course you must see Virginia."

Peter received the news of the job with a roar of laughter. He had seemed rather depressed and *distrait* lately, which made the merriment the more marked.

"It's incredible," he said, "that you should do this entirely of your own accord. *Typing.* You *can't* type, by any chance, I suppose?"

"Of course I can," she said haughtily. "It is much better to work than to moon around the way you do."

"Do mind your own business, there's a dear Sarah," he said with cruel kindliness.

"And you mind yours, about me."

"Well, we won't *wrangle*." He drifted off with his beautiful loping step.

Breakfast was early, so that Sarah could catch the "good" London train. She couldn't eat, naturally, but the undivided attention of all at table was mercifully deflected from her, for Bronwen had another review this morning. Its presence, stuck on a green slip of paper, subtly distorted breakfast, so that even Tom's dish of prunes seemed in the thrall of literature. Bronwen read it to herself as she sipped her coffee and munched toast, but did not for some while offer it for general inspection.

"Bracken will meet you at the station, darling," Elisabeth said, whispering. Bronwen's reviews had the same effect on her as being in church had.

"I know." Sarah nodded. Don't rub it in that I can't be let out alone.
. . . Nervously, she lighted a cigarette.

"Darling, I shouldn't smoke without eating first." Elisabeth had,
after all, noticed the lack of appetite.

"Oh, it's a horrid little cigarette," Tom said, rubbing his eyes as if
they were full of smoke.

"Do leave me alone, everyone," Sarah said desperately.

She was excessively neatly dressed, as she imagined the perfect secretary should be; her old black suit scrupulously brushed, a white blouse
which she thought of as 'crisp,' new stockings, and the wedding shoes.

"Would you care to read this, Daddy?" Bronwen asked, passing the
review across the table.

Mr. Jones cast his gentle sombre gaze upon the words, meditatively
stroking the silken ledge of his moustache as he did so.

"Of course the man doesn't understand properly," Bronwen said.

"They never do, quite, my dear," he smiled.

"Is it rude?" Tom asked morbidly.

Mr. Jones passed the review to Elisabeth who murmured her way
through it, without committing herself to actual words. Then Peter
languidly picked it up.

"M'm . . . He seems to like your prose all right, Bronwen, but your
verse isn't his cup of tea."

"Not his cup of tea!" Tom seized on his own cup, jealously, with
both hands. "Of course it isn't his little old cup of tea!"

Sarah and Philly exchanged glances. They felt vindicated in their
lack of appreciation for Bronny's poems. Sarah felt it to be a good omen
for the day.

"I must go." She swept to her feet without waiting to see if Bronwen appeared discomfited by her brother's betrayal of the reviewer's
opinions.

"There's plenty of time yet," Elisabeth said.

"No, there isn't. I haven't done my face," Sarah said fiercely.

Bracken was waiting when the train drew into the station. He wore
a clumsy brown overcoat that made him look as if he were in disguise.
Behind his glasses his eyes were clear, cold, and kind.

"There was no need for you to meet me," Sarah said breathlessly,
tumbling out into his arms.

"Of course there wasn't," he agreed, rather taking the wind out of
her sails.

"I've found some more of the memoirs," she flung at him, as they pushed their way out of the station. "Only yesterday—I didn't tell anyone. When I get settled down here, I'm going to fit it all together and see if it makes a whole."

He nodded encouragingly. What an unsuitable typist, he thought. "You'll have lunch with me?" he asked formally.

"Yes; my appointment isn't until three," she said grandly. "Where could we go?"

"Anywhere you like," he said expansively.

"It doesn't matter where." Sir Giles wasn't in London, there was no chance of coming across him lunching fashionably, so it didn't matter where. "Somewhere with music, perhaps," she suggested tentatively. "How lovely London looks," she said as they passed from the green light of the station to the pale sunlight beyond.

He could not imagine anything less lovely than the drab grey streets here; but there was a bright flower barrow not far off, so maybe it was that which gave her the illusion of grace. He hailed a taxi and hurried her away to surroundings of more authentic charm.

She stared out of the window, not speaking. I am in London alone, except for Bracken, who hardly counts, because he leaves you alone. He *does* leave you alone, severely alone, even in his thoughts sometimes.

"Where did you get that funny coat?" she broke her silence.

"I brought it with me from the States."

"I thought so." She smiled briefly. "Your clothes *are* funny and American, although *you* don't seem very much so."

"Less than a gangster, anyway?" he suggested gravely.

"Much less." She laughed suddenly. "Do you disapprove of my taking this job?"

"Not if you want it."

"I do want it. Not because I like working, but because I want to get away from everything." She wanted him to be impressed; wanted, even to confess the story of her love to him.

They reached the restaurant which he thought would please her: colourful without too definite a vulgarity, vivid flimsy fare that she would find satisfying. Her nose quivered with delight as they went in; her body, moving close to his, seemed taut and brittle with urgent acceptance of all that the moment offered.

"I have introductions from Lady Pansy to people in London." She opened her powder compact as they sat down and glanced in its mirror to see if her prim-seductive little black velvet hat were in danger of sliding off the back of her head. "And then I expect I shall see Sir Giles Merrick when he comes home."

Bracken was ordering the lunch, and did not take up the invitation of her remark. The pale pretty room took her eye. "Could we have a little wine, Bracken?" she asked wistfully.

"By all means, if you don't think it might endanger the securing of the job."

"I'm sure it wouldn't."

The lunch was far more successful than either of them had expected it to be. She could close her eyes, in swift self-deceiving winks, and imagine herself with someone really exciting, not Bracken with his red tie, his cold eyes, his soft voice, the man who had written fairy tales for her when she was a child.

Over coffee and a cigarette he seemed so perfectly sympathetic with her mood that she decided to risk confiding in him wholly.

"Bracken, do you believe love is very important?" she delicately led up to it.

"Very," he said.

"I wasn't sure you would. You often seem so remote, so . . . polar."

He smiled. "Do you mean *love*, or the single track of romantic love, young love, calf-love?"

"I mean love. There's only one sort really, when you get down to it," she said blithely. "Being *in* love, you know." (The sort that Mrs. Moody had horridly classified as "sex". . . .)

"I'm not a very good modern authority on that kind," he said mildly.

She sighed. The summer light was caught in sea-green swirls within the restaurant window curtains. Silver glowed and glass shone. The people at the other tables stood out with a remarkable clarity, as if each group made a separate tableau, not animated yet infinitely expressive. The wine had not gone to her head, of course, but it seemed in some way to have heightened her thoughts.

"You must have a very dull life," she said compassionately.

"Not in the least," Bracken said. "You know, we have lingered rather long. We shall have to be thinking of your appointment. Will you meet me for tea when it is all over?"

She hesitated. It would make it seem more than ever that she wasn't capable of taking a step by herself; but on the other hand tea with Bracken might be as good as lunch with him had been.

"Yes, if you like," she said graciously. She rose from the table. "There's a moustache like Mr. Jones's over there. On the right, by the door. Now that sort of love I do *not* approve of," she said decisively.

Bracken was left to decide for himself whether she meant moustached love, middle-aged love, or step-parental love.

A slight shower came on while he was waiting for her at the meeting place they had arranged. London briefly quickened in new movement, figures scurrying, umbrellas opened, mackintoshes appearing. He waited patiently, expecting her to be late. Then, with the rain ceasing, and little pink puffs of cloud twinkling across the sky, he saw her coming. She came headlong, one long hand tenderly holding the back of the ridiculous hat which might at any moment leave its perilous perch; and she came with a smile that was merely herself, telling nothing of either victory or brave defeat, only dwelling on tea to come. She waved to him, which was quite unnecessary, as she was almost up to him by then, and her fingers practically caught his nose in her salute.

"The situation seems rather bad," she said in a voice of fantastic sobriety, as she danced up to him. "I've been reading the newspaper placards from the bus. (I *did* get the right bus.) You'd think someone could do something about it." She thought almost indignantly of Sir Giles, rushing off to keep some foreign fires burning instead of attending to the home ones.

"Yes." Bracken brushed the situation aside, waiting for her personal news.

"Aren't you *upset*?"

"Nobody would pay any attention to my plans for world salvation, I'm afraid, so I reserve the right not to be upset at this particular moment."

"How *selfish* of you." She was shocked. One had always believed in Bracken's ungoody-goody goodness, in all circumstances of living.

"At this moment, I want to hear how you got on."

"Oh, yes, of course. Oh, I got it."

"You got it!" His unflattering amazement turned to unflattering suspicion. His mind was as squeamishly filled with fears of white slave traffic as Mrs. Oxford's might have been had she been present to hear Sarah's words. "Whom did you see?"

"Oh, quite a nice woman, who said I would do."

"Just like that?"

"Yes," Sarah said simply. "She said seeing that I was so young I wouldn't mind doing little odd jobs around the office sometimes."

"And would you?"

"Oh, no."

For the moment she was unquenchable; so he took her in to tea. It had been beyond possibility that she would get the job; but she had got it. There was really nothing left to say on the subject. He did not even make the effort to inquire when she began work. Neither did he comment on the favourable fact that a woman appeared to be in charge of the office.

A tenuous simpering orchestra of strings greeted them as they entered the warm friendly interior of the café. The atmosphere was of after-cinema dalliance, a rest and some tea after shopping, respectable rendezvous of friends and relations. Flower decoration burst irrepressibly all over the place. The squeezed appearance of too-abundant blooms in corsets of too-narrow vases would have been enough to make Elisabeth faint. Trolleys of opulent oozing cakes and mountains of sandwiches took Sarah's politely indifferent gaze, as they passed to their seats.

"Oh, but this is lovely!" she said radiantly. "I am sure I am going to be happy in London." She added, a sober line running through the radiance: "As happy as it is possible for me to be."

He smiled at her across the table decorously mounted with palest pink china. He had a lovely smile, she thought without sentiment; but its vanishing left him all the more remote; its fading was the sun going in over the sea, leaving the water a dead grey. Yet he never lectured, never tried to reform; and he entered whole-heartedly into the seriousness of choosing sandwiches from the trolley.

"How Philly would enjoy this," she said warmly. She poured the tea, but did it scarcely to the manner born, her beautiful ineffectual hands dabbling vaguely from jugs to teapot.

It made her sad to think of Bracken going back to America, with the probability that they would not see him again for a year or two. The past seemed to flow through her on waltz waves wafted from the little orchestra. Her egg-and-cress sandwich took her back, back, in the first bite, to a similar wet-dry eggy taste on a blowy spring picnic long ago, herself lost in a dream of Bracken's fairy tales, the friendly picnic sounds subdued to the cold thrilling terror of a wizard's spells.

"I don't think your fairy tales could have been very good for young children," she said comfortably.

"I don't suppose so," he agreed.

Dreamily, she looked through him, still conjuring the past. Back to the time when Bracken was some sort of professor at one of those smaller and improbable American universities, and of his suddenly throwing all that up and going off as an explorer and then never returning to his old life. Perhaps he *was* rather romantic in his own way. The music was soft and drowsy now, somehow seeming to dwell on Bracken's past, bringing to life the soft drowsy town hidden deep in American mysteries of habit and custom, not old, but veiled over with sympathies for things old. Sarah stared into her cup. . . . I see eucalyptus trees—I don't know why—and very broad white pavements with very clearly marked light and shadow. . . .

"You call pavements 'sidewalks' in America. . . ." she said, out of her dream.

"Yes," he said, not knowing whether her words were a question or an explanation. He made no attempt to seek the dream leaps of her mind. "Will you have any more sandwiches?"

"I'll have nothing more." She gave up the idea of cake, suddenly afraid that Bracken might see her as a mere Philly or Christopher. She felt that her vivid illuminated swift vision of him entitled him to some adult mark of respect from her.

She chose to pause with her appetite still in full flight, as it were; to refuse cake, in tribute to Bracken's arrival at full-grown estate in her mind.

"Yes, I had lunch with Bracken and tea with him, *and* he put me on the train," Sarah repeated patiently. She was the centre of interest, yet lacking the dignity the position should have given her.

"Then that was all very satisfactory, so far as it went," poor Elisabeth sighed.

"It went much farther. I got the job."

"Yes, darling, but—"

"There is no 'but' about it. I begin on Monday."

"But you have nowhere to live!"

"Oh, yes, I have. Before I met Bracken for tea, I went and found myself a room." Her own resource still dazzled her. Never mind that the address that Mrs. Billing at the office had given her had proved to be a warren of heart-sinkingly tiny, dreary, grudging little rooms. Never mind that, when she had achieved her purpose of finding somewhere to live in London.

"Julian and I will have to go and see what it is like."

Sarah frowned. "There's no need to interfere with people's liberties. It is a nice room. Anyway, I can always leave it if I don't like it."

"You will have to have an allowance, in any case, darling, so you might as well have somewhere pleasant to live," Elisabeth insisted, still suspicious.

Sarah said nothing. But she had firmly resolved to accept not a penny from home. *Anyone* could live on two pounds a week, surely, if they were broad-minded enough not to mind being a tiny bit squalid occasionally.

It was difficult to realize it had really happened. Philly had never noticed before that Fontayne could give such an empty feeling, as if dwarfs moved reluctantly and insignificantly through its far too spacious area. Tiny dwarf groups going their own ways, never warmly mingling: Tom ringing the changes of hours with Miss James and Mrs. Moody, dividing his work and play; Mother and Mr. Jones still depressingly self-contained in their garden honeymoon; Bronwen perpetually frowning into little notebooks; Peter always off on his own. In a Sarah-less, Christopher-less world Philly wandered bereft. Even the Rudges had gone away for a holiday on some of the triplets' money. It didn't seem a very good idea, with the new Rudge still only on the way; but that wasn't any business of yours, as Sarah would have pointed out if she had still been here. You came back and back to the stumping fact that Sarah wasn't here. She had gone away on Sunday and now it was Tuesday, with the awful weight of Monday's undigested wholeness left upon you.

Philly put on her wide-brimmed straw hat and walked aimlessly down to the town. She took her letter to Christopher (telling him of Sarah's flight) to send off from the post office, but this was scarcely an excuse in itself. The long street looked secret to her eye, as if only Sarah's presence had given it real life. She found a few coppers in the pocket of her light coat (she couldn't remember how they had got there) and went in to spend them at the haberdashery on a couple of reels of sewing silk; but more for the sake of talking to someone than because she really wanted them.

Mrs. Pratt was in one of her bad moods, as it happened, so Philly didn't tell her about Sarah. And when Mrs. Pratt snapped: "Would there be anything more?" she felt ashamed at having to admit that there wouldn't be. The only propitiatory thing she could suggest in excuse was that Mrs. Pratt needn't wrap them up.

With the red and the white reels in her hand, Philly went out to the street, to find her big straw hat had justified the day and that the sun had come out. Bob Norbett also came out; from the wine shop, to talk to her.

"Sarah's gone away to work," she burst out unhappily.

"You don't say!"

"I do. It's true."

"Well, cheer up, Miss Philly. Work is good for everybody, you know."

"Not for Sarah," Philly denied, with conviction.

"What is she doing, if it isn't rude to ask?"

"She's a secretary," Philly said, in her simplicity believing this.

"Well, that's good work, you know," Bob said, probably thinking of some of his own voluntary charitable labours in that field.

"But she can't spell," Philly said miserably. "None of us can. It's a family failing." She added scrupulously: "Not including the Joneses, of course!"

"You're lonely, that's what it is, Miss Philly. Why not come and help in our Socials? Read to the kiddies or something. You like kiddies, don't you?"

"No—yes, I mean." She couldn't admit to Bob that "kiddies" was one of the words she and Sarah felt you simply couldn't use, like another of Bob's favourites: "bubbly," for champagne. She was afraid that Bronwen would wholeheartedly agree with them on these points, but even that could not alter her opinion. Small children and babies she usually did get on with very well, but for "kiddies" she had almost as haughtily instinctive a distaste as Sarah could have felt.

"You'd like it, I daresay."

"But I couldn't read aloud!" Even this supporting of a conversation with Bob, without help, was an ordeal.

"It's surprising what you can do when you try, Miss Philly. Well, I must get along. Give my regards to Miss Sarah when you're writing."

"And what will she do if a war comes on suddenly?" Philly demanded, as if she spoke of a shower of rain.

"Ah, that's where none of us knows where we'll be," Bob said darkly. "I don't know, I'm shu-er." He stared up and down the tranquil street, his eye just pausing to see how his window display of soft drinks looked. "No, that's what none of us knows. It's not given to any of us to comprehend the workings of the Universe."

They were not very cheering words, Philly felt, to speed her on her way home.

Sarah could scarcely believe it possible for anyone to feel so tired without collapsing altogether. This, after only two days of it. When one thought of it, days fading into weeks and weeks into years, it was enough to make one faint on the spot. Years of Mrs. Billing being play-ful and overpowering, years of walking the stone steps to that fifth-floor office—because one was afraid to work the lift oneself—and year after weary year of listening to the other two girls being dashing and supe-rior. For of course there was no question of giving up and going back to Fontayne. . . .

Not that there weren't comforting aspects of the affair. One of the comforts was that Mrs. Billing's office was in such a muddle already that Sarah's presence could do little to make it worse. It appeared that Mrs. Billing ran some sort of business that she referred to as "mail order," which necessitated the use of only one chaotic little room with an adjoin-ing apology of a room for the two dashing superior girls, one of whom Mrs. Billing spoke of as her "secretary" and the other the "first typist."

So far, Sarah had not had to look a typewriter in the keys. Her time had been employed in wrapping up horrid little samples of Mrs. Billing's patent medicinal and facial-unguent wares. So politely non-committal were the completed packages that Sarah had misgiv-ings that many who had sent for digestive aids would find themselves saddled with undesired complexion packs. The typewriters clacked professionally on while she continued unambitiously wrapping and sealing—with Mrs. Billing, enormous and stifling, usually close at hand, nodding and smiling from the sheath of her huge sustaining bulk. There was no mistake, no incongruity, in Mrs. Billing from head to foot. Her bosom was immense, but so were her feet; her mouth was a great clown-red balloon-tyre effect, but her great pale prominent eyes were not abashed; her hair was an uncut brassy crowning glory, but the brave flare of her ginger eyebrows was not dismayed. When she stood up she almost hit the ceiling, and when she sat down she overflowed her chair with a generous abandon.

"I've taken quite a fancy to you, dear," she told Sarah, before the first morning was out. "Sometimes you have to work a bit overtime, but you won't mind that. In business you have to take the ups with the downs."

Sarah said, No, she wouldn't mind.

At the end of the exhausting day her room lay in wait for her. She came in and stood staring at its already painfully familiar unfamiliarity. Her bed looked as if it were standing on stilts, the meagre coverlet leaving its bare enamelled shanks horribly naked. A colossal old washstand dwarfed the narrow room, its marbled slab seeming unnaturally varicose-veined. A dismal flowered curtain concealed the corner where her clothes hung. Cold grey linoleum ran in hillocks across the floor, a dreary sea-sicky undulation. The little window seemed to grudge the light.

Sarah could not have said with truth that she cared for her room.

She lay on her bed, when she came in, and took from a paper bag the food she had brought for her supper. In spite of her independence, she put off the ordeal of going out again at night to find some café in which to eat. The thick buttered roll, with a layer of aggressive mouse-trap cheese running through it, she ate with surprised relish. The banana to follow tasted somewhat stodgy; she was glad she had got an apple, too.

When she had finished her meal she thought she would write a gay casual note home, and then begin to fit together the erratic parts of her father's memoirs. But first she had to spend some time brushing crumbs off her bed (one mustn't use it as a dining room again) and then she drifted to the scrap of mirror over the terrible washstand, and began to comb her hair into a new style which made her look older and more responsible. More lipstick might be used, too, but not, of course, those astonishing blots of rouge worn high on the four cheeks of her young fellow workers.

By the time she had finished her experiments, she had begun to feel extremely tired. The idea of going to bed seemed extraordinarily pleasant. Just to drift away and forget about everything . . . forget Mrs. Billing and overtime and samples, and simply drift on a cloud of dream. . . .

Peter, when he paused to think of it, felt sorry for Philly. He congratulated himself on the delicacy of his perception that, for Philly, Sarah's departure might have been years rather than days ago.

He found her sitting on the terrace, reading one of her perennial boys' papers, her cat on her knee. She gave a little jump when he suddenly spoke. Bad, he thought; no natural ease, no *savoir-faire*.

"You ought to be out meeting more people," he said, without preamble. "Sixteen!—and scarcely been out of your native village. It is a great mistake, you know. It leads to all kinds of things."

What kind of things? . . . Philly wondered unhappily. "Where is there to go?" she asked politely.

"Nowhere here," he admitted gloomily. "It really is too bad." Too bad about his father's heart, in more ways than one; too bad about his own interrupted inspiration; too bad that Sarah's preposterous wild-goose-chase of a job should leave one to feel more aimless than ever. "It can't go on, this summer idyll," he said scathingly, aloud. "It is time to be *getting* somewhere. Obviously nothing is going to be done through July and August, but after that—"

After that? Philly hung alertly on the pause, but nothing else was said. After that? Why, Mr. Jones might persuade Mother to do anything; to follow him to the ends of the earth, with all of them; to Hollywood, perhaps, to live in the bowl. . . . She saw it as being like the dwarfs' house in *Snow White*, everyone running around to brisk tunes. . . . And Fontayne left empty, quite alone, the winds going through it.

"It is bad for you to have no male society," Peter went on. "You don't want to grow up *gauche* and awkward, Philly. In America, girls of your age are already quite sophisticated. They feel no ridiculous inhibitions in the company of young men. They simply accept them. You do see that is the right, the *only*, attitude, don't you?"

"Yes," Philly agreed miserably.

"I'm glad you do." He gave her his warm alive smile approvingly. "And you're quite lovely in your way, you know. You ought to care about your appearance more. That childish little slide pulling back your hair is a mistake. You're sure you don't mind my talking like this?"

"No," Philly said.

"If you took more interest in yourself you'd soon find people took more interest in you."

"Yes. . . ." It was like those beauty notes Sarah read in Mrs. Moody's paper. She had never thought anyone truly said things like that.

It was rather cold on the terrace. Peter smiled, shivered, and departed. Philly sat on, watching a faint prickle of goose-flesh spread over her fair arms. She tried to go back to reading her paper, but it was no use, she couldn't concentrate.

Sarah had occasion to type an address on an envelope, while Mrs. Billing was towering near her.

"Not very snappy at it, are you dear?" she said, her tone not going anything like so far as to suggest Sarah had got the job under false pretences.

"I'm not used to this machine," Sarah said weakly.

"Oh, well, I've plenty of other little jobs for you to be getting on with," Mrs. Billing said kindly, leaning slightly, like some majestic Pisa. "Cheer up, dear. You'll make out all right. Always keep a smile handy, that's what I say. That's right! Our sunshine girl, that's what she is—eh?" Mrs. Billing wagged an immense roguish finger and thundered into the other room.

"Our sunshine Sally," Lily, the first typist, said, devastatingly solemn.

Sarah's smile remained, frozen stiff.

"Where did you learn to twist people round your little finger, Sally?" Joan, the secretary, inquired sarcastically.

"I haven't—I don't—" Sarah said.

"You have to do something, I suppose, to make up for lack of efficiency," Lily said. "What's on your mind?"

"I was wondering where you went for lunch," Sarah said, striving to keep friendly.

"Why?"

"Because I haven't found anywhere convenient yet." Somehow or other she had managed to spend far more than she expected. The five pounds that Mother had forced on her before she left (one knew in one's bones that it had come straight from Mr. Jones) was vanishing at a spectacular rate. London was an extraordinary place for *dwindling* money; the two pounds a week already seemed far less munificent.

"You can come along with me, if you like," Joan said unenthusiastically. "If it's good enough for you."

"Of course." She blushed.

"Though I can't think why you couldn't find a place yourself, considering there are thousands of Lyon's," Joan added witheringly.

Philly saw Lady Pansy standing in the front courtyard of the almond icing, where she had stood that other day before Sarah went away. But it was not raining today.

"Hello, there! It's my young friend, isn't it?" The voice was imperious. "Come in and talk to me."

Reluctantly, Philly entered the garden.

"Sweet creature. How pretty you look."

"I'm not Sarah, you know." She wanted there to be no mistake.

"Nobody said you were. Just come in and . . ." She beckoned with her floating veils.

"Do you want me to fetch you some cream?" Philly asked, nervousness taking her back to a former request of Lady Pansy.

"Cream?" Lady Pansy raised her powder-camouflaged eyebrows. "I want you to look at this." She thrust a little bottle at Philly. "Do you think that's too dark?"

"I—I don't know—" Oh, it was nail polish. . . .

"Just run over my nails, then. Just one coat."

Philly, who had never performed this formidable task in her life, took the little brush in a trembling hand. It was like being asked to paint a masterpiece without having had even one painting lesson.

"Pretty child," Lady Pansy said, holding out her hand. "Why don't you do your hair up on top?"

First Peter sneering at her slide, and now Lady Pansy—

She made a tentative blob of scarlet in the centre of a broad thumbnail and carefully skirted the half-moon. "Will that do?"

"Perfectly, darling. When you've finished I'll do your hair for you. I'm very good on hair."

There was no escape. When the nail operation was completed—the final effect a little blurred—an excuse about its being nearly time for lunch was not accepted by Lady Pansy.

"It will take no time," she said. "I have my little spirit lamp."

So irresistibly did this suggest Aladdin and a genie (the more so for the Chinese lacquer finish to the inside of the house) that Philly waited to see what it could be. The result was not only disappointing, but also embarrassing. A smell of methylated spirit, a fainter one of burnt hair, and the sight of Lady Pansy wielding clanking old-time curling tongs and, finally, the sight of your own head in a mirror, an outbreak of golden-brown curls above your forehead, frizzed high like froth.

"There!" Lady Pansy said.

The "there" was unmistakably one of success achieved. It was a good thing she said it; otherwise Philly would have begun to say on no account to bother, and that it really didn't matter at all, she could wash her hair when she got home. Given her cue she said instead: "Thank you very much."

She got away, then; ran flying away from the almond icing into the road.

"Where are you going?" a robust voice demanded.

It was Mr. Lupin.

"We haven't met for a long time," he said. His eye ran up her appreciatively until it came to her hair. "The gods defend us! What have they done to you!"

"I didn't do it—" She returned his dismayed stare.

"I should hope not! Another victory over nature. This is what civilization has come to."

If he meant that the last straw that broke the back of civilization was her hair, Philly thought the statement somewhat sweeping.

"You must get it put right at once. At once. Then I shall paint you."

For a brief desperate moment Philly wondered if she could contrive to wear her hair like this for ever, just so that Mr. Lupin might be thwarted.

"We haven't seen you, lately," she said meekly.

"No." His old-baby face turned glum. "No. . . . I've been seeking the past. Bah!—I'm nothing but a sentimentalist."

Philly noted with awe that he really did say "bah!"

"The past's crock of gold you'll never find, child. When you think you've caught it, what do you find instead?"

Philly knew. Pubs full of the wrong sort of people, the people who weren't like Mr. Lupin; people who wrote "modern books" and drank the wrong things and never quaffed deep of the authentic wines of life.

"You find sham, everywhere," he answered himself. "You find 'bottle parties' in fetid atmospheres, you find 'cocktail parties' of the *intelligentsia*"—he underlined the word with scorn—"and you find each man selling himself for a mess of—of—" He had run out of words suited to inverted commas.

Philly waited politely for him to finish, but there was nothing else except a suspicion of a "bah!"

"I'm afraid I have to go now," she said.

"Yes, go, child. Go and take down that damnable scaffolding and let's see the wind blowing free in your hair again. And then come to me and I'll get your golden-morning look on to canvas if I have to die for it."

"Thank you," Philly said, not quite appropriately. "Sarah has gone to London, you know."

"No, I didn't know—but I might have known it. Why must they do it? The talented and the beautiful all tumbling after will-o'-the-wisps and mirages—and what to show for it in the end?"

"I don't know," Philly admitted, feeling something was expected of her. "She hasn't got to the end yet, I'm afraid." He laughed suddenly, his boisterous beer laugh. He let her go. "Relinquished" her was the word for it. He tramped way down the dusty road. Tramping through vineyards . . . Philly thought, hurrying off in the opposite direction. He should have been; but his little feet would meet nothing more lush than a chance daisy or so, all the way home to his cottage.

CHAPTER NINE

A WEEK had gone. A whole week and she was still alive.

Sarah hovered between self-congratulation and despair. If a week were over and lived through, the rest could surely be no worse than repetition. One could bear it. Just go on and on, until at last this became recognizable as life. How weak I am, she thought sorrowfully; anyone could do my job standing on her head . . . except me. . . . One of the few satisfactions left in what had once been life was that she had not touched the money that her mother and Julian Jones had sent her since she began work. Receiving her first week's pay she had felt that the proper thing would have been to have some sense of pride in achievement. The first money she had ever earned! She said it over to herself, with a carefully-placed exclamation mark at the end; but it was no use; she simply didn't seem to have the mentality that responded ardently to the joys of being a woman of independence. The exclamation mark toppled over and became only the deadest of full stops.

She did not go home for the first Week End. It might have looked like the thin end of the wedge of a permanent home-coming. Besides, she was sensitive to the fact that the job showed in her face. All the little packets she had wrapped up, making an alarming sort of glaze in her eyes; and even the ghost of the terrible sunshine Sally smile on her lips; and a perpetual *pricked* appearance about her ears, as if—tiny though they were—they must for evermore flare alertly for Mrs. Billing's commands.

There was overtime on Saturday, in any case. Lily and Joan went off for their Week End at the lunch hour, but Mrs. Billing said Sarah wouldn't mind staying on a while to finish her little jobs, would she? Sarah, hypnotized by the bulk of her employer, said, as usual, that she didn't mind. She rushed back from lunch to find Mrs. Billing herself, a magnificent figurehead at the prow of her industry, sailing through the half-holiday afternoon with a sublime unconsciousness of any private concerns.

"Come along, dear. Get on with some of these. Can't have our clients waiting, can we?"

"No," said Sarah, thinking of all the mystical legion of indigestion sufferers and those crying out for face packs.

"Such a nice day, too," Mrs. Billing went on, with unintentional cruelty. "Makes you feel brisk to see the sun so gay. You might clear up that corner, dear. It's a tiny bit *chayotic*, isn't it?" She smiled her great roguish smile. "Business is a question of discipline, you know."

It might be the question, Sarah thought, gazing hopelessly around her; but, if so, it didn't appear to be very satisfactorily answered. *Was* work ennobling? . . . With a prudent idea of beginning cautiously on last night's wages, she had lunched off a couple of nauseating buns and a cup of urn-vitiated coffee. Did I ever really like buns? How one matures with experience! I used to eat buns for *pleasure* at home—

"Now, dear, look snappy! We haven't got all day."

"Haven't we?" Sarah said, with a sarcasm that went over Mrs. Billing's great curl-crested head.

"We'll have a cup of tea here, just the two of us unless your boy is waiting for you, is he?"

"No," Sarah said coldly.

"You have a boy, I suppose?"

It is as bad as Mrs. Moody . . . "No," she said, still coldly; thinking of Sir Giles; wanting to cry.

"Oh, you ought to have a boy. Lily and Joan have one."

"One each, or one between them?" Sarah asked wearily.

"One each, of course. What an idea!"

"Yes, wasn't it?" She sat down by a packing case of samples, and fell into a dream. Tonight she would go on fitting the memoirs together, and then she would get them published . . . and that would be the end of these horrid little boxes of powder . . . she would walk out and never return—

She dropped a packet; chalky dust scattered over the floor. "Clumsy!" Mrs. Billing snapped.

"I'm terribly sorry—"

"Well, it's no use crying over spilt milk. Scoop it up."

"I think—I'm afraid—it's rather dusty."

"Nonsense! Everyone has to eat a peck of dirt before they die."

"But not a whole peck at once, surely—"

"Sally!—scoop it up," Mrs. Billing said inexorably.

*　　*　　*　　*　　*

She had badly wanted to buy some stockings, but could find no shop open when she was at last released. Not even a provision shop; but there was always the ever-open ham-and-beef shop on the corner near her lodgings. She could still taste the stewed black office tea and the tinned milk for which Mrs. Billing seemed to have a morbid passion, and the biscuits whose green flourish of decoration might have been either rigid cream or a tentative tracery of mould.

The steady late afternoon light astonished her. The heat of the city was flat and gentle, almost kindly. It suggested the odd idea that to some people London might be quite a friendly happy place. A momentary self-pity caught at her throat, disastrously resurrecting the flavour of the long-past luncheon buns.

She achieved, by her hit-or-miss method, the right bus today; it took her within a street of her dwelling. Walking the last bit, slipping through the still air and light, she saw a glaze of sprightliness over the drab buildings, even upon the usually sinister areaways leading into secret depths of unknowable existence; but not touching herself. She alone walked still in the dismal pattern of servitude to Mrs. Billing. What could I eat tonight? Whatever I get it will be cold and sad inside, like me. A cold sad sausage, perhaps—

The light struck steadily through the glass panels in the lodging-house door. It seemed to irradiate the very smell of the hall. There was a letter from her mother. She pulled it from its envelope and began to read it as she went upstairs. It took her mind off all the closed doors she had to pass on implacable landings, doors bolted hopelessly against the world by defeated beings. They must be that . . . and more and more defeated, the higher one went.

Steeped in Fontayne, Elisabeth's words flowed tranquilly, her mind already accepting the London job, even though her gentle heart had not yet done so. "Bracken said you looked very well when he saw you. . . ." One sensed the relief in Mother. Bracken was to be trusted, his judgment final. If Bracken, keeping an eye on the prodigal daughter, said it was all right—Did I really deceive him? Perhaps. The nice meal he gave me was such a surprise to my stomach; it seemed to bolster me up, right in the awful middle depths of the week, when both the beginning and end of it were out of sight. I *was* cheerful, on that supper. It was better, that evening, to have my stomach bolstered up than any amount of spiritual cheering-up. "Bracken said you looked well. . . ." *Good!* . . . Fontayne hadn't budged an inch. At its emotional centre, even the flower room must now be perfectly calm.

She came into the ironic sunlight upon her room. The swinging mirror on the washstand had turned its face up to the ceiling; reflecting the whitewashed blankness, like despairing whites of eyes upturned. "The enclosed letter came for you this morning . . ." *What*—where? Her fingers dipped frenziedly into the envelope again. She might easily have thrown it away. It was scarcely any surprise to see Sir Giles's writing, then. Dipping into a bran tub you expected a proper prize. Even so, she had to—as Mrs. Moody would have said—get her breath before she opened it. It made her sick to look at the paper bag of ham sandwiches she had brought in. What a waste of ninepence! she thought in a mournful exclamatory aside, before she remembered that nothing mattered. He was in London again and nothing else mattered.

Of course it was not much of a letter as letters went; but it was far, far more than she had expected. Just to read that she was "his dear Sarah" and that he was "hers sincerely" would have been something. All the little text between was like some extra treat, a tidbit of exquisite delight. The thing was (she paced wildly up and down the miserable strip of linoleum), the crucial thing was that he need not have written at all. He owed her no letter; this was simply and solely out of the blue, out of the kindness of his heart. . . .

She ran out of her room, down to the landing with the telephone. If I hadn't had twopence I would have done nothing about it; but I *have*. . . . His telephone number was on his letter. She did not even have to look it up in the book. The landing smelt of mice and cheese, in a callous combination. She heard the pennies drop down into the box, then her own voice speaking; but she never knew how she achieved Sir Giles, as she finally did, at the other end of the wire.

"I've just had your letter sent on to me," she plunged desperately across his own opening words. "You see, I live in London now."

"You do?" (How oddly more encouraging this sounded than "Do you?" would have done.) She answered: "Yes, I do. I work here now." "Where?" he asked. "In London," she said. (*Why* wasn't she a sparkling telephone conversationalist? But even Sir Giles seemed almost at a loss.) "Then we must meet," he said, after a pause, "when you have any free time." "Oh, I have—" She caught back the words. To be over eager, Mrs. Moody's paper had more than once said, was one of the besetting minor sins of femininity. Yet what was sin, minor or major, compared with the prospect of a solitary and bunned-up Sunday? The house flapping around one with ghostly unseen Sabbath life, furtive parcel-carrying comings and goings, sinister sounds of gas-ring cookery, smells that made you hungry and then took your hunger from you. . . . Sarah shivered on the landing with eerie light falling through green curtains covering an abortive little window stranded between floors.

"I hope it is pleasant work," Sir Giles said.

"Yes, thank you. I hope Europe was all right."

"Slightly peevish, I'm afraid."

"Yes." The demon sitting on Tom's shoulder; breathing down Mr. Harbrittle's neck. . . . "I wonder what will happen."

Sir Giles did not seem prepared to go into this, at the present moment.

"I suppose I ought to have brought my gas mask with me."

"I suppose you ought," he agreed, without very urgent interest. "We'll meet one day soon, then?"

"Oh, yes. I *am* rather lonely." How caddish . . . what a horrible bogus remark, putting him at a disadvantage.

"You wouldn't be free for tea tomorrow—?"

"Oh, yes, I would; perfectly free."

"Then shall we meet?"

They arranged it, somewhat crisply, as if it were a business appointment. Tea seemed a sadly negligible pause for him to choose among the edible punctuations in the day. One would never have associated him with tea as a meal. Think of Sir Giles and cosy buttered soggy crumpets and jam layer cake: why, it was almost like sacrilege. Yet he had said *tea*, as if not only the hour but the actual meal existed. It looked, unhappily, as if he had not thought meeting for a drink would be a suitable suggestion.

Even so, in spite of tea, the sunshine in her room was utterly transformed. She tilted back the mirror: saw the ceiling swing away, saw her own face astonishingly clear and vivid in the bumpy insane glass. And, strangely, her appetite had come back at a rush, so that she ate the ham sandwiches with zest, and the ninepence was not wasted after all.

As a social occasion it might have been classed as a success, but as an hour for mellowing and maturing friendship it seemed a disastrous failure. Yet she could not see that she was to blame. Even her stockings, though not strictly socially presentable, could not be blamed for everything; and the rest of her appearance was quite happily at its best. The bun diet had left no marks on her, it seemed. Step by step she

achieved the various stages of her toilet, from the determined penetrating of the sinister geysered gloom of the bathroom to the final fluffing
of powder on her nose.

She took a taxi to the hotel, which was only *just* not the hotel of the
wedding breakfast; no more than a good stone's throw separated them,
and in intent and purpose they were one and the same. This sense of
dream-like familiarity tended to allay her nervousness. The full green
assurance of leaf in the park buoyed her up. Gates and railings caught
the light. Flowers confined in strict segregated beds made one aware
of a tidiness in London, streets clean-swept, windows shining crys-
tal-clear from the tall hotels (myriads of window cleaners hidden
somewhere in obscurity) and the Sunday quiet like some extra furbishing and burnishing in itself.

She got out of the taxi, her legs trembling. I shall eat only one cake,
at the most; perhaps none.

The hotel interior had the green-gold shimmer of the park, but
softer, more cunning. One swam through the liquid-like softness, only
just did not drown in it. Like a helpless fish, a cherished hot-water fish
in a fragrant tank, speeding smoothly with scarcely the flicker of a fin—

"Hello." Sir Giles touched her arm, restrained her with gentle force
from swimming straight past him. He gave her his beautiful candid smile.

"Hello. . . ." Coming up for air, she could scarcely breathe.

"This is my young cousin, Benjamin Crossley."

"Is it?" she said piteously, not turning her eyes from Sir Giles, but
already woefully conscious of an alien presence.

"How do you do?" the cousin said.

He had nice bright chestnut hair and nice blue eyes and a nice
smile. Oh, it was monstrous! He could not be more than twenty-three
or so, she decided indignantly. "How do you do?" she returned frigidly.

Sir Giles did not seem to know there was anything wrong. This must
be how he went through Europe, she thought bitterly; never admitting
even to himself that everything wasn't going smoothly; hypnotizing
whole nations with a plausible word and an easy gesture.

It was like the restaurant where Bracken had given her tea, but on
a more fashionable scale. The orchestra tippy-tipped so unobtrusively
that there was danger of it melting altogether into silence. Even as the
wafers of sandwiches were so elegant that there was danger of their
attaining the ultimate of silver-fineness and vanishing into thin air. Yet,
in spite of these achievements of refinement, the situation was *gross*.
It might as well have been a treat at the Zoo, with all the attendant

miseries of a jolly uncle whose only earnest desire was to please, cost him what effort it might, exhaust and drain him though it would; of jolly buns and peanuts for the child to give the animals and keep her amused; and of a jolly new playmate unearthed for her and brought along to join in the fun. . . . How *could* he be so horrible, so crude?—whose subtle diplomatic words had run like honey over soured cities.

Not that he was in the least at a loss now, his voice no less confiding than when he had called her "his dear girl," at Fontayne. He inquired of Fontayne, as of an old friend. He asked after all, including Bronwen. He had seen a review of the book. His brilliant eyes twinkled at her, drawing her into the hinted conspiracy of a joke.

"I believe it is doing quite well," she said listlessly, not to be drawn.

"The young author is only twelve or thirteen," Sir Giles then drew in his cousin.

"It's a bit steep when it comes to children writing books, isn't it?" the young man smiled.

At any other time and place, Sarah would heartily have agreed. "It depends on the life you've had," she now said.

"How is *your* life?" Sir Giles asked. The tea had arrived and with a disarming little gesture he had invited her to pour it.

Both chair and table were too low; this seemed to affect her sense of balance. She felt far too free and unmoored from the behind up, and far too cramped and distorted from the behind down. Pale round blots of tea dripped on to the silvery-green cloth.

"You must put sugar in for yourselves; I don't know what you like," she said aloofly. "Oh, my life"—she stared down at her minute rose-budded plate that made a mockery of the very idea of appetite—". . . there is nothing very nice about my life, I'm afraid." Why pretend? Why sparkle with all the new-discovered joys of working in London, as she had meant to do, if Sir Giles had been alone? She had meant to save his face at second hand, as it were; to confess her own failure would have been to confront him with the necessity of accepting that such a thing as failure existed. But now she did not care, had no desire to flatter him by padding him in the cotton wool of her solicitude.

"I'm very sorry to hear that," he said instantly, seriously sympathetic; as if to shame her.

Cousin Benjamin Crossley drank his tea and said nothing. His hair ran to red-gold at the temples, an authentic Old Master hue shared by the Rudge triplets, but somehow rather embarrassing in a young man.

Sarah sipped the subtle China tea which she thought smoky and horrid. "I thought I wanted to get away from home, but I don't think it matters much where you are." All vestiges of shyness had vanished in her disappointment. "If you are depressed, change of scene doesn't help a lot."

"I find it can," Sir Giles contradicted gently.

"Not if the change is to a horrible little office, with an enormous giant to see you never leave off working for an instant," she said expressionlessly.

"But how ghastly!" the red-gold cousin exclaimed.

"Oh, you get used to it." Her eyes challenged them: I'll tell you all, but don't dare to pity me.

"To most things, perhaps, yes, but not to giants," Sir Giles said, with moderation.

"It's a female giant." Against her will she began to feel a bit bitter; even wanted to smile, but didn't. "In the room where I live, there's linoleum on the floor. It sticks to your feet when you get up—"

"You don't *sleep* on the floor?" the cousin interrupted, prepared for anything after the giant.

"Oh, no. I have a bed. It stands on the tip of its toes and never rests. It gives me cramp in the back of my legs just to think of it." She *was* amusing Sir Giles, after all, though not in the least in the way she had intended. She eyed his profile. You see you needn't have been so cautious; you wouldn't have found it awkward to be with me alone. . . .

"But how did you find such an appalling place?"

"The giant recommended it. But I don't really mind anything but the bathroom. It is always full of fog—or if it's steam it is dead cold steam—and there are always great pools on the floor which you have to leap, and the geyser rumbles and rumbles and you know it's only a question of time until it bursts."

"But you *can't* go on living there," the cousin burst out, while Sir Giles seemed still to be framing his protest.

"Oh, yes, I can." She was high in spirit now, aloft in a sort of blithe fury. "Lots of people have to. Why not I?" (It was like Philly, saying all people should be equal. . . .) "Living at Fontayne is so *soft*. You sink into it, as if it's a sort of warm mist."

"I'd prefer it to the geyser fog," Sir Giles said judiciously.

"Actually it's no longer a question of *preferring*. I have to earn my living. Or—if I don't—live on nothing at home, without independence."

"Independence has its points," Sir Giles admitted.

"But surely you could get a better job." The cousin brought the matter down to a more practical basis. "With your looks, I mean—" He paused diffidently. "I suppose it is awful to be a mannequin or anything like that—but some girls don't seem to mind it, even do it for fun, and surely the pay would be better—"

"I never thought of a job like that," Sarah said simply. To her horror she found she had absent-mindedly eaten an éclair and a beguiling little pastry while she had been talking. "Of course I am also in London to see what I can do about my father's memoirs."

"Oh, yes, how are the memoirs?" Sir Giles inquired pleasantly, as of another old friend.

"I seem to have them all, but they are still in an awful muddle."

"We must see what we can do with them."

Her heart began to beat madly at his words. He must mean they were to meet again, cousin or no cousin. "Yes," she said sedately, "we must."

"Do you ever go to theatres or films?" Benjamin Crossley asked.

"I haven't, in London."

He didn't say any more, but she felt his gaze hanging over her. Could it be that he admired her? She couldn't bring herself to care much whether he did or not; though at any other time she might have been as pleased and flattered as when the young man in the blazer had tried to pick her up on the beach.

As if he read her thoughts, Sir Giles said: "You know, it really is all wrong for you to be living like this by yourself."

"No, it's quite all right. My mother wouldn't let me do it if it weren't quite all right." (One mustn't admit how quelled Mother was, being undermined beforehand by the Jones situation.) "And you mustn't think I mind. It isn't as if the geyser is important compared with wars and things."

"There is not a war on here and now," Sir Giles said, keeping almost religiously to the point.

"But you know what I mean," she appealed to him. "I am always having to remind myself of things like that, because I don't *respond* very well to hardship, not even mine, and certainly not"—she smiled candidly—"other people's. I'm afraid I'm a carnal sort of person."

They both stared at her.

"Oh I don't think it's what I mean." She stared back in horror. "What I mean is, I don't respond terribly well to spiritual kinds of things. Nice food and drink make me feel much better—more *good*, I mean—than any amount of *trying* to be nicer."

"It all sounds rather alarming," Sir Giles admitted, but he smiled.

"But all the same, I do keep on trying to consider other people." It isn't true; look how I didn't consider Mother; but then, she didn't consider us, when she married Mr. Jones. . . . "I'm afraid most people are really selfish," she said aloud. "Perhaps that accounts for wars," she brought the theme neatly back to the edge of the geyser: that woeful subject that had run morbidly, concurrently, in her mind with war.

Long-threatened calamity had come to be. Philly was sitting for her portrait to Mr. Lupin. Outdoors; in tribute to the golden-child-of-the-morning subject. She sat in a pose of unnatural naturalness beneath a meagre sapling of an apple tree, the only one in Mr. Lupin's cottage yard-cum-garden. She leaned lightly back on her arms, her head raised. At least, the "lean" had been light at first, but was now tearing the muscles in her forearms. If she could have kept silent, it might have been bearable, but Mr. Lupin expected to keep up a running, not to say leaping, conversation. He flung colours on to his palette from tubes as he flung words into the air. He made painting so virile an occupation that to all intents he might as well have been a butcher handling great mounds of meat with such a relish that nobody could have accused him of squeamishness. If Philly had had time or eye for the miseries of any but herself at the moment, she might have spared a pang for Mr. Lupin so tirelessly and boisterously proving that painting need not be an occupation for the effete.

"Tell me when you're tired," he called out.

She smiled faintly; knew she wouldn't dare.

"We must get as much done as possible now while the sun is just right. The warmth of tone is perfect now. All right?"

"Yes, thank you." She thought the grass was rather damp from last night's rain, but did not like to mention it.

His poky little week-end cottage humped an ungracious back to Philly's view. Mrs. Rudge had once gone in to oblige him, but never again, she had said, not with all those empty beer bottles to stumble over and empty tobacco tins doing the can-can (as she had picturesquely phrased it) down the stairs after you, making you run for your life.

"They didn't mind you coming?" Mr. Lupin waved a brush vaguely in the direction of Fontayne.

"Oh, no." The Joneses had been surprised and—Julian and Peter—amused by the portrait; and Mother, wholly failing to understand her agonized point of view, had said it might help her to get over missing

Sarah so much. Even Mrs. Moody had failed her, saying it would do her good to have someone new to talk to. That Mr. Lupin wasn't new—was that most unnerving thing, an unripe acquaintance of quite long standing—nobody understood.

Terrible as was the posing, that which Mr. Lupin called the "break" was even worse. He led her into his dreary kitchen, where he opened a bottle of beer for himself and stood holding bottle and glass in either hand, taking a gulp and then filling his glass to the brim again, as if he were racing against time. He offered her beer, ginger ale, lemonade, in turn; and looked rather hurt when she refused all. He hadn't shaved this morning. The sun glistened on the stubble of beard on his babyish chin.

"I shall have bread and cheese and an onion for my lunch," he said with a sort of pride. "English women can't cook. I remember a little inn—by Gad, I do! Snug-set in the wine country, where the . . ."

Standing there, watching him quaff (the very noise he made was an indubitable quaff), she fell into a dream. One of the old waking trances she used to share with Sarah before everything went wrong; before Sarah went into the life that never stopped for trances, and before she had committed herself to reading aloud to the village young. The more you went on growing up, the more awake life seemed to get. Even now the dream wouldn't last, with the damp reality of the kitchen intruding. What a mess Mr. Lupin's crockery seemed to be in, you couldn't help noticing, piled high and dirty in the sink. An egg had been dropped on the red-flagged floor. This theme—the yolk part of it, at least—was taken up again in the ravelled wool of Mr. Lupin's pullover. She had to restrain herself forcibly from offering to bring him some eggs laid by her hens. This unnatural strangling of an instinctive impulse had the effect of making her more unhappy than ever.

Still worse did she feel when Mr. Lupin, vanishing for a moment, reappeared with a couple of little books which he handed to her.

"You might like to have these," he said. "Some of my bits and pieces, collected. Caustic stuff, you know, but funny, I believe. There are several rather nice bits lampooning some of our 'moderns.' Forthright stuff." Forthright, perhaps, but (as he gave them into her hands) somewhat wistful little volumes.

Philly turned a page or two, wondering what to say. "Are they . . . epigrams?" she asked cautiously.

"Jupiter, no! None of your polite swill of epigrams for me. Something more robust than that, I hope, child." So robust that the words must have hurled themselves off his pen, whirling and spinning, blowing clean

winds of ridicule through intense intellectuals and la-di-da poseurs. . . .
Mr. Lupin stood foursquare in his eggy pullover against decadence.

"Thank you very much," Philly said, closing the book firmly. "I—I'll
keep them until I get home."

Out of the darkness had come light. Mrs. Billing, Lily, Joan, the
powders in the little boxes, the very geyser itself, were dazzled, transformed. Even when Lily said sarcastically, "Our Sally gets to be more
and more of a little ray of sunshine," she still went on smiling, unhurt,
unheeding. For Sir Giles had not left her sunk in the pit of that polite
Zoo tea, from which she had had scarcely a hope of being extricated.

Only four days on, only ninety-six or so hours forward from that
time, he telephoned her. It was the merest chance she ever knew it,
for the telephone rang and rang before anyone answered it, and again
it was only chance that she happened to be on the stairs when an
unknown voice called up, "I think it's for you," (how did it know?) and
left her in merciful peace to attend to the call.

"You are very elusive," he began. It sounded oddly flattering, though
it meant nothing but that she was too poor to have her own telephone.
"How are you getting on?" He went straight on: "Has young Ben been
in touch with you?"

"No," she said, surprised.

"Oh. How are the memoirs?"

"I'm afraid I haven't looked at them since I saw you." Considering
how few times I've seen him, I always seem to be on the telephone with
him. . . .

"What are you doing now?"

"Nothing." One could not warm up to conversation without seeing
him in the flesh.

"You've had dinner?"

"Yes." Had she? Here on the shadowy landing with the mice-cheese
smell, she lost count of time. Yes . . . she had left work ages ago, had
eaten fruit, a bar of chocolate, and what the ham-and-beef man sold
under the name of savoury pie. It had tasted all right at the time, but
now, with Sir Giles on top of it, as it were, she felt rather sick.

"You weren't in bed?"

"Oh no." I'm being so awful and stodgy. . . . I'll regret it to my dying
day. . . . "I *hate* going to bed early."

He laughed. "Would you like to have a drink with me. Well, no, not a drink, but a cup of coffee, say, at the Café Royal?—and we'll talk of the memoirs."

"Yes, I would like to." She snapped out the words, fearful that there would be a break in them. "I love going out in the evening, but I never do."

He laughed again. "I'll call for you—"

"Oh, no. Oh, please don't. Please let me meet you. I'd much rather."

"Very well," he agreed quickly.

She was gratefully certain he had remembered the geyser and had put two and two together about the probability of corresponding ills. He gave her minute directions as to the spot where she would find him (Bracken couldn't have done better) and rang off.

As soon as she saw him she forgave him without reservation for the Sunday tea with the cousin. He had probably done it from some mistaken sense of chivalry, not cautiousness; just as he now said, as he greeted her:

"It really is quite preposterous that you should be wandering around London on your own."

"I don't wander much," she said truthfully. She stared around her at the stuffy redness of surroundings from which he had stepped forward to meet her. "Is *this* Café Royal?" The resemblance to the interior of Copley's Green was striking.

He laughed. She thought she would give anything to know exactly how to make him laugh, but she did not think she would ever be sure. He put a hand beneath her elbow and propelled her gently forward. The big, noisy, drab, smoky room into which she was led surprised her again. It was less like Copley's Green, seeming bleak rather than stuffy, but was hardly less overwhelming. It didn't suit Sir Giles's precision of dress and manner. Not that he didn't look artistic enough (his striking black hair with the individual little shelf at the back alone made him eligible for that distinction), but his whole personality seemed too energetic and decisive for the place.

"How is the giant?" he asked, as they sat down. "Young Ben was immensely amused."

"Was he?" She had thought he seemed more worried for her than amused; but that wasn't the point. It amused Sir Giles now to think his cousin had been amused. She was surprised how easily she could see this, and see a very heart of indecision in his decisiveness; he wanted young Ben to have telephoned her, to prove she had been a success, and yet was rather glad he hadn't, or at least had not got hold of her.

It was extraordinary how clear and adult she suddenly found her thoughts to be. . . . Not that he treated her, now, as adult. Without even asking her if there were any special drink she would like, he ordered coffee for her. But when it came, in a glass, with the white added to the black from a huge continental-looking can, she felt stimulated, nearly intoxicated, merely by the sight. She did manage to say, however, gravely and to the point:

"I'm practically on the verge of being eighteen, you know."

"Really," he said, smiling again.

"Your cousin is very *young*, isn't he?"

"I suppose he is," he agreed.

That was settled, the Zoo tea party washed clear, dismissed. Sir Giles, perhaps taking some cue, offered her a cigarette, which she accepted. He asked her how the state of independence was getting on.

"It is better than some things."

"Much better than being a débutante, at least."

"Yes." This point of view had not struck her before, but now she was sure that he was right. Obviously he would not dream of taking out a débutante. "Except that a débutante might have a telephone of her own," she added thoughtfully. "I gather from the difficulty this evening that you haven't?"

"Not even a proper share in one. It's not even on my landing. And it smells of mice and cheese." Hearing him laugh youthfully and simply again she knew she was back into the swing of entertaining him. "The landing does, I mean. The telephone smells of my old mackintosh that I left behind at Fontayne."

"Fontayne in the rain would be very attractive," he said, as if he were speaking of an imaginary place.

"When will you come again?" He won't, and can't bite my head off, so why not ask?

"When do you go again?" he countered "Soon, I expect. Next Week End, perhaps."

"I might be able to drive you down."

"That would be nice." So quietly said, an achievement of modulation, cigarette poised. One must not attempt to bring the suggestion more firmly down to earth. "The giant tries to keep me for over-time on Saturday, but I expect I could escape if it were really urgent."

"Poor Sarah," he smiled.

She took another sip of coffee to steady herself against the joy of hearing her name on his lips. It was queer how she had fallen by chance into the right manner toward him. Her minor tragedies of living appealed to him in an unexpected way. She struck the correct balance. If she had *looked* the part of woe, in addition to speaking it, it wouldn't have done at all. It was only because she looked perfectly *un*-downtrodden, she now realized, that he could bear it. He doesn't mind my suffering all kinds of discomforts, so long as I can make them sound comic, she thought without dismay.

"But what do you *do*?" he persisted, his interest genuine, complete. "You have friends in London?"

"Well, there's Bracken, of course."

"The explorer, yes." He had Bracken tabulated, frozen stiff in his role for ever, whatever other occupation he might take to. "But all this—none of this, I should say, is exactly exciting."

"No."

His eyes didn't move from her; he was observing, really seeing her. It was the keenest, most exciting, scrutiny she had ever undergone. She stood up to it with self-possession. It was no use pretending she had a full brilliant life.

"You must certainly meet a few people," he said casually. In her new shrewdness, she wasn't sure this half-promise would ever be fulfilled. She was sure he found her most agreeable in the solitude of her comic sufferings; among other people she might lose her point.

"Lady Pansy Bysshe—she's staying near Fontayne now, you know—has given me some introductions, but I haven't done anything with them yet. She told me to go and see her niece in a flat that is all windows."

"Oh, Virginia Welwyn, yes."

The clatter of the great room came up and enclosed them for a minute in separated silences. A scraping and booming that was worse than—better than—an orchestra. Through a haze of smoke she watched his face, so far away in silence, so beyond recall. "You're very elusive," he had said. Ah, but it was he, it was he who was that.

"Do you remember the . . . dance?" she breathed.

"I do," he said, with as astonishing a solemnity as if he were promising to take her in holy matrimony.

"I don't think there could ever be anything quite like it again," she said.

"Perhaps not," he agreed gravely. "Such occasions are not born of plans."

"No." She sighed. "We began to break up a bit after that."

"And I'm afraid we'll have to break up now," he said as if she had said her words in the nick of time for him to cap them gracefully. "I have an appointment in a quarter of an hour's time."

"Oh, yes, of course." She blushed. She might have guessed him to be a man who would still bristle with appointments at nearly ten at night. She jumped up too quickly, knocking over her coffee glass, crashing down the gently built up nostalgic memory of the spring night of the dance.

He took her back by taxi to her dwelling place, and tactfully did not even glance at the dismal façade before he was into the vehicle again and driving away.

Going slowly up through the various smells to her room, Sarah felt that the slice of evening had been a decided success, and yet that she felt very faintly depressed.

"Sarah says she is coming home this Week End and can Giles Merrick drive her down," Elisabeth informed the breakfast table, looking up from her letter.

Philly's heart sank. The first Week End; and not alone.

"By all means, I should think," Mr. Jones said, "can't she?"

"I don't see any reason *not*," Elisabeth in turn appealed to him, "do you?"

They always went on like that, until they were absolutely sure they were doing what each other most desired. Perhaps that was the worst of two people getting together, neither of whom would hurt a fly, Philly thought. It tended to slow down all ordinary domestic routine almost to a standstill. On the other hand, it could not be said that either Mother or Mr. Jones wasted much time on considering their respective children. Marriage seemed in this respect to have hardened them both. Bronwen wailed that her father was far less attentive than formerly; and Mother was in some ways even vaguer and less noticing than she used to be. And this was in summer when the garden more or less ran itself. What it would be like in autumn, when gardening presented more crises, Philly couldn't imagine. If there *were* an autumn, she added to herself, no longer sure of anything.

"Sarah!" Tom exclaimed, as if he had forgotten her existence until then. "Well I never! Will she come to lunch?" he asked formally.

"You heard that she was coming for the Week End, darling," Elisabeth said patiently.

"If she's coming to lunch, can we have parsnips?" Tom asked, undaunted.

CHAPTER TEN

THEY LEFT London in good time. Sir Giles had said casually, "You must get the morning off," and somehow, miraculously, as if buoyed up by his own confidence, she had done so.

He drove with unthinking ease, talking nearly all the time. She sat very upright beside him, her eyes usually resting on his hands on the wheel. Even gloved, shapeless in crumply pigskin gloves, his hands were (she sought a phrase) . . . a joy for ever.

Rain was washed broodingly over the sky, but so far it was holding off from earth. He had said Fontayne would be nice in the rain, but she couldn't agree. Oh, let the weather be a blaze of glory (she squeezed her hands fervently between her knees), so that everything could and would take a cue from it.

"You won't mind there being nothing to do?" she asked anxiously. "I've brought the memoirs back again"—there was something wistful in the confession, as if Marcus Fontayne's ghost were returning like a homing pigeon—"so perhaps we could get down to looking at them and find out if they are quite all there." Whether they were complete, she meant, though it sounded as if she doubted her father's literary sanity.

"I'd like to do that very much," he said.

Sarah sighed with relief. It was as if a thing regarded purely for utility and profit had suddenly shown itself to be an entrancing toy. With luck, if it rained, Sir Giles would play with it all the Week End. And, once in order, what might not the memoirs bring? Not only money, but a return of her father's name to fame. The very thought of being able to offer him such a tribute aroused dormant filial pride in her. It was a pity all her memories of him were such inconsequent ones. How nice it would have been if she had possessed intimate little gems of his reputed wit. As it was, her only positive impression left of him was that he had seemed to prefer cats to children. Perhaps this accounted for Philly's somewhat wearing devotion to Ernest.

"Do you believe in heredity?" she asked, rather sadly. "I mean, it must be disappointing when it doesn't work out right. It would have sent my father frantic to realize that none of us was ever going to improve in intelligence. The *only* thing we seem to have inherited is a liking for cats." She stared at the masterful gloves sliding gears and pulling things out and pushing things in. "I suppose he was very clever?"

"Very, I'm sure."

"But not as clever as you?" she suggested delicately.

"My dear Sarah! He was in line for the very front rank, I am confident, if he lived. I am merely the back stairs of politics, as it were." He smiled modestly, candidly. "The *below* stairs, if you like. Dreadfully knowledgeable about the more sordid sides of my masters' business."

To Sarah, it sounded even more exciting, more deviously thrilling, than if he had confessed to being the front stairs themselves.

"We're nearly there!" she said, surprised. All at once she felt herself take on a new personality; not the girl hanging devotedly on Sir Giles's words, but the eldest independent child, bringing down a friend for the Week End. The vision was brilliant, intoxicating, rain or no rain.

Philly had been sent up to the schoolroom to see if Tom were presentable enough to take lunch with the family. It was a delicate mission, because Tom, though really preferring to lunch with Mrs. Moody (Miss James luckily liked to eat in solitude), was, nevertheless, inclined to be on his dignity if he thought there were any question of his being "inspected." He could have the subtlest appreciation of the difference between a mere friendly glance and an inspection.

Miss James and Tom sat at opposite sides of the old school table, its surface scarred and seamed with lines of disillusion. It had suffered so much from youthful vengeance against boredom. A vicious cut made by Christopher's penknife could still be seen running deep in the centre, though time had camouflaged it with dried ink and the fluff of blotting paper. Miss James's clear little Dresden china head rose up against a background of cretonne window curtain, her guileless rimless glasses catching the light. She and Tom could not be said to get on well together, but for days, weeks, could exist in a passive state of armistice between flares of active war.

"What do you want?" Tom demanded of his sister. "We are boiling down arithmetic."

"Tom, what do you mean?" Miss James's little withered rosebud of a mouth formed into a minute oval protest.

"Mrs. Moody said that all that arithmetic boils down to is putting two and two together."

"You will perhaps allow me to know more on the subject than Mrs. Moody does." Miss James in turn allowed herself a narrow edge of lady-like sarcasm.

"I just came to remind you that Sarah will be here for lunch," Philly said tactfully, her unobtrusive scrutiny having passed Tom as fit for company. Indeed, he looked full of well-being and beauty, she thought, the fascinating blond feathers of his hair traced demurely across his high Fontayne forehead.

"I'll be there," he said, promptly closing his books.

Philly went downstairs again. A sense of peace invaded her. There was no question of going on with the week-end posing, with Sarah here. And there was the possibility that Sarah might be able to elucidate the mystery of the little books Mr. Lupin had given her to read. Vaguely, she imagined they must be full of quips and fun, but where to find that fun she did not begin to know. Peace was added to by Bronwen and Peter both being out. In a few minutes—except for Sir Giles Merrick's presence, and the lack of Christopher's—it might seem nearly like the old days. She was wearing her gingham, newly washed, and expertly pressed by Mrs. Moody; she herself had attempted no new dress-making in the fortnight since Sarah went away. Only a fortnight . . . yet it was time unmeasured.

Still more, when Sarah came in, was she conscious of the immense clots of time which mere days could hold; dollops and dollops, more than you could ever possibly digest.

Wearing her wedding frock and her high-heeled wedding shoes, Sarah came into the hall with Sir Giles and stood there looking about her as if she were a politely interested visitor.

"Sarah!" Philly said in an agonized whisper, and flung herself forward.

It was all right, then. Even Sir Giles stood momentarily forgotten, only Cruddles to esteem him at his proper worth.

Not that Sir Giles minded in the least. He enjoyed the reunion of the sisters, as if he were watching some pretty scene in a play. They were really absolutely charming, he decided with a quite boyish enthusiasm. Sarah startlingly seemed to his eyes to grow lovelier each time he looked at her, as if she were . . . yes . . . *ripening* at a perhaps alarming speed. He felt pleasantly hungry, and hoped they kept a good cook.

Philly turned to him and shyly shook hands.

"Where is Mother? Where are the Joneses?"

"In the garden. Shall we go to the terrace?" Philly said, feeling horribly like a hostess.

Sarah was annoyed. How like Mother to go grubbing in the garden at such a time, probably doing something tense which she pretended couldn't be left: pricking plants in or out, or whatever the intricate things were that you did to them at some time or other during the year. . . .

Cruddles gave them to understand that drinks would be served on the terrace. Either Mr. Jones had given directions for this or Cruddles was behaving in a way beyond the bounds of hope. Either way, Sarah felt she would have liked to embrace Cruddles, if merely for entering into the spirit of things so beautifully.

"What a delightful view it is," Sir Giles, gazing down from the terrace, said; the perfect guest, which was no more than he or anyone else would expect him to be.

Ernest, drowsing in a meagre patch of sunlight, aroused himself with flattering alacrity and rubbed himself slowly in and out between Sir Giles's legs, a thoughtful expression on his face.

"Oh, I didn't know you had arrived. Sarah, darling!" Elisabeth came up, rather breathless, hair rather disarranged, wearing her glasses (quite unnecessarily) and her dreadful predatory-clawed gardening gloves.

"Hello, Mother, darling." Sarah scrupulously kept all trace of disapproval from her voice, but managed dexterously to tuck a wisp of hair behind Elisabeth's ear as she kissed her, and to whisper that she had a faint smear of earth on her cheek.

Mr. Jones came up while Elisabeth was dithering with the tray of glasses Cruddles had brought out. He dealt so efficiently with the drinks that Sarah greeted him with far greater warmth than she had intended.

For a few minutes life simply spun on an apex of bliss, the sun breaking through clouds, glasses tinkling, talk a satisfying continuous buzz, laughter frequent, the promise of a "visitor-lunch" just around the corner of appetite and time. . . . Truly, Sarah thought, it was at life's most ecstatic moments that you unreasonably felt you could die happy.

The sun did just dim a little when Bronwen plodded on to the terrace, but not even her presence, festively clad in one of her new heavy white silk frocks, could take the splendour from the day. Not even the fastening of her pale gaze on Sir Giles and her immediate buttonholing of him with some obscure literary conundrum could spoil the enchantment that stretched in unending grace toward tomorrow evening.

"You aren't feeling too tired after all this work you have let yourself in for?" Mr. Jones asked, quite anxiously, as he gave Sarah a drink.

"It is an interesting job," she said, with faint reproof. And yet she had to admit that sometimes he showed greater virtues than the mere negative one of not hurting flies. The easy way he passed her a drink should surely be a lesson to Sir Giles with his cups of tea and coffee. "One doesn't really mind working hard." To speak of "one" rather than "I" seemed to put Mrs. Billing at one remove from shattering reality.

"Good," Mr. Jones said, smiling under cover of his moustache. "So long as it's what you want—that is the important thing for young people, I believe, to do what they want."

This too generous creed accounted for Bronwen, yet he still stuck to it. . . . Sarah marvelled at such simplicity. Yet, put at a disadvantage by his generosity of manner, she could only smile at him and say that it was kind of him to say so.

They were all gathered on the terrace now, including Tom. Unfortunately, and for no perceptible reason, Sir Giles appealed to his sense of humour; his laughter ran away down the garden, a startlingly mature, though meaningless, commentary. Well, he never did! His dark eyes fixed themselves unwinkingly upon the guest. Even after his mother had presented him, and Sir Giles had actually shaken hands with him, and there could be little further doubt in his mind that the visitor was on the usual sphere of the human species, Tom still continued to gaze at him as if his like had in fact never yet been seen on land or sea.

Sir Giles himself was conscious of this scrutiny before any of the others. It touched him on a peculiarly sensitive spot: for, whereas he knew—more or less—where he was with babies, and believed he was sympathetically fairly well up on adolescents, he would frankly admit that children between, say, five and twelve defeated him, left him floundering between the two stools of infancy and puberty. And if there were one thing Sir Giles disliked it was floundering.

"Do you go to school?" he asked, endeavouring to break the spell of Tom's dark gaze.

"No, I have Miss James. But Mrs. Moody showed me how to boil down arithmetic."

Sarah, coming to Sir Giles's rescue, heard the remark.

"Mrs. Moody is rather too fond of boiling things down," she said. She had never quite forgiven Mrs. Moody for saying that all that love really boiled down to was sex.

"Do you like arithmetic?" Sir Giles asked, glad of Sarah's elder-sister presence.

"It's *insubbortable*," Tom said, in a macabre voice.

They went into lunch. The dining room, which was by nature dark and uncertain of itself, today trilled and carolled with joy; yet not so much, Sarah had to admit, with conversation as with flowers. Nobody could shape flowers to such speaking mirth as Mother, when she put her mind to it. She had done this for Sir Giles . . . how sweet she was. . . .

Sarah cast a glance of such devotion and gratitude upon her mother that, on catching it, Elisabeth fumbled for her glasses, not able to believe her modest naked sight.

The lunch was just sufficiently tinged with formality to be right, Sarah felt. Even the sexes, four of each, around the table, helped the illusion of perfection—although Tom hardly held up the male side, of course, especially with his knife and fork in the wrong hands, and more or less upside down at that. Still, there was much, much, to commend the scene. There was Cruddles behaving like an efficient ghost and miraculously suggesting a trail of lesser ghosts giving power to his elbow and ever at his beck and call. . . . She was content to let Peter and his father take over Sir Giles, at the moment, on the subject of music and art. She could afford to be generous, with such an endless invitation of hours before her. She opened her ears to oblique confidences from Philly behind Mr. Jones's back.

With the melting of Mrs. Bale's regulation summer-visitor-ice-pudding in the mouth, all formality melted, too. This was as it should be: the afternoon left free from restriction of those social holdings back that were like people who hovered in doorways, saying "After you, please . . ." Left free for words to come out in any order they chose.

Sarah stared dreamily across the table and out of the window, not even bothering very much whether it would rain.

"There's Digby, recking not his own rede," she remarked, the words no longer meaning anything except that Digby wasn't getting on with any work.

"What a charmingly elusive description!" Sir Giles laughed.

"Yes, I suppose it is—" The words struck her anew. "Why was it, Bronwen?" she asked, quite kindly, loving everybody at this happy moment.

"You seemed to have strained the allusion, somehow," Bronwen beamed, in her element. "But I should think it must be because he the primrose of dalliance treads."

"How true!" Elisabeth sighed.

*   *   *   *   *

Philly got Sarah alone for a minute or two when she went up to her bedroom after lunch, to powder her nose and critically to survey the back of her hair with the aid of a hand mirror.

"It looks . . . grander," Philly said tentatively, respectfully.

"I had it set at a hairdresser's. I think the style is called a semi-page-boy. Do you think it's nice?"

"Very nice." Her eyes, as well as her voice, full of deep respect, Philly gazed at the dark silken length of her sister's hair falling very smoothly until a fascinating and very professional swerve laid a deep kink in it just above the shoulders. "It looks like a film star."

"I'm glad it's all right—because I couldn't afford it," Sarah said calmly. "What have you been doing, darling?"

"Oh, Sarah, it's been awful! I've been posing for Mr. Lupin."

"I don't see anything awful about that. But I certainly never thought he'd remember to ask you again."

"But he did. I would have had to go again this Week End, except for you coming."

"Is *that* why you were so pleased to see me?" Sarah asked, none too pleased herself.

"You know it wasn't, darling. But the picture isn't all—he gave me some little books. Wait—I'll show you." She went to fetch Mr. Lupin's painfully impulsive gift. Sarah was engrossed in her hair again when she returned, but graciously turned to attend to her sister's problem.

"Well, they are just two high-brow little books, obviously," Sarah said, with sweeping casualness.

"But they're *not*." Philly's distress deepened as she began to feel Sarah could not help her. "You know he doesn't like high-brow people," she added, in a sort of impersonal reproach.

"Then why this?" Sarah demanded, and read aloud: "'Mr. Osmund Kedger-Grope has just published his newest and slimmest book of verse. His inspiration for the first poem in the volume—entitled with simple candour, "First Poem"—came from prolonged contemplation of his friend Mr. Godfrey Wygod's tremendous imaginative painting of a pair of cloth button boots and a large lemon cheese tart, the latter of course symbolizing the sun setting on one of life's unfortunates, the former the drab reality of—'" Sarah broke off; demanded triumphantly: "What can all that be but high-brow? You know modern art is always obscure. *And* poetry." She laid the book aside, as if the whole matter were now satisfactorily cleared up.

"But I tell you he *isn't* high-brow," Philly still insisted, her distress not lessened. "He hates 'moderns' and 'intellectuals.'" Unconsciously she used Mr. Lupin's inverted commas for the words.

"Well, whatever he is or isn't, I can't waste time discussing it all day," Sarah said impatiently. "Just tell him you thought the second book was even better than the first, if you have to say something."

This light brushing aside of the intrinsic puzzle of the matter, not to mention the blatant insincerity of the actual words, shocked Philly into silence. Silent still, she followed Sarah downstairs.

The telephone rang as they reached the hall, and Sarah ran to answer it. It was Mrs. Oxford. Without preamble she said: "Come to tea this afternoon, dear. I must hear all about London." As if London existed only through me, Sarah thought. Her reply was hesitant: tea with Mrs. Oxford had always been more or less a royal command. "It's very kind of you, but I have Sir Giles Merrick here—"

"Bring him, too, of course," Mrs. Oxford said. For the first time in her life, Sarah felt her old friend really had rather a cool nerve. As if Sir Giles would jump at the chance of being dragged out to one of the Oxford teas—"Pansy and her niece will probably drop in," the old lady added. That, naturally, made a difference; suggested something of the legendary Fontayne house party that had never taken place. "Thank you. I expect we'll drop in, too," Sarah said, as graciously as Mrs. Oxford herself could have said it.

Sir Giles also received the idea graciously. It was an admirable plan, when one came to think of it, killing two birds with one stone: killing the threatened void of aimlessness in the afternoon, and killing off the possibility of Bronwen tagging on. Neither Bronwen nor Peter would be paid to pay social respects to Mrs. Oxford since that evening she came to dinner.

"Are you coming, Mother?" Sarah asked.

Elisabeth turned a wistful glance toward the patch of garden that had occupied her attention in the morning.

"Don't bother. I expect you'd rather stay here," Sarah said. Her grown-up indulgent tone might as well have made it "play" instead of "stay." It relegated Elisabeth, if not to the nursery, at least to the nursery garden. "And you won't be coming, Philly?"

Philly hastily said, "No," feeling this was expected of her.

It was as simple as that. . . . The first part of the afternoon passed without a single awkward pause, the memoirs not yet called upon in their capacity of reserve strength; and at four o'clock Sarah and Sir Giles got into his car and drove down to Mrs. Oxford's.

As soon as she saw her old friend again, Sarah felt ashamed of her moment's criticism of her. Kissing the withered violet-scented cheek, all the old deference returned. And to see Mrs. Oxford's reception of Sir Giles was a revelation of ceremoniousness allied to a sort of august playfulness: her tone recomposing his character for him, the public man blended skilfully with the charming little boy he must once undoubtedly have been.

"Only the two of you?" She looked round in vain for attendant representatives of Fontayne.

Before Sarah could begin to make excuses, however, Mr. Harbrittle arrived. Mrs. Oxford's diamonds encompassed his frail yellow hand. "I think you know Giles Merrick," she said.

Relinquishing his Panama hat, his cane, and his frosty social amiability, Mr. Harbrittle said sharply: "I think I was the first to have that pleasure in this part of the world." He made his old neighbour's presumption seem a geographical rather than a social solecism.

"Ah, of course," she said blandly. "He is staying the Week End at Fontayne."

"Indeed." Mr. Harbrittle stared full at Sarah before turning his complete attention to Sir Giles.

Rain rattled suddenly and sharply against the window; like some immediate retribution, Sarah thought, for one's having stolen Sir Giles from Mr. Harbrittle. Now, it would be no use trying to cajole him into talking of his middle chapters, middle Europe, or anything else; in a studied monumental fashion, he was engaged in sulking.

Emily came in and said how-d'you-do all round, politely, then sat down on an edge of chair, bent low over a tortuous bit of knitting, fingers flying. She knitted in a loose end of hair from one of her plaits, but was glad to find nobody had noticed this comic bit of by-play. Grandmother, preparing the ritual of silver kettle on patent boiler, had luckily forgotten her existence for the moment.

"I did not even know you had returned to England," Mr. Harbrittle said to Sir Giles in a refrigerated ice-cubed sort of tone.

"I never know where I'll be," Sir Giles said easily.

"The situation could scarcely be worse, I suppose?" Waiting for the exact inspired moment to snatch the kettle from its moorings, Mrs. Oxford gracefully left herself open to correction.

"Scarcely," Sir Giles agreed cheerfully.

"When one thinks of it"—she lifted the kettle, heated the massive silver teapot with a swift rinse of hot water, dexterously turned it over a slop bowl, measured a properly meagre quantity of "her" China tea into it, poured water in a long steaming spout from the kettle held high from an angle of steep fingers and diamonds, finally shut the teapot lid with a reverence only less than that she employed for closing her Bible at the conclusion of a chapter—"when one thinks of it, that we should be sitting here, still concerned with our civilized trivialities, it seems extraordinary to realize that we are neither more nor less than sitting on a volcano." Nothing less like a volcano-sitter than Mrs. Oxford presiding at her nests on nests of little tea tables could possibly have been imagined, so it was hardly surprising that nobody was overcome by horror in contemplation of the immediate future.

Emily hadn't heard. She had drifted out of the room, though her thin little body remained perched on the edge of her chair. Disembodied— yet with a fine feeling of solidity—she mounted her white steed, with a courtier to ride on either side. One of these was her cousin, a prince who loved her from the depths of his chivalrous heart. Out beyond the palace gates and up the white road to Adriana's Tower, the sunlight on the tiny peaked hat set slantways on the Queen's blue-black mass of hair. Emily breathed the beautiful impossible scents of the morning that made even the Queen say she felt lifted out of herself. The land was patched with unknown flowers that Emily had not yet had time to invent for this particular spring season, being too busy with the conversation of the courtier prince. But she knew exactly what the view was from the top of Adriana's Tower down over the distant spread of the great city of Pompadella. The Queen gazed down, down, *down* through the shimmering sun, monarch indeed of all she surveyed—

"Emily, don't plait your legs!"

Obedient to her grandmother's command (the Queen still leaning lightly on her cousin's arm) Emily unwound her sharp-boned legs from the tortured attitude which high altitudes of imagination sometimes induced them to assume, and went on gazing at the ineffable pearl-pink view of the far City.

Sir Giles looked suddenly across at Sarah and smiled. She had been happy enough merely to be near him, but his swift little intimate regard lifted her once more on to the highest plane of bliss. Quiet, now, don't whisper it . . . but he does seem to realize I exist. He does more . . . he looks at me as if he knows and likes me well. . . .

Lady Pansy arrived, followed by Virginia Welwyn, hatless and dressed with a surprising simplicity; until one looked again and saw how consummately the simplicity was underlaid with cunning. Even Lady Pansy seemed to have been curbed of some of her scarf-mania in her niece's presence. Her light tweed was a very French sporting English ensemble, and her row of palpably false pearls had a peculiarly chaste elegance all their own.

"Don't have fresh tea made, Bunty," Pansy said, kissing her friend on either cheek. "I *like* mine stewed. Ah, Joey, how are you?" She raised her furry powdered clown's eyebrows at Mr. Harbrittle.

"My tea is quite incapable of stewing, Pansy," Mrs. Oxford said sternly.

"Giles!" Pansy turned aside. "You must come and see the extraordinary house Virginia has taken. You know my niece?"

"Of course he does," Virginia said, going over to stand beside him. "Yes, it's quite a bilious sort of house, but I'm only here for occasional Week Ends."

The worst of being both rich and good-looking, Lady Pansy thought, was that it made one liable never to see anyone else's point of view. It did not seem to enter Virginia's head that her aunt had to bear that biliousness the summer through. . . .

"Hello," Sarah said shyly, abruptly.

"Hello!" Virginia flashed her wide brilliant smile. "What have you been doing?"

Not knowing that this was simply a gambit to display undemanding interest, Sarah did not know where to begin to say what she had been doing since last she saw the lovely Mrs. Welwyn in the spring.

"She has become a working woman in London," Sir Giles answered for her.

"But how marvellous!" Virginia said admiringly.

"She works for a giant," he elaborated.

"Things like that never happen to me," Virginia smiled. "Once when I was very young *I* thought I'd like to work. Just one of those ideas of the very young, you know." Her violet eyes looked gravely up from beneath her perfectly-painted lashes. "I think it was some sort of idea of finding out how the other half of the world lived. *You* know." (Her "you knows" were oddly inviting and appealing.) "I hired myself out as a sort of Mother's Help, I think it was, to a wee wifie type of person in a woeful cosy suburb. *You* know. It wasn't so much an experience as an absolute *revelation* of dreariness." Her wonderful smile suddenly lifted the rueful corners of her mouth dazzlingly. "I do admire people who can find anything as exotic as a *giant* to work for."

Sir Giles and Sarah both laughed; but she felt she did so under false pretences. They couldn't know a giant could be quite as dreary as any wee wifie if it were in the person of Mrs. Billing.

"If you're in London, you must come and see me," Virginia said. "And you, too." She looked at Sir Giles. "None of my friends ever comes to see me. I think I must have one of those devastatingly sordid complaints you read about in advertisements. *You* know: why one's friends drop one like hot bricks. Stories in pictures, from degrading beginnings to wonderfully happy endings. There can't be any other explanation of why I'm always left severely alone."

Only somebody who lived constantly surrounded by popularity and friendship could possibly say such things, Sarah thought enviously. She could see in her mind a glamorous picture of Mrs. Welwyn's many-windowed flat, people always "dropping in" and having a drink and talking, nobody in the least formal. How lovely. . . .

"How is that sweet gruff brother with the fair hair?" Virginia asked.

"Christopher? Oh, he's at school." She felt personally flattered by Mrs. Welwyn's remembering him. "He'll be home soon."

"Give him my love when you see him."

Sarah knew that she would do no such thing; it would embarrass poor Christopher far too much; but all the same she was grateful and would pass on some slightly expurgated version of her words to him.

"If you have finished tea, Emily, you can go and play," Mrs. Oxford said. She thought the child seemed unsuitably engrossed in grown-up conversation.

Emily, who had known nothing of what was going on around her, rose from the edge of her chair and left the Queen riding like the wind back home to the palace. There was a Ball that night, at which she would wear a sumptuous jewel-sewn crinoline. Emily hitched at her meagre skirt, feeling the languid pull of the crinoline against her legs.

"Emily!"

"Yes, Grandmother?" She turned at the door.

"Your skirt, child!"

Sighing, Emily gave up the ghost of her regal panniers and realized that the scrappy tartan pleats of sad reality were ignobly tangled at one side in one of the garters holding up her best black silk stockings which Grandmother liked her to wear on tea-party days. A shocking expanse of thin white leg was revealed to all the world of Mrs. Oxford's drawing room.

"I despair of that child ever learning any of the *graces* of living," Mrs. Oxford said, when her granddaughter had departed. "*Squirming* is an attribute of the young which I find difficult to endure."

Nobody could approve of Mrs. Oxford's cruel-to-be-kind bullying of Emily; which was not to say that anyone ever defended the child against her grandmother. What they would have said (had they ever said anything) was that the whole thing was too easy, not exactly cricket on Mrs. Oxford's part, because Emily never threatened for a moment to stand up to it.

The whole party soon began to break up after that.

"Perhaps I'll see you at church tomorrow," Virginia said, slipping away so unobtrusively that it was almost incredible she could at the same time command the room in doing so.

Did she mean it? Sarah couldn't decide. Church and Mrs. Welwyn didn't *seem* to go together, but one never knew. That Lady Pansy went to church Sarah knew, because Philly had told her of being called into the almond icing last Saturday for the purpose of redoing Lady Pansy's nails a paler and more decorous shade in readiness for Sunday's service.

Sarah was still pondering the question as Sir Giles drove her back to Fontayne. The rain fell steadily, despondently, now. The evening's promise became faintly tinged with threat.

Looking back, there was no certain mark dividing promise from threat; not even any certainty that fulfilment had been tamer than either threat or promise would have seemed to suggest. But the thing that fulfilments ought not to do was to peter out; which was what the Week End did.

Saturday evening, in spite of the rain, did not entirely fall to pieces; but the exciting feeling of being the important independent daughter did. The atmosphere of Fontayne disintegrated all but the most willful alien egos, so what chance had anyone with the mere home ego which was shared, in a way, by all the family? Sir Giles, naturally, did not suffer from this disadvantage. Indeed, he held up his end against all comers, against Joneses as well as Fontaynes. He had so much time and sympathy for all of them that an obvious consequence was that his time and sympathy for Sarah were, by comparison, scamped. Before the evening was out, he was in danger of becoming that most lamentable, least exciting proposition, a friend of the family.

Not that he himself diminished in exciting qualities for an instant; which made things all the more exhausting for Sarah. If it had not rained, there might have been opportunities for escape . . . showing him the rose garden in the warm twilight, for instance . . . but, as it was, the dismal truth was like nothing so much as a prolonged game of Happy Families.

Sarah knew she would never forget the malicious cheerful rattle of rain on the windows; the feeling of being shut up with emotion, piling up until you thought you would burst. Like the Brontës . . . she thought; a dark turgid concentration on close-knit family life.

The house looked shabby, artless, out of step. His bedroom, she knew, was the one with the canopied bed; but even that seemed an empty gesture. He must have seen beneath the pretence of Fontayne by now. Mount Olympus indeed! Even Mr. Jones perversely made no attempt to prove he was clever. Nothing less like a fiery artistic genius could have been imagined than himself in his mood of tonight. He was nothing short of *benign*, Sarah thought indignantly, his gentle melancholy eyes going from one to another of them, pausing longest on Elisabeth. If he went on like this there would be no hope of his ever getting another engagement—or whatever it was conductors got—and he would simply sink into Fontayne and leave no ripple. Music might be in his bones, but it looked as if he were going to allow it to set stiff in them.

Peter was polite and attentive, but an underlying moody restlessness was apparent to Sarah. And Sir Giles's was such a superior brand of sophistication to his—so easy and unstressed —that the boy was at a disadvantage, reduced within himself.

If one could only assume a Virginia Welwyn manner, and say with simple candour, "We're going off by ourselves to examine the memoirs, so be sure none of you disturbs us," how easy life would be; but one couldn't. He would not even allow his eye to be caught. It was like having a panther in the room, as large and lithe as life, yet willing to lie back with its head against a shabby cushion and blink its eyes in sleepy brightness at Mother knitting a horrible endless garment which had long ceased to have any semblance of probability.

A log fire burned in the huge drawing-room grate, setting up an unseasonable spectre of autumn, depressing in spite of the warmth. Even before ten o'clock, Elisabeth gave a couple of unpardonable little yawns. Retirement was in the air then; inescapable. The summer cold of bedrooms cast chill presaging breaths, ghostly draughts through the warm air. And was there the least likelihood in the world that the bath water would be hot in the morning?

Sarah knew that nothing had gone wrong, that Sir Giles had fitted in well—all too well—with Fontayne, but that neither was everything perfectly right by a long, long way. Had anyone ever thought of placing special literature by Sir Giles's bedside, even? Flowers there would inevitably be—but a back stairs of politics could not live by flowers alone.

Tom had gone early to bed, followed surprisingly soon by Bronwen. Philly, with Ernest taking up three-quarters of her chair, had nothing to say. To be the eldest of a family was a tragic thing, Sarah thought; it meant that all one's youth was attuned to the presence of children, one's own individuality swallowed up in the whole puerile design of life for the young. . . .

The yawns were contagious. Conversation had petered out and left one enormous amorphous gape in sway. Sir Giles said quite casually, without apology to himself or anyone else, that he was going to bed.

Philly went in to Sarah's room early next morning, still in her dressing gown.

"Bronwen has gone down to the other bath and is taking all the hot water, I expect, so if I have one now there may not be any left for him."

"*What* are you talking about?" Sarah said crossly, sitting up in bed and rubbing her eyes.

"I told Bronwen to use our bathroom, so that he could have the decent one in peace, but she took no notice. She rushed off to get there before he did."

Tears welled in Sarah's heart and nearly reached her eyes. She felt that nothing more depressing than this sordid bath-scramble could possibly be imagined.

"If you mean Sir Giles," she said tonelessly, "I wish you wouldn't call him 'he.'"

"Sarah darling,"—Philly eyed her with a maternal sort of anxiety—"aren't you happy in London?"

"No," Sarah said, weak and cowardly from a disturbed night and this dismal bath-water overture to the day.

"Do you hate your job?"

"Yes."

Philly's strong slim golden arms, so pleasing to Mr. Lupin's robust artistic eye, flung themselves fiercely around the tense form of her elder sister. She felt painfully protective, supporting the slight shoulders, feeling the silky fall of Sarah's hair across her arm. "What is it, darling?" she whispered, rocking her gently, as if she were a baby.

"Oh . . . everything. The two girls—the secretaries—laugh at me and sneer at me, and when they are a bit nicer to me it's even worse. They call me"—she paused on the enormity—*"Sally."*

"You must never go back," Philly said, as if that decided it.

"Of course I'm going back. Don't be silly." Wearily, Sarah slid back the bedclothes. "I might as well get up."

"What shall we do about baths?" Philly said, seeing it would be useless to argue.

"Oh, I don't care. I shall go dirty. What does it matter?" She was feeling terribly Russian. "Wouldn't it be the utterly last straw if Mother and Mr. Jones went in for a baby?" she suggested, sinking into an ultimate Siberian gloom.

"They couldn't," Philly said firmly, though she was struck not altogether unpleasantly by the idea; but for Sarah, she might even have dwelt lovingly upon such a theme. "They couldn't," she repeated. "They're too old."

"You never know," Sarah said darkly.

It was raining; had obviously continued all night and would go on through all the morning. Breakfast seemed soaked in its long monotonous plash. The terrace and stretching lawn were dressed in a sloppy uniform of grey; even the waistcoats of robins looked drab.

Sir Giles, hot plentiful water or not, looked marvellous. Sarah's heart reluctantly lightened a fraction as his eyes met hers fully and exclusively as he said good morning. Loving him a little less, how happy one might have been. Then, to look at him would always have been bliss and never torture. Why can't I see him just as a handsome fascinating man and leave it at that? She gazed at him across the table, trying to fix his image temperately. But it is no use. The whole *point* of him is that it is more torture than bliss to be with him. Even to pass the toast to him—

He smiled at her as she did so. "Are we going to church?"

"'Are we?'" she echoed stupidly.

"You ought to, if only to hear the excruciating church organ," Peter said.

"Shall we go?"

"Do," Elisabeth said. "It's time somebody did."

Sarah stared at her coldly. What a way to treat Sir Giles, as a mere useful unit to fill up a depleted congregation!

Elisabeth wondered what she had done now. She had got up feeling so pleased with the soft prolonged fall of rain, but nobody seemed to appreciate it except herself and Julian.

Bronwen was glowering at her plate of cereal. Even Peter had lost his normal playful gallantry toward Elisabeth this morning; which was a relief, in a way, for she had grown a little tired of his persistent whisking of her chair into position for her. Courtesy was all very well, but when it developed into something like musical chairs it became a little wearing, though naturally she would not have dreamed of letting Peter know this. . . .

"You'll come to church with me, then, Sarah?" Sir Giles said boyishly.

The question was delivered so flatteringly and exclusively to her that her unreliable heart took a wild upward leap, preventing the logical descent of a piece of toast from mouth to throat. For a moment, her larynx throttled, she felt as if all her mechanism had gone seriously wrong. She didn't know how she at last got words out with grave precision:

"Yes, I should like to do that."

"I shall come to church," Tom said, smiting the top off a boiled egg with one fearful blow.

"You will not," Sarah retorted furiously, before she remembered to camouflage her motives and emotions.

"Well, I never!" Tom eyed her in placid wonder. "Well, I never did, in all my born days! Fancy trying to *stop* anyone going to church." He was slightly shocked by this reversal of all accepted Sabbath rules.

"Of course Tom can go, if he wishes," Elisabeth said.

Sarah stared at her fixedly. How could any human being be so dumb—in the sense that Lily and Joan at the office used the word?

"Let Tom stay here this morning," Mr. Jones said unexpectedly. He caught Sarah's eye, but hastily let it go again. Whatever his artistic perception did or did not understand in this delicate situation he did not desire to be led into any closer conspiracy.

"Very well. You stay here, Tom," Elisabeth instantly agreed, it being Julian's suggestion.

"Very well. Tom will stay here," Tom said, his eyes fixed on Sarah, his mind gradually working round to a true interpretation of the matter. "You needn't have been afraid I'd come with you," he said, making himself all too clear. "I would have gone on my little bikikle and I would have met Mrs. Moody for church." Mercifully, he at last transferred his gaze from Sarah to his egg. "But never mind. Tom will stay here."

* * * * *

"I'm afraid it's all very boring for you," Sarah said, as they walked through the rain to church. It no longer seemed any use pretending the Week End was a dazzling success.

"On the contrary, I find it most restful and charming," Sir Giles said, like someone out of a book.

He must be used to disguising his feelings, so she was not convinced. But she felt happier now. Walking with him in the light rain was a sweet experience. She was glad they had had time for the walk, instead of rushing down in his un-Sundayish car. Here was peace now, deep and green, even her heart beating tranquilly. Only once did it threaten to get out of control again; when she saw a raindrop poised on his thick dark lashes like some preposterous tear. She kept step with his long-legged paces, as if in duty bound to do so. She was sorry that his beautiful brown suède shoes would probably be marred for life after this rain; though perhaps it was just as well they should be toned down a little before they reached church, as it seemed unlikely that anything quite so worldly had ever crossed the threshold into the sober aisle.

Several people she knew saw them go into church together: Bob Norbett, and Mrs. Pratt from the haberdashery, and Mrs. Oxford and Emily. The service passed like a dream. The church (very High) usually had suffocating-sweet traces of incense in the air; but this morning, standing, sitting, kneeling, Sarah was aware only of that indefinable, elusive, manly fragrance emanating from Sir Giles himself. Shaving soap, expensive tobacco, light seemly tweed . . . she wasn't sure where it began or ended. Rain trickling down the outside of the feeble stained-glass windows made them more blurred than ever. She prayed for him. *Whatever happens, I hope he's always happy because he needs to be.* . . . Mrs. Oxford and her granddaughter were in the pew just in front. Emily's bowed nape of neck, where an undecided little fluff of dark hair escaped from her rigorous plaits, was oddly pathetic. Her poke-bonnet sort of headgear shot up surprisingly from her peaked little forehead. Mrs. Oxford wore a dissimulating ledge of wig under her own high-perched hat. The sermon limped on, unspectacularly. Sarah threw heart and soul into the singing of the final hymn.

The churchyard smelt damp and acrid as they walked out through it. The atmosphere was morbid, single-minded; concerned with death. Rain fell in deliberate intrusive drops straight down the back of one's neck, from what Tom called the funeral trees. It was spine-chilling, actually as well as metaphorically. No cheerful bustle of departing congregation, its mind with but a single thought of the pleasure of the midday meal, could drag the churchyard from its melancholy contemplation of mortal frailty. That it should matter so vitally whether or not Sir Giles smiled was quite beside the point. Death and corruption and then everlasting rest were the proper point. . . . . Sarah shivered.

Away from the churchyard, it was better. Virginia Welwyn appeared from nowhere and lightened the morning with her brilliant smile.

"Hello. I didn't see you. Were you there?"

"We were," Sir Giles said.

"Isn't it sinister? That odd smell, and the fumed oak or whatever it is. *You* know. The bats in the belfry seem to be practically in your hair all the time. You must come and have a drink with Aunt Pansy."

"Will that be all right?" Sir Giles courteously deferred to Sarah.

"Yes, I think so. We can walk back quickly. The almond icing is quite near here."

Neither Sir Giles nor Mrs. Welwyn knew what she meant, but didn't bother to ask. They discovered mutual friends—in conversation, not in the flesh—between the church and the house, and discussed them contentedly.

"I have had a terrible morning," Lady Pansy greeted them.

Sarah waited for details of disaster, but none came. The Chinese interior of the almond icing flowered hospitably. The door of a cocktail cabinet swung open, like the front of a dolls' house being removed in a ruthless display of an intimate interior; but instead of the dolls' home life being revealed, one saw only the life of Mrs. Welwyn's country Week End in bottle on shining bottle inhabiting glass compartments.

"It's a rest," Virginia explained. "I like to come here for a day and a night and simply go *slack*."

Lady Pansy, who had expected and hoped to preside over interesting batches of week-end visitors, gave her own individual brand of sniff. "Where is the other one?" she asked Sarah.

"Philly? She stayed at home."

"H'm. She should have kept her hair on top, as I did it."

"Yes," Sarah agreed, not knowing the key to her cryptic remark.

"She would never be a profile beauty, but I believe something *good* could be made of her front face. Personally, I dislike profile beauties; they are usually far too cold. I was never one myself. A front-face beauty always enjoys life more, you will find."

215 | BENEATH THE VISITING MOON

"Do they—does she?" Sarah said; lost. To make a profession of beauty must be a very exacting thing, she thought. She had not realized that angles came into it in such a crucial way.

"Now you, I would say, can make a compromise between the two. You should be able to vary the statuesque with the vivacious. In some ways that leaves you more free. You don't attain perfection from either view, but neither is there any obvious flaw."

"I see," Sarah said, trying to sound intelligent.

"Virginia is of the same type. In fact"—her eyes beneath the untidy jut of eyebrow passed critically from Sarah to her niece—"you are quite alike, really. You both have the fined-down look that is admired now. It has an appeal, though personally I feel it is quite irrelevant to beauty." Lady Pansy shrugged her massive shoulders that had regally cushioned so many compliments as they had gone in at one ear and dropped out at the other, in the magnificently unthinking days of her youth. Like a magnolia, she had been, full and ripe and white. . . . She took up her cocktail glass and refused herself the solace of a sigh.

Sarah passed from a stage of flattered pleasure at being likened to Virginia to a sense of obscure woe. To be oneself could be oddly comforting even in the midst of misgiving, but to be cast ever so faintly in the image of another was somehow a dangerous thing. She could— but only just—see what Lady Pansy meant. That "fined-down" look; but only by chance possessed by oneself; in Virginia, a deliberate . . . yes . . . *pruning*. And everything that went with pruning (she thought vaguely of her mother in the appalling gardening gloves): the tender care of every detail, the training through years. No, it wasn't exactly comfortable to come anywhere within the orbit of Virginia's perfection, even if she were not really any better-looking than oneself, perhaps. The thing was, one would never tire of watching her, but only rarely had one the patience for any lengthy self-scrutiny. Virginia's movements would never know painful urgency. She would come and go with herself exactly as she pleased, and never get lost. She was cool in just the way she intended to be, her smile ready to her need with all the warmth in the world. Her complexion was cool and assured; her colouring warm of violet eye and of bronze lights flecked through brown hair. Her hands, Sarah thought quite humbly and without false modesty, were by nature almost as beautiful as one's own, and by art even more civilized and elegant.

Mrs. Welwyn caught her watchful glance and casually left Sir Giles to cross the room to her.

"Is that all right?" She pointed childishly at Sarah's glass.

"It's very nice, thank you," Sarah said primly, smiling.

"I'm glad," Virginia said, as if it really mattered. Lady Pansy had dragged Sir Giles off to look at the unnecessary back staircase which still held a morbid fascination for her. "He's nice, isn't he . . . Giles?" she said easily.

"Yes," Sarah said, with a surprised feeling that she scarcely knew of whom Virginia spoke. Even in her thoughts she always saw and felt him formally as "Sir Giles."

"I don't know why we meet so seldom," Virginia went on vaguely. "You must be sure to come and see me in town."

Together, did she mean? It was all so friendly, but so offhand. Sarah felt her throat ache with doubts. She put down her glass still half filled. She couldn't manage the drink, after all. It wasn't only that it didn't seem to settle very well on the top of church; Sir Giles was mixed up with it, too, making it taste sharp with misgivings.

She was glad when he returned with Lady Pansy and came to her side. "Oughtn't we to be going?" he asked, with that surface play of diffidence that so well became the reality of his full assurance.

"Yes, we ought," she said, glad for him to say it first.

A more than usually at-sixes-and-sevens atmosphere was apparent to Sarah when they returned to Fontayne. The weight of the persistent rain lay heavy not only in clogged gutters and drains, but was a spiritual burden, too; yet it was more than that. Mr. Jones seemed rather more *distrait* than usual as he offered Sir Giles a drink and accepted his refusal. Mother was not to be seen, and after a minute or two Mr. Jones vanished, too. Tom, inventing on the drawing-room rug in front of the renewed log fire, was not very helpful. There was never anywhere to go, when it was too wet for the terrace. For such a rambling house, it could seem singularly cramped and awkward. The "excellent accommodation" of those advertisements, laboriously written out so often in one's mind, was proved in this event to be the barefaced lie one had always half suspected it of being.

"Do you like weddings?" Tom looked up from his inventing to ask of Sir Giles.

"I don't think I do, very much," he smiled. "Do you?"

"I don't know," Tom said mournfully. "That's what I'll never know."

This was all somewhat beyond Sir Giles, yet he contrived to look sympathetically interested.

"Don't be silly, Tom," Sarah said brusquely.

"I'm not silly. I looked *forward* to that wedding." His grudge against Sarah for not letting him go to church this morning had deepened to include former things he held to her discredit.

"What wedding?" Sir Giles asked, innocently encouraging.

"Mr. Jones and my mother," Tom said, with dignity.

"And they didn't let you go? Too bad."

"He did go. But he didn't—well he didn't feel too good at the ceremony," Sarah explained. "Through no fault of his own," she added with scrupulous fairness.

Tom smiled tenderly at her. He suddenly, and rather thankfully, found that he had forgiven her for everything.

Philly slipped into the room and said, in a rather stagy aside to Sarah: "Bronwen has gone to bed."

"Why?"

"She suddenly came on a horrid piece about her book, in the Sunday paper," Philly said, as if it were something that had leapt out and bitten Bronwen.

"Did she?" Sarah felt a little more cheerful again. "What she calls a review you mean?"

"Yes. I saw a bit of it. It said: 'Far be it from my intention to be cruel to children, but this is pretentious nonsense,'" Philly said, all on one breath and note, without censure either for the reviewer or Bronwen.

Bronwen lay on her bed and sobbed. Her whole body heaved and quaked; there were no half-measures in her giving way to grief. She wished she had never written a book, she wished that she were not a girl, and she wished she could die. The curtains blowing at her open window were soaked with muddy outdoor tears.

Sarah, coming in with a kind word on the tip of her tongue, to hide the slightly morbid streak of her curiosity, received a wrong impression of the scene. Seeing a half-empty bottle on the bedside table, she interpreted Bronwen's plight over-dramatically. With something almost like respect in her voice, she asked:

"You weren't trying to . . . end it all, Bronwen?"

Bronwen raised a tear-swollen face. "I've got indigestion," she said feebly, not wanting Sarah to know she cared about the review.

"Oh, is *that* what the bottle is for? I can give you some powder stuff to take that is probably better than this." (Automatically, unnecessarily, she pushed Mrs. Billing's wares, even now, out of hours.) She picked up the bottle.

"Don't!" Bronwen cried. But she was too late.

Sarah was already reading "Reduco" on the label, and was forming her own conclusions. "You mustn't take this. It's very bad for growing girls," she said virtuously.

"Leave me alone. Go away!" Bronwen entreated. It was the ultimate blow, the most ruthless tearing away of covering to the Achilles' heel; that Sarah should know one had ever for a moment even *wanted* to be thin. . . .

Sarah felt an unaccountable pang. She put down the bottle and gazed down at the disordered pale dried-seaweed hair scattered in a veil over Bronwen's face.

"I knew a positively *enormous* girl who got quite thin when she was a bit older than you," she invented rapidly. "There's nothing unusual in being a bit . . . plump. I believe *I* was," she lied unconvincingly. Then, unable to control the generous impulse, she rushed on: "Surely you don't take any notice of what people write in papers. Why, when the Rudge triplets won that prize, the paper just said anything it liked, regardless of truth."

"You don't understand," Bronwen said haughtily, sniffing. "Reviews aren't like that."

"But surely you don't believe what this one said?"

"No, of course not."

"Well, then—"

Bronwen waved her fat hands with the ghost of their usual bravado. It was no use. You couldn't expect a Philistine like Sarah to understand.

"Promise you won't take any more of that stuff, anyway," Sarah said, with a nearly Elisabeth-like concern.

"All right—I won't," Bronwen promised ungraciously. It had made her feel ill, in any case. Mopping her eyes, she gulped convulsively. "I wish I weren't a girl."

"Would you rather be a boy?" Sarah asked incredulously.

"No. I just don't want to be a girl."

"But you have to be one or the other," Sarah said; honestly believing this.

"All I said was that I don't want to be a girl. I think it's perfectly horrid."

"Well, it's too late to do anything about it now," Sarah said, utterly perplexed by the workings of her stepsister's mind. "I'm going down to Sir Giles now. Do bathe your eyes and come down to lunch and be sensible."

"I don't want to come down to lunch." She hesitated, her pale red-rimmed eyes hovering over Sarah. "But you could bring me a morsel up here, if you would. The underdone part, you know, if it's beef. And I think I saw a chocolate mousse being made, so I'll try a little of that afterwards."

Sarah was smiling as she went downstairs. It was surprising how her sudden generous feeling for Bronwen had also made her feel quite warm and indulgent toward her. She felt in a hazy, benign, adult mood; most comforting.

Neither the mood nor the comfort lasted. Sir Giles was in the hall at the telephone, she saw, as she reached the foot of the stairs. There was something *up*, she was sure: that respectfully taut look about the jut of his shoulders, the tense planes of his clear-cut face half turned from her. "Yes, I'll come right away, sir." Down went the receiver with a masterful bang. He turned and walked straight into Sarah, who stood consciously and desolately eavesdropping.

"My dear—" Half laughing, he put out his hands to ward off the full collision. She stood within the shelter of his arms and gazed anxiously up at him. "I'm sorry, I shall have to go at once. My chief particularly wants to see me." He smiled tenderly into her eyes. "Something slightly urgent—"

What did he mean—"slightly urgent"? She shivered in his clasp. His beautiful voice makes you notice when he says *slipshod* things. It might have been me, saying that. I can't bear it. . . .

"But you'll stay to lunch?" She kept her voice cool, not to be unfair to him.

"No, I must go at once. I shall get a sandwich on the way. I'm very sorry to go—"

"Are you?"

"It has been delightful. Where is . . . your mother, everyone?"

"I don't know." She still gazed at him.

Gently, he removed his hands from her shoulders. "I'll see you in London, of course, shan't I?"

"I hope so," she sighed. It did not seem to have occurred to him that she might drive back to London with him now, instead of staying out her Week End at Fontayne.

"I *am* sorry I have to go."

Without warning he bent toward her and kissed her cheek. She hadn't even time to enjoy it, so unexpected was it. She stood as if transfixed. Even when he turned away in vague search for Elisabeth, she could not move. She saw that, taut again, he was speaking to Cruddles. She felt utterly alone and bereft, in spite of the kiss. Somebody opened the front door and the green rain light was intensified, the flowers in the great hall vases seeming to stretch up and outward as if seeking to be quenched by the wet morning weather. Transfixed, she felt the hall awake to the full sad bustle of departure.

"It's no use mooning around doing nothing," Mrs. Moody said. "Why not sit down and cut out a blouse. I've a nice dressy piece of lace here that would be just the thing."

"I don't want a nice dressy lace blouse," Sarah said flatly. "I can't imagine anything I'd like less."

"You'd find it would come in, duck."

"I hate things that 'come in,'" Sarah said implacably. "What are you doing here on Sunday, anyway?"

"I thought I'd just run up and iron your mother's lonjy."

"Oh." The word was no mystery to Sarah; indeed, it was far more expressive than the affected word "lingerie" could ever be. Mother's lonjy was very fine and patrician and beautiful: her one real luxury, apart from the garden.

The big ironing board and the lesser sleeve board were up and in position in the sewing room. Mrs. Moody was nothing short of an artist at pressing clothes. All specially treasured garments, coming limp from the wash, were brought miraculously back to life by the cunning even pressure of her hand upon the iron.

"I would have gone back with him if I'd been you," Mrs. Moody said, testing the warmth of the iron against her face, so close that it almost singed her moustache.

"Oh, you would?"

"Yes, I would, duck," she said, undaunted by Sarah's tone. "It's out of sight out of mind with some of these fine fellows."

"I can't imagine what you are talking about."

"He's very well set-up and handsome, I'll give you that, but I shouldn't be surprised if Number One doesn't always come first with him. He's too old for you to bother about, anyway, duck; though I must say when I was a girl I didn't give twopence for the young ones if there was a likely older one about."

As if it mattered what Mrs. Moody would or would not have given twopence for. Her idea of an "older man" had probably been a nice steady widower in a cloth cap. . . .

"You're looking a bit peaked with that London job, love. Do you get yourself enough to eat?"

"Of course," Sarah said haughtily.

"Be sure you spend all that allowance they give you."

Sarah was silent. She was beginning to fear there was no way out of taking that advice. It was incredible just how far the dazzling sum of two pounds a week *didn't* go, when it came to the point. . . .

Mr. Jones, too, urged her, before she left, to make full use of the allowance, and more if she needed it. She felt humiliated, yet grateful. "Or if"—he hesitated—"you would rather give the job a rest for a while—"

As if you could expect jobs to wait for you while you rested! Had the man never heard of unemployment? . . . "Naturally I should not dream of doing that," she said indignantly.

Mr. Jones did at least take No for an answer; which was more than Mother did. She went over and over the same ground, weeding it of all arguments in favour of the job. "It isn't as if you are doing anyone in the world any *good* by working, darling."

Sarah kept stubbornly silent. Tears had been so ominously close since the moment Sir Giles's car had swung out of sight that she dared do nothing that might raise her emotional temperature.

"It's so lonely for you, too. There is nobody for you to see except Bracken and—now—Giles Merrick. I do hope he continues to take a little notice of you—"

For some reason these would-be hopeful words, as Elisabeth gazed short-sightedly at her with a sort of perplexed compassion, infuriated Sarah.

"Do you think he has nothing better to do than run around as a sort of nursemaid to me?" she demanded fiercely, before the tears threatened her eyes and throat again, and she had to turn and escape.

"I can't think what has come over her, lately," Elisabeth said sadly, staring after her. She was infinitely glad that Julian was close at hand to stroke her arm gently, with the kind of comforting gesture she understood and appreciated perfectly. "Sometimes I think she is turning out like Marcus. Which is hard on her, because *she* has no politics to vent herself on."

CHAPTER ELEVEN

IT RAINED and rained. The streets never seemed clear of moist summer mud! July was nearly always a wet month, people said; as if that were any comfort. The monotonous pattering sound, and the damp swish of traffic, laid a sense of desolation on the heart. And each way the gaze turned it met bad news. Every newspaper headline was a cold wet smack in the eye. The end of the world is at hand. . . . Mrs. Billing's arch tantrums were nothing much, compared with that; still, there they *were*, and the world was not yet quite gone.

Sarah sped and scurried, drooped and dreamed, through the days. Another week gone.

"You want to buy a mackintosh," Lily said, with brief condescending kindness.

"Yes," Sarah agreed. I don't want to buy one. I have one at Fontayne—and, in any case, they smell. . . . But for Lily to talk to one at all was an honour, not to be argued.

She shivered uncomfortably through the damp-warm summer days. What if the war really did come? One agreed with everyone that it got to look more and more like it, yet one didn't truly *expect* it to come. Not enough, that is, to try to remember where one's September-crisis gas mask had gone.

Half-heartedly following Mrs. Moody's advice she bought some bargain lengths of material and began to make dresses during the long light lonely evenings in her room. But, without the sewing machine and Mrs. Moody to do the pressing, they were not very successful.

There were a few letters. Philly wrote faithfully; but, as the school holidays loomed, Christopher came to life with increasing frequency beneath her pen. She prepared herself, his twin, for any call he might make on the sympathy of her thought or word. Sarah had an old horrid feeling of being pushed a little way into the cold. Not that Philly loved her less than Christopher; but that, willy-nilly, she was held for ever in the thrall of being his twin.

Julian wrote rather apologetically and sent her some extra money, which she angrily put aside at first; and then took out and spent on silk for an evening frock, and wrote a gracious little note to thank him. It was surprising how much easier it was to be beholden to him now that one no longer imagined him to be very rich.

She heard, too, from Sir Giles's red-gold cousin, Benjamin Cross-ley. His was a large sprawly boyish hand, very different from Sir Giles's decisive intelligent script. He said he had telephoned her, but hadn't got hold of her (which was scarcely surprising), so was writing instead, to ask if they could meet for dinner and a movie, perhaps. If she could manage it, would she give him a ring at this number?

Listlessly, she did. Even for the sake of being able to talk about Sir Giles, she wasn't sure she wanted to go out with his cousin. She shrank from being asked whether she often saw him. To admit that unfin-ished Week End, and the fact of not having heard from him since, was almost more than she could bear. Still, it was a free meal, she thought, as callously as Lily or Joan could have done. They grew quite zestful over the matter of free meals; and she was beginning to understand the point of view.

Benjamin improved by lack of comparison with Sir Giles. Cousins were usually unsatisfactory people (Sarah decided with her own brand of logic), but he was quite harmless except for the red-gold ripples of his hair. He gave her a pleasant dinner, and seemed to have no diffi-culty in making conversation, although it was never of the obviously manufactured kind such as Peter's was when he was on his best behav-iour. He encouraged her to take all the *hors-d'oeuvres* offered, and did not seem embarrassed when she did. And, contrary to expectation, he did not press for information as to how well she knew his cousin.

They talked of her job during the *hors-d'oeuvres*, and again he urged her to find something more suitable.

"It wouldn't be any better," she said flatly. "I wouldn't be suitable to any job."

"Do you *have* to work?" he asked, but not inquisitively.

"Yes." She smiled at him and was astonished at the way he seemed instantly to mirror her expression. She was being "attractive" to a man. It was too easy, meant nothing. . . .

"You're not the type for work," he insisted.

"What type am I?" She thought that it was a mild form of flirting, the words flying lightly between them.

"I don't know—You're too . . . delicate."

"I'm very strong." She smiled again; watched his inevitable mirror-ing grin.

"I don't mean that, exactly." He gave it up; offered her a cigarette.

"Not in the middle of a meal," she said, slightly shocked.

"I suppose you go to a lot of parties and things?"

"No." That seemed wrong, so she added with a demure sort of cautiousness: "It depends what you mean by 'things.'"

He laughed. "No, but you must be terribly popular is what I really mean."

This ready-made reputation half alarmed, half thrilled her. Why shouldn't it be true, though, except for the fell circumstance of upbringing . . . ? Somewhat arrogantly, she stared down at the newly arrived next course of her meal.

"I'd no idea when Giles asked me along that day that you would be like you are," he went on ingenuously.

"Did you think I would be some sort of freak?" she asked sharply.

"I didn't know," he said simply, puzzled. Then he smiled. "I probably would have, if I'd heard of the giant first."

They had reached a firm easy friendliness. She felt no anxious tension in his company. If words flagged, she had only to smile and the even balance was restored. It was the same at the cinema. They agreed contentedly on merit; and censured with similar light ridicule. It was a comfort for Sarah not to have to be on the alert against offending good taste, Benjamin having no more regard for the quality than she had. They enjoyed the feature film simply because it seemed to them amusing; and both would have thought it an insult to the film industry to look for more than the pleasure of being entertained.

It was raining when they came out to the cinema foyer. They hesitated, watching puddles glow fitfully with yellow light from car lamps. London loitered in a summer ease, tolerant of the rain. The damp did not quite destroy an elusive summer perfume on the air.

"I enjoyed it very much," Sarah said, her eyes on the dark crowd surging out to the open air.

"Yes, it was good." He smiled, hanging cheerfully on the promise of her answering smile. "Could we—have you time to come and have a drink somewhere?"

It was a silly thing to say: had she *time*? . . . "I don't know," she said, no less silly. She was surprised that, having enjoyed the evening, she yet did not want to prolong it.

"The Café Royal—" he began tentatively.

"No," she said decisively. "No, I must get home." One would think there were no other place in London but the Café Royal.

He looked disappointed. "I'll see if I can get a taxi then." He flung himself into the crowd with an athletic swing.

There was nothing to say, as he took her home. He already knew the distressing joke of her dwelling place, and did not choose to harp on it now.

"I'm afraid this is terribly out of your way," she said politely.

"Of course not." He could not see if she were smiling. He laid a light chivalrous arm across her shoulders. "Perhaps you'll spare me another evening soon," he said.

"Yes, I will." She held herself stiff, yet did not in the least mind the conventional pressure of his arm. Only when she saw the familiar outline of the row of houses which tightly encased her own unhappy habitation did she diffidently withdraw herself and relax a little. "Thank you very much. Good-by."

"Good-by—" He had no time to do more than blurt out the one word before she was gone.

The week-end rain, of which Philly had hoped so much, was no respite after all. Mr. Lupin took rain in his stride. He telephoned to say the rain would cease by eleven, so would she be down at the cottage then? Wheeling out her bicycle, looking up at the sky, she sadly saw the clouds roll back, obedient to his prediction, and a thread of blue appear.

He greeted her jovially, making her feel ashamed of her sick apprehension for the morning's art.

"You deserted me last Week End," he pouted.

"I'm sorry, but as Sarah came—"

"I quite understand," he said kindly.

Encouraged, she murmured: "And when Christopher comes home for the holidays I'm afraid I shan't be able to come."

"It will be all finished by then, I promise." He was eyeing her with his remote art-eye. "And how did my tilting against Bloomsbury amuse you?"

She had no idea what this meant, but clutched thankfully at the clue in the word "amuse."

"I think it's very clever," she said steadily.

"They really are the limit, such people," Mr. Lupin went on school-boyishly. "They know I'm always out for their blood and it infuriates them." He said this with a bloodthirsty complacence, as he began to clean his palette of stale colours, in the kitchen.

"Yes, I expect it does," Philly agreed, feeling this was expected of her, though what Bloomsbury blood was and why Mr. Lupin should be out for it she couldn't for the life of her imagine.

"I'll get a rug for you to sit on, in case the grass is damp," he said thoughtfully.

"Thank you." As it had been raining all night and had only just ceased it seemed not unlikely that it would be soaked rather than merely damp. "I wore the same dress, because I didn't think you'd want me to turn up in a different one," she said, with an intelligent regard for the demands of art; although the short white frock was really rather shamingly grubby by now.

"Glory be, no," Mr. Lupin said. "Praise the gods, you don't go in for 'fashion.'"

The worst, most unnerving, part of Mr. Lupin, apart from the inverted commas, Philly decided as they went through the kitchen doorway into the garden, was that there were so few possible answers you could make to his conversation.

Bronwen had laid aside her second book for the time being. She would have liked to think she was merely resting on her laurels, but the truth was she felt more as if she were sunk well into a stupor. It wasn't that her career was proving actually discouraging. She had had a very nice letter from Mr. Tulsey to say he was pleased by the number and quality of the reviews "our book" was getting. Yet she could not help but feel a little grudging toward him for having quoted in his advertisement the opinion: "The spirited humour never flags."

"Wit," yes, she would have accepted as a proper tribute, but "spirited humour" was not in the least what she had meant to convey in her work.

Such worries, added to the memory of that painful scene at which Sarah had been a witness, warped her original enthusiasm for the opening of her second book. She had thrown away the bottle of Reduco, so now had no incentive to get up early to study her shape with a hope that the previous evening's dose would have had visible effect. Now, there was no longer the faintest reason to suppose the "too, too solid flesh" would in any way have "melted, thawed, and resolved itself into a dew." Yet (in spite of Sarah's first distasteful jumping to conclusions, that Sunday morning) Bronwen had not as yet seriously disputed the "Everlasting's having fixed his canon 'gainst self-slaughter"; but had merely reserved her right to agree how "weary, stale, flat and unprofitable seemed to her all the uses of this world."

The rain was a cloud dropped low upon Fontayne. It seeped everywhere, through windows, down chimneys, and into the soul.

*   *   *   *   *

Mrs. Billing, with a brutal flash of charm, said that if Sally couldn't get to work a little earlier in the morning they would have to see about it. A menacing tower, she threatened at any moment to crash down and crush her victim in a thousand pieces.

Sarah felt she no longer cared, come what might. Being a giant's drudge might be funny in the abstract, to amuse Sir Giles, but, as he showed no new interest, that was neither here nor there . . . Mrs. Billing asked rather sharply if Sally had heard. Yes, she had; but she had thought she was on time, unless the hour of arrival had been altered. Mrs. Billing gave her to understand that that would do, and that her mind didn't seem to be fully on her work, lately. For two pins Mrs. Billing would give her a taste of what work *could* be like.

For two pins, Sarah thought, she would walk out and take the first train home. Ignominious defeat . . . not to be thought of! She knew deep down in her bones that it was only a question of time before she came to it, but so far the knowledge was only a fitful lodger in her mind and had not yet taken up permanent abode there.

Rain slopped on the green summer evening. Sarah flitted through the bedraggled city, took meek seat upon a bus and prepared herself to be thankful that another day's work was done. Meek she was, but not quite meek enough: the thankfulness tipped with impatience that turned to anger and then to a dead flat sadness. She knew that she simply could not bear to return to her room.

She got off the bus and boarded another. Where did Bracken live? A quiet square, a backwater, a retreat; oh, happy Bracken outside the world. . . . She felt old and disillusioned, compared with him. An unnatural twilight was shutting out the day, blocking the sky with formidable slats.

Bracken wasn't in. She was allowed into his clear cold rooms; "chambers" was the word for them. She sat down on the edge of an upright shiny chair, her desolate bewilderment deepening. The twilight flowed into the impassive room, striking deep green improbable lights into the seemly furnishing. Her heart began to beat with a painful slow thudding.

She sat so quietly that Bracken didn't see her when he came in. The hard glare of the light as he switched it on made her blink and then give a little cry.

"Sarah!" His sparse eyebrows rose up from his cold kind eyes.

"I . . . trespassed." Her heart died down. Bracken was so undramatic, wiping his glasses, putting them on again. He took the wind out of loneliness; made it a proper thing, not something to bear with horror.

"Good," he said, taking off the comical overcoat.

"You want to buy a mackintosh," Sarah said, finding relief in passing on Lily's condescending advice.

"No, I don't," he said mildly.

"Oh, Bracken!" Very quietly she began to cry.

He did not comfort her; not even to the extent of appearing to "let her have her cry out." There was no question of his leaving her alone out of charity. When her sobs had ceased, disconcerted, he put out his small neat hand and took one of hers into his peculiarly heartening clasp. Even now, he offered no mere facile comfort, but seemed to thrust back upon her the burden of personality her tears had falteringly tried to discard.

He was, in fact, dismayed; selfishly so, he thought, but was not absolutely sure of this. His love for her, for all of them, was so nicely, clearly, placed that he hated to see her ruthlessly hurl herself out of his picture. Her brittle quivering form was enlarged, out of focus, on his sight.

"Will you have dinner with me?" he asked, as if it were a last resort of comfort, although in fact he had no intention that his tone should suggest this.

"Here?" She looked around, the cool severe room striking her consciousness again.

"If you like. I can get meals sent up."

"I'd like to," she said soberly, her tears ceased now. She made no apology, but put her handkerchief firmly away in her handbag as if to assure him her emotions would not again overwhelm her.

He went to the house telephone and ordered the meal. She sat down quietly (as if she were decorously leaving him alone to his prayers) and waited, her hands clasped in patience.

"Won't you take off your hat?" he said, turning to her again.

"Oh, yes." She pulled it off, no longer tender with it, though it was still her best. "How horrid everything is," she said; but resigned, not protesting.

"In particular?"

"*Everything* in particular." She frowned at him. "You wouldn't understand. You will go back to America and give some niggling little lectures and then you will prepare for another expedition to some improbable place, and then you will go and burrow in the ice or heat for ages, and you won't care at all whether the normal world has come to the end or not."

"What is the normal world?"

"Oh, it's no use talking to you, if you are in this polar mood," she said wearily. Yet she was relieved, really; he did not fuss her with brisk sensible counsel which would have insulted the unfathomed well of her grief. Because of that she dared to give him her confidence: "It isn't only the world," she admitted candidly. "I'm also very unhappy myself."

The silence, then, settled down upon her, a solace in itself. She looked about her, not positively awaiting an answer. The tall room, the tall full-curtained windows, the books let deeply, secretively, into angular slots in the wall, and the pale ball of electric light breaking free of its severe pearl-white shade: it seemed to her the height of comfortlessness, but so unconsidered as such that it achieved an aloofness of grandeur not only for itself but for those who sat within it, too. She did not dare now to speak of her loneliness.

"When are you going, Bracken?"

"Not until the end of August, probably. I have a number of things to do yet."

It was no use bothering to show interest in the things he did. He "spoke" sometimes, she knew, at obscure dry little societies of this or that. He had dry crusty acquaintances that one wouldn't be seen dead with. It was odd what a clear actual part he played in one's life because, if one got down to it and analysed Bracken, he was truly little but a crank. He conducted his life from some inscrutable basis, had no obvious nice feelings along the lines of trying to do good for his fellow beings (as Sir Giles, for instance, certainly tried, with all that tireless scurrying around Europe and so on), but merely retreated frequently not only into remote physical solitudes, but also into the cold final solitude of his mind.

Yes, friendship with Bracken was one of the most incomprehensible things in all the varied mysteries of life.

The dinner was unambitious, unexciting. They sat down at a little white-clothed table in the centre of the room.

"I'm afraid I'll have to go home to Fontayne," she took courage to confess, halfway through the meal.

"Yes?"

"Yes. I'm no use. I'm no good at work." She stirred the salt madly around in the cellar.

"Is that all that's worrying you?" he asked, as if he might as well have it all at once.

"No. No, it isn't." Her eyelids still prickled uncomfortably with the remembrance of tears. "I'm a failure in every way. I'm not . . . popular."

He looked at her intently, but did not smile. "There doesn't seem any reason why that should be so," he suggested mildly.

"No, there doesn't, really, does there?" she agreed candidly. "But it's true. It isn't exactly that I haven't any sex appeal"—she thought of Benjamin, who had written again to her, but whose almost sentimental little letter she had not yet answered—"no, it's not so much that I haven't *got* it as that I don't know how to direct it."

"It sounds rather tricky," Bracken said.

"I'm afraid it's true." She took her gaze off him, allowing him to continue eating as she turned her eyes to her plate. "I thought Americans always ate exciting food in private," she said, as if it were an indecent and yet intriguing habit.

"Not always," he denied modestly.

She sighed. "I'm in love, Bracken."

The confidence broke sadly, but not shyly, over the unimaginative fare. Bracken was forced, as if for very decency's sake, to lay down his knife and fork. He took off his glasses, leaving the naked frosty blue of his eyes full upon her.

The manservant came in with the sweet. The impersonal service, unobtrusive and efficient, was so different from Cruddles's that Sarah's attention was momentarily sidetracked.

"You call sweets 'dessert' in America, don't you?" she said on a note of woe, as the man quietly closed the door behind him.

"You seem to have some remarkably specialized scraps of information about the States, honey," he said gravely.

But she knew, by the way he tagged "honey" on to his words that he was less solemn than he seemed. He used that endearment only when he was deliberately—as they had always referred to it—"being American."

"Don't you ever complain at the uninteresting food?" She glanced disparagingly at her plate.

"I don't very often eat here."

"That's no excuse for junket that doesn't junk," she said sharply. "Yes, it's quite true—I'm in love."

"Do you want me to ask about it?"

"I don't think so. I know you don't know anything about love," she excused him. "I just felt I had to tell somebody, and I'd rather it was you than anyone else."

"Thank you," he said, with complete sincerity.

She swallowed some of the more than ordinarily spineless junket and separated stones from stewed fruit. Tinker, Tailor, Soldier, Sailor,

Rich Man—Her heart lightened faintly. At least, she supposed Sir Giles must be fairly rich—?

"If you don't want any more, I'll let him clear away."

"No, I don't." She got up. "*Hopelessly* in love," she said.

"You're sure of that?"

"Not absolutely," she confessed, amazed to find this was in fact so. "But it seemed hopeless this evening, with the rain and all the gloomy news and everything. Mostly, I think it's hopeless. It's Sir Giles Merrick, if you'd really care to know," she said wearily, impersonally.

"Oh, yes," he said, as if he were making a mental note of the fact.

"What do you think of him?"

"From the little I've observed of him, he seems a very attractive, dynamic, and charming man."

"Yes, that's what I think," she agreed listlessly.

The man came in again to clear away. She stood by the window, looking out on the twilight that had scarcely changed except to become imbued with authenticity. The rain had ceased and soon now the day would be truly gone. Greenish clouds tumbled down from a brief flickering pink. The room faded behind her as if, in spite of the constant glow of artificial light, it had died off into the night. She thought of Bracken's fairy tales, so diabolical and at the same time so reasonable that they outlasted the memory of all other books in her mind.

"I think I'd better go, as it has stopped raining."

He did not try to dissuade her.

She stretched up to a too-high mirror, to put on her hat.

"I read a lot of American books. That's how I happen to know a lot about your habits."

"Oh." Her tone, he thought, suggested bird watching.

"I read all kinds of books, you know, though nobody ever seems to believe it."

"I believe it."

"Good-by, Bracken, darling. It was very nice of you to have me."

"Shall I take you home?"

"No, thank you. You can give me some money for a taxi, if you like. I don't seem to be in the mood for a bus. Although I *do* know the route perfectly well. Thank you." She looked at him, her eyes level with his, and saw his lovely cloud-dispelling smile. "I'm sorry to be such a bore."

"I don't think you could ever possibly be that."

"Yes. Those in love are boring to those who aren't. Will you come to Fontayne again soon?"

"Yes. Will you be there?"

"I might be. It depends. Good-by, Bracken." She kissed him.

She went out to the muted evening, down steps sharply white in the dusk. Bracken had offered her no solace or advice, but all the same she felt a great deal better.

Mrs. Billing said that as the typing hardly came up to scratch—now did it?—she had better take a week's notice. She seemed to offer it on an invisible silver platter, ceremoniously, with an arch-hint of congratulation in it. There were no personal feelings in it, none at all, she added, as she had enjoyed her sunshine Sally's presence no end. At first, that is. Little Sally had been just a tiny bit naughty and sulky lately, hadn't she? Not quite so sweet in the matter of all pulling together, which was all in the day's work, after all. You couldn't expect to get on if you looked down your nose at any wee bit of overtime that happened along. That, added to the typing not coming up to scratch—

Sarah experienced a sense of deep ignoble relief. To get the sack was at least one degree less abject than to give up of one's own accord. The sack, unless for something really reprehensible, was something out of one's hands, like an undeserved visitation from heaven, such as being struck by lightning.

Only another week, she began to think, dazed, as if she had been released unexpectedly from a term of lifelong servitude. The sun began to shine almost at once, after that. Even Mrs. Billing's packs and powders, from being things with which one would live out one's life, became suddenly, by comparison with such a fate, imbued by charm and novelty.

Sir Giles's note brought her abruptly back to panic for this slothful attitude in herself.

"Why don't we meet?" he wrote. "You are still very elusive. Could you bear to come to a party with me? I'm afraid it will be awful. Don't ask me why anyone should give a literary arty-party in July" (as if she would dream of asking him anything so irrelevant) "but if you don't hate the idea of it too much, do come."

She nervously crushed the letter into a ball, then smoothed it out tenderly. The date! It was all right; this week, while she still had her job and a legitimate reason for remaining in London.

Not until she saw him again did she think of that one chaste kiss she had received upon her cheek from him. It had been frozen out of her mind by the misery of his sudden departure from Fontayne, and only when she came face to face with him once more did she thaw into memory. She watched his smiling lips, fascinated to think they had ever, for an instant, touched her face.

"You look lovely," he said, but without the inflection of intimacy that his own recollection of the kiss might have excused.

She was wearing what Mrs. Moody called her semi-evening frock, which was, alternatively, the dance-before-last dress. It was considerably less odious than compromises usually are, in spite of the neck that had never quite decided whether to be high or low. Her hair, regardless of expense, had been reset in its professional mould. She wore no ornament, but the memory of the kiss seemed to burn on her cheek like some out-of-place jewel.

"How do you get on with Benjamin?" he asked, as they stepped over the party threshold.

"He seems very kind," she said kindly.

"No more?" He smiled half teasingly, yet she felt as if his ears were pricked quite gravely for her answer.

"Oh, much more, I am sure, but I don't know what. He wrote to me, but I'm afraid I haven't answered yet. We saw a very good film together."

"So I heard," he said, as if he had made it his business to know, even as it was his business to poke his finger with polite inquiry into European pies. He tucked his hand under her elbow to lead her into the full fray of the party.

She thought, at first, that it was the most exhilarating experience, so far, in her life. To swim into high festivity, lighted with subdued artistry, yet with long cool curtains as yet undrawn against a long cool London view, was a triumph of mind and matter exquisitely at one. *If only I can keep my head and appear intelligent*—People converged, lingered and talked and smiled, and drew apart. The view hung neglected at the window, like some respected but unexciting Academy picture; nobody looked at it, each guest having far too much to say to all the other guests. The host and hostess, if such there were, never were revealed to Sarah. The etiquette of acquaintanceship with Sir Giles did not allow her to entreat him not to leave her for an instant alone. Proud false pretences demanded she should appear perfectly capable of standing on her own two feet. Cautiously, she allowed herself to be anchored to a glass which held something that might have been champagne. *Surely this is what I have always hoped for . . . a truly convivial scene, as Bron-*

wen would say. . . . Yet she was doubtful, the glass trembling a little, so that she dared not lift it to her lips.

"I don't know anyone here," she said, as if she might have done so.

"I'll find some people for you," Sir Giles said, with an air as of waving a wand.

"Oh, don't trouble. I'm very happy." That is idiotic. You come to a party to be social, not happy.

"I'll find you something to eat," he said, drifting away, leaving her painfully desiring to drag her anchor in track of him, but not daring to do so.

She was marooned, cast up on a forlorn stretch. Even the view was rapidly shadowing into obscurity. The thing was, to stand poised as if one liked it, as if this were an appointment with exquisite frivolity that might never be met with again. Think how Lily and Joan, giving much even for a free meal, would have envied one this brilliant drink in hand and the promise of brilliant food to come. Or wouldn't they . . . ?

"Glory be. Is this how you squander your emancipation?"

Sarah turned her head and saw with a sort of thankful dismay that Mr. Lupin was standing beside her.

"Oh . . . how are you?" she glared at him from force of habit.

"You're too good for this sort of thing," he said confidentially, raising a warning chubby finger.

Although she had not been enjoying the party, she strongly resented this remark. "Why do *you* come?" she challenged. "Is it"—she glanced at his easily balanced brimming glass—"for the wine?"

"The wine?" He followed her glance. "God forbid!"

Conversation languished. In a moment he would drift away, as Sir Giles had drifted. I must *blandish* him, she thought desperately, and said aloud: "I hear you are painting a fascinating portrait of my sister." The words, spoken, were surprisingly satisfactory, suggesting some magnetic sophisticated sister, as emancipated as herself, who was always being hung on the line or whatever it was, and who made reluctant appointments for her sittings with the painter in a richly bound little engagement book.

"I'm painting her as she is," Mr. Lupin said, as if Sarah could take it or leave it.

"Then it must be very good." She thought with an odd sharp tenderness of Philly, longed for her; and then, as sharply ridiculing, imagined her here, wearing the charade curtain. "I thought you hated . . . intellectual gatherings."

"I do," Mr. Lupin agreed mournfully, but made no attempt to justify his presence here.

Sir Giles returned, carrying a plate of nauseating-looking little wafers covered with something that resembled blackberries. He handed the plate to Sarah as if he had achieved some definite goal.

Sarah introduced Mr. Lupin with informal adult ease. Sir Giles smiled delightfully. It was scarcely to his discredit (with his subsequent European peregrinations to take his mind off lesser things) that he had no idea he had met Mr. Lupin at Mr. Harbrittle's house in the spring. Mr. Lupin, with nothing so crucial on his mind, remembered perfectly, however, and this took down his opinion of Sir Giles by several hearty masculine pegs.

Sarah ate the blackberries which were astonishingly made of fish and which made her so madly thirsty that she took her drink at one stupendous draught and then stood with the glass shamingly empty in her clasp, as if it were panting for more. Mr. Lupin took out his pipe, with a lowering glance around at the rest of the company, a schoolboy's "dare" in his watery blue eyes that said, "Stop me if you can." . . . Sir Giles took the opportunity to slip away and greet a tall handsome intense young woman.

Sarah waited for mortification to spread through her in an only less than fatal rigour; but it did not happen. Her limbs and brain, in fact, attained an almost too fluid sense of ease. Her anchor no longer held her. The empty glass bobbed like a cork in the unpurposed movement of her hand.

"Shall I get you another glass of that sweet and repulsive liquid?" Mr. Lupin asked.

"Yes, please," she said, airily amazed at herself for being unquelled by his censure of the drink. "But no more salty blackberries."

He was gone before he heard this caution. She was alone, but uncaring. She smiled at several people within smiling distance, in a sort of distress signal (though she was no longer distressed) that asked for rescue before Mr. Lupin returned. A stoutish man with an incredibly tanned face bore down on her just in time.

"And how are you getting on?" he beamed.

She beamed back at him.

"What a close night for festivity."

"Yes. . . ." She nodded dreamily. And what a close shave at escaping Mr. Lupin. "Do you write?"

"I'm afraid not. Only publish."

"Oh." Would you publish my father's memoirs? No, one didn't quite dare to ask it. "What name to you publish under?"

He laughed on a flattering note, as if she had said something funny. "Tulsey and Flewkes."

"You aren't—you wouldn't be—Mr. Tulsey?"

"As it happens, I am." His sun tan creased in another fabulous smile.

"I'm Bronwen Jones's stepsister," she said accurately, unemotionally.

"Oh, really," Mr. Tulsey said, not so much as if it were brought home to him what a small place the world was as what a positively claustrophobic place it could be. "Really, now—Well, I will say that I predict a remarkable career for her. Remarkable," he insisted loyally, as if he meant to pull his weight if it killed him. "Immaturity can be charming, charming, so long as it doesn't go on too long. Is she"—he glanced quickly over his shoulder—*"here?"*

"Oh, no," Sarah said happily.

"You are the family representative?" he smiled.

"I am no relation to Bronwen, except"—she eyed him fiercely—"by totally artificial bonds."

"I quite understand," he said understandingly. "May I get you a drink?"

"Thank you, but I have one coming." She waved a consummately careless hand.

"You don't write, then?"

"Of course not." She bore him no malice for the suggestion. "My father wrote his memoirs."

"Indeed. Who did them?"

"He did them himself." She smiled, her mind still floating lightly free of malice.

"I meant, who published them?"

"Nobody. They were lost. I found them among his papers."

"Indeed. I wonder Miss—er—Jones didn't mention this."

"He was no relation of hers," Sarah said coldly. "We don't discuss one another's affairs. We merely happen all to live together, but on no more than a sordid domestic plane."

Mr. Tulsey, who had had several drinks, had a swift horrifying vision of a great many unfortunate young step-relatives in cramped sardine proximity. Sarah, for her part, was enchanted by her mournful phrase. The party was improving by leaps and bounds. She began to feel hungry as well as thirsty, only drawing the line at blackberries.

"My father was Marcus Fontayne."

"Indeed," Mr. Tulsey said.

She forgave him for not bothering to remember what Fontayne had done and been. Nobody had time for everything, she thought charitably. Publishing was probably a very harassing business.

"He was in politics with a future before him, but unfortunately he died before he got to the future," she said gently.

"Ah, yes, of course." Mr. Tulsey resurrected Fontayne to memory, and immediately laid him back to rest in a reverent lavender obscurity.

"Perhaps I could send you the memoirs to look at?"

"By all means," he agreed with automatic geniality.

Sarah was entranced. It was as easy as that! Yet Bronwen had made such an appalling fuss about getting a book published. . . .

"Bronwen hasn't spent that thirty pounds yet that you gave her." Her tone reproved him for his reckless misplaced generosity.

"Hasn't she now?" Mr. Tulsey was shaken, utterly unaccustomed to hear what his authors *hadn't* spent. "How did you like the prodigy's book?"

"I haven't exactly read it," she admitted.

He smiled. "Is poor Miss Jones a prophet without honour—?"

"What?" She saw Mr. Lupin rolling down the room like a stage sailor. "I see my drink coming," she said in thirsty self-congratulation.

"Well don't forget to send me the novel," Mr. Tulsey said, as he turned away.

"I won't forget." She was no less grateful than if he had remembered it was memoirs. Mr. Lupin had given her the drink and vanished again. She walked boldly toward Sir Giles and the intense lady, with every intention of separating them, but when she got there he too had vanished, leaving the lady alone. One had to say something.

"What a beautiful party," she said, with sincerity, enclosed now in a shining expanding bubble of bliss.

The tall dark handsome lady smiled intensely.

"I know Mr. Harbrittle," Sarah said, staking her claim in literature. "Joseph Harbrittle," she added, familiarly.

"Oh yes." The lady smiled with bitter-sweet indulgence. "He's quite out of *touch*, you know. I beg you not to take too much notice of what he says about your stuff."

"My stuff?"

"Your writing—"

"But I'm not a writer," Sarah indignantly denied.

"Oh." The lady seemed half relieved, half disappointed. "Oh well . . ." She drifted away.

Sarah brought her drink down to the level of the lower line of trimming on her glass. Somebody had drawn sea-green velvet curtains over the windows. The room had a glistening heat. Surely it hadn't been like this all the time.

Her dislike for the fish-blackberries was suddenly tinged by a darker and more personal hate. How like fate to thrust them on her in those first moments when she had been too shy to refuse them. Chance was a terrible thing. But for the chance of death her father might have been more or less a Cabinet Minister (if chance had made it the kind of Government he liked) and the Joneses might have been wrapped in oblivion so far as she was concerned, however notorious they chose to make themselves on their own account. But for chance—She caught sight of a fresh glut of blackberries advancing to her on their sinister little wafers, piled on a tray carried by a waiter of sorts; and hastily turned her eyes away.

The room revolved on some devilish axis. It was all space peopled by contorted yet formal figures. Heat lay like congealing grease on the July night. Let me sink through the floor and be heard of no more. . . . The loathsome buffet loomed on the edge of space. Steer clear of that as though it were the plague. Imagine anyone wanting to *eat*. It wasn't enough to think of never going to another party (that went without saying), but the thing was that the remotest likeness to conviviality would never be sought again; never while breath was in the body and power in the will. But this resolution was no use now when both body and will had vanished even as Sir Giles had done.

Without sensible awareness of what she did, she continued to take responsible-looking sips at the remains of her drink. Not for an instant did her disconnected consciousness connect it in any way with her present sensations.

Her aimless glance suddenly focused with terrifying precision on a highly intellectual face bearing down on her. She turned swiftly and found that she was face to face with Bronny's Press.

"Hello, there," he said lightly, never forgetting a face, even if it had not been such an attractive one.

"Hello, here," she said dazedly.

"I didn't know you moved in such an urban swim."

Nothing could have described her feelings with more accuracy. *Swimming. . . .*

"May I get you another drink?"

"No, thank you." She breathed with measured care.

"How is the author?"

She stared at him. "Very hot, I should think." He had the two-dimensional look of the village on a bright flat day.

"It's pretty oppressive here, don't you think?"

"Yes, I do," she said with an ominous steadiness.

"Shall we try to find a cool spot?"

She knew that wasn't possible, but she followed listlessly in his languid wake. Doors opened, and a staircase stood poised unexpectedly, as if Bronny's Press had nonchalantly thrown it up, an Indian rope-trick specially adapted for a London house. They sat down on the second lowest step. They were on a sort of landing, but it was as elegant as any room, with flowers surging from vases and bowls with a chaste abandon worthy of Elisabeth. Sarah thought with a sad remoteness of her mother, as if the innocent life at Fontayne had been swept beyond any possibility of recall.

"I always think stairs were made for philosophical discussions," Bronny's Press said.

"Were they?" she said unhelpfully. It was certainly cooler here. If only he didn't expect her to talk—

He was silent himself for so many moments, in which life began to assume something like the proportions of normality, that Sarah's gratitude to him at last persuaded her into the politeness of speech.

"What if you lived in a bungalow?"

"What if I did?" Bronny's Press countered unintelligently.

"You'd have to . . . eschew philosophy, I mean." What a heavenly word, "eschew," she thought with a pride that couldn't have been greater if she had this moment invented it. Life wasn't really so ghastly, perhaps. It depended how and where one looked at it.

"Yes, I suppose I should." He laughed. "How did you get here? I just drifted in; but I suppose I ought to see if there's anyone worth noting." His next crisp dynamic column loomed threateningly. "Of course I much prefer assignments I can get my teeth into."

She wondered briefly whether he considered he had got his teeth into Bronwen. The stair on which she sat was now quite stable and reliable beneath her. She felt toward Bronny's Press the passionate gratitude of one saved from shipwreck.

"There's Sir Giles Merrick here," she said helpfully.

"Yes, I saw him. But he's overdone."

Even this reference to her love as if he were an unappetizing piece of beef did not wholly destroy her gratitude. However, she did say, with a bracing return tinge of ice to her tone:

"Oh no, I quite see you couldn't get your teeth into him if he's over-done." Her mind took a logical leap. "Do you ever feel you loathe food to the depths of your soul?"

"Usually," Bronny's Press said, with a youthful dyspeptic pride.

"I did, just now. And now I don't."

He looked at her with mild pity for such digestive inconstancy. "Of course you're very young," he said excusingly. "We had better trek to the buffet." He made this sound a considerable enterprise, while at the same time disparaging it.

Sarah took a strip of mirror from her evening handbag. Although she had recovered, her face had one or two unfamiliar green lights that seemed to her rather interesting. The inside of her head and stomach felt light and free, capable of anything.

"We must meet some time," Bronny's Press said, as if they weren't meeting now.

As he was drawing her to her feet, both her hands in his, Sir Giles appeared.

"I've been looking for you everywhere," he said, with an irritabil-ity so undiplomatic and so nearly parental that Sarah was abashed on his behalf.

"You vanished," she said weakly.

He did not even trouble to reply to this highly exaggerated statement.

"Good evening," Bronny's Press said, with as much respect as if Sir Giles were still beautifully underdone.

"Do you feel all right?" Sir Giles gazed at Sarah's face as intently as if it were a map of some European State that had been inconsider-ate enough to change hands, thereby marking in its possessions in an entirely new colour scheme.

"I felt rather funny—but now I don't." She looked around to find she was now alone with Sir Giles.

"Who was that man?" he asked.

"It was Bronny's Press. It is funny how people crop up."

"There were several people I would have liked you to meet, but you are probably tired by now." His tone made it seem that all his selection of people were utterly above-board, while Bronny's Press was some-what clandestine as well as tiring. "We'll just slip away, if you're ready."

So unnerved was she by this exasperated un-suave de-suèded Sir Giles that she dared make no protest.

The proud cool houses, withdrawn upon the night, left the little garden within the square as free as if it were a companion in nature of some boundless country park; as if one could walk and walk and never reach its end.

They came slowly down the steps of the party house into a serene warm well of the summer night. The sky's navy blue was ticked here and there by stars. In the air hung the gathered perfumes of the day, dust and roses and petrol and still-damp soil.

"It didn't rain today," Sarah said.

There was nothing particularly worthy of an answer in this remark, so Sir Giles said nothing. Sarah paused on the pavement, her hands on spiky railings, her gaze penetrating the sweep and trickle of the gardens through the trees.

"You will catch cold," he said; but his voice was less impatient than it had been.

"No. What beautiful gardens," she murmured on an ecstatic purr that would have done justice to Kew.

"Where the residents exercise their dogs, I imagine." His glance belittlingly followed hers.

His remark simply rolled off her; she went on staring raptly. Used, now, to the sober glow of lamplight in the square, she could make out several minute flower beds. She rested her chin on the spikes with such a dangerous semblance of abandon that he felt quite alarmed.

"Are you quite sure you didn't drink more than was good for you?" he suddenly demanded.

She turned her face sideways from the spikes and looked gravely up at him.

"I never said I was quite sure I hadn't."

He deeply regretted having brought her with him. He wanted to shake her. Instead he took her hand. It flowed like liquid against his palm. She was as sweet and insubstantial as . . . his mind went contentedly blank.

"But I hardly left you for a minute—"

"*Didn't* you? How time varies." She shifted her gaze to the chaste line of houses, with glowing fanlights sending out patrician-homely assurances of life. "I wonder if they put out milk bottles on their front doorsteps or hide them somewhere at the back."

"I haven't the least idea," he said crisply.

"You aren't cross with me?"

"My dear girl, don't be absurd."

"Please don't be, because I am going home for good, and it is doubtful if we shall ever meet again."

"But naturally we'll meet." He held her hand a shade tighter. "But it's time you went home now."

"I think railings were *made* for philosophical discussions, don't you?"

"I have never known any railings that discussed anything, philosophical or otherwise," he said crushingly.

A thin cat, grey with night, danced across the square. Sarah relinquished philosophy and thought of Ernest.

"My sister has a cat, but I haven't got one."

"Would you like one?" He felt himself rapidly slipping into her inanity.

"I would rather. I wouldn't let it sit on the bread-board." This oblique commentary on the home life of Fontayne took him yet another step farther away from his adolescent hero-worshipping of Marcus Fontayne. Perversely, it took him one step nearer Sarah. A figurative step, that is, for he was already actually so close to her that there was not even half a step separating them. The orderly lamplight in the square sent out little golden rivulets of radiance which outlined her face and form in a most pleasing way. He forgave her morbid clinging to the mouldy gardens; and then, when she spoke again, regretted forgiving her.

"I suppose we couldn't go to a coffee stall?"

He looked unobtrusively sick. "It's nearly midnight."

"I know," she agreed blissfully. "That's just the right time, I should think."

The coffee stall, when found with no little difficulty, was not one of the more glamorous specimens, Sarah decided. No top-hatted society vagrant hung tolerantly upon its edge, chatting lightly with the underworld. A dispirited-looking man tended an urn, with one cabman as customer. Sir Giles ordered two cups of coffee. Sarah quenched her still persistent and rather depraved thirst with the thin hot liquid that tasted of nothing but sweetness. She was now extremely hungry again and would have liked to try one of the sausage-rolls piled on the counter, but, seeing Sir Giles had not even glanced at his coffee, let alone tasted it, she did not like to suggest this.

"Thank you very much for the party. I did enjoy it," she said.

"I'm glad you got on so well." His voice was chilly. "To whom did you talk?"

"Mr. Lupin, Bronny's Press, and publisher, and a writing-looking lady," she said simply. "Then there was an Aldous Huxley sort of character who looked as if he might be going to talk to me, so I turned away." She sensed an attitude of surprise in Sir Giles, so she added with dignity: "Oh, I read a lot, you know."

"What did the Aldous Huxley character say?"

"He didn't exactly speak. But you know how you feel with book-character sort of people? You never know what shatteringly clever things the author may have thought of for them to say."

Sir Giles, now quite in the dark as to whether they were on the plane of fiction or fact (he was perfectly willing to discuss any aspect of literature, but not if it made sudden and unwarrantable leaps into actual life), had nothing to say for several moments. Sarah continued to sip her disgusting beverage appreciatively.

"Only the Author of his Being, in this case, one imagines," he said at last, making a manful little joke of it, in capital letters.

"God, you mean?" Sarah said seriously. "Oh, no, it's not in the least like *God*, the kind of author I mean. Much more . . ."

"The professional touch?"

"Yes—*much*."

He laughed. She was in her proper role of female Jester again, making a king of him. Even the coffee stall was bearable, from such a point of view. Though not for long. Still laughing, he put a light arm around her and lightly kissed her cheek.

"Sweet Sarah, it is time you had some rest," was all he found necessary to say in persuading her away from that perfectly horrid haunt.

CHAPTER TWELVE

SHE HAD NOT told them exactly when she would reach home. And when she got there, primed for the cherishing and coddling which defeat, far more than success, would always earn one at Fontayne, she found Christopher had already arrived to steal her prodigal thunder.

"But how did you get here, darling?" Elisabeth asked, from the midst of a highly unorganized unpacking of her elder son's clothes.

"By the conveyance, of course. Why don't you leave that to Mrs. Moody?"

"Yes, I suppose I ought to," Elisabeth sighed. "Christopher is having a late tea. You had better go and join him."

"I don't feel like a late tea."

Elisabeth eyed her anxiously. "Are you tired?"

"I am, a bit," Sarah admitted grandly. "There was a very late party the other night and then Sir Giles and I went rushing around to coffee stalls and things. It was marvellous fun, but it *does* leave you rather tired." She had decided it would be unthinkable to have the faintest ghost of a tail between her legs if it meant being fobbed off with her brother's disgusting end-of-term high tea.

"Christopher had an appalling report," Elisabeth remarked unemotionally.

"I'm not surprised," Sarah said gloomily. "We are all born failures." She was already reconsidering the theme of triumphant débutante fun among the coffee stalls, which might be difficult to keep up for long. "Like the Brontës." She felt more Haworth than Russian today.

"But they weren't failures." Elisabeth searched unsuccessfully for the fellow to a deplorable sock that had just enough holes for her fingers to make a mitten which she now absently wore on one hand that she held up.

"They must have *felt* they were, in all that gloom, so it comes to the same thing."

"How is nice Giles Merrick?" Elisabeth asked enterprisingly.

"I wish you wouldn't refer to him as 'nice,' Mother. It's so damning."

"I'm sorry," Elisabeth apologized, although she was still convinced that "nice" was a nice word. "Do come and have a cup of tea, darling, even if you don't want anything to eat."

Downstairs, her brother and sister drew her into a heavy bread-and-jam atmosphere. Philly, who had already greeted her, sent out a little smile that hovered like a moth upon her as she came into the room where they were eating.

"Hello," Christopher said casually. "I wondered where you'd got to."

"It happens that I have only just come home."

"Oh, yes, you've been away, of course. It must have been horrid in London. Have some tea."

He infuriated her, his smooth fair hair above his high Fontayne forehead, his serene grey eyes, his sweet mouth indented even deeper than usual at its corners by a faint shadow of jam, his ears lying as neatly flat to his head as did hers and Philly's, his thick fair lashes that, again, resembled Philly's; everything about him at this moment infuriated her.

Philly looked at her anxiously; poured out a cup of tea for her. It seemed a pity that the bliss of having everyone together was so soon being spoilt. She was torn between the two; whether to placate sister or brother. Sarah won; because Christopher was more like Philly's own self, and so his feelings were the less to be considered.

"Will you tell us some more about that party, darling?"

"Which one?" Sarah asked.

"The one where you met all the people," Philly said unilluminatingly, patiently.

"You look very smart," Christopher said, having just noticed this. "Awfully glamorous." He had no idea she was offended with him. He stared at her with an only slightly ridiculing admiration, one half of his face distorted with bun.

Sarah smiled, against her will. It was the way he said "awfully glamorous" on such a brisk unimpassioned note—Philly saw the smile and her spirits rose.

"Mr. Lupin, when I saw him, was hideously smug about your picture. I suppose it's really a complete mess," Sarah said to Philly.

"I haven't seen it. I told him I couldn't go any more when you and Christopher came home. And I don't see that Bob Norbett can expect me to go on reading to the village children now—"

"Good Lord, how ghastly and bogus for you," her brother said sympathetically.

"Poor Philly." Sarah smiled again as she thought what torture that public exhibition must have been to the younger girl. "What did you read?"

"I couldn't think of anything, so I read some of Bracken's fairy tales—"

"*What!*" Sarah pounced frantically.

"I knew that no one could do anything except love them."

"But how could you? *Bracken's* stories for the miserable village children!"

Philly went pale with distress, but tried to stick by her action. "They loved them. I knew they would."

"That isn't the point." Sarah's eyes seemed to shoot out blue sparks. "Bracken's stories couldn't possibly love *them*."

"You shouldn't say such snobbish things—" Philly began, then faltered. "Oh, darling, it can't hurt you that others should read them, as well as us."

"You don't understand." The blue sparks had changed to ice. "I wanted to have them still rare and exclusive, to hand down to my grandchildren."

This argument, descending to generations unborn, seemed to Christopher to be rapidly degenerating into a wholly bogus state. He rose from the table, bending to take a final drink of tea as he did so. The afternoon bloomed with a late unexpected burst of sun.

"I think I'll go and look round. Has anything been happening?"

"Don't ask me," Sarah answered, although he had been addressing Philly. "I've been away."

"Well, Peter seems rather upset and Bronwen is in the Throes, as she calls it, and Ernest is moulting rather a lot," Philly said.

"Oh, yes, how is old Ernest?" Christopher belatedly asked. That he did not also inquire more closely about the Joneses did not mean that he had now anything particular against them, but that they were too new to his life for him to have much time for them on the first day of a holiday.

"He's all right, except for the moulting."

Tom opened the door with that crafty delicacy of touch that suggested he would make a dexterous safe-breaker.

"Another tea, and I never knew it," he said dolorously. "How-do-you-do, Sarah?"

"Hello, Tom."

"Have you come home for ever?"

Sarah didn't answer. Tom looked mad, she thought dispassionately, his eyes full of self-contained dreams.

"Can I come with you, Ick?" Tom called his brother this only on special occasions such as birthdays and brand-new holidays.

"No. I'm taking out my bicycle. You couldn't keep up."

"It's a very nice little bikikle," Tom said absently.

"Stay here, Tom," Sarah said, suddenly thinking she loved her little brother with a tender eldest-sister love.

Tom smiled at her suitably and fondly, but said firmly: "If this other tea is quite over, I think I might as well be getting back to Mrs. Moody."

There was change, but no change. Fontayne received the little differences of daily life with its own supreme indifference. Green with rain, it now turned its face to the sun again, ripening in a proper and orderly full summer maturity. The fruit in the little orchard was making ready to crown the season deftly. The garden looked tidy in a bloom of heat; but one was not deceived. Fontayne was going its old desolate way in its old stubborn insistence on brooding over the past. Now, it seemed to make not the faintest invitation to a purchaser; it cast out no tiniest wile to entrap some energetic new-blooded unwary admirer. It had given up the ghost, turning a sardonic eye on all idea of good clean sweeps and fresh beginnings. The old corrupt vision of grass growing up through the floors of the house, of spring pushing inopportune daffodils into the drawing room at the terrace edge, was in full sway again. The whole place was well away with its dark sweet pattern of decay.

Within the spell, Sarah yet made one or two rather mechanically frantic efforts to evade it.

"If Mr. Jones doesn't hurry up and begin conducting again soon," she said anxiously to Philly, "there will be nothing left to conduct."

"There won't be, anyway," Philly unexpectedly said. "He says the war will begin at any moment."

"He knows nothing about it." Sarah felt she was the authority on the subject, knowing Sir Giles, and having more recently been in London than the others. Yet privately she agreed with Mr. Jones. Perhaps Fontayne also agreed, and for that reason had decided to give up the last ghost of a chance of revival.

The little daily incidents, springing from the inanition of Fontayne, nevertheless continued with an almost insolent sprightliness. Individualities rioted, regardless of doom. Bronwen, abandoning neat notebooks, scattered erratic loose sheets of inspiration through the house. And something, as Christopher said, was Definitely Up with Peter. The quality of constancy was upheld in the unvaryingly close knit tender devotion of Elisabeth and Julian, in Tom's passionately unimpassioned cleaving to Mrs. Moody, in Philly's regard for Ernest, and in the undeviating frost of eye and speech that Cruddles bestowed upon Bronwen.

To quarrel for long with Philly was impossible, so Sarah was forced to forgive her for her wanton betrayal of Bracken to the village young. Besides she was so beautifully accommodating in the matter of being impressed. Sarah laid out her conquests like jewels before Philly's tender gaze.

"Bronny's Press wanted us to meet again, and Sir Giles's cousin absolutely insisted on taking me out the evening before I came home."

"Is he nice?" Philly asked. She did not mind young men so long as she could view them, as it were, by proxy.

"Yes," Sarah said crisply, conveying Benjamin to her own private patch beyond the pale of true fascination. "Very."

"What did you do?"

"We went to the cinema near our hotel." She meant the one where they had stayed before the wedding.

"Did you see 'Lord Curzon'?" Philly asked.

"I don't think so. Is there one?"

"Oh, Sarah, surely you remember! Black and white and having rather a lot of kittens."

"Oh, yes," Sarah laughed. "You are ridiculous, Philly," she added, in an indulgent adult voice.

A thing that neither Sarah nor anyone else had expected was the sudden social flowering all around Fontayne from the beginning of August. Even before that, for July was trailing its last languid days when Virginia Welwyn started the phase by driving up to Fontayne one afternoon of sullen heat. She came straight to the terrace, where they were sunk into the day as if they were permanent fixtures in it. Her disconcerting air of indolent energy made her unreal, a being from another world; she was cooled by an atmosphere of iced stimulating cocktails, energized by the clear simple quality of physical possessions, motivated by her life-long reasonable demands for unreasonable things.

"Hello." Her smile had a ravishing certainty of the welcome she would receive. "I came to see Aunt Pansy but she seems to be out, taking all the keys with her. There was nothing but the car or the horrible garden to sit in, so I came here." Not even a pretence that she was paying a friendly call on them. Just making use of them, but so sweetly certain she would be welcome that she was in fact exactly that, not even Bronwen grudging it to her.

Sarah was enchanted. The day had badly needed something to break it up and give it quality. Mrs. Welwyn, in the devastating clarity of her slim print frock, provided exactly what had been lacking.

"You know my stepsister and stepbrother?" Sarah said, graciously admitting the relationship.

Virginia gave another brief dazzling smile. Sarah felt a thrill of satisfaction. The Joneses had approved of none of the Fontayne acquaintances until now.

"I saw you at a remarkable dance here in the spring," Peter said, gracefully arranging a new deck chair and cushions for her.

"Oh, yes. *Wasn't* that fun?" Her soft little drawl gave him no chance to decide whether there were any mockery in it or not.

Sarah, vaguely conscious of his suddenly youthful desire to impress and his new uncertainty of how to do so, was more enchanted than ever.

"But what happened to your giant?" Virginia asked, seriously, turning to Sarah with all the astonishing show of interest of a royal personage remembering to inquire after a negligible subject's somewhat revolting complaint.

"I got the sack," Sarah replied, trying to put a disarming Welwyn note of candour in her voice, but rather overdoing it.

"How depressing for you. Perhaps I could help you find another."

The suggestion was as insubstantial as the invitation to drinks at the many-windowed flat. She would be delighted to see you if you went there, but she wouldn't do anything *about* it.

"My father and stepmother have gone out," Bronwen said ceremoniously. "They will be sorry to miss you."

Philly had offered only a smile to the general sociability; and Christopher not even that. He sat angrily hunched into his jacket, as if he had dislocated his neck. He wished she would go. If she sat around all afternoon everything would get hideously irked. He was glad she didn't seem to recognize him. He couldn't have borne it if she had said something bogus about that dance.

"I can't imagine what Aunt Pansy does all the time, can you?"

Nobody had any ideas to offer, except Philly, who knew she spent a lot of time changing the colour of her nails, but she was too diffident to mention this aloud.

"Do drift in, if you're anywhere around," Virginia went on. Her detached yet tender violet glance went to each of them in turn. "I may come down for more than a Week End myself. I'm not going abroad. All this war talk is such a dirge. I'd rather stay here if it is going to creep into everything. *You* know."

Mention of war reminded Christopher briefly of aeroplanes and his face was momentarily rapt-lively with dreams until he remembered to glower again.

Sarah was excited. Virginia Welwyn's coming down might mean anything, even a party at Fontayne. Even Sir Giles's being inveigled down again. The summer was shot through belatedly with hope. She did not connect war with the realization of this desire; and even if she had done so would not at the moment have been depressed by the macabre association.

Bronwen was wonderfully subdued. She had never before been known to meet anyone new without mentioning her book within the first five minutes. Today, any word she spoke was devoted solely to the welfare of the guest. It was Bronwen who asked if she would have tea, though it was barely three o'clock, and she who received the refusal as a hostess who had but done her poor best. She did not even mention that she had been to Hollywood.

Virginia treated her neither more nor less as a child than she did any of them. She stayed little more than half an hour, but the impression of her visit lingered much longer. The perfume she wore was an astringent-sweet essence that vitiated all the flower scents for long after she was gone.

They were silent for a while after she had casually waved them farewell and gone off to her car. Peter had had every intention of escorting her to it but, when it came to the point, did not do so, defeated by the sweet oblivion of her manner. They heard the subdued high-bred throb of the engine and then a swooping sound as the car nosed its way down the drive. After a few moments Christopher sniffed the air and ostentatiously blew his nose.

"I hope we aren't going to have the holidays messed up by Aunt Lady Pansy's loneliness," he said gloomily.

"You never object to going to see Mrs. Oxford," Sarah objected, not very pertinently.

"That's different. Aunt Lady Pansy seems pretty gruesomely bogus, what I've seen of her."

"Her niece, at least, is enchanting," Peter said, in delicate command of his normal gallantry, now that she was gone.

"It is good to meet someone of the world again, after all this time." Bronwen cast a thoughtfully baleful glance around the terrace.

Bronze clouds shifted across an exhausted-looking sky. There was thunder in the air, still and brooding, cherishing Virginia's perfume as if it would never let it go. Sarah's mind settled down to a fantastic embroidering of probability.

Elisabeth found them all still there, an hour or more later, when she came up the garden with Tom's hand in hers. The placid amicable picture seemed right and proper to her gentle eye. Mentally, she had gone on tiptoe, the last day or two. It was too good to be true. Sarah at home again, Christopher on holiday, Peter less frequently wrestling invisible demons at the piano, Bronwen (here one tiptoed with most Agag-like care of all)—yes, Bronwen wrapped in a fresh creative benison and not a *sign* of indigestion; and the household bills, shared and mastered by Julian and by him reduced—if not actually, at least spiritually—to a satisfying state of subjection. If the daily paper had not hung over the morning like a guillotine ready to cut it to shreds, how simple life would have been.

"Were you in the garden all the time, dear Elisabeth?" Bronwen said courteously. "If I had known, I would have come to search for you. We had a charming visitor." Bronwen had as sincere a respect and appreciation for Elisabeth as Elisabeth herself had for Bronwen's Muse.

"Really, Mother, why are you always *somewhere else*?" demanded Sarah, who had no such nice regard for the conducting of filial-parental relationships.

"But who was it?" Elisabeth peered about the terrace as if she expected the visitor might still be skulking there.

"The beautiful Mrs. Welwyn," Peter said. It was as if a breeze had arisen in the stagnant day and blown a high-glossed page of a fashionable magazine across the garden.

"Oh, dear," Elisabeth said, with a conscientious effort at disappointment.

"You don't care a bit," Sarah said, not deceived. "You'd *far* rather be weeding with Digby."

"*I* was weeding with Mr. Jones," Tom said. He was the only one who still openly and to Julian's face blandly called him that. He had never forgotten and never would forget Sarah's taunt that he would be calling him "Daddy" in no time. "We weeded and weeded and a little old robin came and watched until little old Ernest came up and ate him."

"You mustn't tell lies, darling," Elisabeth said absently. It would never have occurred to her to doubt Ernest (whom she had trained from kittenhood to do no more than unambitiously stalk a bird now and again) and to believe Tom.

"And then Mr. Jones squodged a worm with a trowel by a mistake when it got in the way," Tom went on, unabashed. "It was half dead and half not dead," he added, as a matter of general interest.

"Please!" Bronwen shuddered.

"It was a very nice little worm," he said, offended.

*   *   *   *   *

In spite of Elisabeth's feeling that all (with the exception of the world) was well with the world, Sarah was not so docilely accommodated to circumstances as her mother imagined. Never, before this, had she spent so much time spread supinely in the little orchard looking up at the sky. Surely, in kissing her a second time, Sir Giles had set a seal of custom on the tricky frail proceeding. Having once begun, was there any logical reason why he should not go on and, in going on, increase inevitably in fervour? But unless she were always on the spot, how had this happy state a chance to be? In books, these tedious geographical details were seldom found. Partings, in books, were contrived merely for the sake of subsequent meetings; never all up in the air and unorganized like this. Emotionally, lovers might temporarily be allowed to drift poles apart; and even physically it might happen; but always for a reason.

Of course, when I said we might never meet again, he said but naturally we would. Yet what does that mean? In the natural course of events? . . . but, also, I shall die in the natural course of events. That is really no comfort at all. . . . (The orchard around her, slowly thickening to maturity, was no comfort. The memory of his kiss was more of an anguish than a comfort.) And if I write to him again it might begin to look rather obvious. In no circumstances could I write.

Her eyes unfocused, busy with inward images, she began to devise a circumstance which might suitably excuse a letter to Sir Giles.

Julian was alone in the drawing room, in perfect accord with its tattered grace. It maddened Sarah, as she came in from the terrace, to see him mildly engaged in reading sheets of music. It wasn't so much the fact of its being music that sent her into a cold sweat of fury (she was fairly broad-minded about that) as that she couldn't remotely imagine the emotions of the peruser. She felt exactly the same exasperation when she saw Mrs. Moody nodding and smiling her way with intelligent comprehension through some dark inscrutable knitting pattern.

"I was thinking about my birthday—" she began breathlessly, trying to control her helpless anger.

"Yes?" He looked up, benevolently attentive, but Sarah was not entirely appeased; she saw sharps and flats, crotchets, quavers, and those even worse things with many-pronged tails, still dancing in his glance.

"Of course if there's a war, I wouldn't want anyone to bother about anything so unimportant as a birthday," she said moderately.

"And if there isn't a war?" he prompted, with a gently melancholy insistence, the quavers dying out of his dark eyes as he gave her his whole attention.

"Well, in that case, I thought—I wondered if—as I shall be eighteen (it is no use talking to Mother) it might be possible, as I have never in the slightest degree come out, as they say, without any particular trouble to anyone (Cruddles is much better at looking after things than he will admit), for me to have a tiny party of some kind."

Following Sarah's intricate but controlled fashioning of phrase with no more ado than if it had been a mere wilfully tortured extra-modern score, Julian nodded sympathetically.

"It seems a good idea."

"When *we* discuss it, yes"—she acknowledged him her equal—"but Mother never keeps to the *point*. She says that nobody would come, as if we were lepers, and that, alternatively, nobody would enjoy it if they did. I think it's a mistake *never* to have a good opinion of oneself, don't you?" Not that it is any use appealing to him about Mother, as he dotes on her so much—It happens that I have *lots* of friends. I expect I could rake together enough even for a little dance."

"Then let's have a little dance," Julian said, with admirable promptness.

(If only he and Mother could be kept apart, there was a chance of getting something settled; but never if they got together and began idiotically deferring to each other, while life simply sank away and died around them as they tenderly unravelled their separate feelings until they were utterly sure they corresponded, when they would slowly and carefully knit them up again in a single shared design. . . .)

"Good." She pounced on the decision, pinned it down. "The end of August will be a good time, because we shall still be able to sit on the terrace to cool off between dances." She saw pale festive dresses fluttering like moths in the darkness, and heard a saxophone out-hooting an owl across the velvet stillness of the night. "It will round off the summer," she said, as if it needed only a final shaping to make it perfect.

"By the beginning of autumn we should all be ready to begin life again in earnest?" he suggested, his smile shaping the sombre edge of his moustache quite playfully.

"Yes," she approved. Including him, if he can find anything to conduct . . . but that is *his* business to worry about. . . . "Then shall I just tell Mother we have fixed it all up?"

"Do, by all means," Julian agreed, with simple cordiality. "But on no account bother her with it."

"I shouldn't dream of doing so. I shall arrange every scrap of it myself. Thank *you* very much for bothering." And for taking the crotchets out of your eyes and concentrating on me, she added silently, as she left him.

The summer had its second wind. The roses, temporarily dispirited by the July rain, were now born again; and in rebirth were fuller, finer, more confident than before. From the upper windows of the house, the distant blotch of colour seemed freely mixed with Chinese white. Elisabeth loved those thick pale chalky tints that could be so opulent as well as delicate. Sarah, too, took a voluptuous pleasure in the great spread of colour, blending in a slow subtle shading from flat white to the dark pink that nevertheless was still blotted with an under dress of white; but she, with the others, hated the affected finical names that made the roses seem to mince in your mind when you thought of them. The names came trippingly, fondly, on Elisabeth's tongue, poems ingenuously spoken; but to all the children it was an embarrassment, as if you had a great many distinguished guests ever lodging on the far edge of hospitality.

Up from the rose garden, this side of the posturing yews, tall shaggy hollyhocks made a bright little wilderness, with shadows lying in long lines like palings overthrown. The wistaria bloomed again, hanging in great bunched drops in the formation of clustered grapes; opening in a minute intricacy of lapping petals, expanding and deepening in colour, and then slowly retracting, turning pale, meeting death halfway. Down by the deserted Cedar Ring, where the ruins of ruins kept a meagre vigil of a few large misshapen stones, wild flowers began to bloom in neglected papery seedy grass, paradoxically in order with the whole of that unnurtured patch; scattering the free field-breath of poppies that flew clear red rags in the path of the sun. Digby kept the August lawns in trim, making a neat downward pattern for the eye from house or terrace, but now there began to spread a tired yellowish glaze across the green.

Sarah did not tell Bronwen either that she had met Mr. Tulsey or sent the memoirs to him. She waited patiently for the moment when chagrined surprise should burst upon Bronwen at finding she was not the only card up the sleeve of Messrs. Tulsey and Flewkes. It was a theme that helped to occupy the time when she was directly thinking neither of the letter she would write to Sir Giles nor the promise of her birthday. Indirectly, she *was* thinking of these things all the time, but gradations of thought are inevitable, and occasionally the sensational subject of the memoirs came out on top.

Bronwen had kept to her promise to discard the Reduco, but had consoled herself with a new bracelet bought with her own money (that bounteous "advance") which she disparaged with a passionate fondness that the other girls did not understand. "It's appallingly rococo, isn't it?" she appealed to them, her voice almost trembling in its withheld emotion, her pale eyes passing over it in caressing contempt. Then why did she wear it, if it were appalling? they wondered. How or why it was rococo they neither knew nor cared. But Philly, in her own mind, dimly connected the whole thing with delicious stuffed pike.

They did not, in any case, waste much time over the matter. The appalling rococo bracelet sank into the general scheme of things, even as Bronwen herself had done. While Sarah had her party to brood over, Philly had her portrait and Mrs. Rudge to bother with. The new Rudge baby beat Mr. Lupin's invitation to view the finished picture; but only just, and by rights should not have done so.

Philly rushed on to the terrace, one morning, leaping obliviously over Bronwen's sheaf of rough notes spread as if to bake on the warm stones, and reaching Sarah with a final astonishing bound.

"The excitement of the triplets' prize has made Mrs. Rudge's new baby get born a bit soon. It suddenly happened last night—"

Sarah looked up from Mrs. Moody's picture paper which she had managed to snatch early, virgin as it were, the seamstress not having had time to look at it before she set to work. At this moment, Mrs. Rudge was as nothing compared with a diabolical murder that had belatedly come to light.

"What a *delayed* excitement," she said sarcastically. "It is terribly affected of her still to get shocks from such old news. Mrs. Rudge makes awful fusses about having babies, as if it's interesting. She's disgustingly boring, too. She *will* tell you about what she can and what she can't 'fancy'—I suppose she is seizing her only hope of anyone ever taking any notice of her." She said this with an impersonal contempt, but without knowing her suggestion could apply with devastatingly appropriate truth to millions of mediocre women.

"Oh, but, Sarah, being boring about it isn't the baby's fault. It is sweet—"

"You haven't seen it."

"I have. I was down by the haberdashery after breakfast and I saw Mrs. Rudge's neighbour and she took me in to see it."

"Good heavens." Sarah put down the murder and began to laugh. "What on earth did you want to go poking in and looking at it before it got properly aired and seemly?"

There was a flurried sound of papers being gathered together and the sight of Bronwen shooting away down the garden as fast as her short fat legs would carry her.

"What's the matter with her?" Philly said, startled.

"She probably didn't like all those dreary baby details. She thinks it's sordid."

"But it isn't sordid," Philly protested, bewildered. "It is only rather small—but it will grow. It will probably get as pretty as the triplets."

Sarah laughed again, her eye already edging back to her paper.

"I expect you have ruined Bronny's digestion for the rest of the day. She will probably stay and brood in the kitchen garden for hours."

"Well, she's taken her writing with her, anyway," Philly half excused herself. "And she has the appalling rococo bracelet to console her. But it's a sweet baby, truly, Sarah."

Peter came up out of his moodiness to listen with unexpected amiability to Sarah's plan for her party. He said sympathetically, with nicely balanced melancholy and malice: "I don't wonder it is sending you frantic to stay here after you have once been on your own. You must have *something* to tone down the agony."

"Then why do you stay here?" she asked.

"But what else is there?" He gave his Gallic shrug. "I don't choose to live in a garret for the sake of my music. Besides, it wouldn't help it. The theory of hardship is out of date."

Sarah, thinking of Mrs. Billing and the lodging-house geyser, said sharply: "Hardship isn't exactly a *theory* when it comes to the point."

"Artistically speaking, I naturally meant," Peter said loftily.

"Do you miss . . . Claudine?" she breathed.

"What?"

"You know." She blushed, but struggled on. "Your New York . . . friend."

"Oh, Claudine," he said, as if correcting her on the name. His eyes avoided hers. "Naturally—but what can one do? One cannot live on memory alone." His dark eyes slanted with a fugitive suspicion over her. "However, let us not discuss my woes. How many people do you propose having?"

"Well, all of us," Sarah began unenterprisingly, "except Tom. Christopher doesn't dance badly. And Bracken and Mrs. Oxford and—"

"They aren't exactly young," he said mournfully.

"That's only a beginning." She glared at him. "Mrs. Welwyn, if she'll come, and Benjamin Crossley and perhaps Bronny's Press and Mr. Tulsey and of course Sir Giles Merrick. And Mr. Harbrittle often has people down during August, so he might send someone along. He had an Indian Prince at Christmas—"

"It all sounds somewhat . . . hypothetical."

"It is nothing of the sort," Sarah said, with all the more conviction for not being able to remember at the moment what the word meant. "And I suppose we'll have to ask Mr. Lupin, and Virginia Welwyn would be sure to bring someone glamorous as a partner if she comes, as I don't expect there'd be anyone here she would want to dance with, except Sir Giles and"—she smiled—"perhaps Christopher, if he would let her."

Peter would not for anything have allowed her to see how her unintentionally rude neglect of himself as a suitable partner pricked at his pride.

"One needs to look at the thing as an intelligent whole."

"Of course it will be intelligent. We shall have a real band. I'll let your father arrange that, as he knows most about it," she said kindly.

"How nice of you," Peter said, with such a poised deadly irony that even Sarah was aware of it.

She hurried on: "Cruddles *rises* to events like that. I can leave masses to him. And even Mrs. Bale is more bearable when she has something to go on. We'll use the ballroom, of course." Even to speak the festive word was as if to renovate the great barren place within her mind; to see it glow from a light within itself, the tarnish transformed to a patina of pure gold, the crust of ages burnished with a high light of frivolity.

The letter to Sir Giles was written, torn up, rewritten, sealed, stamped, and actually waiting panting for the post when she heard from him. Over and above the expensive crackle of his note paper, she could hear her heart thundering like a herd of cattle (and no ordinary cattle, but some Wild West stampede of steer, no less) as she smoothed out the page tenderly. His words were so effortlessly right, humour touched with rue and invisibly underlined with a faint sweet nostalgia. He was so sorry she had left London without giving him more chance to see her . . . it had been so delightful to have her with him at that party, and even her preposterous coffee stall seemed almost charming, looking back. . . .

It was far too good to be true. He had written to her for no discoverable reason except that he had wanted to. And now she could destroy her own letter full of humble plea, and write again with a playful imperious demand that he must come to her party. You simply must come . . . the way Virginia Welwyn would say it; blatantly, without guile.

Sick with joy, she dashed off her reply, not altering a word. She was inspired, uplifted, dauntless.

When she had finished, she was trembling with heat and bliss. She bathed her forehead with eau de Cologne, as if she were inducting herself into some mystic rite. Her eyes burned with a fanatic blue zeal; it was scarcely credible the others would not notice, but she didn't care. The gong sounded for lunch. She couldn't imagine where the morning had gone; she stared at the dim pink roses of her bedroom wall paper as if they might hold some key to the mysterious fluctuations of time.

It amazed her to see the others sitting with a calm inevitability around the dining table, the solid warmth of the day seeming to be laid in layers upon them. As if they had always through eternity been here, the aroma of roast beef wafting over them. Roast beef . . . Sarah felt herself faint within her own sensibility at the thought, though she was not exactly not hungry. But *roast beef.* . . .

The carving knife flashed blue and bloodthirsty against the steel. Roast beef at the start of an emphatic August afternoon. Had no one any reticences? There could be little real integrity in the vaunted artistry of the Jones temperament while they could all enjoy beef so much. . . . Tom brooded in "his" chair (guarded with no less possessiveness than Mrs. Oxford's responsible vouching for the Bible), his eyes darkly repelling the sun, the fair crest of his hair riding the fair light of the day triumphantly. He sat at Julian's right hand, the shadow of the carving knife playing in a macabre stripe across his oblivious face. Philly and Christopher sat side by side, arrestingly alike in this physical and emotional pause before eating. Bronwen and Peter sat opposite, more civilized and diffused in their attitude toward food, but certainly not antagonistic to it. Elisabeth faced Julian, wearing her reading glasses for no known reason. The sun caught the glass, destroyed her expression; her eyes, if one had not known otherwise, might have been bleak, fierce, anything. Her hair, rinsed through and through with light, was as fair as Tom's. Philly's and Christopher's hair had a warmth that was almost like darkness by comparison. Mr. Jones passed plates with parental zeal, for all the world as if he had never waved a spectacular baton and had never been without six children; and for all the world as if there were no Cruddles skulking in his pantry when he might have been here whisking dishes with professional ease.

Sarah took her place opposite Tom, on Julian's other hand. The eau de Cologne momentarily overwhelmed the heavier domestic smell of beef. She was conscious with pride of something alien in her presence: knew that she could eat, and yet remain utterly withdrawn.

"Where did you go all morning?" Christopher's grey eyes studied her incompletely, seeing the surface Sarah only.

"I was in my room." She made a meditation of the explanation, her words peeping from a strict nunlike privacy. Disturb them if you dare.

Tranquilly aware of the devious snub, Christopher turned his attention contentedly to his plate. Horse-radish sauce—good! The thrilling nasal pang brought on when you ate too much of it was more symptom than savour, but it was, to him, a highly satisfactory sensation.

"Mrs. Oxford rang up and asked some of you to go to tea, if you liked," Elisabeth said, absently helping herself to gravy which she didn't like. "Oh, yes, and Mrs. Welwyn, too. She said she had arrived early for a Week End with her aunt and she wondered if any of you would like to go on a—on a *trip*, she said, to the sea tomorrow. It seems an extraordinary idea of pleasure, in August, but I didn't say that to her, and I said I'd tell you." Having done her duty, Elisabeth began to eat.

"But why didn't you tell us at *once*?" Sarah glared at her. "Of course we'll go."

To Elisabeth's astonishment they all seemed to agree with this.

"You might never have told us!" Sarah couldn't get over it. "We might have had an utterly aimless Week End when there was no need for it. We might never have known we could have a trip—"

"But I *have* told you," her mother remonstrated gently.

"Thinking of Mrs. Oxford reminded me of Lady Pansy and then of her niece."

"That was the merest chance—"

Gazing round the table, Elisabeth realized they all agreed with Sarah's censure. How peculiar they were—"But she meant the *town*, darling," she emphasized their popular seaside neighbour. "I don't know why anyone should want a hot smelly trip there in August." She sighed, her eyes still travelling round the table. None of them—not even Bronwen—seemed to agree with her. "She said perhaps you'd telephone if any of you felt like joining in."

Sarah leaped from her seat. "I'll go now. I don't want any more to eat."

"I'll do it," Peter said, slipping gracefully between her and the door. But she was already ahead of him before they were into the hall.

"Will you want to go, darling?" Elisabeth, still interested in the inscrutable workings of the children's minds, asked Bronwen.

"I shall go," Bronwen said deliberately. "Virginia Welwyn is a very attractive, fashionable, amusing person. Will you pass the butter, please, dear Elisabeth?"

"She's rich," Christopher said. "She has a particularly decent car. She must be pretty rich, I should think."

"I like rich people," Tom said simply.

"She obviously goes only to the completely top people for her clothes. You can always tell," Bronwen said impressively.

Sarah came dashing in again.

"She says to bring anyone we like and have fun," she announced half triumphantly, half accusingly. "As if we knew anyone funny to bring. I expect she will bring someone lovely and fashionable who will talk about things in the swim. It will be agony—but worth it."

Gradually, they all drifted away from the table until only Elisabeth and Julian were left. She took off her glasses and blinked. The table, confused by the passage of the meal, was fussy with scattered bread crumbs, crossed knives, napkin rings, an overturned pepper pot, empty glasses. The low bowl of roses in the centre was the only thing with any precision of purpose left. Julian, contemplating the cheese with gently abstracted gaze, said nothing.

"I wonder if other people's children can possibly be as vulgar and snobbish as mine," Elisabeth said at last, wistfully. "As *ours*," she corrected herself, with no intention of wounding Julian, but with the sudden realization that between his and her offspring there was sadly little to choose in the matter of innate fineness of feeling. "In the swim . . ." she wonderingly echoed Sarah's words, as if she were holding up to the window some flimsy scrap of rag and seeing the light do its worst with it.

If only I *could* get someone down—Not Sir Giles, of course, as I have just written to him; that's out of the question. But someone? There is

Benjamin, but—He doesn't work on Saturdays, I know. If I wrote now—or telephoned after seven for a shilling. Nobody could object to that. I'd cut him off the instant the pips went—

In the end she decided to write, more because long-distance telephoning unnerved her than because she thought the shilling too extravagant. He would get it in the morning, if he were there, and could come straight down if he chose to. She had no special regret that it might all be somewhat rushed and uncomfortable for him. Her sense of having, even though very slightly, the upper hand with him gave her a sort of bland ruthlessness so far as his feelings were concerned. If he wanted to come, he would do so, difficulties or not.

She said casually to her mother, at tea on the terrace (it was one of those days that seemed nothing but meals):

"I have invited a friend to join the party tomorrow." Elisabeth paused respectfully in the midst of tea pouring. "Do you mean Giles Merrick, darling?"

"No, Mother, I don't. I mean his cousin. I know him quite well."

"Oh, I didn't know." Knowing full well that it wasn't the thing to say, she yet could not stop herself asking: "Is he nice?"

"Yes," Sarah said flatly, as she had answered Philly. "Very. Perhaps he could stay all the Week End if he comes?"

"Why, of course, darling." She felt somewhat shocked by Sarah's untypically cavalier manner. "Is he like his cousin?"

"Not in the least. He's only about twenty-three and he has red hair and he's just come down from Oxford and he's got a mediocre sort of job like stockbroking or something."

The others, together with various wasps, flies, birds, and Ernest, began to drift toward the terrace. Philly heard with misgiving the description of the young man, now looming with ominous reality. She looked upon the whole plan of the picnic as a mixed blessing.

"He sounds very nice and suitable," Elisabeth said mistakenly.

"Suitable for what?" Sarah frowned.

"I mean," Elisabeth said, putting milk in Bronwen's tea, although she should have known that nothing annoyed her more, "I was afraid you would not get to know anyone in London and would be so lonely—"

"Then why did you let me go?"

"You know I didn't want to, darling," she said weakly.

"But the point is, you *let* me. And you have got it all wrong. It isn't difficult to get to know people in London—far from it." She was suddenly annoyed by her mother's innocent complacence, although she had earlier been glad of it. "After all, anything that could have happened to me might have happened then," she said, not very concisely.

"I know, darling. But I did at least trust you to be sensible."

"But that might not have been any use." Sarah was by now thoroughly roused to an abstract indignation, ready to play the role of stern zealous parent as well as impetuous child. "Once, a terrible man followed me. He was *terrible*. He looked like a—a"—she hovered in search of some ultimate denunciation—"like a commercial traveller, I should think. It was awful. He was practically breathing down the back of my neck. And then you say it is difficult to get to know people in London!"

"Well, darling, I . . ." Perplexedly, Elizabeth knew that the tables had been turned on her, but as she didn't know what tables they were she was completely at a loss.

She felt quite glad when Peter gave an ill-natured laugh and took the tortuous conversation out of her hands.

"How long did the commercial traveller keep on breathing down your neck?" he asked ironically.

"As long as he dared," Sarah retorted. "Until we reached a policeman." She looked pityingly at Elisabeth. "Mother is so unsophisticated that I don't suppose she has even even seen a commercial traveller."

Elisabeth, who had not known this held the key to sophistication or its lack, was silent. She thought rather wistfully of the unpleasant sights she *had* seen: the snake house at the Zoo, Boris Karloff, and even Lon Chaney in the old silent days . . . but she didn't suppose these would vindicate her, so she wisely said nothing.

"Bronny wants her tea un-milking," Tom said, catching his mother's wandering eye.

"If you don't mind, dear Elisabeth. A cup without milk."

"Oh, of course, darling. I'm sorry." Less than usual did Elisabeth know where she was. Julian hadn't joined them for tea. It was surprising how she relied on his mere presence.

"It doesn't matter at all," Bronwen said patiently. She sniffed delicately at a rose she had plucked to stick in the tight solid bosom of her heavy white silk frock. As she did so, a little worm came curving insinuatingly out to her nose. She screamed and dropped the rose, worm and all. She was too shaken to say anything about the worm in the bud, and could only murmur with awed horror: "And it looked so sweet, so beautiful, my poor, poor rose . . ."

"I can't see any difference between worms and roses," Tom said implacably.

"Don't be idiotic, Tom," Christopher said, although he couldn't exactly feel sorry the worm had gone for old Bronny.

"I don't see any difference *at all* between worms and roses," Tom repeated.

Elisabeth was intensely glad that Cruddles chose to appear on the terrace just then, for Bronwen's sallow face was beginning to flush darkly, but she knew from experience that it would be useless to try to get Tom to placate her now. He obviously believed in his own remark and would defend it to the death. She wondered (parenthetically, between the arrival of Cruddles and his first words) whether Tom might be going to turn out one of those terribly modern artists who saw things—genuinely, presumably—in shapes and hues not natural to them. But she hadn't time to go into this distressing notion now.

"A gentleman called Mr. Lupin is here to know if anyone would like to come and see the picture," Cruddles announced.

"The picture?" Elisabeth repeated, still thinking of Tom allied to subversive art.

"And if they do, will they come now, as it won't be here after today," Cruddles went on impatiently.

"Oh . . ." Philly said, in an imploring murmur.

"Ask him to come out here," Elisabeth said.

"He's not here in person," Cruddles explained, now assuming an awful patience, "but on the telephone." He began to walk away. "I'll tell him you'll be down on your bikes in a couple of ticks."

Philly went dramatically white beneath her golden tan: but it was no use. Sarah was already making a move, if a contemptuous one, in search of her bicycle.

"If we're really going," Peter said, "I'd better get the car. I don't somehow feel I'd make a very favourable impression on the artist if I arrived perched on the step of Philly's bicycle." He gave the word "artist" a faint suggestion of sceptical emphasis, to be on the safe side.

Mr. Lupin had hung Philly on his private line. She dwarfed his stuffy uncomfortable little living room, a golden child of the morning scarcely in keeping with the tired tobacco-dulled atmosphere. Leading them in, he inquired whether their parents were coming, and, as nobody seemed to be in any hurry to bother to reply, Philly at last said nervously: "I'm afraid not," without explanation or apology.

The heavy late afternoon light beat in at the fussy latticed cottage window with a peculiarly evil glint. The whole room had a lowering expression, forbidding, in spite of the tenant's jolly no-nonsense country-parlour furnishing, and the crush of honest books that conscientiously knew no brows either high or low. There was a faint musty smell that Philly vaguely connected with tramping through vineyards, but which was actually due to the bad-tempered windows having long ago clamped themselves shut and refused all efforts to prise them open.

They stared up in silence at the highly coloured Philly, embarrassingly nearly as large as life. The actual sun, struggling to get in, and the bland undeviating sun that played over the picture, made a confusion of light that dazzled the eye with a sort of double-focus intensity; this moment's sight was tagged mystically by Mr. Lupin's boisterous constant vision through the days he had been painting. One felt how he simply had not *allowed* the light to flag for one instant, had held it inexhaustibly orange, pitched to his stubborn demands.

"It's terribly true to life," Bronwen said at last, without any intention of personal insult to Philly.

It was, in a way. In spite of the sun and the glaze of perpetual triumph in which the figure was cast, it was an extremely plausible portrait of Philly. Not a hair out of its accustomed place, and even the slide abhorred by Lady Pansy and Peter in full guileless view. The rich fair hair, the fair lashes glinting in the sun, and the arms and throat washed over by an oily even tan.

"May one ask where is its destination?" Peter inquired.

Mr. Lupin smiled mysteriously, the Royal Academy lurking as a probability on the quirk of his lip.

"Isn't the pitch just slightly *high* for any light ever seen in this benighted land?" Peter went on, his tone courteously blaming the English climate rather than the artist. It was more than high . . . it positively screamed . . . he thought privately.

Tom had stood in silence, his neck cricked, his eyes upturned to the picture, his hands in his pockets, his mouth thinned out in unchildish concentration, his blond quiff pulled forward on his formidable brow. He might have been preparing himself for either a tremendous sneeze or some huge affront of laughter, but finally he broke his silence in so muted and comfortable a tone that it was as if an expected lion had come in like a lamb: and a particularly docile lamb at that.

"There now—isn't that a sight for sore eyes?" Tom said.

A furtive giggle, in which even Philly joined, ran through the room. Sarah took the note high, outside furtiveness, glad to laugh and to

reduce the whole thing to absurdity. Imagine anyone *seriously* painting Philly. . . .

"She was made for highlights," Mr. Lupin went back to Peter's
remark, refuting it.

Philly blushed, wondering if the agony would ever end. It was a
double agony, not only her true self but her portrait self in the pillory.

"I shall always paint her in strong light," Mr. Lupin said.

Philly believed her ears, but only just. It wasn't over . . . it would
begin again and go on and never end . . . pose after pose outlined by
incredible sunlight, summer after summer until youth at last had
mercifully passed her by. . . .

"Gosh," Christopher said. The word was solemn, awed, an "amen"
that gave up his twin meekly, knowing she couldn't be saved.

Only Peter and Bronwen chose to go home by car. The others
walked slowly back through the dusty aching sweetness of a day that
did not mean to die. It had gone on and on, and would go on and on,
simply flattening out without transition to the night. The foliage of
the season—full to bursting, the coarsened green taking up the light
thirstily, bruisingly—still looked unquenched, as if purity not only of
form and colour but of the atmosphere as well had vanished for the
rest of the summer. The chalky dry road sent up cloud after little cloud
of powder to lie wearily on shrubs, dusting the veins of leaves with a
detailed sort of slovenliness. It was like a face powder strayed on to
brows and lashes, Sarah thought, careless and yet giving a contrary
impression of being carefully brushed there. Cottage gardens billowed
and lolled with flowers going rollickingly to seed. At this rate, one felt
there would be nothing left by the end of the month. There was a shocking appearance of nature's squandering which Sarah, again, thought
would distress Mrs. Oxford's sense of parochial neatness and prudence
if she had noticed it. In her mind, too, she could see her old friend
running a disapproving finger along the leaves of close-set domestic
hedges, and shaking her head sadly at the adhering dust. The green
wainscot of the countryside was in a deplorable condition . . . one could
hear her saying it, clicking her teeth a little. . . .

They plodded in silence.

"Gosh," Christopher said, finally.

Philly felt pinched with anguish; wanting to take a bold plunge of
protest against Mr. Lupin, yet wanting to defend, shrink back within
the secrecy of pretending none of it mattered.

"Do you think it's like you?" Sarah asked.

Philly felt naked and ashamed. "I don't know . . ."

"It's like her," Christopher said. "But it's pretty bogus all the same."

The anguish turned to desolation. I'm bogus . . . Philly whispered to herself; I'll never be the same again. . . . Ahead, she saw that first imposing vista of the Fontayne gateway, solid blocks of pale grey set with the wrought-iron gates, feathery tracings of black against green. It was bogus too; seeming to be what it was, yet nothing of the sort.

"It's going to be fine tomorrow," Christopher said.

Philly thought of the picnic-to-be and the possibility of Sir Giles's cousin. The day, all around, looked familiar and gentle to her eyes, but all the same it now became infused with doubt. She did not see how she could put off for much longer the unhappy climax of being grown up.

CHAPTER THIRTEEN

THE GRASS SPRAYED dew on Philly's bare ankles as she came up through the garden after feeding her hens. Ernest's sleek coat was sprinkled with shining moisture. The slanting lawn was burnt to a thirsty yellow no dew could quench. Burnt to a frazzle, she thought; and wondered what a frazzle was. The morning was too fair by far. Nothing now could stop the picnic save Virginia Welwyn's incalculable whim. Carefully carrying three brown eggs, Philly knew quite definitely that she didn't want the picnic; not like this, all on top of her portrait, with no interim for readjustment to the idea of being bogus. Sarah's voice, flying down from the terrace, confirmed this certainty.

"Benjamin is coming. He has just telephoned to say he is on his way."

Philly was saved from answering by the arrival of Mrs. Moody coming to a full stop in mid-pedal as it were, her bicycle still seeming charged with excessive vitality even after she had alighted.

"You *have* got a nice day," she said to Sarah, who went to meet her. "Your friend will have a good view of the countryside."

"I don't imagine he is coming for a view." Unwittingly, she played right into Mrs. Moody's hands; left the opportunity wide for inevitable retort. "As if I thought he was!" Mrs. Moody exclaimed in her most pointed nudge-in-the-ribs tone. "If you ask me, young fellows who like looking at views are as bad as those that hold them. Plenty of time for all that when you've passed the twenties. I've brought back your undies. They're all right now." Her voice rode triumphantly across the morning. "You'd joined up the wrong seams. I put it right in a jiffy. You can begin wearing them right away." Philly heard the chill civility in her sister's response: "I don't want to, thank you. And need you shout everything across the garden?"

Unabashed, Mrs. Moody disappeared into the house.

"Where is everybody?" Sarah asked, as Philly approached, balancing the eggs on her cupped palms. "We are supposed to be at the almond icing at noon."

"Bronwen's gone up to her room to get a poem off her chest." Philly's tone put this at the same unemotional level as a bout of indigestion.

"Well, I hope she gets it off quickly, because she always feels sick for half an hour after a poem, and we don't want her being sick at Lady Pansy's before we even start the picnic. Why she has to have a poem this morning I can't think." Sarah made an inopportune birth, rather than indigestion, out of her stepsister's inspiration.

"And Peter dashed down to the village as soon as he'd finished breakfast."

"You know, I think Peter is acting queerly, and I think Mrs. Moody suspects something. She looks awfully lavicious when his name is mentioned." She gazed at Philly, who seemed unimpressed, and tried again: "She has a lavidious expression when she speaks of Peter."

"She has that when she speaks of almost anyone," Philly said, understanding Sarah's meaning. "You won't leave me alone with the man, will you?"

"If you mean Benjamin, no, I won't; but I shouldn't think he could frighten even you." Anxiously, Sarah hoped he wouldn't appear over-young. It was important that Virginia should class him, if not with Sir Giles, at least not with Christopher.

Indoors, there was an air of leisured activity that irritated Sarah. The close little breakfast room, with the remnants of the morning's meal still on the table, was filled with passively hostile interests. Elisabeth was still at the table, getting through the morning's news in one prolonged gulp, the paper propped against an unsuitably cheerful tea cosy, her eyes peering nervously over her glasses into naked disasters. Her attention was rooted to the interminable leader that went on and on with scarcely even a comma to break up the cruelty of the world. She would not let in the light that was Digby waiting for the orders of the day. Let him wait, she thought sternly, until she could conscientiously say she had done her attentive best by horror. Let the flowers wait, too. Not to mention the children.

Christopher was tinkering with an obscene-looking bit of his dismembered bicycle, drenched with oozing oil. Tom, of all things, had chosen to set out his puerile painting outfit on one corner of the table.

"I hope everybody realizes we are going on a picnic," Sarah said reproachfully. "Benjamin is dashing here at top speed."

A powerful black roadster charged across Elisabeth's painfully alert perception of the news. She jumped up, only halfway through the leader, not even waiting for a full stop. "I'd forgotten, darling—"

Bronwen came in. She looked slightly damp with heat but not, Sarah was glad to note, particularly sick.

Tom was painting with passionate concentration, digging into all the crudest colours to the limit of his brush and grooving the paint with its metal base, washing away each tint with contempt almost before he had gathered it in a rich globule at the brush tip; impatiently shaking the water from it after rinsing, sucking it with insolent disregard for hygiene, then flaying his palette once more with ghastly undigested mixtures of hue.

"*Why* do you paint?" Bronwen asked, the insult made threadbare by her tone, not the faintest suggestion of sincere interest to cover it.

Without any attempt to defend or justify his art, and whisking his brush madly around the glass of muddy water, Tom said: "I like the *sloppery* sound."

Benjamin's hair was even more noticeable at Fontayne than in London. . . . Sarah saw nothing but that when his little car pulled up near the house. She advanced toward him with a cool "hello," but it died on her lips as he took an extraordinarily *alive* basket from the car seat and held it out to her.

"Giles sent this for you."

"Oh, but—" Really this wasn't necessary, God. I was feeling quite pleased with life without this, but . . . "But when did you see him?"

"I happened to ring him up to tell him I was coming down here, so he said I might as well bring this. It's a cat of sorts." On the signal, an indignant wail shattered the hot heavy peace of the garden. "He said you said you'd like one of your own."

With steady fingers (as if to be given exotic pets by well-known figures in the social and political swim were all in the day's play) she unstrapped the basket and in silence watched an angry slim beige creature leap out and spin contemptuously away from any threatening caress and then sit down sedately at a distance while it let out an automatic wail or two.

"It's a Siamese," Sarah said, almost reverently.

"He said you'd like it," Benjamin said doubtfully. "He said to tell you its name is Sanka."

"Like it—I love it!" she cried, her eyes as blue and fierce as the cat's. Her emotion was so strong that she wanted to burst into tears. Instead, she said: "He thinks of such unusual gifts," as if Sir Giles were in the habit of bombarding her with presents. The cat was docile when she picked it up and held it, but it continued to give its automatic blood-curdling yells. "I asked you down for a picnic but"—she gazed into Sanka's eyes with a bizarre sort of mother love—"I don't know that I'll go now."

Benjamin felt as if he had been betrayed by his own will to please. Far from reacting favourably upon himself, the gift had alienated him from the simple pleasure of a country Week End. "They're very independent creatures, I believe," he said wistfully.

"That isn't the point." Gathering the cat into her arms, Sarah led the way into the house. "You must meet all the family," she said over her shoulder. He was certainly nice, and useful at a pinch, but one did not waste undue sympathy on pinches, particularly not if they had such embarrassing baby curls.

It was Cruddles who saw to it that Sarah did go on the picnic, in spite of Sanka the cat. It appeared that in some middle distance of his inexplicable youth Cruddles had been what he called a party to the ways of Siamese. He promised Sarah that if she left the cat with him for the day he would have her so civilized by evening you wouldn't know her. Doubtfully, yet gratefully, Sarah left her pet to him. The malevolence of Sanka's expression was softened somewhat by her worried frown; Oriental pride mingled with a shocked what's-the-world-coming-to fretfulness.

Benjamin said, to each new person he met, what a lovely old house it was. There seemed a great many new persons, each younger than the last. He came to Elisabeth with relief; but she did not remain. Even as she spoke to him she was edging away; as if a curtain had gone up too soon and left her inopportunely upon the stage. He knew nothing of the morning paper's leader lying reproachfully, half read, across her conscience. Poor young man, so terribly suitable in age and physique to defend his country in war . . . she was thinking; but he did not know this. She peered at him severely, almost as if she blamed him for being young and in such good shape for slaughter; but he had no clue to her expression. Nevertheless he thought she must be a perfect person to have for a mother. No wonder, he thought with simple sentiment, that Sarah was so nice. . . .

The continental almond icing flourished in the blistering sun. For once, its bright roof cut the sky on a clear burning line of authentic Riviera blue. Not only did the house preen, but Lady Pansy, also, was in her element. She moved in a mid-morning party atmosphere, as if she were the focal point of all the countryside.

Virginia was stowing picnic baskets in her own car when the Fontayne party drove up in Benjamin's car. As they all got out—seven of them including the red-gold cousin—Virginia stood and laughed.

"Have you all come!" She laughed *at* them, in a way that would have been cruel in anyone else.

"I've brought someone," Sarah said quickly, as if this excused her.

They went into the house. Lady Pansy swept across the Chinese interior, with Emily's hand in hers. "Virginia rang up Bunty and insisted this child should come, too," she said, but as if she personally couldn't imagine why. Emily, limp-pawed, was passive and amiable in her grasp. "I'm afraid Bunty doesn't know how to bring up children. *I'd* let 'em all run wild as savages." Lady Pansy had never had any of her own, savage or otherwise, so could let her theories, at least, run rampant. "Who is that young man?"

Sarah said he was Sir Giles Merrick's cousin, but Lady Pansy's gnawed-looking incredulous eyebrows showed no faith in the truth of this. She snatched Philly's arm and forced her to meet her eyes. "You've got that hideous bit of celluloid in your hair again," she accused.

"It's a nice little kirbi-grip," Tom said, outstaring Lady Pansy.

"Where do you think I would have been if I had curbed or gripped my hair?" she demanded of Philly, ignoring Tom.

"I—I don't know," faltered Philly. (She had known nothing good would come of the day.)

"You don't know? But surely you know about my hair?" She stared from face to face. A hush fell on the room. Her tone suggested something more than a legend, something more concrete and impossible to refute, such as the Pyramids or the Great Wall of China. "Why, there was so much of it that it used to be washed in three separate parts, one part a day, so that it shouldn't be too exhausting for me. Once a month.

We didn't—luckily—think it good to wash hair more often than that, then. I remember that the first three mornings of my honeymoon were spent in washing it. My husband was astonished."

Everybody present felt that this was the very least he could have been.

Virginia had no picnic escort, after all. How *like* her, Sarah thought, when one had braced oneself for someone terrifying and superlative. She moved coolly within the aura of her dazzling smile. Her manner was the same for all of them, including Benjamin, with perhaps an extra shade of sweetness for Emily. Privately, Virginia called Emily the petrified orphan, a description which induced a half-ridiculing tenderness in her.

Emily herself, in such close proximity to the godhead of Lady Pansy, was painfully conscious of a form of ghostly sacrilege in being able to observe in detail one who had unconsciously received her prayers for so long. Seeing Lady Pansy smoking opulent and most irreligious-looking fat cigarettes and tossing off a bright unholy drink, Emily blushed again and again in alternating chills and heats of shame.

"We must be getting off," Virginia said vaguely. "We don't want to miss the worst of the day." She smiled briefly. "*You* know."

"You must all come here for hot drinks when you return," her aunt said.

They fitted themselves into the two cars. Sarah slipped into the seat beside Benjamin's driving one, but was not sure she wouldn't rather have gone with Virginia, if only to prevent Peter from sitting by her. Philly sat between Tom and Emily in the back of Benjamin's car, sandwiching their alert neutrality. It was a disaster to Emily to find Tom in the party, but she bore it meekly. In the back of Mrs. Welwyn's car, Christopher and Bronwen found themselves incompatibly placed together.

A picnic is a great thing for lowering the vitality and heightening the more hostile of the emotions. Polite pretences are apt to go by the board. Virginia had no pretence, except of the most blatant and blandly undeceiving land; and Benjamin had none of any sort. They were the only ones who enjoyed the day simply and without any of those emotions that are odiously called "mixed."

On and off, all day, Sarah thought of Sir Giles's cat. (Given to her, it was still, at the base of its existence, as it were, a possession of his.) From now, life—which had so many false fresh starts—began once more anew. Not only had he remembered words she had spoken, but had also made it his business to supply a positive answer to the need they had expressed. She shifted impatiently on the hot leather seat beside Benjamin. The triviality of the day's project, in the incessant yellow pattern of the weather, filled her with dismay. Love was baulked by such petty barriers: she felt she could more easily have borne it if the barriers had been sinister implacable things.

The country, narrowing down to a sparseness of colour and shape near the sea, seemed marked off for autumn, though as yet untouched by it. Sarah clenched her hands and beat a futile little tattoo on the gay cotton lap of her frock. If we don't have the house party—the dance— soon, it will be too late. I feel it in my bones. Not only autumn, but—Her mind jibbed against some invisible sharp edge of disaster. Nothing would happen . . . but anything *might*.

Philly, retiring into her bogus shell, ceased to be a bulwark between Tom and Emily. The two children had nothing to say to each other, but the girl's open and almost speaking fear of the boy was a subtle invitation to him to abuse that fear; not because he was a bully but because it was the kind of secret pensive not-batting-an-eyelash drama that he found impossible to resist.

In the other car, the light conversation between Virginia and Peter gave an appearance of general ease. Bronwen chimed in at intervals, but Christopher said nothing at all. With his hands between his knees, he stared out at white milestones and flying verges of fields and dry shrivelled hedges. A ripe smell from one of the picnic baskets made his mouth water, but not sufficiently to make the picnic itself worth while if it meant sitting by Bronwen for years.

The first view of the sea was seen from high land. It had a distant tepid charm, robbed of colour, nearly white beneath a sun haze. It was seen at an unfamiliar slant of propriety: it looked a *nice* sea. Tom said this aloud. The others in Benjamin's car felt a backwash of Tom's surprise. Not the vulgar sea they knew, but painted in within the landscape with a seemly colourless flatness: just sea, dignified.

Virginia stopped her car on that peak of land. Benjamin drew in behind the still insolently puffing exhaust of her superior motor.

"I think we'll have lunch here. Would it be a good idea? And *descend* later?"

No one would have dreamed of going against her whim—which was so much slighter than an actual plan. And the way she emphasized a subsequent descent made the promise less a visit to the sea than an excursion into some outskirt of hell.

Full of nice restraint though the sea might be, they found, as they set out lunch on the ground so high and dry above it, that its smell was still intrusively heartening. The scrubby grass, threadbare in great patches, had a desolate neglected appearance. The slope was perilous, the lunch cloth laid at a laughable angle, its formal stiff white glaze affronted. Cups, saucers, plates tipped as if to the motion of a boat on high seas: yet there was the nice quiet sea, obliquely placed below, to refute such an impression. An acrid seaweed smell came up and flaked away the country smell into unimportance. Eyes might still discount the sea's proximity, but nostrils could not, even had there been any wish for them to do so.

"Now we shan't be long!" Tom said, rubbing his hands together in self-congratulation.

"It was awfully kind of you to provide all this," Bronwen said to Virginia, awed by the lavishness of the picnic. She eyed them respectfully, those Lucullan Fortnum hampers. To eat civilized food again would be an inspiration in itself. She swallowed appreciative saliva and the unspoken opening lines of a new poem.

"Picnics are fun, I think," Virginia said simply, "when one can get the right people."

Peter was helping her unpack bottles and glasses. He was rather disappointed to find nothing but tame "ades," lemon and orange, and cold green sickly lime; but he put a good face upon the discovery, and merely said: "What an incredibly meretricious shade lime juice is," as he held the bottle to the light.

Virginia didn't answer; only Bronwen nodded appreciatively. Emily was content with the task she had been given: unwrapping knives, forks, spoons. Even when Tom's shadow fell across her, she did not quail.

"Is your granny coming?"

"No." She looked up, her eyes shy, dark, startled. Tom was a blond dazzle before her. "How could she—now—even if she wanted?"

"She has her little old legs, hasn't she?" Tom said sternly.

Emily had never considered whether her grandmother had legs or not. But, if she had done so, it would not have occurred to her to imagine them used in pursuit of a picnic party. Polishing each fork on a cloth before she laid it down (a trick that would have shocked Mrs. Oxford by its suggestion of someone tainted by vulgar humble house-proud zeal) she eyed Tom timidly, ingratiatingly. She was not sure she believed he would punch and ill-treat her even if he had the chance, but she did wish he would go away.

"You're sitting on an ants' nest, you know," Tom said.

Emily raised herself on her haunches and looked at the innocent earth intently for a moment, and then sat down again in the same spot. Undismayed by her lack of confidence in him, Tom tried again: "I shall bathe on top of my lunch."

"Shall you?" Cutlery lay shining and alert, ready for use.

Christopher felt happier now, making himself useful, free of Bronwen. Mrs. Welwyn unceremoniously shoved a pile of plates at him. The slight breeze blew back her hair: her appearance better matched her manner now; he felt all right once more in her presence. "For God's sake look where you're going!" she laughed. He smiled back, relieved. He breathed deeply, walking steadily with the plates. He felt thirsty, suddenly happy, released somehow within himself. Downward, the cliff crest jutted like an angry ancient eyebrow over the sea.

Emily looked up, as he lowered his burden gingerly to the slanting cloth edge. He smiled at her, too, his natural unthinking chivalry coming uppermost once again. She felt herself to be saved, the big fair grey-eyed boy more than cancelling out the little fair dark-eyed boy. Smiling up at him, her thin cheeks darkened by emphatic mirth-sad creases, she began to drift away in the wake of cloudy thistledown. Away and away to the island where she would live alone when she was a lady as old as Grandmother. She would have the People of her Country there, invisible to any eyes but her own. And there she would live out her days, with no one to interrupt—

"If your granny hasn't any legs, how does she stump it?"

"Shut up, Tom," said Christopher, who saw no point in his brother's considered query.

The combined inner gratitude of the party toward Virginia was immense. Amid the scattered crumbs of picnic, repletion reached from the stomach to the mind: set in as if to last all the rest of the day. Even Benjamin (used as he probably was to proper food, thought Sarah) had shown appreciation. The smell from coffee, taken in a civilized way at the end of the meal, cloaked warmly the starker sea smell. The party was no longer alone on its eminence. A motor coach was parked at a ponderous slant, and groups of people, dark, light, noisy, were scurrying about briskly. Nobody minded this end to privacy; indeed, it brought them back to the purpose of the day, which had been to mingle with seaside crowds. They had made no attempt to make a nice clean picnic without attendant litter. To have done so might have been to feel superior to the motor coach: and this, in the blazing heat of the present, would have seemed a waste of time as well as a pity.

Virginia lay flat on the ground, unself-conscious, dark glasses not disguising her but seeming to enrich her identity. "I shall live in the country for ever," she said, to nobody. "Not the real country, but this half-in-half. A gritty little house, with motorbuses thundering past the front and sandy marigolds and lines of washing at the back . . . *you* know." Her laugh melted in the heat. "Every moment of my existence dusty and garish, all my neighbours minding my business for me. I shall 'take up' something suitable. Yes—I know—I'll take up hair-dressing, and I'll catch one of the buses every morning down to the town. I'll *perm* people in the biggest, classiest hotel on the front. I'll be sweet to faces and catty behind backs. I'll have a neat attaché case. . . . Where did the cigarettes go?" She groped, still lying down. The sun glasses were bland brown discs, giving a quite appropriate expression to her elegant face.

"Is she always like that?" Benjamin whispered to Sarah; amused, puzzled.

"I don't know her very well—but I think she is." She felt a bias of pride at being able to provide friends who were not only generous but humorous. "She does what she likes."

"No inhibitions?" He smiled, saying that.

"None," she agreed seriously. She thought of Sir Giles's cat, to keep her from feeling jealous of Virginia's utter freedom of being.

"I don't know that I—" He didn't go on. His eyes sought the peeping bit of sea; his hand pressed abruptly down on Sarah's fingers. "I think she could be rather alarming."

"Oh, no," she said quickly, pleased for him to feel faintly quelled.

"Is there some *idea* behind this picnic?"

"Not that I know of," she said haughtily.

Still puzzled, he gazed around the scrubby waste of land and wished they might have stayed in the lovely old place Fontayne . . . Sarah's home. He thought happily of it as her background. It vouched for her, as her charming mother also did.

"We think this sort of thing is fun," Sarah went on, still haughtily. For once, she associated herself, open-eyed, with the Joneses among the others. *They* also thought it fun.

"I shall bathe now," Tom said, standing up, eyeing the meagre strip of sea with hypnotic gaze, as if he expected it instantly to expand to his very feet.

"I could do with a bathe," his brother said.

They all began to stir a little against the threatening weight of somnolence. Bronwen started up from an exquisite open-mouthed doze; saw her poem riding away into oblivion, unrecapturable. Christopher sat up and saw Virginia lying close to him. For a moment, only halfway out of a sleep coma, he studied her closely, pinned to his own curiosity as his gaze was pinned to her. To see the faint rhythmic movement of her breathing astonished him as much as if he had seen a doll come to life. She had taken off her short white linen jacket and her head now rested on it, but her short hair ruffled over its edge and sprayed the stubbly ground. The boy felt, in a strange way, dismayed: that the jacket should be harmed and that her hair should touch the earth. It did not strike him that she might observe his scrutiny through the dark glasses; to him, she was a blind face, with a blind red mouth and a blind mind. Yet he did not see her as bogus now. He felt as kindly to her as when he had remembered her in the days after the Easter dance, when she had treated him as a human being. He was not sure, now, whether he had wondered about her only once or twice, or many times, after that. He knew that all the paint of lips and nails had embarrassed him. It still made him wince when he thought of it, but he did not notice it as much as he had.

"Well, are we going to bathe?" His placid voice, not yet quite broken, ran up on an urgent crack. He heard it himself, and it made him laugh. This proved to him that an early protesting impatience with the picnic was gone from him now.

"Will someone gather up the things?" Virginia murmured, her initiative gone.

Emily began happily to stack crockery. Nothing terrible was happening; she was getting through the day. Mrs. Welwyn was a kind lady. Tom sat at a distance; his expression was distant too. Philly came to help Emily. They shared a momentary cosy impression of domestic ease, there in that dry unstable setting. Philly forgot her portrait and the fear that she might have to talk to Benjamin. Presently, perhaps, she would swim with Christopher. Her spirits had begun to rise after the motor coach had arrived. She had liked watching the people bustling around, setting about their own picnic, had liked, too, the cheerful fizz of their voices on the buoyant air. She was pleased for so many people to be enjoying what she enjoyed: the zestful taste of outdoor food and drink, the sun seeking out every cranny of exposed flesh, burning you to a beautiful frazzle. Thinking this, she knew how such thoughts would annoy Sarah. If she imagined for a moment that the motor-coach people could really be feeling things in just the same way that she, Sarah, was experiencing them, she would be furious. It had been the same with Bracken's stories for the village children, Philly thought shrewdly, with guilty remembrance.

"I've wiped the plates with tissue paper," Emily said.

Philly looked at her with admiration. It was the sort of thing none of the Fontaynes would have thought of doing.

Peter's cool olive face seemed to repel the sun's rays. This gave him a melancholy air of aloofness, as if it were a spiritual matter rather than one of pigment. Every sophisticated gambit he had tried on Mrs. Welwyn had been thoughtlessly laughed out of his control. He didn't know where he was. He had smoked too many cigarettes, and felt, as well as looked, melancholy. The summer, he thought, had gone from bad to worse, financially, emotionally, artistically.

"I suppose we have to stay with all the others all the time?" Benjamin said wistfully.

"Of course," Sarah said firmly. She was dimly aware that her deepening sense of power with the young man was bad for both of them. If he were less anxious to please, how far more ready she would be to do so—She knew that her discovery so soon of this vulnerable streak in him was disastrous to him: she would abuse her own feelings for the sake of being able to abuse him. It was a pity, because (she realized with a cold clear Lily-Joan-Mrs. Billing sort of acuteness) he was a very *useful* young man to have. But such perversions of friendship were natural to her, and she did not see how she could go against nature. . . .

They came to the sea. Here, at its edge, they saw it exhausted, no longer in the least nice. It was polluted by August, without grandeur, sporting wearily with the ever re-accumulating refuse of holiday. "I think," Virginia said, looking abstractedly down her nose, "that we had better move on somewhere, hadn't we?"

Half-reluctantly, they turned back from the scummed edge of the sea and walked across a peopled space of hard torrid sand, threading their way with difficulty among haphazard portions of anatomy wilting in the sun. You never knew where you would trip over an apparently disconnected hand or foot. It was about here, in the comparative solitude of June, Sarah remembered, that the young man in the blazer had tried to pick her up.

"I suppose the pier would be impossible?" said Bronwen, loathing her surroundings with so fierce a zest that she was enjoying herself more than for weeks past.

"I'm going to bathe," Tom said.

"You are not," Sarah said flatly. "You wouldn't want to bathe in that crowded dirty water."

"Why wouldn't I?"

Emily was afraid, her knees trembling. It was the noise, not the people. Gulls swooped and shrieked. She defensively placed her hands over her ears. Like that, she got through the living mass of the seashore fairly well. The secret silence encouraged her own world. She would live quite, *quite*, alone on her island—

The others had stopped. With head bent, ears closed, Emily had gone on a pace or two ahead before she noticed this. A donkey, laden with a large top-heavy child, came between her and the others. The donkey's expression was as patient, as shut in, as her own. She skipped timidly past its hind legs to rejoin the others. Against the grey cliff face, a Punch and Judy show was in progress. Emily opened her ears suddenly to the noises of reality and to the terrifying dream sounds that came from the little high bright box of a stage. In spite of the heat, she felt a swift coldness in the tips of her fingers and toes, and her nose had a pinched tight feeling, as if it had been suddenly frozen blue. She *would* not look—Her eyes came back, drawn by the crude shocking colour, the vicious movement, the sinister posturings. She clasped her hands, but there was no prayer in her. Lady Pansy would receive her prayers, and that would never do. Fright brought back the taste of cucumber that had been in her salad at lunch. Here, the sand was softer, so that her feet sank helplessly and her shoes filled with its dry spray.

Tom's laughter, near, startled her to her depths. It was a sacrilegious mockery for which he would never be forgiven. "It's a very nice little Punch and Judy," he said pensively. She trembled for him as if he had spoken the ultimate blasphemy. The last wanton phase of terrible drama had set in. Emily clenched her hands. It could not go on much longer because there would be nothing to go on *with*. The high gabbling quaking voice of Punch must fall silent because he and life could not both go on. The sticky rubbery smell of concentrated humanity by the sea made an ominous impression of thunder in the air.

Virginia glanced at the petrified orphan and saw her tense, rapt; as if she couldn't have enough of it. Even when a stiff blood-red curtain dropped down on the peep show, and the tight-pressed crowd began to drift away, Emily didn't move. Virginia took her hand, humorously plucking at the child's trance: "I'm afraid I couldn't quite bear to wait and see it all over again . . ."

"Couldn't you?" Emily said politely. She pulled her sand-filled shoes along with difficulty. Her bones felt very old. She thought of her grandmother's aged legs with sympathy. Her heart still fluttered at her throat, whirring at the cucumber like a mower cutting grass; but now she felt more sad than afraid.

Their backs to the sea, they wound slowly up a trickling cliff path. Halfway up, they sat on a seat and shook sand from their shoes. All engaged in the same action, they felt peculiarly intimate and friendly. A smell of wilting tar came down to meet them, a reminder of the town above. They came to the top, opposite the largest hotel, glass-pavilioned, palm-fringed, insularly exotic. Cars throbbed by, little toy-like buses trundled smoothly. "Buses—well, I never!" Tom said; and indeed there was something extravagant in the sight; these urban vehicles of utility almost cheek-by-jowl with fantastic Punch.

"I suppose the pier *would* be impossible," Bronwen said, again.

"Entirely," Peter said. The joke of the town was no longer fresh. "I'm sure you'd like to get away, Mrs. Welwyn, wouldn't you?"

Virginia did not resent his solicitude, but—worse—she was indifferent to it. If she could have seen herself as an ill-used young woman dragged by a tiresome swarm of children, she would have been enchanted by the vision; but she could not. She still held the hand of the petrified orphan, but from no motive of sympathy, merely because she had neglected to relinquish it.

"Why not some tea?" she said, with that lovely appearance of deferring to opinion, which deceived neither herself nor anyone else.

"Tea!" the Fontaynes echoed.

"Tea with the funeral trees?" Tom added hopefully, pointing at the pavilion.

"Those are palms," Christopher said scornfully. "You never saw *palms* at a funeral."

"If we go there, it is sure to be tea with music," Philly whispered happily to Sarah, forgetting that Benjamin, on her sister's other side, would be sure to hear.

"Yes, I know," Sarah said impatiently, thinking of the musical Zoo-tea with Sir Giles and his red-gold cousin. Treading the centre of a metal-studded safety way across the road, she wished she had stayed with Sir Giles's cat.

The glass pavilion held the unexpected spectacle of a tea dance. The place was so light with day that every colour in the room stood out with a terrible clarity, as if Mr. Lupin had painted it. Even the dressy afternoon frocks of girl dancers had a dubious quality that was not in their material or style but in their highlight. This was a new world, jolly but restrained. It bore no relationship to the teeming pageant of the sands. Tom was exasperatedly conscious of himself as a little boy, his surroundings all wrong. The funeral trees were not the slightest consolation. He stared down resentfully at his scrubby knees, the whole room offending him, and his little-boy naked knees also offending him in relation to the room.

"I should like to go and wash my hands," he said with a formidable cold formality.

"You are a nuisance, Tom," said Christopher, knowing the task of playing escort would fall on him. He blushed with dismay at the prospect of leading Tom across this huge shining palace room.

"I'll take him," Peter said, with one of his unexpected impulses of discerning generosity.

"I think these must be the modern equivalents of what used to be called tea gowns," Virginia said, her unconsciously insolent sympathetic eye travelling slowly around the room. "*You* know."

"Do you go in for mass observation?" Peter could not resist pausing to ask, in another attempt to draw her attention to him.

"I shouldn't imagine so," she said sweetly, innocently.

"Hurry up," Tom said implacably, urgency muted down beneath the overwhelming all-enveloping quality of his disdain.

Virginia began to talk pleasantly to Benjamin; about London, about Giles. Sarah listened happily, satisfied with the easy words and the background of polite dance music and the *shush-shush* of feet on the polished floor. She and Philly smiled dreamily at each other across a waving pattern of heat and sound. The sea's influence was upon the room (all this *swimming* light could come only from the sea), but, again, it might have been nice sea. Here, it was idealized, a mere backcloth for luxurious sandwiches and cakes. Emily recognized cucumber sandwiches on an advancing trolley, and the sight brought her heart into her mouth again; but already she associated her fear as much with cucumber as with Punch, which meant that she was slowly recovering.

Virginia had not removed her sun glasses. "You pour out," she said to Philly, flashing her a swift intimate smile beneath the blank eye masks. Filled with a great weight of responsibility Philly rose clean above her diffidence and performed the duty expertly. "I shan't pour out Peter's and Tom's till they come back," she said seriously, thinking out her future moves with grave generalship. "We shall need some more hot water."

"Could we dance?" Benjamin said, aside, to Sarah.

"Oh, no!" She was still brooding over Virginia's remark about "tea gowns." The hotel was smart, but . . . somehow, somewhere . . . it struck Virginia as being funny. Sarah resented the fact that Benjamin, a presumably sophisticated young man, did not seem to see this.

"Why don't you two dance?" Virginia said, laughing across the table at them.

Sarah would not meet the young man's eye, but she at once rose and stood stiffly waiting for him as her partner.

Peter and Tom returned. Tom's disapproval of the room was tempered by interest in the food trolleys; but he was still offended. "I did wash my hands, too," he said resentfully, refuting a suspicion he felt in all of them. He displayed his freshly scrubbed and somehow forbidding hands as evidence. "It was purple soap in a pink cake dish, and it made purple froth. I had a towel to myself. It was a very big room with green walls, but the lavatory had white walls. I—"

"Shut up, Tom," Christopher said.

"It's a *tango*, Peter," Bronwen said, a cosmopolitan light in her eyes.

"How quaint," Virginia smiled. "My mother used to dance it in the War, in a large hat and a hobble skirt. They called them tango teas, I think." For her, the tango was English, comic, and dated.

"Oh, but it's still danced all over Europe," Bronwen said courteously, unintentionally presenting a whole continent in a slumbrous-frivolous light. "Peter and I used to do it." She sighed for the lost lovely days of her departed youth. "I'd love to try just once again, Peter," she said nostalgically.

The nicest thing about Peter was his niceness to his sister. In spite of mounting hope that he might have been allowed to dance with Virginia, he rose at once to Bronwen's demand. Christopher thought that he would rather die than drag that bulk around the floor. But it happened that Bronwen's fat was full of rhythmic guile—to music, she moved like a feather blown upon a wind of song.

To Christopher, on his third sandwich, Virginia said: "*You* are my partner, aren't you?" and smiled again, recalling the dance in the spring.

"I can't do tangoes," he said, agonized.

"We won't dance it as that, of course," she said, still unable to treat the idea of tango seriously. She stood up and he unwillingly followed her. It surprised him, as once before, to find that he was taller than she.

Philly was left with Tom and Emily and the neglected cups of tea. "I shall bathe on top of my tea," the boy announced, staring at Emily.

An incredibly smart young man paused at the table and bowed to Philly. "Excuse me—but were you by any chance thinking of dancing?"

"I—" Her tongue clove to the roof of her mouth in a paralysis of horror. He took her silence for assent and held out his arms. "I—I can hardly dance," she unclamped her tongue sufficiently to say.

Far from discouraging him, the admission seemed positively to inspire him. "I promise that with me you will dance," he said solemnly.

So like a sacred vow were his words that to refuse him now would have been to desert him at the altar in the very midst of his promise to cherish her for ever. "Go along, Philly," Tom said maternally. "I'll keep my eye on the little old teapot." The young man smiled whitely beneath his black strip of moustache. "Yes, come along," he said persuasively.

Christopher forgot his own agony of reluctance to dance in seeing Philly trip off with a stranger. He steadily breathed in Mrs. Welwyn's amazing perfume and steadily avoided her eye. Her neat glowing necklet of pearls described for him everything unnerving that the word "débutante" could mean. Of course she must have got over being a famous débutante by now, but she *had* been one.

"You see, it needn't be a tango," she said. They were moving smoothly, unspectacularly.

"No." He cleared his throat, ventured: "Look, Mrs. Welwyn. Over there. Philly . . ." He laughed; a shaky gruff little sound. Looking, she grew weak with laughter. She was a child with it, younger than Christopher. He became a little anxious. "Look, Mrs. Welwyn—-ought I to—"

"No, my dear, leave her alone."

"But she—" He paused to master a difficult turn, and didn't continue. In a cowardly retreat he abandoned Philly to her fate. Himself, he found with simple selfish fervour of relief, was not really hating the dance at all. "Have you—have you been flying, since?" he spoke again. The sun glasses faced him blankly.

"Since?" she echoed. "Oh—since we last danced together, do you mean?"

"I—yes, I suppose so." He could have kicked himself. But it was what he meant.

Sarah didn't see Philly at first; and, before she did so, she was involved in a personal despair. The first burst of tango ceased and another began as encore. "It's *La Paloma*," Sarah said, surprised by her recognition. "We have it on the gramophone." The emphatic formal rhythm, the bland decisive tune, reminded her unreasonably but vividly of Sir Giles. Frustrated, she felt the arms of his cousin like a prison about her. Nothing ever came out right, whatever Mrs. Moody and the magazines said to the contrary. . . .

"You must come flying with me," Virginia said simply, to the boy. His spirits surged as if he did in fact believe her implicitly. His gratitude was directed straight at the person who had treated him as a human being and who had stayed stubbornly in his mind even when he was at school. For this, he could overlook that she had made him dance with her and that she had been a famous débutante. It was a relief to get that straight in his mind, and to feel it was not necessary for him to be ashamed of liking her. If he could just *believe* he believed what she said, he need not despise himself for liking her.

"That is awfully decent of you, Mrs. Welwyn," he said earnestly. . . .

"Do you mind not holding me so tightly, please, Benjamin?" Sarah said coolly.

"I'm sorry. Most people call me Ben, you know."

"Do they?" As if it mattered. *La Paloma* had taken the heart out of her. What, even, was the gift of a cat if he never came himself. Soon, the beautiful Sir-Giles-smell would begin to fade from her nostrils and she would no longer be able to call up his vision at will. What was she doing dancing in a seaside hotel with funeral palms, and not with him? There must have been something she could have *done*. She did not believe he would come to her birthday party.

"Do you believe in Free Love?" she asked, in abrupt capital letters.

"It sounds rather . . . post-war, doesn't it?" He smiled faintly, scenting a joke, but not sure of it.

"I don't know what you mean." She was the more annoyed with him because the book in which she had recently found the phrase was one with a cover depicting a girl with an Eton crop and a frock with a waist at the hips, and with an explanatory tag under the title, "Frank exposé of post-war moderns . . ."

"Don't you like dancing?" He was as unsure of her mood as of the joke.

"That isn't the point." The point was, she had never really and truly expected to *marry* Sir Giles, so one ought to face the alternative facts.

Until now, her imagination had refused to take her beyond the first thin end of the wedge of love, but one could hardly go into all this with his own cousin. . . . *La Paloma* beat on unrelentingly.

Bronwen and Peter continued to move through the encore with a beautiful singleness of purpose. Her fat cheek dumped against his shoulder, she murmured: "Peter . . . wasn't it lovely when we were young?"

He knew what she meant; didn't smile. "I'm afraid such times will never come again."

Virginia took her head from Christopher's shoulder and removed her sun glasses. He was astonished to see the deep violet of her eyes after he had grown used to the brown blank discs. It was no longer easy to escape her glance. He felt a void in him that he attributed to hunger; he had reached only his third sandwich when she dragged him off to dance.

As if she sensed some protest in him, she asked: "Are you bored with this?"

"No, Mrs. Welwyn. I—"

"Still, perhaps we'd better have some more tea."

An anguish of compunction seized him. He would have hated her to imagine he wanted to dance with her in the first place, but now that he was doing so he could not bear her to think he might dislike it.

Tom sat opposite Emily, now and again stroking the teapot handle to prove he was still guarding it. His dark gaze oppressed the little girl, branded her with the image of Punch. His very glance could browbeat her, not a word needed; in which he was more subtle than Punch. She smiled, shamelessly on the defensive, ready to give in spinelessly, without a murmur, on all subjects, including her grandmother's legs. "I won't ever come here again. It is like a bath," he said.

"Yes—"

"Do you have baths?"

"Yes, of course."

"There's no 'of course' about it," Tom said, nettled. "I have them when I have to. I lock the door. I don't let anyone in. Sometimes I don't use any soap at all," he said with pride.

"Oh, don't you?"

"No, I don't. But sometimes I do." He looked down at his grubby knees, brazening them out, as it were. If he were willing to accept this horrid bath-like room, the room had better not do anything but accept him. "They have purple soap and froth here."

Philly approached for the third time the haven of her table where her own little brother and nice little Emily sat. True to his word, her terrifying partner had made her really dance, but this was no consolation.

"Please—" she begged desperately, setting a brake upon his persuasive steps. "I think I had better sit down now—"

"As you like." He looked suddenly pained. "But, as I understood it, we were booked for a round ticket of five."

"*Five* dances?"

"That's usually the shortest session," he explained patiently. "Most people, one finds, don't want to chop and change partners every five minutes."

He sounded as hurt as if he really wanted to go on dancing with her . . . she couldn't make it out. . . . "Well, you see, we have to go soon. Thank you very much," she said wildly, digging her heels in, not budging an inch beyond the table. He released her, but did not move away.

"I wish that little old man would sit down," Tom said pointedly. "Or go away."

Virginia and Christopher came up, and then Sarah and Benjamin, so Philly never knew what the single effort of Tom's words would have achieved. There was only one thing to be thankful for in the terrible developing situation: which was that Bronny and Peter did not witness the first abysmal depths of her humiliation.

On the way home, sitting again between Tom and Emily, she took out the living nightmare from the back of her mind and looked at it self-torturingly. The others might forget, but she never would. The way that Mrs. Welwyn had taken it so casually, as if it didn't matter a bit, had only made it worse. She had smoothed it all down so perfectly, and the young man had gone away subdued by her charm and her practical handling of the matter; but none of this made it really any easier to bear. They were all (even Bronwen when she heard) so tactful about it that Tom's burst of unthinking brutality was almost a relief. "Philly's partner had to be *paid*. —well, I never," he remarked, when it was all over and they were walking away from the hotel.

Miserably, now, she wondered if Virginia had paid for all the five dances, the . . . session, as the young man had demanded. It was the sort of thing you couldn't possibly ask about, however grateful you were to Mrs. Welwyn. The car ran on through the exhausted summer weather. Philly's partner had to be paid . . . Philly's partner had to be *paid*. . . .

Returning, Christopher sat beside Virginia. His twin's woe had released the last of his taut conventional distrust of a woman who was over twenty, but not, he supposed, yet thirty. Of course he was sorry for Philly, but it was *funny*. Now, he did not wait always for Mrs. Welwyn to address him first. Of his own accord he asked her how much her car did to the gallon and what was its maximum speed.

"I suppose the Fontaynes have never seen a professional dancing partner before," Bronwen remarked to her brother. "They simply don't know how to cope with anything outside their own narrow little lives." She sighed again for her departed youth.

"You'll stay all the Week End, I hope, Ben," said Sarah, gracious now, busy covering up Philly's lapse.

"I'd like to, yes." With the evening of Saturday already here, he had not imagined he would do anything but stay. He smiled. "I'll help you tame your cat."

"I shall attend to her by myself," she said, dedicated. She no longer believed implicitly—after the long, hot, ego-disintegrating day—that her birthday party would come to pass, but Sanka at least she had. All my life long I'll have her, at least. . . . She forgot that a cat's span of existence did not match that of the average human; that she might yet be left to a bereft old age.

Philly dreaded her homecoming all the more because of her knowledge that Mrs. Moody was there. It was too much to hope that she would have departed before they reached home; even as it was far too much to hope that she would not have wormed out the dancing partner before many minutes were gone.

Mrs. Welwyn dropped them at Fontayne, but wouldn't stay. She waved her sun glasses at them and smiled as she drove away. They could all sense the prospective gaiety of her evening: whatever she did, even if she spent it alone with Lady Pansy. But each, privately, chose to imagine an informal little party lightening the Chinese interior of the Congtinental.

Nothing was ever as you expected. . . . Braced for the slinky re-emerging of her dancing partner, Philly found that the house was not keyed to his reception. Fontayne's atmosphere had been worn down by events during your absence. It was queer how life went on even behind your back, and how it always surprised you that this should be.

Sarah and Philly automatically went up to see Mrs. Moody as soon as they got in, leaving Benjamin to fend for himself. Elisabeth and Mr.

Jones were not to be seen. Mounting to the sewing room, Philly could already feel her dancing partner slowly being drawn out of her, like an interminable piece of chewing gum.

Mrs. Moody was whirring the machine, but she stopped dramatically as soon as she saw them. "And what sort of a day have *you* had?"

"Very nice. Where's Sanka?"

"Cruddles has her. Bale won't have anything to do with a foreign cat, she says. All I can say is it's a good thing Ernest was duly neutered."

"Sanka is too young for that sort of thing, anyway," Sarah said loftily.

"Don't you be too sure. Never be too sure of who or what's too young." With the born conversationalist's dexterity, Mrs. Moody had her theme exquisitely at her fingertips. "They *do* say," she went on quietly, well able to afford to play down to her thunderbolt, "that our Peter has got Gertie Wiggs in trouble and that her pa's going to make him marry her."

"But he can't have!" Sarah protested.

"Don't you be too sure," Mrs. Moody repeated lasciviously.

"I mean, he can't have *got* her into it," Sarah explained, "because she always *has* been in it."

"That's neither here nor there—"

"Oh, but it ought to be!" Whatever one thought of Peter, this seemed an undeserved fate. *Gertie Wiggs* . . . with her rolling eye and gait. . . . But, all the same, how *horrid* of Peter who should have been faithful for ever to his romantic if reprehensible New York Claudine. . . .

Philly felt terribly sorry for Peter; all the more so for his having removed her so blessedly from the limelight. What he saw in Gertie Wiggs, who had trailed disconcertingly around the village for as long as Philly could remember, was his own business. To go down and face him now, with the knowledge of his doom upon you, would be unbearable.

"Isn't there *anything* else he could do but marry her?" she beseeched.

"There usually is," Mrs. Moody said, with a sniff.

Benjamin stood alone in the hall. He had stood there for minutes, simply waiting. Nobody took any notice of him. The little boy appeared and disappeared. The girl Bronwen, with head bent and a pile of books under her arm, plodded briefly across his view, to vanish also. The butler person came and looked at him and went away again. Presently Sarah herself rushed downstairs, absent-eyed, and shot past him with the merest glancing explanation: "I must find Mr. Jones. I must hear what he's going to *do* . . ." before she, too was gone.

Smoking nervously, the young man wished his hostess would appear. But for a long time nothing more happened and he stood there in the eerie greenish light of the hall with only the distant wail of Sanka for company.

CHAPTER FOURTEEN

PETER NEVER DID marry Gertie Wiggs (as Sarah, telling the story in later days, said) because she ran away with a man in a travelling fair, reputed interesting condition and all, the next day; but that, as Mrs. Moody had it, was more Peter's good luck than good management. His guilt remained unproved—or, rather, it remained unproved as his exclusively; and, as the one thing Gertie had never been was exclusive, Sarah felt that her point that nobody could *get* Gertie in trouble was more or less satisfactorily dealt with.

Nevertheless, the *affaire* Wiggs was another nail in the summer's inevitable coffin. Not only did one feel removed to a disapproving, yet respectful, distance from Peter, but that distance would soon be actual as well as moral, for he was not to be kept penned to Fontayne once the summer was over. It was not yet decided where he would go, but go he must. A quiet life, as Mrs. Moody, with a gleam in her eye, again had it, didn't exactly seem to suit him.

The Benjamin Week End was *distrait*, to say the least of it. What with Peter's eclipse (he retired into what Mrs. Moody grimly called a belated monastery for several days to follow) and Bronwen's attack of nausea on dimly suspecting the cause of this retreat, and Elisabeth's remorseful feeling that she *ought* to have found him some nice girls to play tennis with, even if he *had* thrown the idea back in her face, and Mr. Jones's emerging into what Peter, when he heard of it from his sister, labelled as that rare and parentally alarming thing, a spiritually *pronounced* fortissimo, and Sarah's exalted concentration on Sanka, and Philly's brooding over her paid partner, and Christopher's near memory of Mrs. Welwyn, her car, her bogus lips and nails, and her half-promise of the freedom of the skies—what with all this, Benjamin's Week End had a great many loose ends. Tom alone held humour flagged high throughout Sunday; and Tom's humour was not a thing to put even the most confident guest in countenance with life at Fontayne.

The summer was full of the nails of its doom. The picnic, that full emotional day, accomplished the semi-final knocking in. The final hammering home was reserved for the birthday party which, from being no more than what Peter had called hypothetical, gradually assumed the proportions of certainty.

Elisabeth, watching the morning papers as they followed one another with crisis cynically capping crisis, felt that the race between the birthday and the full flower of disaster would be very close; but she did not interfere with any of the mounting Fontayne plans.

Sarah spent the Sunday afternoon of Benjamin's visit in writing to thank Sir Giles for Sanka. It was, she said, the perfect birthday present; and added urgently: "You *will* come to my birthday party, won't you?" Oh, God . . . the shadow of prayer fell over the words, making them at least spiritually indelible. . . . You will *make* him come, won't you?

After completing the letter, she spent the day in soothing and crooning over Sanka, who eyed her with bland blue sardonic gaze, while graciously accepting devotion. Poor young man, Elisabeth thought as she watched Benjamin in the cold of Sarah's devastatingly kindly indifference, not only so ripe for slaughter, but also so ripe for feminine rebuff. . . .

Even in that Week End, listless and *distrait* though it was with divided interest and lack of interest, Fontayne seemed to begin rising to what might very well be its last occasion. An onslaught of turning out bedrooms started (some people would come only for the dance, but some would undoubtedly stay: why else call it the Week End?) and, outdoors, the gardens seemed to put on nothing short of a midnight spurt. One went to sleep on the night of the picnic with all the debris and the fluff of August going through a squalid phase, and awakened to see a fresh patina over everything, a sleek delicate brilliance that caressed the eye. Mentally, Sarah stroked and patted; Fontayne was making one of its timely resurrection bids, which meant nothing really, and yet was comfortingly deceiving. It was . . . almost . . . 'this desirable residence' of the crafty advertisements. Momentarily, the weeds growing up through the floor were stemmed in the very birth of imagination. Stemmed, the desolation turned off into victorious channels and, suddenly, it was no great effort to see Fontayne as that Mount Olympus of more prideful days.

"I'm glad it has been such nice weather for you," Sarah said kindly, on that Sunday evening of Benjamin's departure.

"Yes, the weather's been all I could wish," he agreed sincerely. "Such a lovely old place. It seems a—" He was going to say "a pity," but he was not sure where the pity lay.

"And you'll be sure to come for *the* Week End?"

"Thank you." Her emphasis suggested it *would* be less absent-minded and disconcerting than this one, he thought rather bewilderedly.

"And bring anyone you like," Sarah supplemented lavishly.

"Perhaps Giles could come—"

She stared. "Come?" The chill edge of query was directed painfully at herself as well as him; but this he could not know, nor that her marrow was as frozen by doubt as his was by her forbidding tone.

The renewal of garden, the furious furbishing of house, were to be accepted with tantalizing reservation until the query was answered. There was a pause at the very heart of the heart of that busy clock-work of activity until one knew. The unseasonable spring cleaning, with Mrs. Rudge (happily recovered from the new baby) to the fore, might, even in the very pace and bustle of it, be proved nothing but a hollow mockery. Time itself hung fire, the hours creeping sickening things, until one knew. Come . . . ? The purpose and the being of celebration *not* come . . . !

Mrs. Rudge was a talisman against the paid partner. Not once, in her presence, did Philly think of him. He could not live in the pungent atmosphere of floor polish, virile soaps, astringent mops. "You wouldn't hardly think it possible there could be so much conglobber in such a big house, would you, Miss Philly?" The more the better, Philly thought so long as the freely used vigorous bracing cleansers could take her mind off the humiliating immediate past. "Doesn't the baby mind being left?" she asked again and again. "Not him. Catch him missin' his mornin' beauty sleep! Not nohow!" A proper Rudge baby, the new one was already taking beauty with professional seriousness, if only in sleep. "No, Miss Philly—if I couldn't get off and shake an outside duster now and again I'd begin to regret I'd ever taken on an 'ome and 'usband." To Philly, the shaking of any duster, even an outside one, seemed a modest enough form of dissipation, but it appeared to satisfy all Mrs. Rudge's needs of expressing herself.

These days, she did more than "come in." Swooping after cobwebs in the derelict ballroom, and gathering great panfuls of dust before she got down to the polishing, she found release for her libido, thereby freeing her home life from all manner of possible neuroses. At home, she explained to Philly between swoops and sweeps, it never seemed worth getting down to one big proper tidy through, but here you had something to *go* on, something to show for it at the end. Husbands were all right, and babies were all right, but there was a lot to be said for getting taken out of yourself now and again.

Peter stepped cautiously, bit by bit, as it were, from his voluntary retreat. It was not so much being a moral leper that worried him as having to act up to being one, for very decency's sake.

"It doesn't seem to have changed him much, though," Philly said, puzzled, thinking how far more changed she herself was by her portrait and her paid partner.

It wasn't the first time with him, you see . . . Sarah wanted to tell her, but she refrained, thinking it not a suitable subject for younger sisters. Nevertheless, Gertie Wiggs, though gone, was not forgotten. She left behind her a spirit of unrest. Against Fontayne's integral unchangeability, change was in the air. Peter's delinquency forced him willy-nilly upon adult notice. I shall be the next one, Sarah thought, setting herself firmly in line if not for moral leprosy at least for the full view of sharpened parental attention.

"We don't want to embarrass him by looking as if we have taken it *in* too much," she said, in a kindly meant camouflaging tone.

"Oh, no, of course not." Philly agreed quickly.

It was Bronwen who was not to be consoled. Nothing could make her swallow Gertie Wiggs in a sophisticated spirit of tolerance. The best she could do was to pretend to understand less than she did. This entirely went against the grain of her nature, stemmed the flow of her inspiration, and involved her in a sharp embittered attack of indigestion.

The appearance of Sarah, radiant-eyed, at her bedroom door, a morning or two after the flight of Gertie Wiggs, did nothing to speed her recovery.

"Shall I write to Mr. Tulsey or would you rather do it?"

"Write to him?" Bronwen paused in the brushing of her hair, which was dragged in long sulky curves over her shoulders.

"To invite him. We must get *down* to the Week End."

"I thought you *had* got down to it."

"Well, yes, but—" No use to explain to Bronwen that only now—only this morning, in receiving Sir Giles's acceptance—could she really get down to it. No need to enlarge on the sweet wistful mocking note being so like his sweet wistful mocking dynamic personality. She had herself scarcely taken in the separate phrases yet; merely the fact of his acceptance. Something about "our sacred institution the British Week End, come what might," and that he promised to get down at least for the birthday dance itself.

Come? . . . but of course he would come . . . ! Now, at last, the Week End was properly on its feet.

"Why Mr. Tulsey?" Bronwen asked suspiciously. One result of Peter's being revealed in his true colours was to make her suspicious of everything. She half expected sex to raise its ugly head even here, even in the innocent relationship of Mr. Tulsey with her career.

"Well, he is obviously used to Week Ends," Sarah retorted, "his face is so tanned."

"But I don't think I want to be seen in my home life by my publisher," Bronwen said mournfully.

"If you don't invite him, Mother will," Sarah forced her at the very pen point to agree. "And you know he'd rather have a pretty literary note from you."

Bronwen went on stolidly brushing out her hair against the light that caught the authentic seaweed hue and emphasized it.

Mrs. Oxford agreed to go the whole formal hog of the Week End, even to sleeping at Fontayne if that were what was needed to ensure the necessary leisured tone of the proper house party. Asked by Sarah what was the true clue to the conducting of a successful house party, the old lady said that, so far as she could recall throughout a long career of such events, she had always *dawdled*. Nothing could better have pleased Sarah than this dissection of pleasure. She saw decorative people dawdling down to breakfast on Sunday, unthinking leisure the very keynote of their existence. That her inner eye dressed them in elaborate ground-sweeping morning gowns with pouched bosoms and high tight lace necks was merely a natural sympathy with Mrs. Oxford's instinctively early Edwardian presence; a complimentary mental embroidery that had nothing positively in common, except manners, with her own neo-neo-Georgian birthday.

"And, if your mother would not feel it out of place, I should like to bring Emily with me. Even though she remained in the nursery most of the time with your little brother, she could at least absorb some *sense* of adult pastimes and begin to learn how to conduct herself in the normal usages of society."

Sarah was so flattered for Fontayne to be called society—even if only "the normal usages of"—that she would have welcomed a guest far more awkward than Emily.

It was through Mrs. Oxford that Sarah learned how sincerely sympathetic to the dance were Lady Pansy and her niece. The word had gone tactfully out to Virginia that if she could and she should bring a party of her own dazzling friends down for the dance they would be welcomed with the most open of open arms.

The party taking shape, Peter was more and more inclined to forget he was a contaminating influence and to range himself on the side of the angels and innocents. And nobody, except Bronwen—and possibly Mr. Jones—took this amiss. Elisabeth was only too pleased to forgive. Besides, he was so helpful in doing his best to bridge what Elisabeth persisted in viewing as nightmare gaps in the young people invited. Name after name he brought out in amiable asides to Bronwen.

"There was Kasnov. He was young and amusing and I think he danced and I'm almost sure we have his address."

"I hardly think he'd go down here," Bronwen said steadily, "unless he has deteriorated since we saw him."

"The point is whether *we* could swallow *him*," Sarah glared at her.

Kasnov was dismissed and Elisabeth gave another sigh.

It was no use asking Bracken to bring anyone. Sarah resented the fact that Bracken let them down so badly as an American, if not as a human being. Any normal American would have had the decency to be a dashing, dauntless steam-heated sort of person: but not Bracken. It seemed unfair that one's solitary American should refuse to conform to a single one of the standards that the movies had so properly and efficiently set up.

"Why can't Bob Norbett come?" Philly asked.

"Oh, would it do?—I'm afraid it wouldn't." Sarah felt a depression in the most sensitive part of her stomach because it wouldn't do; and she dared not meet Philly's eye. "Lady Pansy knows him, for one thing. She said what a nice young man he was—"

"*Well*, then—" Philly challenged.

"But . . . *across the counter*, she meant."

"Oh, Sarah!"

"I know things shouldn't be like that," Sarah agreed, discomfited. "But the point is they *are*."

"They won't be, much longer," Philly said darkly, more wounded than she could ever have been on her own behalf.

"Oh, if you're going to start being prickly just at the very beginning of my party—"

"I'm sorry, darling," Philly said quickly, humbly. "I was forgetting it was your party."

"Bob wouldn't come, anyway," Sarah said rather wistfully hanging on her sister's response.

"No, I don't suppose he would," Philly agreed. But it was all wrong, her expression still said. There was something utterly wrong somewhere.

Bracken arrived the day before the dance, but everybody was glad to see him because he introduced the party spirit without of course in any way being the party itself.

"Those who are coming to dinner and to stay, we expect to arrive any time during tomorrow afternoon," Sarah explained the arrangements to him. "More will come later, of course, just for the dance. I hope you *have* remembered to bring your evening clothes?"

"Yes, I have," Bracken said meekly.

"I'll show you the ballroom after tea," she promised. "You'll never recognize it. It looks almost *lived-in*, if one can say that of a ballroom."

Bracken was in one of his warmest moods; as accommodatingly interested in the resuscitated ballroom as he was in the antics of Sanka.

"Nobody really appreciates her except me," Sarah confessed; "but, then, I couldn't expect anybody to understand the sentimental interest."

Privately, Bracken thought he had never seen anything that looked less concerned with sentimental interests than Sanka. Her fawnings and archings were as free from genuine humility or desire to please as a caliph masquerading as a beggar in his own kingdom. Her proud worried face had no trusting belief in the milk of human kindness, but merely an unimpassioned suspicion that humanity could be quelled into subjection by a pair of sardonic sapphire eyes. Fawning gracefully, almost abandonedly, against any leg that offered, Sanka yet frowningly reserved herself in unfathomable fastnesses of essential privacy, with little opinion of most things and of Ernest none at all. Mrs. Bale, who had always guarded the kitchen tabby from Ernest, now took to guarding Ernest from the heathen cat Sanka. Behaviour at Fontayne was more complicated and tortuous than ever, Bracken thought.

Here, he was used to having little or no notice taken of him, so he had none of the feelings of odious neglect that Benjamin had known. He would not have blamed Sarah if, with so imminent an anniversary to live up to, she had been least upon the scene of any of them; but, next to Philly, she was the most attentive to him. She even confided to him the appealing history of her dance frock.

"*Julian* gave it to me, Bracken," she said, her voice shaken with emotion. "The loveliest thing. A model. It doesn't mean anything to you—as a rarity it's wasted on you—but I do assure you"—she paused earnestly—"I've never seen its like before. It's white; but not too white in spirit, if you can know what I mean. It is . . . perfect."

She remembered, with self-approval, the dignity with which she had accepted the overwhelming gift.

"Thank you very much indeed, Julian," she had said whole-heartedly, for the first time treating him as an absolutely definite person, with all the appurtenances of thought and feeling proper to a fully-fashioned human being. Dexterously, she had skipped straight from treating him as a near-stranger to accepting him in the perfect light of adult understanding. It was a formidable jump; but she took it in her stride, with no intention of looking back. (Come what may, as Sir Giles said.) Bygones would be bygones. Even the taking of one's mother in marriage could, viewed from the right and charitable angle, be a bygone that had turned out better than one could have expected. His white model of a peace offering, diffidently proffered and graciously accepted, was the symbolic adjustment of at least one family relationship.

In kitchen, drawing room, garden, ballroom, a driving effort was apparent. Sarah wandered from one spot to another, hands clasped. Now if only it keeps fine and if only the war doesn't begin. . . . Cruddles was up to his eyes, as he said. Whenever Mrs. Moody was not in the house, Sarah sent telegrams to remind her of tasks she might have forgotten. Thanks to Julian, she had no dressmaking to do for Sarah, but she had made Philly's first authentic dance frock, a flowery silk whose large jaunty pattern Philly already hated by the first fitting; but as she was going to hate every moment of the Week End, anyway, the dress seemed no more than a small extra to despair.

"I think *anticipation* is the most unbearable thing," Sarah confided to Bracken, that day of his arrival. "You won't mind using the bath on our floor, will you? The luxurious one is reserved for the proper week-end guests."

Bracken said he wouldn't mind at all.

Saturday itself, which was the birthday and the day of the dance, began too soon, Sarah felt. First, there was that tedious polite period of receiving the family gifts and showing suitable pleasure. Actually, and somewhat mortifyingly, the only present to which her heart went out in genuine joy was the heavy and barbaric but sophisticated necklet with which Bronwen presented her.

"It's beautiful . . ." Sarah murmured, stroking its hard bright chunks and cubes. "It's a bit like the appalling rococo bracelet, isn't it?"

"What?" Bronwen scented an insult, not realizing that Sarah used those words as a mere mechanical description. "Well, yes, it *is* rather baroque, but that is how they are worn now."

"Of course; and that's what I love," Sarah said sincerely. But, all the same, it was a somewhat shaking experience to have to begin the day on a note of such genuine gratitude to Bronwen.

The house, on tiptoe with expectancy and polish, was an uncomfortable place to be in until it was released on festivity. The birthday sandwich lunch, taken in the schoolroom, improved nobody's temper; especially as Benjamin inopportunely arrived in time for it, with the friend he had promised to bring to swell the ranks of the dance.

"You did say to come early?" he asked diffidently.

"Oh, yes," Sarah said flatly. "If you don't mind cold things and sandwiches."

"No. I saw Giles. He said he would get here."

"I know," she said coldly. Somehow, it didn't feel like the Week End, though all, including Mother, were doing their best. "I don't imagine the war is likely to begin between now and this evening." But it would if it could, just to spite me. . . .

"No," Benjamin agreed, but doubtfully. "A lot of people think it's sure to be here by the end of the month, though."

"That's not *tonight*, anyway." She was on the verge of tears. She could eat nothing at lunch; but it was the dance, not the war, that dried up her appetite, then. Benjamin's young man friend was more of an embarrassment than an asset. He looked as if he had been brought here on false pretences when he discovered that Sarah was the only grown-up girl of the family. He eyed Philly with sulky contempt, to make it plain to her that she had no part in his general scheme of attractive femininity. Philly actually smiled at him in relief to find this was so.

Mrs. Moody presided at the scrappy schoolroom meal. She and Tom were the only ones really in their element. Tom could not bear to see even Benjamin's sulky friend looking as if he weren't enjoying himself.

"Would you like to have a pull at the little old wishbone with me?" he asked ingratiatingly, holding out a licked-shaggy portion of chicken carcase.

"No, thank you," the friend said politely.

"Will you help me when the band arrives, please, Julian?" Sarah said, using his name with as pretty an air of familiarity as Elisabeth could have done. "I won't know what to say to them."

"I'll do or say anything I can," he smiled. It sounded as if she thought he knew some special suitable chirps of encouraging language to use on dance bands. . . .

Bronwen had sent astray the sulky young man's calculations on femininity by embarking on an adult conversation with him about America, whence he had lately returned.

This fat child solemnly telling him that Manhattan was a place where she felt particularly at *home* was highly disconcerting to him.

"I must go to America," Sarah said carelessly, feeling that she ought at least to hold the conversational reins on her birthday. "Do you think I'd go down well in America, Bracken?"

"I think you'd go down very well, honey," he said gravely, slyly.

Bronwen, not to be done out of the limelight, slipped in: "Honey, you shall be well desir'd in Cyprus; I have found great love among them. Oh, my sweet, I prattle out of fashion, and I—"

"You certainly do," Sarah cut her short, embarrassed by the endearments, even at this quoted second hand.

"I want some lemon cheese tart," Tom said.

"You can't have any, duck," Mrs. Moody said. "Wait for the birthday cake this evening."

"I won't be there. I'd rather have lemon cheese tart now."

"There isn't any, duck."

"There isn't any!" he repeated, wounded. "I'll have to have another suck at the little old wishbone, then."

"I must go and get on with things," Sarah said, jumping up, finding the school room insupportable.

* * * * *

The day dripped a slow steady warmth, but the sun was not often visible. Sarah and Philly went down to the little orchard to gather fruit. The walled space seemed overwhelming, bursting with ripeness. Sarah remembered lying beneath the apple trees while they were yet blossoming, reading Sir Giles's first letter.

"Being eighteen is making me feel a lot older already," she said, plucking a plum with a responsible gesture.

"Is it, darling?" Philly was already so anxious about the day (that it should be a success and that she should not be called upon to try to be one) that she could express little further anxiety.

"And then the war-high branch."

"Don't let's talk about it today, darling."

"That doesn't prevent its being *there*, ready to pounce," Sarah retorted severely. "I wish I knew exactly what Sir Giles did."

"Oh . . ." She was still thinking of him, then. . . . "Isn't he somebody's secretary?"

"That's so vague," she objected, as if it were Philly's fault. "I hope those coloured lights are going to show. All the trees are so horribly high." This, too, might have been Philly's fault.

Sanka, brought down the garden by Sarah, contemptuously flirted her black pencil tail at Ernest, who had followed Philly. He watched her unmoved, the sun flecking his eyes with sleep. She rose on her black silk stockings and pirouetted, her eyes intent and frowning on a butterfly, her front paws cutting the hot air with swift capricious dabs. Ernest, not amused, yawned and buttoned up his eyes for slumber.

"Do you think it would be a nice idea to put a little basket of fruit in each guest's bedroom, or do you think it would look affected?"

"I don't know," Philly said unhelpfully.

The afternoon gathered speed at a distressing rate, with so many things left to do, and yet such an awesome sense of empty spaces that would never be filled.

"What shall we do, Peter?" Elisabeth whispered, from the midst of her social anguish, entirely forgetting the barrier of moral leprosy that still separated her from her stepson. "Nobody will come. One or two couples dancing in that great room—what a nightmare! Of course if we are all going to be bombed by next week, an empty ballroom is hardly important—but, all the same, poor Sarah. . . ."

"Don't worry." Peter gave her hand a reassuring little squeeze. "The Deverings and the Peels faithfully promised me they would turn up. And there are *lots* of them, and they're inclined to bring *others*." He passed over the coming war as a subject unsuitable for further commiseration.

"Thank you, darling," she said gratefully, Gertie Wiggs or no. "I know you've done your best."

Bronwen came up to where they stood at the door of the empty ballroom. For her, the place had been ruined. She stared balefully in at the transformed room, frivolous with flowers, all prinked up in a pink-ish glow to make a birthday holiday. All the magic tarnished glory was gone, the green shabby light banished to make way for this—this *blanc-mange* atmosphere. . . . Bronwen scowled.

"Mr. Tulsey seems to have arrived, and that old Mrs. Oxford has got hold of him," she said.

"Oh, dear. . . ." Elisabeth sighed. "Wouldn't you like to go and amuse him, darling?" she suggested mistakenly.

"I don't see that because Mr. Tulsey happens to be my publisher, dear Elisabeth, I should have to amuse him in private life." She had not forgiven him for quoting in his Sunday advertisement that her spirited humour never flagged.

It was much to everybody's surprise that Mr. Tulsey had plumped for the Week End instead of merely the dance. Sarah heard of his arrival, also of Mrs. Oxford's and the dance band's, from Cruddles, who raced down to the orchard with the information.

"I don't know what you're up to down here," he said irritably, "with every other one of us up to our eyes."

"I'm coming," Sarah said, crushed, no longer feeling eighteen to the full.

The band, she found, was at least as touchy to handle as Bron-ny's Press's photographer had been. (Bronny's Press himself, far from coming for the Week End, or even the dance, had not even bothered to reply to the invitation. No wonder people said you could not trust what you read in the papers. . . .) The band leader looked the ballroom over with disapproval. "I should think the acoustics must be rotten," he disparaged.

"They are Georgian," Sarah said, refuting "rottenness."

"It is only the truly ancient part of the house that is beginning to go to seed at all." She outstared him firmly.

When the band had at last become reconciled in some way to playing at Fontayne, Sarah went in search of Mr. Tulsey who had been taken in hand by Mrs. Oxford. Already Sarah was beginning to regret having given her old friend the run of the Week End. It was not only that she would probably expect to have the best bathroom solely for her personal use, and that Tom refused to harbour Emily in his schoolroom for long, but also that—in spite of her advice on dawdling—she seemed to have no intention of allowing the hours to go their own sweet way.

Sitting in the drawing room, she talked through the open window to the publisher, who was outside on the terrace. It was impossible for Sarah to get him alone to hear what plans he had made for the memoirs.

"Many happy returns, my dear child." Mrs. Oxford left a violet-scented kiss on each of the girl's cheeks. "This should be one of the happiest days of your life."

"You forget the war in the offing," Sarah said.

"Offing?" Mr. Tulsey sighed. "I should scarcely call it an offing." His sun tan seemed a mocking masquerade of joy.

"It is a pity you have no conservatory, Sarah," Mrs. Oxford said. "I never think a country dance is quite complete without one."

"Dance?" said Mr. Tulsey, who seemed to make a habit of repeating words from others' phrases and tagging a query on to them. "I hope you don't expect me to dance. I have a wooden leg, you know."

"No, of course I didn't know!" Sarah flung at him, nearly in tears once more. "Why couldn't you have said?"

"Of course, if I had known your affection hung by a leg, so to speak—" smiled Mr. Tulsey, who made light of his more personal intimate misfortunes.

"Naturally I'm very sorry to hear it," Sarah said, seized by compunction, but not sufficiently in its grasp to forgive him wholly for being so inconsiderate. "Have you always had it?"

"No, not always, but for a long time."

"I never noticed it at that party."

"No; it's a surprisingly good one, really," he said cheerfully, as if she had complimented him.

Mrs. Oxford, who had begun to feel the conversation had indelicate implications, said: "I've left Emily with your governess, dear, but perhaps she could come down to tea."

"Of course," Sarah said absently, "but I'm afraid Cruddles doesn't seem to be concentrating much on tea. I'll go and see—" She escaped, still resentful over Mr. Tulsey's false pretences.

Passionately, she wished Sir Giles would arrive and fill in this horrible hiatus with the all-encompassing charm of his being. His bedroom was ready and waiting to house him for the Week End, but if he didn't come soon she would know he was to be here for no more than the dance.

Philly and Christopher had retreated to have tea in the schoolroom. Emily was still there, and Tom, with the governess, Miss James, who had just returned to Fontayne from her summer holiday, her little pink china face burnt by the inconsiderately torrid sun of Italy, where her sister lived.

"Only *just* in time," she kept repeating. "Another moment, and I'd have been caught up in the toils of war."

"Get away with you!" Tom said, with that admiring sort of half belief that was open to be wholly convinced.

"Don't be rude, Tom. Give the little girl some cake."

"No, thank you," Emily said, stricken, tasting cucumber and seeing Punch again at the mere sight of Tom.

"I don't know about this dance," Christopher said slowly. "There's a bogus sort of feeling hanging around, just as there was on the day of that wedding."

"What wedding?" Tom demanded suspiciously.

"Well . . . *the* wedding, of course." Christopher realized with a start that it had been his mother's, and that it hadn't really turned out too bogus, in spite of his forebodings.

"My mother's and Mr. Jones's," Tom persisted accusingly, *"and I don't remember anything about it."*

"Shut up. It's all over long ago, anyway. You'll have to tie my tie, Philly. I hate that rotten dinner jacket, anyway. How like Sarah to let us all in for this." He added gloomily: "On the eve of war, too."

"The eve of Waterloo . . ." Philly murmured dreamily, biting into a large piece of cake. She might as well make a good meal, as she doubted very much whether she would have the heart to eat anything at the dance.

"Ernest has been sitting on my gas mask. It has old mouldy fur all over it. I won't like to take it back to school in such a state." Rebelling inwardly against the tameness of his own words, he finished pensively: "If I go back to school."

"Of course you'll go, dear," Miss James said jumpily. "It is our duty all to behave utterly calmly, with order in our minds and hearts—" Christopher's sweet, brooding, unheeding expression stopped her short.

"Are you going to have the partner you paid, tonight?" Tom asked Philly.

She blushed to the roots of her hair; and even the palms of her hands seemed to flush. Now the moment would soon come when she must don her long flowery dance dress and put a little powder on her nose and let Sarah squirt her with scent from the new spray that had been one of the birthday presents. And then she would have to go downstairs and hear the band strike up and the dancers begin to patter in the ballroom; and then, sooner or later, someone . . . Mr. Lupin or Sir Giles's cousin or even Sir Giles's cousin's friend . . . would ask her to dance and then she would be lost, quite lost. . . .

Drowning in monstrous conjecture, she clutched at a copy of *The Magnet*, and sheltered herself amid a pale rain of cake crumbs in the Fourth Form Remove.

Sarah began to dress. The day, which had been very heavy with uncertainty even in its weather, was going down to a perfect summer night. Mrs. Moody hovered in the shadowy room like some weighty well-upholstered moth.

"Don't put all the light on until I've put it on," Sarah said, meaning her frock. "Then we can get the full effect all at once."

"He did turn out princely when it came to a pinch, didn't he, duck?"

"Who?"

"Why, Mr. Jones, of course."

"Yes, he's nice."

"That Madam Bronwen notwithstanding—?"

"She can be all right, too . . . sometimes. She gave me a lovely appalling rococo necklet. Baroque, I think she called it."

"H'm. . . . *Now* let's see, duck."

They were both half inattentive to their own as well as one another's words, all their true attention reserved for the frock. Mrs. Moody switched on the full glow of light and the shallow breadths of the vari-coloured evening fell away from the clear hard interior of the bedroom. Sarah saw herself in the full-length mirror inside her wardrobe.

"It's . . ." Her voice sank away. "I do look nice, don't I, Mrs. Moody?"

"You look beautiful."

Sarah sighed. Let the night begin.

"He won't have a chance, with you wearing that—"

"Oh, don't. . . ." She couldn't bear the encouraging joke; besides, it was surely unlucky to labour the point. But . . . don't speak . . . he *will* like me in it. . . .

"Now my face." She stirred from her trance. "You'd better cover me up with something in case I spill powder." Mrs. Moody dexterously arranged an old soft sheet around her shoulders, and she giggled for a moment at her reflection. "I look as if I've been preserved for the future, like a valuable couch in a dust-sheet."

They both laughed again briefly at the idea of her as a valuable couch, but there was something rapt and solemn in the very midst of their mirth. Their words came in abrupt low snatches.

"It's a lovely night. You'll be able to sit out on the terrace."

"And watch the coloured lights, if they work. I don't think they will. Could I wear the appalling rococo necklet?"

"I shouldn't, duck. Keep it pure and simple, I should."

"But I hate looking simple—"

"Not this way—not in a model, you don't."

"No—perhaps you're right. I have the flowers for my hair. Wasn't it *odd* of Peter to send to London to get me flowers for a present when we have so many here?"

Mrs. Moody sniffed. "I daresay it was that sort of conduct that got him where he *did* get. Though I'm not saying these gardenias, or what they are, aren't much more like a dance than anything you'd pluck fresh from a bush around here. They set off dark hair no end."

"I hope Philly's getting on. You had better go and see she doesn't put her dress on back to front."

"M'm—I will when I've got you done." She took the flowers from a soft mossy bed within the elegant cardboard box. "This cluster for the corsage, this one for the coiffure," she said grandly. "You look like a bride."

"Oh, no," Sarah said quickly.

Ready for the dance she stood for a moment by the window, trying to see the garden as guests would see it, as once she had tried to see it from Sir Giles's eyes. Pencilled all over with hurriedly filled-in strokes of advancing evening, she decided it looked properly glamorous, not in the least decrepit. "It doesn't look too . . . moth-eaten, does it?"

"I never knew gardens more full of moths, but I don't say they've eaten much, duck."

Soon, the drive would be gay with the music of approaching cars, gay with formal flitting figures ready for the dance. Unless it was that nobody would come—like Charlie Chaplin's unbearably tragic party in that shabby old silent film, *The Gold Rush*—Oh, no! Oh, no! . . . In a panic she swung round to face the room again.

"Do you hear anything, Mrs. Moody?" She was half pleading. "Anything at all?"

"Hear anything, love?"

"Do you *feel* anyone will come? Can you *feel* there being a party here tonight? We've only got Benjamin and his friend and Bracken and Mr. Tulsey and Mrs. Oxford for the whole Week End. How can we make a dance of them, if nobody else turns up? Particularly as Mr. Tulsey insists he has a wooden leg?"

"Don't you worry, duck. We'll have our dance all right." Mrs. Moody's voice was exquisitely stout and soothing at one and the same time. The night took courage from her tone.

Mr. Lupin, invited in the face of Philly's anguished protest (but after all, he *was* a man, and he *did* dance, after a fashion), arrived earlier than any of the other dance guests; so early, indeed, that he impinged upon the genuine Week-end visitors and became absorbed in their atmosphere of leisure.

"He's in the hall with Mr. Tulsey, who is dressed," Christopher reported, as if this were specially worthy of note. "Mrs. Oxford doesn't seem to have gone down yet, and I can't think where Mother is. Isn't it time you two went down and started being charming?" He and Philly were in Sarah's room now. They were all three ready and waiting. "I've just seen Bronwen," he reported further. "She's wearing a sort of tiara thing. She looks like old Father Neptune."

"Doesn't Sarah look lovely?" Philly said, hitching at her flowered silk, which was, like so many predecessors, too tight under the arms.

Christopher studied his elder sister. "Very glamorous," he pronounced.

Tom opened the door and announced: "Emily and me are coming in to look at your little old dance. She's got another dress, but I shall come as I am," he explained, airily informal.

"Well, you can come in when I cut the birthday cake, though you ought to be in bed," Sarah said. "But we're not having you hanging around after that. I'm not going to have it a children's party, just for the sake of Emily learning the normal usages of society."

"Emily is a very nice little girl," Tom rebuked dispassionately.

*   *   *   *   *

At one moment Fontayne was full of the poignant aching emptiness of too few people busily filling in too great a space with forced words; the next, the hall was full of new arrivals, wrap casting, laughing, chattering, as if Sarah's anniversary had an authentic place in worldly social design.

"Hello," Sarah said stupidly, seeing Sir Giles emerge mysteriously from the midst of Mrs. Welwyn's three carloads of friends.

"Virginia gave me a lift."

"Oh . . ." So he can't possibly be meaning to stay the night. "I'm glad you could come."

"I meant to come, even if it were the last thing I ever did of my own free will," he smiled.

"Is it as bad as that?" She returned his whimsical puzzled green-flecked stare. "I mean, the War . . . taking your free will?"

"Let's talk of you," he said lightly. "Many happy returns of this beautiful day and night."

"Oh . . ." She wanted to cry again. "Thank you for Sanka. She was the loveliest present. I'll love her always." I'll love you always. . . .

She wanted to touch him, make sure he was really there. Even now she could scarcely believe in him, standing there as large as life, in his beautiful evening clothes.

"You look enchanting, Sarah," he said, his eyes intent.

"So do you," she said, not thinking.

He laughed. "Young Benjamin came?"

"Oh, yes. And a friend." She looked about the hall, quickening with movement and colour. "I must go and talk to people."

The Joneses' friends were coming in, too; unfamiliar, but decorative and apparently quite appropriate. But it was a relief to see people one really knew. Lady Pansy and Mr. Harbrittle and even Mr. Lupin. Sarah advanced brilliantly on Mr. Harbrittle, loving him merely for being known to her.

"And how are all you young people?" he asked, with acid geniality. He repelled affection with a suffocating aroma of camphor balls.

"It was terribly kind of you to come."

"This is the last we shall know of unthinking festivity." He meant this to sound captious, but to Sarah the words seemed sweet and dauntless.

Lady Pansy had never been so veiled, so gloved, so royally dappled with mascara. She wore a prankish brocade decked with improbable flares and flounces. "But you look delicious, child, delicious," she said.

Above, in the ballroom, Philly heard the first rippling notes of the dance band. Now, nothing would stop it, no power on earth: the bandleader was a god on his little dais. . . . The flowery dress caught her across the chest, making breathing a delicate operation. Her eyes followed Sarah who seemed so astonishingly at home in the crowd, like a lovely fragile butterfly flitting lightly, unpurposefully. From the corner of her eye she saw Mr. Lupin bearing down on her; and it was only then she gave up the last ghostly hope of deliverance from the dance.

Elisabeth stood with Julian in the ballroom doorway, as far removed as possible from the band. "I hope and *think* it is just what Sarah intended," she sighed, "but one never quite knows. Usually they seem to bear grudges against me for things done to please them." Julian smiled; pressed her fingers in that small private caress she found so comforting. "She will at least never forget the dress you gave her," she said.

The room, roused from the very blight of death, looked as if it would never lie down again. I should never have brought flowers back to it, Elisabeth thought; after this it will be so hard to force it back to the shades again. . . . Flowers put such a bold face on decrepitude. The room flourished, spun with colour and light. How *nice* of so many people to come, she thought, surprised, grateful. Peter had been a great help. She was glad to see him enjoying himself, though of course (of course, she impressed upon herself), he ought to show more conscience. Philly, released momentarily from the horrors of sociability, pranced round with Christopher, the unearthly dahlias of her dress straining at the underarm seams and clashing with all the decoration of the room. She had retreated into some lively-sweet dream, her eyes as full of unconscious tender raillery as her brother's were. She awakened to smile her slow lovely smile at Julian, in passing.

"I hope *she's* enjoying it," Julian said.

"Oh, Philly's so dear and accommodating," Elisabeth said vaguely.

Sarah danced with Benjamin, Sir Giles with Mrs. Welwyn. Everybody seemed to fit in, nobody out in the cold. Lady Pansy and Mrs. Oxford had each a sedentary share in Mr. Harbrittle. Somewhere, Tom and Emily lurked: waiting for the birthday cake.

"Shall we go down on the terrace and see if those coloured lights are working?" Benjamin asked.

"Oh, not *yet*. Anyway, you can see them from the window."

"I love your dress, Sarah."

"Do you?" she said listlessly. Sir Giles looked quite content *not* to be dancing with her. She couldn't even catch his eye. Come to think of it, how seldom she had ever really caught it. "Very well—we'll take a turn on the terrace," she relented proudly. Let him keep his eye.

The night was so sweet and deep and pure-scented that it came as a shock after the heated room. The fairy lights hung raffishly in a near vista of trees. Far above, stars looked cold and chaste and disparaging.

"They were a mistake. They look common. I wouldn't have had them if I had known there would be stars. Bob said there would probably be stars."

"Who is Bob?" Benjamin asked jealously.

"Bob Norbett. You don't know him." Bob had unconsciously heaped shame upon her by being so disinterestedly interested in the Fontayne party. Proffering to him, finally, an invitation to the dance, he had courteously refused, but had very graciously sold them the champagne in which the birthday health would be drunk; and he had said that he personally would cut out the fairy lights as there would probably be stars, and Nature's effects were really always best in the long run.

"No, I don't know him." He watched the starlight lay a faint silvering over her insubstantial dim white figure. He put his arm around her shoulders. "Do you mind?" he asked.

"No," she said politely.

"I don't think they look *common*," he said carefully, after a pause.

"I suppose he's quite old," Sarah said unexpectedly, almost blithely, from the midst of harboured woe.

"What?"

"Your cousin . . . Giles."

"Oh—I really don't know." Disconcerted, he let his arm fall from her shoulder. "Thirty-five to forty, I should think."

"He can't be thirty-five *to* forty."

"But you know what I mean."

"No, I don't know what you mean!" Tears throbbed on her eyelids once more.

Philly sought brief respite with Mrs. Rudge at the buffet in the dining room. She had a genuine excuse for escape: to deliver the message that the cake would be cut sharp at eleven, because Tom refused to go to bed before then, although he was already practically falling asleep with his eyes open.

"You do look nice," she said, amazed to see Mrs. Rudge looking crisp and efficient in a stiff white overall.

"So do you, Miss Philly," returned Mrs. Rudge, always ready to exchange a compliment or a favour. "How's the dancing?"

"I've had two." She smiled bravely. "And I'm missing one now. And supper will take up quite a while. And Christopher and Mr. Bracken have both promised to rescue me if they are free and happen to see any unwitting person coming to ask me for a dance," she said simply. "Be sure to take some cake for the children, won't you? Was it all right for you to leave them?"

"Their Dad's with them. He's quite good with them when you leave him to it." It always surprised Mrs. Rudge nearly as much as it did Philly to realize the beautiful children had a father. "It's a good thing, though, that the triplets aren't old enough to know 'e didn't look after their money better."

"It hasn't . . . gone?" Philly asked, awed.

"Well, it does mostly sort of seem to have slipped through our fingers somehow, Miss Philly."

Leaving Mrs. Rudge, she ran into Sarah and Benjamin returning from the terrace.

"You two dance together," Sarah said, running on ahead.

Cut off from all hope of rescue, Philly abandoned herself to her fate.

Sir Giles was standing almost in the doorway of the ballroom when Sarah got there. Smiling, without a word, he drew her into the dance.

"You absolutely bowl me over, you know," he said, gazing down at her.

"It's the dress. I'm the same as I was." Yet she began to thaw into the ecstasy of hope again.

"It's the dress *and* the wearer."

"Do you remember . . . the first dance? In the Hall?"

"The village hall." He nodded gravely. "I'll always remember this, too."

"Will you? It was terribly nice of you to get here at such a crucial time."

"I wouldn't have missed it for the world."

That light, unmeaning, diplomatic tone . . . how far dared one go toward meeting and believing it? The world, anyway, was coming to an end . . . everybody said so . . . so perhaps his words were not meant to be taken at a full and absolutely pre-war worth.

*   *   *   *   *

Christopher was happy. He did not mind dancing with Mrs. Welwyn. Of his own accord he asked her for the dance and she accepted simply. She was his friend; the picnic lay warm in living memory to bind them in sympathy.

"Mrs. Welwyn, what do you think of all this war talk?"

"My dear, what can one think?" Her dress was a shadowy violet colour, matching her eyes. "What do *you* think?" she asked, as if she cared.

He hastily turned aside from her limpid glance, as if his eyes had been undignifiedly tripped. But he forgave her again almost at once and muttered: "If only I weren't so young."

She did not deplore this remark. "I suppose you'd like to be in it, if anything happens," she said simply, not misunderstanding him, her feelings as crude and direct as his own.

"Yes, I would, Mrs. Welwyn." His heart yearned to her with passionate gratitude because she needed no explanation and wasted no time on futile weighings-up of right and wrong but went straight to the central selfish point he was concerned with.

"One always does seem to be the wrong age for everything one truly wants at any particular moment." She smiled absently, briefly. "*You* know."

"Yes." He gave her his sweet lazy smile. In spite of the shooting pains in him of impatience for his own years not being a match for events, he felt contentment now. It was a pretty good evening, after all. "It's nearly suppertime, Mrs. Welwyn. After this dance. There is champagne."

"Will you take me down?"

"All right, Mrs. Welwyn. If you like." He was cautious with the pride he felt: would not quite give it its head.

Philly went down with Mr. Lupin, because there was no way out of it. He had bluffly insulted her frock, her powdered nose, and her high-heeled shoes—as if painting her had given him a permanent right to criticize her. "I'll paint you barefoot on the edge of the morning, with your arms and hair as free as the wind," he said. There was nothing—nothing, she thought desperately—to save her. Except war; for surely even Mr. Lupin, however robust and virile, would not go on painting with bombs falling all around him. . . .

They went down with others to the dining room, transformed with flowers and food and drink. Tom and Emily had been there some time. "Don't you go to bed before you've had your nice little piece of cake," he warned sternly, keeping a firm yet sleepy eye on her. "No," Emily agreed politely. She no longer feared him, for he was by now nothing but a tired little boy, while she was still alert, lending a gracious secret ear to her favourite courtier. Her white accordion-pleated party frock sat immaculately upon her, but the hours had given Tom a grubby and distraught appearance. She was gratefully alone amid company.

Sarah, coming down with Sir Giles to cut her cake, felt that now nothing could go wrong. His black sleek arm linked with hers was a talisman against defeat. Now I am the centre of attraction, entirely living up to my day. . . .

When they had drunk her health and tasted her cake, the gardens— terrace and fairy lights and all—began to come into their own. Fired by champagne, Sarah felt herself to be a born hostess. Here was Mount Olympus reborn, and she moved among her guests with assurance. She was uplifted, without reticence.

"I think you once gave me a glass of champagne," she said to Mr. Tulsey, handing him one now, and at the same time forgiving him his wooden leg, letting it be a bygone. "When I asked you about the memoirs."

"Oh, yes, the . . . memoirs. Haven't I written about them?" He nodded as she shook her head. "They won't do, you know. Erratic bits and pieces. And dated, too. Storms in departed teacups. Not our stuff."

"But you took Bronwen's book. Surely my father was more important than *Bronwen*—"

"Publishing is not, unfortunately, so simple as that," Mr. Tulsey said mysteriously.

But even this unfair blow could not damp her risen ardour for the night. If she could not resurrect her father's fame, she would find a way to make fame for herself somehow. *Somehow.*

"Come here, child." Lady Pansy caught at the white frock. "How *right* those flowers in your hair are—emphasizing neither profile nor full-face beauty. I could imagine you Virginia's younger sister. You achieve a similar effect. Your type would appeal to the same man."

Flattered, she was for a moment dismayed; as once before for the same reason she had been. The feeling didn't last. "Thank you, Lady Pansy," she said radiantly, in a moment.

Mr. Harbrittle's dry cindery voice sieved words carefully into Mrs. Oxford's ear. "I shall leave before midnight."

Sarah heard, and could not bear that even he should not be loving the night. "Are you still writing?" she asked compassionately. What would he do with Europe now?

"Just a little vignette," he admitted coldly.

Bronwen, in her long black velvet frock, and with her hair falling in a dank straight veil from her little silver Juliet cap (which Christopher had bizarrely seen as a tiara for Father Neptune), hung professionally upon his words. "How do you go about your work?" she asked.

Mistakenly imagining her to be asking his advice, he answered almost pleasantly. "Above all, eschew the smart ephemeral phrase. Write purely, basically."

"I see," Bronwen said, a gleam in her pale eye. To her, the moment was sweet with possibility. Moving her fat wrists until all the bracelets were jangling, she took her time about continuing. "Yes, I see. . . . But think of Shakespeare." (She thought of him, friendlily.) "He must have used a lot of smart new words in his time, and after a while they must have got dreary and old-fashioned, and then—still later—cheap and vulgar, and then ghastly and quaint, and then . . . after years and years and years . . . immoral."

"Quite right, infant," Lady Pansy said, delighted with this reconstruction. "One in the eye for you, Joey," she added inexcusably.

Mr. Harbrittle's parchment face crackled with distaste as he turned a stiff camphored shoulder on the insufferable girl-child.

"That child must go to bed at once," said Mrs. Oxford, turning her hooded eye to Emily, who was docilely eating the last crumbs of her slice of birthday cake. The normal usages of society were long since appeased so far as her granddaughter was concerned.

As the old lady spoke, Elisabeth bore down upon Tom and the little girl. Emily licked the last crumb and rose obediently for bed. With a stiff piece of icing clutched in his hand, Tom gazed up at his mother from a white exhausted waking dream.

"I don't like it," he said loudly.

"What don't you like darling?" Elisabeth leaned over him. "You and Emily must go to bed now."

"I don't like it at all."

"*What*, darling?" She peered near-sightedly, perplexedly, at him.

"People not being the same age."

"But how could they be, darling?" she asked helplessly.

"Why not?" His dark eyes held hers hypnotically. "Why couldn't they? I don't *want* people to die before I catch up. Poor Mrs. Moody, poor little old Mr. Jones. . . ."

"Tom's gone to bed in tears," Philly came to tell Sarah.

"It's always the way with little children if they're allowed to stay up late," Bronwen said complacently. She was still glowing with delight from her skirmish with Mr. Harbrittle. She had never felt better in her life; supper, birthday cake, even a glass of champagne, all taken in digestion's stride and not a twinge to show for it. She even felt less disgusted about the indignity of being a growing girl. Indeed she felt beyond such things, as if she were a goddess sprung full-grown from her father's brain.

"Poor Tom," Sarah said absently. "I think Fontayne is turning out a success tonight."

"The *party* is a success," Bronwen corrected. "Fontayne itself is not concerned with such things."

"Perhaps you're right," Sarah agreed restively.

She thought it was true that the place repelled the power of tonight's innovations: was neither tricked nor persuaded, beneath its guise of mirth. Her heart began to beat more quickly, disturbed. But why need Bronwen have put her finger on it so expertly? This *seemed* all one had expected of it: one didn't want to go delving too deep; hardly even hoped to be more than satisfactorily deceived. Of *course* Fontayne would have the last word . . . but let this gaiety outlast the night. . . .

"For Fontayne itself," Bronwen went on conversationally, refusing to let well alone, "there is nothing left remarkable beneath the visiting moon."

"Oh . . ." Sarah stared at her, dismayed. The too apt alarming phrase, borrowed from she knew not what inscrutable classic griefs, seemed to shift her very soul on a spasm of desolation. "Please don't let us talk of that now."

"Where is everybody?" Philly asked helpfully.

"Sir Giles went into the garden," Bronwen said promptly, "with Virginia Welwyn. What a divine couple they make."

"What do you mean?" The words froze on Sarah's lips.

"Mean? Whatever you care to choose I mean." Bronwen did not take her gaze from Sarah's face. Her eyes brooded, their expression sympathetic, open to the persuasive crosscurrent of emotion in the air. She felt stealthily around in her mind for words worthy to cap another pregnant moment deftly. *"They are not even jealous for the cause, but jealous for they are jealous . . ."* she murmured at last.

The fairy lights made meretricious petals on the trees. Sarah stumbled out on to the terrace, blindly seeking. She caught the hem of her delicate frock on a jagged stone and heard the material tear. But before she could really damage herself she found Sir Giles, and he was blamelessly alone.

"Did you have any cake?" she asked stupidly, breathlessly.

"It was delicious," he said judiciously.

"I'm sorry I didn't behave well at that party you took me to. You were very patient with me."

"I found it delightful, I assure you."

"No. That coffee stall . . ." Her voice sank away. "You must have been disappointed in me."

"My dear girl—"

"And yet you were sweet enough to send me Sanka after that." I'm still his dear girl. . . . "Why was she called Sanka?"

"I believe it's the name of an American brand of coffee."

"Oh." She was bitterly disappointed by the unemotional explanation. "I—I suppose it's suitable because of the coffee stall."

He laughed. "I'd like to tell you something nice, Sarah."

"Yes?" His voice sounded nervous, boyish. The lights *were* common, whatever Benjamin said. But here on the terrace the silky night lay like a lovely frail unending twilight.

"Virginia and I are going to be married."

"Are you?" The fierce cold blue of her eyes upturned to his would have abashed Sanka's own. "How lovely. How simply lovely. How simply perfectly lovely. . . ." Her voice would never stop. She felt it going on and on, but it ran so high that mercifully at last it became inaudible.

"I know you are fond of her," he said modestly, wilfully denying any such place as he himself might hold in her affections.

"I love you both. I love you—" The words came freely, an anguishing relief. "You are the most beautiful person . . . people . . . I have ever known."

The prosaic schoolroom was chaotic with the shape of woe. "But you can't stay here," Christopher said flatly.

"Leave me alone. Why did you follow me?"

"I saw you stealing off. Are you ill?"

"I'm all right." She was tearless, frozen, and on fire. "Isn't it funny?" she said. "Sir Giles is going to marry Mrs. Welwyn."

"I know. She's just told me," he said uncomfortably.

"She has?"

"Yes." He whistled glumly. "Never mind. Cheer up."

"I don't care."

"Cheer up. Never mind."

"Don't keep on! And don't pat my arm."

"I'm sorry." He was surprised, not knowing he was doing so. He felt peculiarly empty and light, in spite of supper. It must be the few sips of champagne. He had thought before, at the wedding, that it had a bogus taste.

"How odd of her to tell *you.*"

"We're friends," he said simply. Again he felt that cold empty sensation in his stomach.

"I believe *you* are sort of jealous, too, in a way," she said wildly, giving up pretence on her own account.

He instantly shut out the odious feminine meaning of her remark, not even glancing at it sufficiently to realize that he could never forgive her for it.

"Never mind. Cheer up," he repeated glumly, and mechanically began to pat her arm again.

"Bracken . . ." Philly whispered across the terrace.

"Yes. Is it time to go back and dance?"

"Yes, I suppose it is, but—Bracken, I'm afraid Sarah's not very happy."

"Isn't she?" he said gently. His heart sank. Cracks were beginning to run across the clear surface of festivity. The blooming air and the peace of the garden weren't enough; wouldn't see the night through, emotionally. "Can I do anything?"

"I'm afraid not," Philly said reverently. "It's Sir Giles."

"Oh."

"We must find her and help her get through the rest of the evening, but without saying anything."

"Yes." It sounded a tall order. He took off his glasses and put them on again. The fairy lights winked frivolously.

Sarah and Christopher appeared from the shadows.

"Oh, you're here," Bracken said lamely.

"It's time the band started again. It must have finished its supper," Sarah said, clear and hard.

Philly sighed with relief. They wouldn't have to try to say anything. . . .

"Yes, we'd better go up. We ought to make the most of tonight," Christopher said flatly. He saw school looming, tame, inevitable, whatever happened. "Isn't this light queer?"

"It's the fairy lights," Sarah said expressionlessly.

"A sentimental vision of twilight," Bracken said. The whole night was that, he thought. It was Austria dancing waltzes before the Great War: Russian princesses in tinkling sleighs before the revolution: English tennis parties, the rattle of delicate china beneath stately trees on a Rupert Brooke lawn. It was the dangerous futile glamour of the unrecapturable. . . . He gave a little laugh and was then ashamed of the sound because they seemed to expect some explanation of it.

"Tonight seems the end of summer as well as the end of the world," Sarah said. Her voice seemed to float, now, quite light and free.

"The last days of Pompeii . . ." Philly breathed from some senseless dream.

"I can never be happy again," Sarah said.

Her blatant personal desolation had given her a peculiar dignity, which no finer subtler diffusion of sorrow could have done, Bracken thought.

"Never mind," Christopher said. "Cheer up."

"I think we had better go in," Philly said, anxious for the disintegrating pause.

"Yes," Bracken agreed, relieved.

He edged them thankfully across the terrace. Above, in the ballroom, there was a re-awakening of the night to its proper theme of joy. The band, refreshed, began to play again.

THE END

FURROWED MIDDLEBROW

Printed in Great Britain
by Amazon

43656641R00185